Convergence

BOOK THREE, LONG SHOT SERIES

MICHELLE GREY

ISBN-13: 978-1530169436
ISBN-10: 1530169437

Cover Art and Design by Cover Me Darling
www.covermedarling.com
Formatted by Athena Interior Book Design and Cover Me Darling

Chapter 1

Jack Mathis incorporated the sound into his nightmare, the shrill alarm screaming a warning that Becky's oxygen levels had fallen. He reached for her, but his arm fell to the cold, empty sheet as he came fully awake.

He licked dry lips then hit the talk button on his phone to silence the racket. "Mathis," he croaked, staving off the worst of the pounding in his head.

"Agent Mathis? Field Agent Randy Martin, Duluth office." He paused as if waiting for an acknowledgment, then filled the silence. "I understand you're the lead on the weather girl case. Looks like we've got a victim to add to the list."

With an inward groan, Jack shoved the sheets aside and sat up on the edge of the bed. The shadowed room tilted. Rubbing his hand over his face, his gritty gaze landed on the finger of scotch left at the bottom of the bottle. His stomach rolled.

"When?"

"Late yesterday. Got a positive ID on her a couple of hours ago. Dana Palmenteri."

Jack squeezed his eyes closed. He wasn't fool enough to believe the killer he'd been tracking for almost a year would vanish, but damn him for intruding on this time. This was his time. Becky's time. He swallowed the bitterness that welled in his chest.

Resigned, he stood, the hardwood cold on his bare feet. "Another weather girl?"

"Sort of. Not on TV, though. This woman was a meteorologist at the National Weather Service."

The agent shared the details. Same MO as the others – all young women, all killed and placed post-mortem in a simulated work environment. But the details didn't matter yet, not until he saw and assessed them for himself.

Jack shook his head, the late afternoon hour on his clock surprising him. "I'll be on the first flight in the morning."

As he tossed the phone toward the bedside table, he caught a strong whiff of himself, and whatever was left in his stomach from last night's binge was damn close to seeing the light of day. He stumbled to the bathroom and cranked the hot water. Under the steaming spray, his nausea subsided and his mind cleared for the first time in a week.

The miserable routine he succumbed to during the holidays might've been cathartic, if it was a one-and-done deal. But it wasn't. This was year seven. And, so far, it wasn't any easier. He could still feel Becky's soft hand as it rested in his, still see the pain in her eyes that the medicine dulled but never vanquished. And on the second day of every January, he could still hear her final, sighing breath.

Jack stayed in the shower long enough to steam the mirrors and shove the memories into their well-worn box. Stepping out, he dried off, then cinched the towel around his waist and went in search of something clean to wear. Once again, he'd climb back to the land of the living, even if the person who mattered most wasn't there.

In front of the FBI field office, Jack slammed the car door and eyed the gray clouds that promised snow later in the day. He imagined the sky looked like that most of the winter in Minnesota. It did last time he was here. The efficient receptionist barely had time to offer coffee and a seat before a young man with short blond hair and obvious Nordic bloodlines strode toward Jack, palm extended.

"Randy Martin. Thanks for getting here so quickly. The vic's in the morgue, well-preserved, thanks to Mother Nature's sub-zero refrigerator. We'll check on her later. Let's get you settled in first."

After a brief handshake, Jack followed Randy down a painted cinder block hallway. "Do you have the final forensics report yet?"

"Should have it later today." Randy swung open a wooden door and pointed to a scuffed desk in the corner. "Your temporary office."

Three heads swiveled toward Jack as he entered the room. The agents looked at each other then, in a rush of scraping chairs, clamored toward him. Randy laughed. "I knew this was coming. Let me introduce you around."

Jack shot him a questioning look but had no time to ask as the winner of the race pumped Jack's hand. "Bob Schilling, sir. It's a pleasure to meet you in person. Is it true that you single-handedly put the pieces together on the Minneapolis strangler case?"

Ahhh...so that was it. A few years had passed, but it had been a big deal up here. Even made the national news for a couple of cycles. Jack started to reply, but a petite blonde who looked like she was fresh out of training jumped in.

"Linda Cole, Agent Mathis." The gleam in her eye bordered on adoration. "We studied that case in my Methods class during training. It was amazing."

Again, Jack opened his mouth but was cut off.

Another handshake. "Incredible work. Hope to crack a case like that myself someday. What was it that sent you in Brown's direction? Doug Jankowski, by the way."

Jack waited a few seconds to see if anyone else would jump in, as uncomfortable with the praise now as he had been when it had first come from his superiors. He'd only been doing his job. Looking at their expectant faces, he sighed and repeated the words he'd said so many times.

"I wasn't looking at him any differently than anyone else. We were leaning hard on his boss, the butcher store owner. So many things pointed to him. But one day, I was in the shop and watched how the kid's hands wrapped somebody's order. God's truth. That was it. For whatever reason, something clicked and I started digging deeper into his background." Jack knew they wanted more, but he'd wasted enough time already. He met each of their gazes. "The lesson, I guess, is never look past anybody. But that case was over a long time ago, and we have another perp to find." He turned to Randy. "So tell me more about where they found Dana Palmenteri's body."

The other agents took the hint and stepped back as Randy laid open the file on Jack's desk and pulled out the photos. "Storage shed behind her house out in Hermantown. Didn't show up for work for two days, so her coworkers became concerned. Local police found her and called us as soon as they saw this setup. Her belongings were shoved to the side. You can see the mock lab best in this photo. I'll take you out there later today."

After he'd reviewed the file, Jack agreed with Martin's assessment. Definitely the same profile: Strangulation and asphyxiation. So how long had he pursued this woman? And how had he connected with her? Did he use email to entice her like he had the others? Or could this be a copycat? It was always a possibility, and this girl was only broadly in the same industry. Jack checked his watch. Better find a hotel room. He was going to be here a while.

Lunch consisted of a cold turkey sandwich, chips, and way more information than Jack wanted about Randy Martin's new girlfriend before they finally headed out to the crime scene. Icicle lights hung from the front of the small brick ranch, the cheery Christmas decorations in the yard jarring against the yellow crime tape that led them around the side of the house to a wooden shed.

Pulling hat flaps down over his ears, a local officer left his vehicle to greet them. "Nothing new out here. Cold as hell, though."

Jack briefly acknowledged the man, his mind already studying the scene. The killer was long gone, of that he was certain. He eyed the gloomy sky again. The coming snow would obliterate their footprints, just like the fresh blanket already on the ground had done for the killer. Jack stepped inside the frozen shed and was impressed that it looked relatively undisturbed. Within minutes, he found what he was looking for. It was the one link that had been kept from the media, removing any chance of this being a copycat killer. A simple piece of paper, partially hidden by the computer keyboard with three printed words: BETTER THAN YOU.

Jack finished his perusal and walked with Randy to the car. "We're good. Go ahead and send the crew in to clean up."

As Jack kicked the snow from his shoes, a red Subaru SUV pulled in behind them. Almost before the wheels stopped, a young man with a notebook and a handheld recorder slipped and slid around the front of his car, hurrying toward Jack.

"Agent Mathis, right?"

The officer monitoring the area stepped out of his car again and sauntered over as Jack studied the eager young man. His hood had slipped, revealing a shaved head that rang a bell with Jack, but he couldn't place him.

"Ken Johnson. I'm with Internet Intelligence, the Source of Virtual Truth." He juggled his notebook then extended his gloved right hand.

"That's the best slogan your boss could come up with?" Jack quirked an eyebrow as he shook the kid's hand.

His cheeks flushed red. "Yes, sir. I mean no, sir."

Jack had pity on him. "How can I help you, Mr. Johnson?"

The reporter's eyes darted toward Agent Martin who waited on the driver's side. "Uh, my boss sent me up here to follow the story. It's another one, isn't it? Like the one in Los Angeles?"

The connection clicked. "You covered that."

Johnson nodded, his grin revealing a gap between his front teeth. "Yep. Must've done a good enough job because the boss heard about this case and sent me asap. What can you tell me?"

Jack mentally cringed. Glad someone had done his job in Los Angeles, because *he* sure as hell hadn't. Three victims. Now four. He had to find a way to get ahead of the bastard.

Yeah, the Minneapolis Strangler case was ancient history.

Shelving his frustration, Jack tightened his hood as the wind sliced through his jacket. "Can't tell you anything right now." Ken opened his mouth, but Jack held up his hand. "Press conference tomorrow at ten. Ask your questions then."

He slid into his seat and out of the frigid wind, as the eager puppy look faded from Ken's eyes. Too bad. Jack's job wasn't to boost anybody's journalistic dreams. He had a killer to find.

Back at the office, he settled in at his make-shift desk and shoved a hand through his hair. This wasn't how he'd expected his break to end, yet the adrenaline coursing through his veins told him this was exactly where he needed to be. *Alive.* He was alive and ready to catch this son of a bitch. He re-read the file cover to cover then pulled out the files on the other cases. He'd reviewed them a hundred times already, but there had to be something he was missing, something they were all missing. There always was.

Chapter 2

The melting icicles dripped from Tori Whitlock's gutters, hitting the ground with the cadence of a ticking clock.

Spring is coming.

She waited for the thrill up her spine for the chase season, and the tightness in her chest from the memories of the tornado that changed her life, but neither came. She blamed the hangover.

Turning to escape the bright morning sunshine that only intensified the grinding headache behind her left temple, she shook out a couple of ibuprofen and tossed them back with a swallow of coffee. She squeezed past the easel in the small kitchen to return to the living room, grimacing at the sleeping man on her couch.

Probably should've made Alan leave last night. He was a decent producer, but he'd gotten handsy after knocking back a few too many shots. She was never vague about her rules, but he must've thought his flimsy excuse about coming to her place to review the applications they'd received for camera operators would translate into sex.

Fat frigging chance. Even if she was attracted to Alan, which she wasn't, co-workers were off the menu. She likened finding a good sex buddy to finding the right car salesman. He doesn't come across as desperate for the sale, only offers the desired options, and doesn't call again until it's time for service.

After another long swig of coffee, Tori settled in at her computer desk and groaned as more than a hundred new messages poured into her inbox. She knew the station was going to rebroadcast their top three shows from last season, but she'd forgotten when. *Damn.* Must've started last night. That meant she'd have to respond to at least fifty. And she'd do it. Not because of the contract demand to help build the fan base, but because keeping the show on the air legitimized her love/hate need to storm chase.

Leaning back in her chair as far as she could while still reaching the delete key, she whacked away at the messages without reading them until she reached a manageable number then began the arduous task of responding. Most of the emails were basic fan stuff or future tornado chaser-wanna-be kids. And most of the responses were as simple as she could make them. "Thanks." Or "Glad you enjoyed the show." Every once in a while she generously pounded out two sentences.

Today there were more than a few random creepers, probably leftover holiday depression bringing it out in people. Wincing at the basic lack of decent grammar and imagination, she trashed those messages before she finished reading them.

Warm breath hit her ear as Alan Reynolds' hands began massaging her shoulders. "Morning, beautiful. What are you doing up so early?"

Cringing at the unwanted intimacy, Tori shifted away from Alan's wandering fingers. "The show aired last night. Episode five if I had to guess. Doing my duty and responding."

His focus shifted in a blink. "Really? I thought they were starting next week. Kick ass. I'll call the station to get our numbers. Have to be decent, though. See any new potential sponsors in there?"

Tori rolled her eyes. Alan would pimp her out in a bikini over a Nascar hood in thirty seconds flat if he could figure out how to get it written into her contract. Which would never happen. "So far no, but you can look for yourself. I need another cup of coffee."

When she returned from the kitchen, the scowl on Alan's face surprised her.

"So, you're putting out feelers to go national?"

Tori raised an eyebrow. It was way too early in the morning for simper, especially from a grown man. "What the hell are you talking about?"

Hurt mingled with the challenge in his eyes. "One of your *fans* is a producer from ABC. *The* ABC. Wants to get together to discuss taking the show national."

Two of Alan's air quotes in rapid succession made her want to break his knuckles as his simper turned to flat-out whine.

"Said that you're too good for the camera to stay in regional programming. Where would that leave me, Tori?"

Tori's shoulders tightened. One more reason to keep her personal life and work life completely separate – or to not have a personal life at all. But, they'd begin shooting in a few weeks and being on the outs with Alan wouldn't make anybody's life easier.

She leaned in and scanned the message. "Cool your jets, Alan. I didn't solicit that email, and I'm not looking to go anywhere. I like it just fine where I am."

His smile told her she'd placated him. He tugged at her waist, pulling her onto his lap. "Good. Because I like it just fine where you are, too."

She shoved at his shoulders and stood. Placating only went so far. "Yeah, well, that's a different subject. We're not going there, Alan. Not today. Not ever. I should've sent you home in a cab last night."

"Come on," he cajoled as he twined a finger through the loose curl that had fallen from her sloppy bun. "You were interested for a minute."

She'd been drunk, horny and lonely, a stupid, dangerous combination. Even if she didn't work with him, Alan's scrawny frame would normally be the furthest thing from what appealed to her. Not to mention he fell well under her six-foot rule. Being tall had its advantages, but it severely limited her choice of partners. She'd tried sex with a short guy once, and once was enough. Thankfully, with Alan, she'd come to her senses before things had gotten out of hand.

"Mixing business and," she tried not to choke on the word, "pleasure would be a mistake. I think the chemistry of the show could be affected."

That got his attention. His hand dropped from her hair as if it had burned him. "You really think so?"

She played into the concern wrinkling his brow. "Absolutely. What if we were involved?" *Gag.* "What if I was so busy thinking about you that I couldn't focus on the job?"

He considered her words then stood and scooted around her toward the sofa. "I see what you mean. You could get distracted by me, which could cause you to get hurt, or worse, and kill the show."

"Exactly. Then where would you be?"

His lament carried. "I'd be back at the public station producing Minnie's Crochet Corner, that's where. Which is why, if you ever even think about going national, you have to promise to take me with you." He shoved his feet into his shoes and looked at her with something akin to disappointment. "You're right. We can't do this."

She smothered the laugh that threatened to escape. That was the trick with Alan. It was only a good idea if it was *his* idea. It grated, but whatever.

"Are you sure you don't want to reconsider Chuck Patterson for the truck one position?" *And...Producer Alan was back.* "His camera skills are good. Plus, he was on the team for three years and knows the ropes."

Tori crossed her arms. "Do you really think a guy who gets his panties in a wad and quits when he's not automatically promoted should be rewarded? He tried to pull the same crap when we brought Cam on last year. Entitled doesn't work real well for me." She paused. "Get whoever you want to replace Chuck for truck two, but I want Tricia Chalmers with me and Cam in truck one. She's got some great footage on her resume."

A long-suffering sigh escaped Alan's lips. "I'll see what I can do." He grabbed his jacket from the back of the sofa. "And remember, Tori. Business only between us from here on out."

She bit her lip. "You got it, Alan. Let me know when you hire Tricia."

Tori plopped into her chair again and sighed. Crisis averted.

Her coffee had turned tepid but she gulped it down, allowing it to chase away the lingering effects from the ridiculous amount of Wild Turkey she'd consumed the night before. She glanced at the email from the guy looking for national talent one more time before hitting the delete button.

She hadn't lied to Alan. She wasn't looking to move up in the world. Living right here with her demons, and an ample supply of bourbon, suited her just fine.

Tori's cell phone chirped incessantly from the kitchen table. She glanced at the caller ID then set down her glass and hit the talk button. "Hey. What's up?"

Dwayne Davidson's scratchy, smoked-too-many-cigarettes voice boomed in her ear. "Missed you, too, kid. Taking advantage of the mid-sixties today and doing a little grillin' out at my place. Steaks and taters. You in?"

In the field, Dwayne was a hell of a driver. Over the past couple of years, she'd gotten him to really start pushing the envelope, most times against his better judgment. And at publicity events, he looked and acted like her very own biker bar bouncer.

But despite her appreciation for him, she preferred the quiet of her own place. As if to challenge that notion, her stomach rumbled, but her innate response won out. Although steak sounded way better than whatever frozen dinner she'd pull out later, Tori declined. "I've got too much to do tonight." She hoped Dwayne didn't hear the lie in her voice. Truth was, she had a date with her favorite bourbon, her remote control, and maybe her paint brush, but that wasn't any of Dwayne's business. "Appreciate the invite, though."

"Change your mind, steaks are on at five."

Twenty minutes later, her phone rang again. This time, Cam's name came up and the corner of Tori's mouth lifted. Dwayne had called in reinforcements. "I know. Dwayne's grilling. Not interested."

Cam countered her surliness with his usual no-nonsense tone. "Too bad. When's the last time you ate a decent meal?" He pounced on her silence. "It's not going to kill you, and it would be good to get the crew together before the season starts. Come on, swap your sweats for a clean pair of jeans, throw on a jacket and get your ass moving. I'll pick you up at four-thirty."

Cam hung up and Tori glanced down at her faded OU Sooners sweats. *Jerk.* She considered leaving but he'd probably track her down. Over the past year, Cam had insinuated himself into her life in little, innocuous ways that surprised her. What surprised her more is that she'd let him. Guess there really was a first time for everything.

Anyone else and she'd have told him where to stick his interfering nose. And she might've told Cam too, if he'd stayed on the line. Hauling herself off the sofa, she pulled the tie from her hair and shook out the thick mass. She tried to run her fingers through the messy curls then gave up and decided that a shower was probably in order anyway.

Tori didn't exactly regret the decision to go, but after a rib-eye, a baked potato with all the fixins, and a half dozen Bud Lights, she regretted changing out of her sweats. Leaning back against the stone seating surrounding the fire pit, she stretched out her too-long legs and closed her eyes, her mind drifting.

"Bobby Nichols says I have giraffe legs," she mumbled, flopping back against the bed.

Vanessa laid down next to her and slung an arm around her waist. "Your legs are beautiful, just like the rest of you."

Tori scoffed at her sister's well-intentioned lie. "You're the beautiful one."

A log shifted and crackled, startling Tori back into the conversation. Her eyes darted around the group, but if anyone had noticed her drifting, they didn't say anything.

"How come we don't have new camera guys yet?" Dwayne swiveled from Cam to Justin Coakley, the meteorologist from truck two. "Don't you all need to break in the new guys in your trucks?"

"We need to meet them, for sure. But the real test will come during the chase."

Tori took another pull from her beer and stood to shake the restlessness from her limbs. "Alan went through a few resumés with me last night. I told him who I want, but he's going to have to make the decisions pretty soon."

"He called you to the office to look at resumés?" Cam's voice was laced with skepticism.

"Of course not." She paused. "He came by my place. What? You got a problem with that?"

"I'll go grab another round from the kitchen." Dwayne retreated from the scene as fast as his large body could take him.

Justin was hot on his heels. "I'll join you."

There was nothing to be embarrassed about. So why was heat climbing up her neck?

Cam's scrutiny was tangible, his words slow. "Alan just happened to come by. To review resumés."

"What's the big deal? We looked at the candidates, had a few shots…"

"He's dying to get into your pants."

"Not anymore."

Cam stood, tense. "You let him –"

Tori matched him eyeball to eyeball and shoved at his large shoulders. "Of course not. We made out for a few minutes before I came to my senses. He knows we won't be going down that road again."

Dwayne and Justin chose that moment to return. Handing out the bottles, Dwayne visibly shuddered. "You made out with Alan? That's just gross. I always kinda thought he played for the other team."

The crackling fire filled the momentary silence. Cam punched Dwayne in the arm, but the comical disgust remained on his face.

Somehow, it all turned funny in Tori's head and she laughed. "Well, I'm not sure which team he should be playing on, but there's a good reason he'd be the last guy picked. Ugh."

Covering his ears, Justin groaned. "TMI. La la la…no details, please. My ears are gonna bleed."

Tori studied Cam's gaze over the top of her beer bottle. He wasn't laughing. "Stop, Cam. You don't get to act that way, all jealous and macho. You don't. Because you had your chance and you didn't take it."

Cam sighed and stood, linking his arm with Tori's. "Come on. You're drunk. And, it's time to go." He thanked Dwayne for dinner, and after a nod to Justin, grabbed Tori's bag.

Tori barely stumbled as she waved good-bye to the guys, then allowed Cam to lead her to his car. But as the passing street lights began to spin, she closed her eyes. "It was a nice party. You know, I don't even like people, but we make a pretty good team," she murmured. "What if the new guys don't fit?"

With a half-smile, Cam reached over and tucked a strand of hair behind Tori's ear. "Told you it'd be fun. And don't worry. Alan might suck at kissing, but he's a solid producer. I'm glad Chuck is gone, and I'm sure whoever Alan hires will be a good match."

Before he made it back to Norman, Tori's breath had evened out in sleep. Cam pulled into her driveway next to her Mustang, then bundled her in his arms and lifted her from the car. Her hair fanned against his shoulder and he breathed in the faint scent of strawberries. Squeezing her a little tighter, he managed to shove his key into the lock and get her inside. Dodging a couple of paintings he hadn't seen before, he settled Tori on her bed, then brushed the hair from her cheek and kissed her forehead. "Sleep well," he whispered.

"Mmmm…care to stick around? It's still early." Tori's words were quiet, but her eyelids fluttered open, the invitation in her soft blue eyes loud and clear.

Cam looked at her for a long second before shaking his head. He tucked a blanket around her. "You saved my life, Tori. And you may not think we need each other's friendship, but we do. I sure ain't willing to risk losing that by sleeping with you."

Whether she'd really passed out or was just feigning sleep, Tori didn't respond, which was typical any time a conversation got anywhere close to emotional. Switching the light off, Cam strolled out of the room. "I'll see myself out. Goodnight, darlin'."

Chapter 3

Tori blinked at the bright morning sun that mocked her through the open blinds in her bedroom, disgust permeating her hangover. Two things were obvious. She should never drink beer to excess. It made her stupid. And, she should never throw herself at the one person who actually meant something to her.

Groaning, she rolled away from the offending light. Oh well, yesterday was over. Not that Cam would make a big deal of it. He wasn't that kind of guy.

She planned to spend her day studying the upcoming weather patterns. Unlike people, at least they made sense to her. She'd been told her uncanny ability to choose the right predictive models was the reason she was so successful during the storm season – the reason her show was renewed for another season. Because she'd get the money shots that could make a viewer hold his breath in fear for the chasers lives.

She'd come about as close to the line as possible on more than one occasion, and someday she'd trip over it. For the past eleven years, she'd envisioned everything about that moment – the smell, the color of the sky, the cold raindrops hitting her face, the awesome energy vibrating in the air, the absolute power that would end her life.

And she wasn't afraid because she knew it was her destiny. She shouldn't have survived last time.

Tori didn't have time for the grief-soaked memories spiraling through her, threatening their special brand of sabotage before she even made it out of bed. They only had free rein in her nightmares.

Squeezing her eyes closed, she breathed deeply for several long minutes. Finally, she hopped off the bed as she pulled her hair into a pony tail, and went to the kitchen where the light was best. Tossing the finished piece aside, she threw a blank canvas onto the easel. She made a pot of coffee, then after laying out her brushes and pouring some turpentine, she added dabs of paint to her palette.

With broad strokes and sweeping arcs, Tori did her best to silence the guilt.

Two days later, Tori settled into the conference room chair, skin tingling, focused. Her early analysis was complete and the season would start in a few short weeks. She lived for the four months from early March through late June, when death was a split second decision away. She didn't even mind the planning meetings, not that they meant much to her. She always went with her gut.

Alan entered the room and Dwayne's laughing eyes swiveled to her. She flipped him the bird and glared him down causing him to hide his laugh behind a cough. Cam shook his head.

With a frown, Alan followed the interaction then cleared his throat. A kid whose curly blond hair and baby face made him look like he was still in high school stepped out from behind Alan.

"First, let me introduce Reece Smith. He's our new truck two camera operator."

They all rose and Tori shook his hand first. "Good to meet you. Hope you're up for the challenge."

Reece's voice was surprisingly deep, eliminating Tori's question about whether he'd emerged on this side of puberty. His eyes crinkled when he smiled. "Looking forward to it. I'm a huge fan of the show, Tori."

Alan made the rest of the introductions, and Reece took his seat next to Justin, across the table from Tori.

"Okay, gang. We've made an offer to Tricia Chalmers for truck one and should hear back from her in the next day or two."

Alan droned on for thirty minutes. Tori caught Reece staring at her at least three times, causing his cheeks to flame every time. She'd have to nip his little infatuation in the bud. No way was she going to start her season with a love-sick puppy in truck two.

"One more thing, then we're done," Alan said.

Tori released a breath. *Thank God.*

"I got a memo from Carly Jackson in HR about a possible threat. The FBI says there's some nut job out there with a thing for weather people." He turned to Tori. "Weather girls in particular."

Tori grimaced. "Pfft. I'm nobody's idea of a weather girl."

Alan set his half glasses on his nose and looked down at the letter again. "The note says this guy sends emails to his targets, enticing them with the prospect of a bigger, better job opportunity." He paused then glanced Tori's way again. "Sounds a lot like the email you got."

Dwayne frowned. "You been reading Tori's emails, Alan?"

Tori leveled a hard gaze at him. "I told him about it, Dwayne," she ground out.

Alan nodded. "Exactly. I didn't think anything about it at the time. But now, I don't know. The memo says to report anything suspicious to the FBI. Have you gotten any more emails from that guy?"

Tori hesitated only a second before she shook her head. She wasn't about to do anything to disrupt the season. "Of course not." She picked up her pencil and started doodling on the pad in front of her. "We done here? I don't have all day to hang around with you girls."

Tori stared at Alan, avoiding Cam's curious gaze.

"Well, if you get another one, you need to let me know. Pronto. Okay, guys. I think we're all set. Reece, get with Justin and he'll show you around."

Hopping up from her chair, Tori made a beeline for the door. "Text me when Tricia signs. I want to go over a few things before the season starts."

Tori power-walked down the long hallway and out the double doors. She almost made a clean get-away. Almost.

Cam jogged up behind her as she unlocked her Mustang. "How many?"

She opened the door and slid into her seat. He leaned in, effectively stopping her from closing the door.

"Tori." Cam's voice lowered as he searched her face. "How many emails have you gotten?"

Turning from his hard gaze, she sighed then shoved her keys into the ignition. "Six. Okay? But I've ignored them all. I highly doubt it's the same guy, but even if it is, I'm not letting him or anything else clutter the next few months. I've got my fingers crossed for an active season. I'll deal with crazy psychos later."

"Really? You're not willing to take this seriously?"

Tori read the edge of fear behind his eyes and patted his cheek. "I'm a big girl, Cam. Do I look stupid enough to fall for some ploy to meet for drinks from someone I've never met? Give me a little credit."

She started the car and stretched for the door handle, forcing Cam to step back. As she pulled out of the station parking lot and glanced in her rearview mirror, Cam stared after her car, arms crossed. She knew that look. Damn. He needed to lose his big brother complex.

Jack stared out the window as fat flakes of snow covered the ground and trees below. The Beltway had been hit hard this winter, and non-essential personnel had been cleared to go home because of the promise of several inches of the white stuff by rush hour. But Jack was in no hurry to leave the office. The weather had already killed his plans to travel to North Carolina for the weekend to visit his friend Garrett and his family, so he had nothing but time on his hands.

Weeks had passed, and they'd cast the net as far and wide as they could. Every television, radio and internet weather entity had been advised, but impatience ate at Jack. So far, the fact that all four women had graduated from the University of Oklahoma's School of Meteorology was the only thing that linked them, and it could be weeks or months before the killer selected a victim. How many people would even remember the memo and think to contact them before it was too late?

Anger mounted. His life felt like a series of endless loops. Professionally, he was a puppet controlled by a murderer. And personally? Hell, he didn't even want to go there.

Garrett's voice grated in his head. *Time to move forward, Jack.*

Several months had passed since Garrett's soul mate had stepped into his life and transformed him from confirmed bachelor into a loving father and undoubtedly, soon-to-be husband. Ever since, Garrett had been all over Jack about finding someone for himself. But it was different for Jack. He already knew what love felt like. He and Becky had begun dating as freshmen in college, married between their junior and senior years, and had a whopping two months of marriage before Becky's illness struck and death parted them the following January.

The snow was coming faster as Jack shelved the bittersweet memories and his thoughts about the future. If he didn't head out now, he'd probably find himself snarled in traffic. He threw on his jacket and gloves and had a hand on the doorknob when his office phone rang. He debated for half a second about letting it to go voicemail, but instead shed his gloves and grabbed the receiver.

"Jack Mathis."

"Agent Mathis. Larry Lewis. Oklahoma City office. I think we may have a lead on your weather guy's next target."

Jack froze. "Let's hear it."

"Tori Whitlock. She's a meteorologist who does a regional storm chaser show based out of here called Vortex. Her producer called to let us know she's gotten several emails that fit the profile."

It was only potential, but it was the first bite they'd had. "You have them there?"

"I do."

"Send them over to me."

Jack gave his email address as he unbagged his laptop, his fingers tapping an impatient staccato as he waited for it to boot up. As his eyes finally scanned the increasingly insistent content of the forwarded emails, potential opportunity turned to excitement. He'd read similar emails a few weeks ago addressed to Dana Palmenteri and the others.

"Excellent work, Agent Lewis. We'll do some analysis on these and touch base the first part of next week."

After hanging up the phone, Jack shed his jacket and forgot all about the storm outside. What was that show? Vortex? He pulled up the internet to check it out. The website's home page boasted links to several tornado chases. Clicking on the first video, he was completely unprepared for the intensity that confronted him. Wind whipped over the camera's microphone, muffling the frenzied voice blasting instructions to her crew.

The video was over before he knew it. Jack clicked on the next one and adrenaline practically jumped from the screen. He'd seen tornado footage on the news, but had never seen people actually chase them. And these people were doing it on purpose.

His fascination led him through the remainder of the videos and onto the bios of the cast. He never got further than Tori Whitlock. He couldn't define what it was about her image that arrested him. Maybe the deep auburn curls escaping her ball cap. Or it might've been her lean curves, more pronounced for the wind that plastered her clothes to them. But both of those things paled against the exhilaration on her face. There was no doubt that, in that moment, she was a woman who was exactly where she needed to be.

Jack shook his head, and with one last look at her intense blue eyes, he closed the website and clicked back into the emails, rereading each of them. He didn't need tornadoes to produce the adrenaline pumping through his veins. He'd wait until Monday to meet with the team, but he believed without a doubt he was finally out in front of the bastard. He'd be damned if there'd be another Dana Palmenteri.

Despite the fresh powder that fell again Sunday afternoon, the three members of Jack's team made it into the office on Monday. His personnel had been shuffled so only Belinda Kane, his profiler, was familiar with the case. But everyone had reviewed the emails, and the planning and strategizing had begun in earnest when the call Jack was waiting for came in.

Bodies edged around the desk as Jack hit the phone's speaker button. "Agent Lewis, you've got the floor. Go ahead and get my team up to speed on Tori Whitlock."

"Sure. Name's Victoria Elaine Whitlock. Goes by Tori. She's something of a local celebrity here in Oklahoma. The fourth season of her show, Vortex, will begin taping over the next few weeks and months. Moved here from Dallas right after high school and got her meteorology degree from OU in three years. She's chased throughout college and developed a kind of cult following on her website. The local station caught wind of her, so to speak, and has cashed in on her popularity."

Jack nodded. "Most of that's on her website. What else you got?"

Papers ruffled. "There's a little bit more on her history. She grew up in southwest Kansas until she was fifteen when her parents and sister were killed in a tornado." He paused. "Damn, you'd think she'd stay as far away from them as she could, wouldn't you?"

Jack remained silent as Tori's image flashed through his mind. He might not understand her motivations, but she sure did. They were evident in her stance against the fierceness of the storm swirling around her.

"She moved to Dallas and finished out her high school years with her dad's brother, Claude, and his wife, Earlene. That pretty much sums up what we have."

"Appreciate it, Agent Lewis. We'll be in touch soon." After Jack ended the call, he pulled up the Vortex website again. "Okay, we need full backgrounds on everyone from Tori on down. Anyone connected to her work."

Josh Fredericks raised his pen. "On it."

Nodding, Jack turned to Heather Ramirez. She was newly graduated and new to his team, but so far seemed competent. "Why don't you go back through OU's enrollment records again now that we've added Ms. Whitlock to the mix and see what you can come up with? Anything that could link these women. Someone they dated, a mutual classmate. Also, get me whatever you can find on her family. Whoever's left. I want every angle covered."

"Will do." She followed Josh out of the office, leaving Jack with Belinda Kane, his profiler.

"You have anything else for me before I go?" Jack checked the flight time on his boarding pass.

Belinda removed her half-moon glasses, her bright eyes sharp in her wizened face. "Not really. Just a reminder to keep your guard up. He's left us precious few clues to work with, so keep that lesson you learned in Minnesota in the front of your head and don't overlook anybody."

Chapter 4

Tori's leg bounced under the table as she waited for Alan to speak. The sweat on his forehead was fair warning that she wasn't going to enjoy this little meeting. "Spit it out, Alan. You're about to hyperventilate."

Chases probably wouldn't start until next week and they'd already had their pre-planning meetings, including the introduction of Tricia Chalmers as their second camera operator. So why another one?

Alan's eyes met hers, but he seemed to be having trouble forcing words past his lips.

Tori's eyebrows rose. "This isn't about Glenn Pritchard, is it? I saw the jerk at the liquor store the other day, and he was gushing about his new show. Said he couldn't wait to showcase his equipment, which I think is total compensation on his part, but whatever. And that he's going to show the world how low brow our show is. But he's full of it. People want to see the excitement, the danger. The only people who care about his findings are other boring meteorologists."

Alan's brow furrowed. "You're a meteorologist."

"True. But I'm not boring. I know what people love about storms, what keeps them watching. They're dying for the close call. It's just like the circus. They want death-defying stunts. And that's what I do."

Alan shrugged. "I agree that Glenn's a storm snob who thinks chasing for the sake of the thrill cheapens the industry, but hey, it works and we've been renewed for another season, so we'll leave that there. This meeting isn't about Glenn and his new show."

Tori checked Cam and Dwayne to see if they were as confused as she was, but neither one was looking at her. She sat back and cocked her head. "Then what?"

Alan tugged at his shirt collar. "The emails. Cam gave them to me. And I gave them to the FBI."

Her head swiveled to Cam, her voice low and menacing. "You rat bastard. I want my key back. You had no right."

Cam's steady eyes assessed her. "Would you have turned in the emails?"

Tori rolled her eyes. "Of course not. I –"

"Exactly. I had no choice but to be the responsible one."

"Responsible my –"

Alan raised his voice, interrupting their spat. "Either way, the FBI thinks the emails are credible enough that they're sending their lead agent on the case down here to become your best friend for a little while."

Fingers dug into the chair's padded fake leather arms as she shot a pointed look at Cam. "I don't need another 'friend.' I've got enough of them already. What's he going to do, live with me?"

"Probably. And chase with you, too."

Tori's chair exploded against the conference room wall as she flew out of it and planted her palms on the table. "Oh, hell no." Her glare should've set him on fire. "I've already got Dwayne freaking out every time the wind blows too hard. The last thing I need is some guy who doesn't know his ass from a hole in the ground screwing up my season." She looked at Cam to see if he was as outraged as she was, but he was checking Facebook on his phone. *Seriously?* Swiveling back to Alan, she fought to keep the rising panic out of her voice. "A. There's no room in the truck. Four is a tight squeeze as it is. And B. You think I can keep one eye on FBI boy and one on a funnel cloud and still do a good job? You think we can get decent footage that way?"

Alan cringed, the battle for sustaining good ratings versus keeping the show's star safe warring on his face. "You'll have room. Guy's name is Jack Mathis. He'll be here in the morning. And to everyone else, Mathis will be a second cameraman."

"What? What about Chalmers? You agreed with me that she was the best person for the job. You offered her a contract. You think the production people are so stupid they won't realize this guy knows nothing about filming? And I need two good camera people in my truck. I can't make the show work without it." Her voice bordered on hysteria. *How could he do this to her?*

Gathering his file, Alan headed to the door. "Chalmers was made aware of the change in plans earlier today. Anyway, the agent's family owns and runs Mathis Productions, one of the biggest independent commercial producers in the country. I checked them out. They've done some pretty high profile campaigns. It's the best place for him to fit in."

"What an amazing stroke of luck." Sarcasm dripped from her words. "But that doesn't make him capable in the field."

"You took a chance on Cam and that paid off. Give the guy a chance."

She was done listening. Her leather bag banged against the back of Cam's chair as she charged past him. "Thanks for all your help. Hope you're happy."

"Somebody has to care if you're safe. And, if you're safe, I'm happy."

She ignored the agitation in his voice and slammed the door on his words.

Tori released a sigh of relief as Mack lowered the hydraulic lift and ran through the laundry list of checks he'd done to make sure her tornado intercept vehicle was ready. She'd spent the past twenty-four hours seething, and it felt good to get refocused.

"She looks great, Mack. Can't wait to put her through her paces." She followed him into the shabby office at the front of the metal building. "What do I owe – "

Words died on her lips as she looked up from wiping a spot of bearing grease from her hand into the most gorgeous pair of whiskey brown eyes she'd ever seen. Mack might've answered, but the blood pounding in her ears drowned everything else out.

Those eyes were part of a damn fine package, too. Tori hoped she didn't lick her lips as she boldly assessed the man staring back at her. Tall and broad shouldered with dark hair that showed the slightest hint of curl against his collared shirt, he looked like the kind of guy who could wear her out and barely break a sweat. And, man, she needed to be worn out. It had been a while since she'd even been on first base, and Alan didn't begin to count.

Her nipples tightened beneath her sweatshirt as she mentally cataloged places in the repair shop that could work for a mid-morning rendezvous. Of course, that would mean convincing Mack and Shelly, his office manager, to take a hike. The stranger's eyes crinkled, and she wondered for a split second if he could read her thoughts.

Remembering her manners and her ability to speak in the nick of time, she gave him a jaunty smile. "Excuse me. Didn't mean to interrupt."

"No problem at all."

Oh, that accent. Definitely not an Oklahoma boy. East coast maybe? Her brain started calculating how she could sweet talk Mack into stalling whatever repairs tall and gorgeous needed. She only needed a day. Her eyes made one more quick, head to toe pass. Okay, maybe two.

"You're not interrupting," Shelly said. "Guy's looking for you."

Her words registered in Tori's brain and shot ice water directly into her veins as the blood drained from her face. *No freaking way.*

"Jack Mathis. You must be Tori. Alan told me I'd find you here."

Tori looked at his extended hand then back at his face. Fate was a cruel bitch. "Yeah, well, he was wrong. I'm out. Shelly, if you would, drop my invoice in the mail." She turned on her heel and left them to wonder what the hell just happened.

———————

Jack tipped his beer back as he lounged on the uncomfortable hotel bed and laughed out loud thinking about the mechanic's face as Tori stormed out of the garage. He'd apologized ten ways to Sunday, but Jack waved his words away. Alan had warned him that Tori was far from thrilled with the arrangement, but Jack wasn't there to be her best friend. He was there to find a serial murderer and keep her ass out of harm's way in the process.

The image of Tori from the website flitted through his brain, but it was nothing compared to the woman live and in person. Her image had provoked him, stirred him. But even in a sweatshirt and jeans that fit her like a second skin, she was hot as hell and had turned his brain to mush.

With effort, Jack shoved his inappropriate thoughts away and finished off his burger as his cell phone rang.

"Jack Mathis."

"Hey, Jack. Josh here. You should have files in your inbox on Whitlock and her coworkers. Let me know if they don't come across."

The new kid was quick. Nice. "Got them right here. Good work."

"Thanks. I had a chance to glance through the file on Whitlock and wanted to run something by you. Did any of the previous victims come from money?"

Jack mentally flipped through the files he'd committed to memory. "No. The first two victims and the most recent were from middle class families. The LA victim had a wealthy uncle, but he wasn't connected to the case. Why?"

"Money can equal motive and she not only inherited her family's estate, the life insurance from her parents' deaths is sitting in a trust and is worth about two million dollars. It's all there in her file."

"Okay. Doesn't fit at first blush, but I'll look at it. Get up to speed as quickly as you can on the other cases, then check with Heather to see if she needs help with the university search."

"Will do, boss."

Jack hung up then unzipped the full workup on Tori. He scanned her history, and although it was sad, it didn't raise any obvious red flags. He clicked into the trust fund record and stopped at the transaction history. Frowning, he scanned significantly large sum withdrawals over the past several years that added up to almost a cool million bucks. He shot a reply off to Josh to find out where the payments landed.

After a few more minutes, Jack closed the file and let his head fall back against the padded headboard, thinking about the woman he was charged with protecting. He'd let Tori go today, but tomorrow he needed to find a way to get on her good side. If she had one.

Tori's eyes followed Agent Mathis as he strode into the conference room and she silently cursed the station president who'd required her presence, and the flutter in her stomach. Killer guns had always been a particular weakness, and the play of solid bicep muscle beneath his light blue button-down did the trick. Then her eyes moved to the real gun holstered against his ribcage and she was reminded of the reason he was there. She cleared her throat and straightened in her chair. So what if he was a walking turn on. He was also going to be a huge pain in her ass.

Jack shook hands with Cam, Alan and Dwayne before turning to Tori. If he was expecting her to apologize for jetting on him yesterday, he could stand there all day. To her surprise, he offered a practiced smile.

"Ms. Whitlock. It's a pleasure to finally meet you."

She accepted the olive branch he offered by not mentioning yesterday's encounter and shook his hand. "Agent Mathis."

Jack took his place at the head of the table. "This is a conversation that most people never have, and never want to have. And everything we discuss from here on out about this case needs to be restricted to the people in this room. To everyone else, including the station staff and even the other crew members, I'll be introduced as your camera operator." He paused. "The person we're pursuing has killed four people. Four women. So far, the only obvious connections between them are the meteorology field and the University of Oklahoma."

He continued to describe the similarities and, vaguely, the crimes themselves. By the tightness around his mouth, Tori felt certain he left out many of the more disturbing details.

Fifteen minutes into the meeting, she laid her pencil down with a sharp click. She got it. He'd been bested by this mystery guy. That totally sucked, but his logic was sketchy at best and she'd listened to it long enough. "Look, Agent Mathis –"

"Jack."

Tori paused then forced a brittle smile. "Jack. This isn't the first time I've received questionable emails from random creeps. I'm a public figure. It comes with the territory. I don't reply. And, in my experience, the losers give up and go away when they don't get a response." Jack opened his mouth to interject, but she rushed on. "Secondly, there's absolutely no way to create a simulated work environment for me. My job is so unpredictable, I don't even know what it will look like from one day to the next. I respect your need to find your guy, but I think you have the wrong girl."

"For your sake, I wish it was that easy. But, you are his next target." Challenge and anger sparked in Jack's brown eyes, matching the hardness in his voice. "In case you missed it, he's killed four women."

He held up four fingers on his right hand and Tori bit the inside of her cheek to keep from letting him know she understood the number without a visual reference.

"Four intelligent, college-educated women living in the twenty-first century who all grew up with a lifetime of knowledge about stranger danger." He sighed, exasperated. "Look, I know you're not stupid, but neither is he. And according to our profiler, he has no intention of stopping. He's a psychologically damaged individual who hasn't finished proving his point."

Dwayne raised his hand, clearly agitated. "Hold on a minute. What about the job thing? I mean, isn't Tori right about that?"

Thank you, Dwayne. Tori crossed her arms and nodded support until she turned to face Jack who was already shaking his head.

"We can't make that assumption. He's shown us that he's willing to change things up. For example, his first three victims were all television weather personalities. But Dana Palmenteri, our most recent victim, didn't share their field at all. That's why we reached out and broadened our search.

"So far he hasn't slipped up, hasn't given us anything. Not even a molecule of DNA evidence. But I guarantee you, these emails are his, which makes this the first time we've had a decent jump on him."

"But – " Tori began.

Jack stood and placed his palms flat on the table, firm conviction in his gaze. "You don't want me here. I get that. But until this guy goes down, you're going to have to adjust."

Tori inhaled deeply once. Then again. But it did nothing for the anxiety building in her chest. Her voice was quieter than she would've liked. "I need to chase. No offense, but your timing couldn't be worse. There's a system developing now that I think will blow up tomorrow. Tomorrow. Do you get that? I don't have anything against you personally, but you're about to screw up everything I live for."

He relaxed into his chair and offered a sympathetic smile. "Your passion for your work is impressive, but it's my job to make sure you *stay* alive."

Jack's direct gaze unsettled her. There was respect there, but something else, too. Like he was trying to psychoanalyze her. That pissed her off. Plus, he'd proven it was a waste of time to reason with him, and they both knew he was going to win this battle. And that pissed her off even more.

Tori broke eye contact, anger heating her cheeks. Looking for another outlet, she bypassed Alan and Dwayne, and teed up on Cam. "I could kill you for this."

The corner of Cam's mouth lifted. "She doesn't mean that," he told Jack before winking at Tori. "But just in case, could you at least wait until they catch the guy?"

"You are ridiculous." She stood, the knowledge that she was completely outnumbered and outmaneuvered, chafing. All four men joined her. Her gaze swiveled back to Jack. "I don't have a guest bedroom, so if you insist on staying at my place, your only option is the couch. And I don't cook."

This time, his eyes held a hint of humor. "I'm sure we'll manage."

Jack followed Tori's car while Cam's headlights filled his rearview mirror. Something different between those two, but he couldn't put his finger on it. He didn't think they were lovers, but it was deeper than the simple connection Tori had with Dwayne and Alan. Made him all the more anxious to dive into Cameron Tate's file.

It was good to have the initial confrontation with Tori behind him. The angst and anger on her face the moment she conceded to the inevitability of the situation made him wish he could snap his fingers and make it go away. But if he could do that, he'd have done it four women ago.

Their caravan stopped in front of a brick bungalow in an older part of town. The homes up and down the street were clean and nice, if a little frayed at the edges. Surprising, Jack thought, given her financial status. He parked behind Tori in the driveway and, by the time he'd pulled his duffel from the passenger seat, she was unlocking her front door.

Cam jogged from the curb across the small patch of brown grass and met up with Jack. "She's just going to need a little time," he said under his breath.

Again, Jack's curiosity was piqued, but Tori flipped on the living room light and motioned them in.

"You can dump your bag over there by the sofa."

Jack crossed the threshold and barely noticed the furniture. His gaze was arrested by the artwork scattered around the room. It cramped the space and, admittedly, he didn't know much about abstract art, but there was raw power in the bold strokes and rich colors he couldn't deny.

"Beautiful paintings," he murmured. "Your work?"

He turned and Tori was studying him, a small frown between her eyebrows. "Yes. And thank you." She turned on her heel. "I need coffee."

Cam followed Tori to the kitchen and the sound of their good-natured jabs filtered back to Jack as he checked out the room. Besides the dated floral couch, complete with hardwood armrests and stiff cushions, the rest of the space was consumed by a computer workstation against one wall, a dark red leather recliner and a small coffee table.

He tossed his bag on the sofa then wandered down the hallway that led to the bathroom and Tori's bedroom. Not a bad layout. At least being in close quarters would make his job easier. Fewer windows, less floor space.

Jack entered the kitchen just as the machine finished brewing.

"You a coffee drinker, Jack?" Cam asked.

"I am."

"Then don't drink Tori's. She'll make you hate it."

Tori took a small sip of the steaming liquid. "I actually like the taste of coffee. I don't have to water it down until it looks like tea or drown it in sugar or cream."

"Same here," Jack said.

Surprise registered on Tori's face for a split second then it was gone, replaced with a plastic smile. "Can I offer you a cup?"

"You'll regret it," Cam warned.

Jack chuckled as he pulled back the yellow curtain from the window. "I'd love a cup, but would you mind if I take a look around outside before I lose the light?"

Tori shrugged. "Knock yourself out."

Cam's eyes followed him. "You want some company?"

"Nah. Just want to get a feel for the place. I won't be long." Stepping out the door to the postage stamp backyard, Jack made a mental note to replace the broken screen door lock. There was no fence, but a storage shed marked the corner of her property, smaller and more run down than the crime scene in Duluth but a stark reminder just the same. As if he needed one. He walked the perimeter of the slab house, his mind replaying each of the other cases. What was the common thread? Was it connected to the university? OU had one of the most highly respected meteorology programs in the country, so it was feasible that it wasn't a connection at all. Nevertheless, he was glad that the case had brought him right here to the home of the Sooners.

He turned the corner then stopped as Cam's voice drifted from the entry. "Are you comfortable with him? Do you want me to stay?"

"Of course I'm not comfortable with him. But you're not real high on my list right now either, so get on out of here."

Jack stepped into the shadow of the roof's overhang as Tori pushed Cam's big frame out the door. Cam turned to her and the light from the porch illuminated the worry on his face. "Joking aside. If you don't feel safe with him, I'm staying."

Tori leaned into the frame, holding the screen door open. "You're being ridiculous. Remember, you're the one who brought him here."

Cam frowned. "Yeah, well. He better know what the hell he's doing."

"Just make sure the guys are ready tomorrow morning. If the system dies, I'll text you. Otherwise, be here by nine-thirty."

The screen door creaked closed, and Jack walked toward Cam as he shrugged into his jacket. "Calling it a night?"

Brushing back the hair teased into his face by the spring breeze, Cam nodded. "Gotta go sometime, I guess." His shoulders straightened. "You've got this, right?"

Jack studied him for a minute. Cam was an inch or two shorter maybe, but probably outweighed him by ten or twenty pounds. In a bar fight, he'd definitely want Cam on his side, but not at a poker table. He couldn't bluff for crap. He was scared. Jack's initial irritation at Cam's question was replaced by a pang of sympathy. He knew what it felt like to be afraid of losing someone.

"I've got this. But I'm going to need help. Yours, Dwayne's, and most importantly, Tori's. I'm on her side, Cam. I just need to convince her."

"Yeah." Cam shrugged, but his voice lost its edge. "She'll get it figured out."

"Well, I'll take whatever secret formula you used to get her to trust you." He was only half-joking.

"Ha. Good luck. Getting her to even like me is a stretch most days. If I were you, I'd shoot for that." Cam stroked his chin. "Start with Master Chen's Chinese. It's her favorite. Number's on the fridge."

As Cam walked to his car, Jack was struck by a surprising jolt of envy. Cam might be afraid for Tori, but at least she was still with him. Jack rubbed the back of his neck and let out a frustrated sigh. Dredging up the past only meant remembering the pain, and he had more important things to do. Closing up and locking the front door, Jack headed to the kitchen as the sound of running water and Stevie Ray Vaughn's *The Sky Is Crying* came from the bathroom.

He leaned against the counter, letting the familiar guitar lick soothe him like it always did. Good for the soul. He grabbed the Master Chen's menu as the song ended and her play list moved on to Robert Cray. Damn, the woman had good taste in music. And food. He perused the menu, suddenly starving. He ordered four entrees, soup, and sides and, by the time it was delivered, he was ready to gnaw his own arm off. If Tori didn't hurry, she'd be picking at leftovers.

"Do I smell – " Tori walked into the kitchen, her eyes darting to the containers of food spread out on the kitchen table then to Jack. Her growling stomach filled the silence. " – Master Chen's?"

Chalk one up for Cam. The guy was a genius. Jack spread his hands. "Wasn't sure what you liked, so there's plenty of variety."

Tori grabbed plates. "Pretty much anything from there. I'm not going to lie. I can eat like a horse, and I'm starving."

"You and me both. On both counts."

Tori opened the fridge and held up a beer. "You allowed?"

Jack smiled and began opening containers. "Absolutely." He caught the incoming can. "Chopsticks or fork?"

"Chopsticks." She chomped off the end of an eggroll, then slid her finger under the remaining unopened containers until the feast covered most of the table. They dug in, filling their plates with rice, chicken and veggies.

After a few bites, Tori cocked her head. "Okay, important question. Crab Rangoon or egg roll?"

Jack gave it serious consideration. "Either. But if I have to choose, I'm going with egg roll."

An approving nod was her only reply as she shoveled in another bite. Jack ate enough to take the edge off his hunger, then sat back and popped the tab on his beer.

Tori glanced up. "You're going to lose to a girl?" she asked as she dug into the half empty cashew chicken container and added some of the contents to her plate.

"I'm pacing myself."

Tori's indelicate snort made him laugh. He'd never met anyone as irreverent as she was, but he had to admit, he found her no-holds-barred honesty refreshing. At least he wouldn't have to guess how she was feeling.

By the time she finished the last few bites on her plate, he was ready to challenge the fragile truce they'd established. But she beat him to the punch.

She wiped her mouth and fingers and sat back in her chair with a replete sigh. "Listen, thanks for dinner. And I'm sorry for being such a bitch today. Like I said, it's nothing personal. I want you to find your guy. The sooner you do, the sooner my life gets back to normal."

"Good. I hope that means I can expect your cooperation." Wariness crossed her features and he held up his hand. "You have a job to do, right? And I told you earlier today that I'd do everything I could not to screw up your work. Now, I'm asking for the same courtesy. Help me catch this son of a bitch, Tori."

Chapter 5

Tori crossed her arms and studied the man across the table. She understood strong motivations, and the fierce determination in Jack's eyes was sexy as sin, but proceeding with his plan meant a much smaller likelihood of her succeeding with hers. The crew had gotten great shots last year, but it had been Cam's first year looking through the lens, and the best footage had come from Jesse Montgomery. Too damn bad his wife's promotion had sent them to Colorado.

Cam had worked hard in the offseason though, so Tori hadn't been too worried, especially because she thought she was getting Tricia Chalmers. She closed her eyes and rolled her shoulders to loosen the knots that had formed. Worrying now wasn't going to help, either. She'd just have to hold her breath on their first chase and see what Jack could do.

With a resigned sigh, she met his gaze. "I still think this whole idea is ludicrous, but I'll do what I can to help you, whatever that means."

Jack slugged back his beer, then his gaze caught and held hers. "It means you answer the next email he sends you. Start a dialogue."

Despite her disbelief, a spike of adrenaline surged. "You want me to bait him."

"He's coming anyway, Tori. He's been very deliberate about his targets – and persistent. But I'm hoping we can set the pace."

"Don't you think it would seem strange to him that I've ignored everything up to now and then suddenly I answer?"

"We'll figure out what to say next time he emails you. The last one was eight days ago, correct?"

Tori nodded.

"Good. We shouldn't have long to wait then." He paused, his eyes never leaving her face. "If there was any other way to draw this bastard out, I'd do it. But I need you, Tori. We know a lot about how he operates, and I promise we'll do everything we can to sting him without putting you in any real danger."

He thought she was afraid. It was there in his posture, in the little frown lines on his forehead. But she wasn't. Even if she believed this maniac was after her, it wouldn't matter. She'd stopped being afraid a long time ago.

Tori leaned back in her chair. "Not much scares me, Mathis. And if it weren't for danger, I wouldn't have a job."

He might've thought she was cocky or just plain full of shit, but he didn't let it show. He grabbed another egg roll and dipped it in orange sauce. "So, enough about all of that. Tell me about the job. I watched the videos online. Pretty freaking amazing."

"It's nothing compared to the actual moment. Hopefully, you'll find out tomorrow."

One minute she was talking about the show and some of her best chases then before she knew it, two hours had passed. She hadn't talked this much about herself, well, ever. She should've been tired but the smoky edge of his voice hit her in all the right places. More than once, she thought about turning the tables on him. It might've been fun to see how far she could get, but she held her tongue.

"You go by Tori all the time or is it ever Vicki? Or Victoria?"

She cringed. "Just Tori. I've never been Vicki and I haven't been Victoria for a long time. Probably never was."

He frowned at her cryptic comment, but let it pass. "What about your family?"

She paused, then shrugged. "Dead. Except for an aunt and uncle. But, trust me, they don't belong on your suspect list. They aren't involved with anything that doesn't have to do with Dallas society."

His direct, probing gaze was starting to grate on her nerves.

"Didn't you live with them for a while?"

"Seriously, Mathis. You're telling me you don't know all of this already? Yes, I lived with them during high school."

"Do you stay in touch with them?"

"No. We parted ways as soon as I turned eighteen. Let's just say it was obvious that they intentionally didn't have kids and didn't want children in their lives."

"And you lost your parents and sister when you were fifteen?"

"Yes." She scraped her chair away from the table. "I think we're done here. All of that stuff is ancient history. Next you'll be asking what kind of diapers I wore as a kid."

Tori fluffed her pillow for the third time then finally gave up the fight. She'd tried to bury herself in the maps and data for tomorrow's storm, but it couldn't hold her attention. Thoughts of her parents and sister bombarded her in random bunches, which was why she never talked about her family. Much easier to keep the lid on that box. But since sleep wasn't coming anytime soon, she leaned over to her bedside table and pulled out her sketchbook and pencils.

Tori blew out a breath, as graphite slid over the paper in smooth, soothing motions. She allowed the soft scrolling pattern to dictate her mood, and her thoughts drifted to the happy memories. The ones of Vanessa and her at Grandma and Grandpa Potter's farm.

There, it had been okay to sit by the water's edge for hours and draw. It had been okay to laugh and be carefree little girls. It was the one place where she'd never had to worry about whether kind words would be followed by a snarky jab, or worse. Where she didn't have to be Victoria. They were good people who'd spent hours in their living room rocking chairs, knitting, and loving both of their granddaughters, not just the perfect one.

It was the only place she wasn't judged a failure.

Vanessa always bent when it came to their parents' expectations, but Tori had never figured out how to do that. Or maybe had never been willing to. She was the upstart. The rebel. The trouble maker. The child her parents regretted.

Tori snapped from her memory and looked at the garish, marred surface on her lap. She slammed the cover on the book, then threw it back in her drawer. Drained, she pushed her hair off her face and closed her eyes. Why the hell did he have to bring up her family? Dead people couldn't kill people. There was zero reason to discuss them.

And still zero chance of her going to sleep. Tiptoeing from her room toward the kitchen, she cursed the creaking door, but her attempt at stealth mode was moot. Jack was stationed at the kitchen table in front of his laptop. She had every intention of being pissed off at him for delving into her past, but damn if he wasn't wearing dark framed reading glasses. And she thought he was sexy before? He looked up over the rim of his glasses, his eyes making a quick pass that burned her from toes to hairline.

"Do you own a robe?"

His question sent a dart of heat to her middle, but Tori hid her smile at the gruffness in his voice as she pulled down two shot glasses and plunked them on the table. "I do."

"You need to start wearing it."

Or maybe not. She turned her back on him to grab the Wild Turkey bottle out of the freezer, the heat of his gaze warming her backside. This arrangement might have some benefits after all. He met all of her basic criteria. And then some.

After pouring for them, she tossed back a shot and nodded toward his computer. "What are you doing?"

He didn't look up. "Catching up on some files. Couldn't you sleep?"

She poured another shot and smiled at the glass ruefully. "Sometimes I need a little help shutting my brain off." Raising her glass she waited for him to join her. After an almost imperceptible pause, he picked up his glass and met hers with a soft clink. Her eyes locked onto his. "Here's to hoping you get your man."

He didn't release her stare. And there was that damn smile again.

"Thank you."

Jack finally returned his eyes to the computer, but focus was out of the question, and it had nothing to do with the streak of bourbon warming his blood. Maybe it was lack of sleep, or hell, maybe it *was* the bourbon, but he was hyper aware of every subtle shift in Tori's body language.

"Tell me, Jack. Is having sex with someone involved with your case against the law?"

Subtle hell. She went from body language to straight up and down English. Jack swallowed hard, but continued to stare at the screen. "I'm ignoring that question."

38

She leaned in, resting her chin on her palm and looking for all the world like she was discussing the weather. "Why? I don't see a ring, so I'd call it a fair question. Is it against the law?"

Jack tossed his glasses on the table then sat back and crossed his arms. "It's not against the law. It's against protocol."

"Have you ever broken that protocol?"

She doesn't quit. And he'd thought he liked that about her? With a hard look, he hoped to erase the tiny smile teasing the corner of her lips. "No."

Didn't seem to faze her. She poured one more shot and tossed it back then rose and rinsed out the glass. "That's too bad."

How was he supposed to respond to that? Jack watched Tori leave the room, the sway of her hips teasing the short hemline of her oversized T-shirt into almost revealing the curve of her very firm, very nice ass.

Holy hell. A nomination for sainthood might be in his future. He adjusted himself after she left the room, his aching hard-on leaving little room for comfort.

After a shower that provided way less relief than he'd hoped, Jack returned to the hard wooden seat at the table and reopened the files Josh had forwarded to him. He'd finished reviewing the files on Justin Coakley and Reece Smith, along with Alan Reynolds' file. Very vanilla. Alan had started at the local TV station eight years ago after graduating from Oklahoma State and has been working his way up ever since. Not so much as a traffic ticket on his record.

Dwayne Davidson's file was a little more interesting. A few scrapes with the law as a younger man, but left the biker gang about ten years ago, coinciding with the birth of his daughter. Divorced but shared custody. Clean as a whistle since.

Jack stood and stretched. It was late, but he needed to finish. He nuked a cup of coffee from the pot Tori had made earlier and then took a drink of the steaming liquid.

He chuckled as Cam's warning came back to him. The coffee was strong, but the flavor was rich. He opened the cupboard and checked the brand. He'd never heard of it, but made a mental note to remember it when he got home. He liked Extra Bold. He took another sip as Tori's blatant questions replayed in his head.

Maybe he liked extra bold a little too much.

With the jolt of caffeine, and a lust kicker, Jack opened the new email notification from Josh. After studying the chart of dates and dollars, Jack shook his head, trying to reconcile the Tori he'd met to the woman who, according to the trust records, had sent hundreds of thousands of dollars for tornado relief efforts to Samaritan's Purse and Convoy of Hope.

He looked at the earliest withdrawal, which happened just months after the tornado that flattened her hometown, and spent the next thirty minutes on the internet cross-checking the dates of the others. Images from some of the most devastating tornadoes in American history flooded his screen: Greensburg, Joplin, Moore, Huntsville, Tuscaloosa, St. Louis, and more.

Jack closed the browser and surveyed the small, simple kitchen. Tori's obviously kept that part of her life secret, and that secret would stay with him, but damn if he didn't want to learn more about this intriguing woman.

The yellow plastic clock above the sink showed one-thirty, and as gritty as his eyes felt, he still needed to finish. He opened the file on Cam and forgot all about charitable donations, and about the time. Jack didn't know what he expected, but it sure wasn't what he found. Cameron Lyle Tate was born and raised in Atchison, Kansas and his juvenile record was sealed. Jack's jaw clenched as he opened the record and began reading.

After he finished, Jack shut down his computer and turned off the kitchen light. He glanced toward Tori's closed bedroom door as questions filled his head. How much did she know about Cam's past? How did he end up here last year working on her show? And what exactly was their relationship?

Cam was the one who'd made them aware of the emails, and he hadn't given Jack any reason to think he was anything but protective of Tori. But there was a whole lot more to Cameron Tate than met the eye. And Jack needed to find out if he was going to be an asset or a liability.

Shoving his hand through his hair, he plugged in the computer to charge. He wasn't getting any answers tonight, and if he intended to be worth anything on the chase tomorrow, he'd have to get some sleep. His gaze slid to the stack of blankets and pillow sitting on the unwelcoming couch.

Well, at least try to get some.

Two things Jack noticed right away. Sometime during his short night, the couch cushions had slid out from under him, mocking him from the floor.

And, his left arm, which was wrenched up under his head, was completely numb. He probably looked like a fish out of water as he flopped around trying to get to his ringing phone.

He caught it on the sixth ring. "Hey, Mom. You're up awful early."

"Early? It's almost eight. That's never early for you." She paused, her voice dropping. "I called your home number and got voicemail again. I didn't want to bother you, but it's been a few weeks since we talked. Are you doing okay?"

Barbara Mathis was an incredible woman with a huge heart, but she was a horrible small talker. He heard the anxiety behind her question.

Jack paused, surprised that the answer she wanted came pretty easy. He was engaged in the case and attracted to a hot redhead he had no business noticing that way.

"Everything's good, Mom. I'm in Oklahoma working. How's everybody doing?"

"Oklahoma, huh? Good. Perfect actually. I was going to ask you to take a few days off and come to New York to talk some sense into Hope, but since our next benefit is in Kansas City in May, it might be better for you to show up there. She tends to listen to you, and that way, it won't quite feel like we're ganging up on her."

Jack went on high alert. He'd always had a special bond with his older sister. "What's wrong?"

"It's ridiculous, really. A development company is building an independent living housing complex. I guess Hope heard about it at one of her classes. Now all she talks about is moving in there later this year when they're finished."

Jack breathed a silent sigh of relief. "So, what's the problem?"

His mother stuttered. "The problem? The problem is that she's not ready."

"I'm sure there'd be a significant battery of skills testing before they'd be willing to offer her a spot." He softened his tone to offset her anxiety. "Do you really think she couldn't handle it? You've spent thirty-five years telling her that she can do anything she puts her mind to. Are you sure you want to undo that work by refusing her this?"

The silence on the line burned his ears, but she didn't shut him down.

"She'll still need you, Mom."

The quiet sniffles on the other end of the line told him he'd hit the bullseye.

"What if they treated her badly? Or took advantage of their residents? Can you look into this outfit that's putting up the housing? It's called Living Beneficial LLC. Sounds more like an insurance company than a development firm. I don't know anything about them, and your father's never heard of them, either."

Jack kept the smile out of his voice. Surely if neither of them have ever heard of the company, it must be second rate. But he appeased her all the same. It wouldn't hurt to do some checking. He jotted down the company information. "I'll see what I can find out. If there are any red flags, I'll let you know. Okay?"

"Okay. So, by Kansas City you'll know something? Remember, second Saturday in May."

Jack swallowed his sigh. That was one of the many things his family didn't understand about his career. It wasn't a nine-to-five deal. He had no idea where his work would take him by then. Hell, he might be long gone from here.

"I'll do my best."

Apparently satisfied, his mother moved on. "So, what's taken you to Oklahoma?"

"Murder." His mind returned to the case, and the woman at the center of it.

"The case you were working on last year?"

"Yep."

"You know your job makes your father and me sick with worry."

"I know, Mom."

"Dad still wants you to –"

"I know, Mom." Jack stifled a sigh and relaxed his shoulders. "But, I'm doing what makes me happy."

It might've been her worry over Hope's situation, or she might've accepted the futility of continuing the argument, but for once, she let it go. Jack accepted his good fortune with a grin. "I better get off the line. Today's my first day chasing tornadoes, and I've been warned that it'll be a long one."

His mom's gasp was followed by a resigned groan. "You're slowly killing your mother. You know that, right?"

"I know, Mom. Love you."

"Good-bye, son," she chuckled. "I love you, too."

Jack set his phone on the table and turned, his eye catching Tori who stood watching him from the hallway, arms folded.

"So, the tough FBI guy is a momma's boy at heart, huh?"

Chapter 6

Tori shook her head as she set up the coffee pot. No one ever told her that listening to a grown man respect his momma ranked so high on the "things that make a man sexy" list. Of course, the plain white tee hugging his biceps and his sleep-tousled hair had to be somewhere in the top ten.

She stopped short, her smile fading. *What are you doing?* Today was chase day. She never let anything steal her focus on chase days, and she wasn't about to start now. If Jack ever decided to give it a shot, she was sure they'd have a hell of a go in the sack, but he didn't have any business intruding on her thoughts right now.

Except he had the power to ruin her season.

The station and fans of the show expected incredible footage. Why else watch it? Anxiety welled in her chest. Had anyone even vetted him to see if he knew which side of the camera to look through? Why hadn't she put her foot down and insisted on Tricia? Jack could've ridden along in the second truck, couldn't he?

The scent of freshly brewed coffee filled the room, centering her, and quelling the what-ifs. After filling her travel mug, she popped her laptop open on the table and pulled up the data again. Still looking good. The familiar tingling started in her veins, crowding out her worry – for the moment.

She'd give Jack one shot to prove himself. If he screwed it up, she'd go to Alan. He'd have no choice but to get Tricia, if she was still available.

Jack rattled into the kitchen and took a big, appreciative sniff. "Mind if I have a cup?"

"Go for it."

Tori watched him pour his coffee then drag some of the leftover Chinese out of the fridge. He was acting like today was just another day. Why wasn't he nervous?

After heating up the carton, he was three bites in before he finally looked at her. "I'm sorry. Did you want some?"

How could he be focused on food right now? "Gross. No, thanks. Chinese is only good the first time around." She continued to watch him. "We're chasing today. You know that, right? Lie to me and tell me you're going to be ready."

A mountain of uncertainty infused her words. Settling across the table from her with his cardboard containers and coffee, he raised an eyebrow. "I am. Are you going to ask me that at least a dozen more times today?"

She borrowed the confidence in his tone as her lips twitched. "Probably."

He nodded. "Thought so."

Tori checked the time on her phone. "The guys should be here soon with the Beast. We need to haul out of here by nine-thirty." She gave him one more look before she left the kitchen. "I hope like hell you can deliver."

Jack sobered as he drained his cup. Finding whoever was killing meteorologists was what he needed to deliver on. But in the meantime, he'd better shoot some damn good footage. It bothered him that she wasn't taking the threat seriously. Instinct was all he had to go on, and everything in him told him he was in the right place.

The distinctive rumble of a big block engine diverted Jack's attention. He took the few steps from the kitchen table to the front door, scooping up his ankle holster and strapping it on in the process. From behind the curtained window, Jack watched Dwayne climb out of the driver's seat and wait for Cam to join him before they headed to the door.

Cam stepped in then walked a circle around Jack. "Looks like you settled in nice. And to think I was worried about you even surviving."

"If it hadn't been for the Master Chen's tip, I probably wouldn't have." He paused. "Did some late night reading. We need to talk."

Cam nodded. "I figured. Just say when."

He headed to the kitchen and Jack tried and failed to reconcile Cam's laid back demeanor with the violence from his past. He shook his head and found Dwayne loitering by the door, looking uncomfortable. For a big man, Dwayne knew how to shuffle.

"What's on your mind, Dwayne?"

He jumped at Jack's question then turned to face him. After another quick look to confirm they were alone, Dwayne leaned in, his voice hushed. "Look, I know it's your job to protect Tori and, by God, I'm glad you're here. But I know that also means you got to dig around." Slow seconds ticked by. Jack had a pretty good idea where Dwayne was headed, but he was taking forever to land the plane. "I got a past. One that I'm not real proud of. And I'd appreciate it if it didn't get around. Big towns have a way of getting real small, and I'd hate for my daughter to have any reason to think less of me."

Jack nodded. "Got it." He knew better than most about burying the past. "The only peoples' pasts I'm interested in are the ones who are looking to disrupt Tori's future."

The older man's sigh was audible. "Well, that ain't me. Tori's like a daughter to me and I sure don't want to see her get hurt."

"Good to know we have that in common, Dwayne."

Cam sauntered into the living room. "Just checked on Tori. She'll be out in a few. She's grabbing her second laptop charger."

Dwayne looked at Jack. "So, what happens next? What can you tell us about the case?"

Jack didn't have any reservations about Dwayne, but he wasn't throwing information around either. He was trying to figure out how to phrase the rejection when Tori walked into the room.

"No, Dwayne." All eyes swiveled toward her. Her words were punctuated by a sharp shake of her head that had her long auburn pony tail playing catch up.

"But –"

"No. And take that look off your face. Mathis and his case are not important. Not today. Not on any chase day."

"But, don't you want to know what's going on? I mean, how do we nail this guy?"

Jack had to give Dwayne points for bravery. Because if the look on Tori's face right now was any indication, he was either dumb or blind.

"You've been my driver since the beginning, and you know I appreciate you." Tori spoke through clenched teeth. "But we're not detectives. We're storm chasers. If our focus is off, we lose. And I'm not going to lose. So are you with me?"

Dwayne didn't look the part, but he was definitely the beta in that relationship. He hesitated a second before nodding his head. "I'm with you," he grumbled, "but that don't keep me from worrying."

The Ford Explorer carrying Justin and Reece pulled up in front of the house and, as they joined the rest of the crew, all talk switched to the storm and the chase plan. Justin and Tori stood shoulder to shoulder, hovering over her laptop, reviewing data. Jack checked his gear and shoved his bag in the back of the truck. He inspected their ride, impressed and a little intimidated by the layer of armored plating and whatever else held the intercept vehicle together. Could this thing really protect them if they ended up getting caught in a storm?

Tori climbed into the front seat next to Dwayne while Cam settled in the back with Jack. There wasn't much room and even less conversation, and the drive through western Oklahoma to the Texas panhandle town of Dalhart should've been boring, but Jack couldn't deny the anticipation building in his chest. Thankfully, his camera was only a generation or two ahead of the ones he'd used during high school and college summers filming commercials. Didn't completely quell his anxiety, though. Would he capture the majesty of the storms he'd watched on the website? Would he even be able to pay attention to the camera in the heat of the moment?

The red dirt landscape gave way to brown and the shifting bank of clouds loomed larger. The sky darkened, obliterating the daytime sun. Tori looked up from the map on her laptop and tapped Dwayne on the arm. "Here. Stop here."

Dwayne pulled onto the shoulder, and Tori jumped out of the truck. Gravel crunched under her shoes as she turned a full circle. The low-hanging scuds teased her. The energy should've been higher, the air more charged. In her gut, she knew what no map or speculative data could tell her. They wouldn't get their super cell today.

"Okay, guys. Hop out." She pointed to her right. "Grab your cameras and set a position over there. We might get lucky and get a couple of babies anyway."

The sky was playing games, but there was some rotation to the northwest that looked promising. Tori almost bumped into Reece as he set his shot on her. "Dude, you need to back up. Stay closer to your truck."

Justin jogged over and shook his head. "I don't think it's going to pop here."

"Me either. Let me refresh the map." She threw on her Sooners ball cap to keep the rain from pelting her face as she circled again then jumped into the truck. "Look. It's moving on us."

"Yep."

Tori leaned out the truck window. "Come on, guys," she barked. "We need to get north and east of this formation. Fast."

Cam and Dwayne jumped in, and Tori bit her tongue as Jack wrestled his camera into the backseat. If they lost their only shot today, she'd kill him. Within seconds, they were off the highway and screaming down a dusty back road.

"Go another half mile or so then get on the next east bound road you find." Before she finished her sentence, the bank she was watching started to lower and form. "Hurry, Dwayne. Cameras, get ready."

After a hard right, Dwayne shoved the truck into park. Jack was seconds behind Cam as he jumped out. They had to be freaking crazy. High winds pulled at him from every direction and frenetic energy swallowed the air.

Tori grabbed Jack's arm. "Get out in front of it."

Something in her voice narrowed his focus. He got behind his camera, the view finder clarifying his shot. He found a great vantage point and held steady against the gusts buffeting him. To his amazement, the small funnel that formed didn't just drop down from the sky. It looked like it lifted from the ground and met in the middle.

He continued to film as Tori's words filtered around him over the wind. "It's going back up. Barely a minute on the ground. Damn it." She came up behind him, urgent. "Jack, over there." His gaze left the remnant of the funnel and followed her finger. "Look at those suckers. Twins coming down."

"On it." Jack spun and set for the new shot, the camera's firm weight settling on his shoulder.

But again, within minutes, the two stove-pipe funnels lost their energy and faded into the clouds.

"Damn it." Tori's ruthless eyes surveyed the sky again before she swung around and slapped the side of the truck. "We're done. With next to nothing to show for it. What the hell happened to the cold front? It shouldn't have been that weak."

Jack studied the turbulent sky, still riding a wave of adrenaline. "Are you sure we're done? What if another one forms?"

All eyes turned to him. Even Reece and Justin stopped mid-load. Cam and Dwayne looked at him as if he'd asked the dumbest question on earth. Maybe he had.

"We're done." Tori's face was a hard mask. Shaking her head, she climbed into the truck. "You just feel it."

The disappointment in her voice as she closed her laptop gave him pause. Whatever this was, it was way more than a job for her. Questions filled his head, none of which had to do with the marvel of Mother Nature he'd just witnessed.

But he held his tongue. The tension in the truck was thick enough without him adding to it. He went back to his camera to review his footage, and forgot he was going to be quiet as a low whistle escaped. "Man, that thing was incredible. I wish it would've held together a little longer."

Cam gave him a sidelong glance and laughed. "This was nothing, city boy. Wait until we get a real storm to chase."

Tori sighed, obviously not sharing Cam's humor. "This should've been a real one. The cold front flat out died. Must've been too much upper level pressure."

She seems to be talking more to herself than them, so no one answered her.

"So, on to the next chase," Dwayne offered.

They drove in silence for all of ten minutes before Dwayne asked again about the case. He shrugged off Tori's glare. "What? We're not chasing now."

Jack jumped in to stave off Tori's reply. "I don't know much else at this point. But I need you all to brainstorm names for me – anyone who might hold a grudge against Tori, or have some reason to want to hurt her."

Dwayne glanced over at Tori. "You tell him about Chuck Patterson?"

"Mathis is looking for a murderer, not a disgruntled former coworker."

Leaning forward, Jack tapped Tori's shoulder. "I'm looking to avoid making assumptions. So tell me about this guy."

Tori shrugged. "Not much to tell. He's a former camera operator who worked with Justin in truck two. His job was to film us as we chase. Like Reece does now. He wanted to work up front and I didn't think his personality would work, so I passed him over and asked for a new person to work with Cam. He got his feelings hurt, so he quit."

"You're forgetting about the little talk I had with him." Cam turned toward Jack. "After the season ended, Chuck kept coming around Tori's place. First it was to plead for his job back, but he got angrier as time went on. I was there the night he was drunk off his ass, yelling from the front yard about how he was going to make her pay."

"When did that happen?"

Cam frowned. "Before Christmas, but after Thanksgiving, I think. I basically let him know he needed to go away. He hasn't bothered her since, unless Tori knows something about it that I don't."

All heads swiveled to Tori.

She held up three fingers. "Haven't heard a peep out of him. Scouts honor."

Jack thought about what he'd read in Cam's file and wondered what kind of persuasion he'd used on Patterson. But that was a conversation he'd save for later.

"Thanks for that. I'll see what else I can find on him. Let me know if anyone else comes to mind."

Cam settled back in his seat and shook his head. "That's a little disappointing. You'd think Tori would have more people pissed at her."

Tori laughed as she reached back and slapped Cam's leg. "What can I say? Must be in a slump."

Without the anticipation of the coming storm, the ride back to Norman seemed to take twice as long as the morning run. Reece and Justin peeled off at the highway exit to the TV station, and Cam and Dwayne beat a hasty retreat after dropping off Tori and Jack.

Tori went directly to her room, leaving Jack to fend for himself. The fast food they'd picked up on the way back had worn off hours ago, so he rummaged through the kitchen cabinets. Tori was right. She literally had no real food in the house. How did she subsist on coffee and crappy frozen meals?

Jack knocked on her bedroom door. "Hey, I'm going to make a grocery store run. Is there anything you need while I'm there?"

"No."

"I'm stopping by the hardware store, too. Want to come?"

"No, thank you."

"Then come and lock the door behind me. Or give me your keys."

The first thing Jack noticed when she opened her door and walked past him was that she'd changed into black yoga pants that outlined her legs and backside to perfection. He blew out a breath and followed her to the front door.

She never looked up from her laptop as she marched to the front door. "Maybe by the time you get back, I'll get a clue about why the storm didn't set up today," she grumbled. She waved her hand with a flourish. "See you later."

Jack stopped with a hand on the knob and waited for her to look up from her screen. "You know this also means you have to let me in when I get back, right?"

Tori's lips twitched and Jack was inordinately pleased to see it. "Do I have a choice?"

He stood on the porch until he heard the deadbolt latch, then slid behind the wheel and checked his phone to find the nearest stores. Round trip, he shouldn't be more than an hour. A lot could happen in an hour, but if his target stuck with his normal strategy, he needed to build rapport with Tori. And then it would be a wait-and-see game. Interactive communication with previous victims spanned anywhere from six to eight weeks before he made his move.

Loading up the cart in the grocery store, Jack replayed the other cases. In interviews, several friends and family of the deceased knew about the emails, but none of the victims ever voiced concerns about their validity. The killer had brilliantly assumed identities of actual people, so the real LinkedIn profiles erased any potential concerns. And Tori hadn't been concerned either. Hell, she'd apparently tried to blow them off completely.

He was anxious for Tori to receive another email, for the dance to begin in earnest. But what if he was pissed that Tori hadn't responded yet? Jack couldn't see him moving on to another target. By the time Jack hit the hardware store, a knot had formed in his stomach. God knew getting Tori's address would be easy enough.

Running through the checkout, Jack bagged up his supplies, his blood pressure kicking up a notch. Hadn't he told Tori he wasn't in the business of making assumptions? He berated himself all the way back to the house, then pulled into the driveway and shut down the ignition almost before he'd slammed the car into park. He pounded on the front door once, then again. "Tori. Open up."

Fear slithered up his spine as he was met with silence. He stepped to the front window and peeked around the edge. A wave of relief surged through him as he saw her at her computer table. He rapped on the window with his keys until he noticed her ear bud wires.

Grabbing his phone, he texted her to let him in. He watched as she picked up her phone and looked up, startled, before running over to the door. "Sorry about that," she said as she pulled it open.

He released the tension in his shoulders and blew out a breath, trying to shake off the foreboding that had gripped him. "No problem. But the penalty is that you have to help me unload."

She rolled her eyes. "Fine."

By the time they stocked the cabinets and refrigerator, Jack was starving. "I'm going to cook some real food. Anything you won't eat?"

"I'm not picky, but don't feel like you need to cook for me. I'm good."

Jack scoffed. "That crap in the freezer can barely be considered food."

Tori shrugged and returned to her computer. "I'm reviewing what little film we got today. Reece's is finished, but I still need to do yours and Cam's. So, if I had a "do not disturb" sign, it would be hanging around my neck."

Popping in her ear buds, Tori settled into her chair and pulled up Jack's file. Truth be told, she was fairly impressed by his shot framing and his steady hand. She spent several minutes playing around with the file before moving on to Cam's work. With a little better direction, Jack might actually manage to keep from ruining her season.

An amazing aroma wafted through the room as she was finishing up, and her stomach grumbled.

"Traitor," she whispered.

Despite her best intentions, she wandered to the kitchen. Her heart did a slow roll as Jack looked up from taste testing his spaghetti sauce. His eyes screamed smoke, and whiskey, and sex.

She leaned against the door frame. "Did I mention I'm a sucker for Italian food, too?"

"Good. Grab a seat. Merlot?"

"Sure." She accepted the glass, trying to resist the urge to be annoyed that he'd set a place for her. He was obviously used to getting his own way.

But, after the first glorious bite of perfectly cooked pasta she smiled across the table, her annoyance evaporating. "This is insanely good. What kind of sauce is this? Ragu?"

Jack clutched his chest. "Sauce from a jar? My grandmother would haunt me from her grave. It's actually a family recipe. Easy, too."

Tori finished another bite then arched a brow. "You're talking to the frozen dinner queen. I have a feeling your idea of easy and mine would be vastly different."

"Well, here's easy for you. Try the bread. Not homemade, but fresh and crusty. Dip it in the olive oil."

Tori accepted the warm slice, her hand tingling where Jack touched. She followed his instruction and the bread was delicious, but the kitchen suddenly seemed too cozy. And their conversation felt too much like silly date conversation. Dating was for boyfriends. She didn't do boyfriends. And in her experience, most guys didn't care any more about the social niceties than she did, which made for much simpler and honest communication. Good sex, and nobody walked away with hurt feelings.

"Very tasty." She took a long sip of wine and refocused. "So. Just finished watching your film."

Jack's eyes met hers, his fork arrested half-way to his mouth. "And?"

She was surprised by the twinge of anxiety on his face. Surprised and pleased.

"You'll do." She laughed as his face fell. "I'm just kidding. It was actually very good. Now, if I can figure out how to manufacture some decent storms, we might get a season's worth of decent footage." Tori rubbed her stomach. "You're full of surprises, Jack. Good videographer, good cook. Makes me wonder what else you're good at."

His lack of response was at odds with the glimmer of heat in his gaze, but he cleared his throat and conceded the staring contest. "There's only one thing I need to be good at right now. Keeping you alive."

"Well, I'd say it's about time you earned your keep."

His keen eyes met hers again as instant tension filled the room. "What do you mean?"

She smiled. "I got an email."

"And you waited to tell me? When did it come in?" That fast, Jack shuffled her out of the kitchen and plopped her back at her computer desk.

"Around four. Glad I didn't mention it sooner. Might've gone without my supper."

Jack stood close behind her, leaning in. His scent, a subtle mixture of spice and male, caused her fingers to mistype her password not once, but twice. "Could you step back? You're making me nervous."

With obvious reluctance Jack took a small step back, his eyes never leaving the screen. As soon as she pulled up the message, he was right back in her space.

"Dear Tori. My executive team will be making preliminary decisions about next year's schedule in the coming weeks. I can't pitch you to them unless I know there's a chance you're interested. Message me at your earliest convenience," Jack read. "Don Sims, ABC. Just like the others. He's fishing. He's still not sure these emails come to you."

"Okay, FBI man." She clicked on the reply button. "What do you want me to say?"

"This is serious, Tori. Type this. Mr. Sims, thank you for your interest. I was going to decline your offer, but my producer and I are increasingly at odds. The creative license you mentioned in your previous emails has piqued my interested. I think I'd like to hear more. Sincerely, Tori Whitlock."

She positioned her mouse over the SEND button, but Jack reached for her hand before she clicked, drawing her attention.

His intense gaze bored into her. "You're getting ready to start the game. Whoever this guy is, he hasn't played until the players are on the board. Now he's going to know you're in. Which means from this point on, everyone you meet is a potential suspect."

Tori punched the button on the mouse and leaned back. "Good thing I don't meet many people in my line of work then. You already know the few people who are in my life on a regular basis, and I'm not much into expanding my social circle."

"What about the publicity event Alan mentioned? Think there might be a couple of people there you haven't met?"

Tori considered the calendar signing she did every year at the car dealership, and she could almost see the gears turning in his head. "Hmmm…guess you'll have to stick to me like glue." She smiled up at him and nudged her shoulder into his hip. "Could be interesting."

He stepped back, his glare almost comical. "It's not supposed to be interesting."

Chapter 7

Jack woke up rock hard. Once his frustration with Tori's nonchalance wore off, his mind spent hours reviewing the open invitation in her eyes and thinking about how *interesting* she would be. Apparently, his body was still obsessing.

He checked the time on his phone, gathered clean clothes, and headed for the shower. He didn't have time for distractions today. He needed to resolve an issue with one member of Tori's inner circle.

After the better part of an hour, the front door opened and closed. Jack jumped up from the kitchen table, hand on the butt of his gun, as Cam walked in. "I forgot you had a key. Let's talk in here."

"No problem." Cam sniffed then scrunched up his nose. "Mmm...Got to love the smell of coffee and turpentine in the morning."

Jack nodded toward an open window. "It was worse earlier."

"Has she been at it long?"

"She was up before I was, but I haven't seen her yet today." Jack motioned to the table. "Have a seat."

Cam lowered himself into one of the chairs. He crossed his arms, waiting for Jack to speak again.

"The other night, you asked me if I've got this, if I'll take care of the threat against Tori. And I do. I will. But I need to know exactly who I'm working with." Jack settled across from Cam and met his gaze. "I'm going to start by saying that, if I had serious concerns about you or what's in your file, you wouldn't be anywhere near Tori. You know that, right?" He paused as Cam continued to watch him in silence. "But you killed a man, and that warrants a discussion."

"Yes, I did. And if the situation were the same, I'd do it again."

"You were thirteen."

"I was big for my age."

"Your mother was still alive when you got home from school."

Cam's jaw tightened, but his voice never wavered. "Yes. There was blood everywhere from the stab wounds, but she was still alive. Still screaming."

"So you opened the door and saw your step-father on top of her."

"Yes."

"Then he turned the knife on you."

"He got me one time. Left thigh. Somehow I knocked the knife away from him."

"And then?"

"I beat him. I don't remember anything else until the police were pulling me off of him and Mrs. Fishbourne, our neighbor, was sobbing, standing over my mother's body."

"And, according to the file, it was her testimony that got all charges dropped against you, right?"

"Yes."

"Seriously?" Tori barked from the doorway.

Jack's gaze darted to her. Man, he was lucky her eyes couldn't shoot flame, or he'd be a pile of ash on the floor.

"Sorry, Cam. Special Agent Mathis has a nasty habit of bringing up issues that are long since buried." She walked up behind Cam and put her hand on his shoulder, her ferocious glare never leaving Jack's face. "Is it too much to ask that you focus on this decade?"

Jack clenched his jaw against the words he was tempted to fire back. He hoped she'd figure out soon enough that he was on her side. It would make both of their lives easier. "It's my job to protect you, Tori." His words were calm and measured as he returned his gaze to Cam. "But it's also important that I protect the integrity of the case. Today's world is different. This situation is different. You're a friend of Tori's —"

"Best friend," she interjected.

"Okay. Best friend. But if something goes down and you get in the middle of it, things could turn out a lot differently for you than they did last time. I've got to know that's not going to happen."

Cam shifted under Tori's hand. "It won't."

Tori shook her head vigorously, reinforcing Cam's statement. The pair reminded Jack of himself and Garrett, and all the times over the years they'd had each other's backs.

"What about Chuck Patterson? How'd you get him to stay away from Tori?"

"I've taken a few photography classes at the community college, gotten pretty good with my long range lenses. When Chuck started harassing Tori, I started doing some digging of my own. Ends up he's got a wife, a mistress, and a pretty serious crystal meth infatuation. All I did was let him know that his secrets wouldn't stay secret if he didn't leave Tori alone."

Jack leaned back in his chair, impressed. And relieved that the tension had receded enough that Tori didn't look ready to kill him. "Nice. His secrets might be out now, though. I got his file about an hour ago and found out he got into a little trouble earlier this year - ended up in county for eleven days. Probably bad for him at the time, but it gave him an ironclad alibi for the murder in Minnesota."

"Good to know we weren't working around a serial killer."

Jack nodded then looked at Tori. "Speaking of our guy, any response this morning?"

Cam's head whipped around. "Holy hell. You're talking to him? When? How often?"

"No answer yet." Tori shot Cam a frown as she poured coffee and joined them at the table. "Of course I'm talking to him, Cam. Well, so far just email. If I don't engage him, how else are we going to get this over with?"

Cam's chair tipped precariously as he made a beeline for the freezer and poured a liberal shot of bourbon, downing it in one gulp. "Anybody care to join me?"

Jack cringed. "None for me. Thanks."

"I'll take one." Tori grinned. "Never too early. Besides, I've been painting since five, so it's practically afternoon anyway."

Cam stuck around for about an hour, pestering Tori every few minutes to check her email. But after he left, the house got quiet. Tori switched on the TV and settled into the recliner. She made it through a two-hour World War II documentary and a show about Area 51 before she became antsy.

She stretched in her chair and yawned. "I can only watch TV for so long. And, I don't have anything left in me to paint today." She looked at Jack, sitting on the couch. "What do you do when you're bored?"

Jack closed his laptop. "Workout. Catch up on the news. Read. What about you? Any games you like to play?"

Tori's face broke into a Cheshire grin. "What'd you have in mind?"

Jack paused. "Board games. I'm thinking board games. Or video games."

"Oh," she pouted. "Never mind then. I thought you'd come to your senses there for a second."

A laugh escaped as Jack stood. "Between the two of us, I'm definitely being the sensible one." He extended a hand to help her up. "Okay. What kind of games do you have around here?"

"What are you talking about? Why would I have games here?"

He cocked an eyebrow. "Deck of cards, even?"

"No. If I wanted to play cards, I'd get online."

For whatever reason, that made him laugh harder. "Come on. Get your shoes on."

She crossed her arms. "Why?"

"We're going to the store."

Thirty minutes later, Tori stood in line at the toy store checkout holding a deck of cards, a chess set, a backgammon board, and a box of dominoes. She bit her cheek to hide the smile threatening to break out across her face. Shopping for toys shouldn't have been fun. Or funny. But Jack was like a little kid, trying to convince her to add this or that to her already full armload.

She'd have grabbed a cart or shoved them off on him, except that he had his hands full with a gaming console and several video games. "You're spending a ridiculous amount of money. I hope you know you're taking all of this with you when you leave."

Jack smiled as he dumped his items on the belt and began pulling games out of her arms. "We'll talk about it later. My guess is that you're going to have so much fun, you'll want to keep them. And I don't want you making any promises you can't keep."

She caught his silly wink and thought about how little he knew about her. Promises weren't ever given or expected.

Jack loaded their purchases into the trunk of Tori's Mustang. "Would you rather go back to your place to eat or go out?"

"I know a little hole in the wall place about twenty minutes from here that has great Tex-Mex. It's not fancy, but the food is incredible."

"Perfect. I'm starving."

Tori settled into the driver's seat and started the car, waiting for Jack to close his door before cruising out of the parking lot. "You're always starving."

"Look who's talking. You ate all the leftover pasta this morning."

She shot him a sidelong glance. "You shouldn't cook so well. I think you're secretly fattening me up to be a bigger target."

The energy flipped in the car and the heat from Jack's searing gaze burned. His quiet words seemed loud in the silence. "Do me a favor, and at least pretend you're taking this seriously."

Conversation was strained, or nonexistent, for the rest of the drive. By the time they got to the restaurant and ordered, she'd expected Jack to come around and relax, but the only time he'd laughed was at a comment by their server. And as Tori sipped her margarita and munched on chips and salsa, she realized she much preferred his laugh to the frown he was wearing.

She sat back in her chair and threw her hands up. "Fine. You win. Look, I'm sorry. Okay? No more lame jokes about your case."

Jack sighed and rubbed a hand over his face. "This isn't my case, Tori. This is our case. You're square in the middle of it. I wish it was all a joke, but your life is in real danger. And if he slips through my hands again, so are the lives of other women."

For the first time, Tori noticed the fine lines surrounding Jack's earnest eyes. How long had he been under the pressure of this case? She wished she'd paid more attention during their initial meeting, but she'd been too busy trying to convince him she wasn't the next target.

Linking her fingers on the table, she sighed. "Okay, start from the beginning, the first victim. I want all the details. No sugar coated bull crap, either. I have a strong stomach."

Jack took a pull from his Corona as their dinner arrived, along with Tori's second margarita. He didn't touch the food, and neither did Tori.

Instead, he watched her, studied her. He was sizing her up. When he began to speak, she released the breath she didn't realize she'd been holding.

"The first victim was a woman named Monica Gibson. She lived in Brooklyn, Ohio and worked as a television meteorologist for the local Fox affiliate in Cleveland. She was murdered in her home. Her dining room was covered with cue cards spewing vile epithets. She'd been strangled and then propped up in front of a foam board that was supposed to simulate a green screen. Her hair had been chopped off and he'd smeared make-up all over her face."

"The case was worked by local officials, but no suspects were ever apprehended. Usually crimes like this are passion crimes. The perp ends up being a jilted boyfriend or husband, but in this case, there was no one."

"How did you get involved?"

Jack swallowed a bite of enchilada. "About three months later, another television weather personality was murdered. This time in Denver. Marcie Daniels. Crime scene was virtually identical."

"But how did you link them? Or even make the connection? DNA?"

"God, I wish. But, no."

His eyes strayed from hers and he was quiet so long, she wasn't sure he was going to continue.

"What I'm going to tell you doesn't leave this table."

She nodded quickly, hoping to keep him from reconsidering his decision.

"The thing that connected them, other than the obvious similarities, is that the killer left behind a note at both scenes that said 'Better than you'."

Tori bit her lip and mulled the information over, intrigued. "Better than you? What does that mean? Is he someone who got passed over for jobs at the stations? Or was there a dating connection between any of them?"

Jack smiled. "You're starting to sound like a cop, Ms. Whitlock. Those are good questions, but we exhausted every possible connection we've considered so far. After the second victim, I got called in to lead the case. Trying to establish a pattern, we realized that the guy had gone west, after a bigger market. So, we shot for Los Angeles or San Francisco as possible next targets."

Tori finished off her plate and signaled for another margarita. "And you were right?"

Jack's eyes turned to steel. "I got to L.A. the week he killed Fran Little. At that point, we were aware of the emails he was sending to lure these women into connecting with him, and I was trying to track down anyone who might be receiving them, but we couldn't make the connection until it was too late."

"Did he kill her the same way? I vaguely remember something about this on the news."

"Yes. Same note left behind, too. After that, we blasted news stations across the country to make them aware of the threat but everything went quiet. It was like he fell off the face of the earth. We believed he'd be back, but there were no leads coming in from anywhere."

Jack tossed his napkin on the table, as if the conversation had turned his appetite. "A few months went by and then at the first of the year, I got the call on Dana Palmenteri in Duluth. I didn't want to believe it was the same guy because if it was, he'd changed the rules on us. But it was him. The note proved it. And every assumption we'd made? They flew out the window. The only thing we know now, for sure, is that all of his victims are women tied to meteorology. So now you know everything I know." His eyes bore into hers. "And hopefully, you understand why I have to stop him."

It was tough to reconcile that she was the next target, but Tori was mesmerized by the story, and fiercely attracted to the hard determination in Jack's eyes. It was obvious that even though he'd never met the victims, their deaths were personal to him. She didn't want this to be her reality, but since it was, there were probably worse people to be stuck with than Jack Mathis. "I do. What a screwed up asshole."

Leave it to Tori to sum up his entire case in one simple, irreverent sentence. He'd have been smart to tell her everything up front. Trust worked both ways, though, and he would need hers, too. It might be a fight, but he'd opened the door and given her every reason to walk through it. Raising his glass, he toasted her. "Couldn't have said it better myself."

After she clinked her glass to his, he looked around the small cantina style restaurant, grinning at the neon velvet paintings gracing the wood panel walls. "Good call on this place. And definitely off the beaten path."

Tori followed his gaze. "Hey, I warned you it wasn't fancy. Just good food."

He met her smile with one of his own, then tossed a few bills on the table. "You got that right. It's getting late. What do you say we skip the games tonight and maybe rent a movie instead?"

"I was up early this morning. Doubt I'd make it through an entire movie." She swayed as she stood and Jack's steadied her with a hand near her shoulder.

"Hold up, there."

"I'm fine. Like I said – just tired." Tori rummaged through her bag for a minute before locating her keys.

Jack extended his palm. She might be tired, but there was a decent amount of tequila in her system, too. "Hand them over."

She opened her mouth, then closed it and dumped the keys in his hand. "Fine by me. I don't like driving at night anyway."

"You can navigate."

As they walked out into the balmy evening, Jack shoved his hands in his pockets. The smooth skin of her upper arm had seared him, tempted him to find another opportunity to touch her.

"I wish you didn't smell so good."

Jack gritted his teeth as he closed her door. Damn if he hadn't been thinking the same thing about her. "Let's get out of here."

Relying more on his GPS than Tori, who'd nodded off within five minutes of leaving the restaurant, Jack finally pulled into Tori's driveway and cut the engine.

"Hey," he whispered, nudging her shoulder. "You're home."

Tori blinked awake and frowned at her surroundings. "Sorry about that. Didn't mean to crash on you."

"No worries. Can you make it into the house?"

She glanced at him sharply. "Of course. I told you I was up early today. Just needed a power nap. I can brew some coffee if you want some."

"None for me, thanks. If I drink coffee now, I'll be up all night. Think I'll just hit the shower and call it good."

Tori nodded as she let them into the house. "I'm going to check my models and see how the next few days are shaping up, then I'm probably right behind you."

Jack did a quick sweep before grabbing clothes from his bag and a clean towel from the linen closet. He was a few steps from the bathroom when Tori called to him.

He leaned around the door jamb. "What is it?"

Tori turned from her computer with a grin. "You were right about his quick response time. Ready for round two?"

Jack hunched over Tori's shoulder and read the email. "Perfect. He's looking for a time within the next few weeks to meet you personally. We need as much control of this as we can get. Tell him your schedule is volatile this time of the year because of the chases, but ask him for a couple of windows that might work for him."

Tori typed the message and hit send. "So now what? We sit and wait?"

"We wait. And watch. The length of time he communicated with the victims via email varied, but we have no idea how much surveillance he did. We know he's coming soon. So we lie low. Except when we control the parameters, I want you out of sight as much as possible."

Chapter 8

After Jack left to shower, his words echoed in Tori's head. The prospect of someone out there, watching her, made her skin crawl. And worse, being a prisoner in her own home would drive her crazy in no time. Especially being trapped with "protocol" Mathis. Oh, yeah. Definitely certifiable.

How could she prompt her adversary to pick up the pace? She picked up her cell phone to check the time, then dropped it on her desk as an idea dawned. What if he thought she was impatient to meet?

Her fingers tapped the keys as she quickly shot off another email to Mr. Sims asking for his phone number so they could discuss the project live. She probably wasn't the first woman to have that thought, but it didn't hurt to try, and she was curious to see how he responded.

Rolling her shoulders to stave off the beginnings of a headache, Tori grabbed her sketchpad and crawled onto her bed. Her margarita buzz had long since worn off, but as she stared at the blank page, nothing creative came to her. She knew better than to try to force it, and she was losing the battle with her headache. A splash of bourbon sounded like a better solution than a couple of ibuprofen. Might help her sleep, too.

She found her lazy bottle at the back of her drawer. The one that kept her from having to walk all the way to the kitchen. Her first shot went down smoothly, so she poured a second one. Eyes closed, she leaned against the headboard, willing the thumping in her temple to go away. She should've known better than to drink margaritas. Tequila always gave her a headache.

The screech of the shower curtain rings across the rod in the next room startled her. She looked down at the unfinished drink in her hands then tossed it back. A shower sounded good, but as she started to tuck the bottle and glass away, she decided that one more shot sounded better.

Tori woke to the smell of bacon. She rolled away from the door and pulled her pillow over her head. Jack really was ridiculous, and he probably already had her place set at the table. As she came fully awake, she remembered the email to Sims and jumped up to check for a response, but there'd been no reply.

As she showered and dressed, she tempered her disappointment with the knowledge that they were a step ahead of him. And until he made his next move, she had one hell of a sexy man to distract her. She considered the day ahead, and a smile played at her lips. No telling what Jack had in store.

Wandering into the kitchen, Tori filled her coffee mug. She nabbed a piece of bacon, nibbling on it as she squinted out the window at the bright blue sky. "We've got to get some storms soon. I swear. I've never seen such a dry pattern. And not just here. All over."

Jack shuffled behind her and she turned to see him placing their plates on the table.

"Come and eat. They'll show up eventually."

After devouring eggs, toast, and bacon, Tori gathered up their dishes. They'd developed a simple routine where Jack did the cooking and she did the cleanup. She was definitely getting the better end of the deal, but it surprised her how easily they'd settled into it.

Jack stuck a skillet in the dish water. "Ready to begin your education?"

Tori didn't look at him as she scrubbed. She didn't have to. She knew his simple question referred to the games he'd purchased. There was no hidden double entendre, but his energy still pulled at her, enticing her. He hadn't always been successful at hiding his interest, but he was much stronger than she was, much more disciplined. As much as that annoyed her, it also impressed her. And it annoyed her *that* it impressed her. How was that for screwed up thinking?

Tori shoved her thoughts aside and smiled as she took the towel Jack handed her. "Sure. Why not?"

After getting thoroughly trounced three chess matches in a row, Tori wasn't smiling anymore. She hated losing. Getting serious, she studied Jack's moves and strategy and at least started making it a game instead of a slaughter.

"How'd you get so good at chess?"

Jack looked up from the table. "My dad. He taught my brother and me when we were pretty young. He liked thinking games. Always encouraged us to think our way out of problems." He moved his bishop. "How about you? What games did you play growing up?"

Tori cursed the tightness in her chest. *He's asking a simple question. Pretend you're a normal person for five minutes and just answer the damn thing.*

"I mostly remember bridge and pinochle."

Jack cocked an eyebrow. "Not what I would've expected."

His expression forced a smile. "Every Tuesday, Thursday, and Saturday at my parents' club. My father either played poker or golfed and Mother met with her women's group. They sent my sister and me off to be entertained, which usually meant crafts or card games. A slow, agonizing ordeal for me. Every time."

Her eyes hinted at the words she didn't say, and Jack pictured a young girl who struggled to fit into a world that didn't allow for her uniqueness. He contrasted his own youth – full of love, and family, and security – to the glimpses she'd given him of her past. He knew better than to let the sadness that touched him show on his face. Pity wasn't her style.

"Did your sister hate it like you did?"

Tori shook her head. "Ha. No. My parents should've stopped with one kid. Vanessa was my parents' idea of a perfect child. She was a pleaser. Never went against the grain. I used to wish so hard I could be more like her, but I've always had a stubborn streak."

"I hadn't noticed." Jack's lips twitched into a smile, but what he really wanted to do was wrap his arms around her and break through her layers of distrust and distance.

Shrugging, Tori smiled and moved a pawn. "Must be slipping. I'll have to make it more obvious."

Jack put a lid on his thoughts. His arms shouldn't be anywhere near her unless it was to shield her from danger.

He caught up to her words and grimaced. "Not necessary. I believe you." He positioned his next piece. "Check."

Her smile was replaced by a frown. Jack could almost see the gears turning in her head as she moved to defend. "Aren't you supposed to let me win?"

He laughed and put her in check mate. "Yeah, right. You'll be kicking my butt soon enough."

"I think it's time for something different. What do you have that I might have a chance at?"

Rummaging through their bags, Jack pulled out the Xbox console. "How are you at shooting bad guys?"

Tori grinned. "Willing to give it a try."

Jack hooked up the unit then loaded the disc and handed Tori one of the controllers. He ignored his body's desire to sit next to her on the couch and sat down at the far end instead. The look on her face as she stared at the controller made him laugh.

"What is this? I thought we were shooting people? This doesn't even look like a gun."

She was a quick learner, though. He was as patient as he could be with his explanations and, in no time, Tori not only had the controller figured out, she was winning the round.

As they started the next game, Tori leaned forward on the couch and went into beast mode. Jack stopped playing altogether as she made five long-distance head shots in a row.

He set his controller down and faced her, arms crossed, a grin spreading across his face. "I've been played, haven't I?"

The mock innocence on Tori's face that dissolved into a fit of giggles was all the confirmation he needed.

"I can't. I just can't," she said in between convulsive laughter. "I'm sorry. I had to have one chance to win. I used to play with Cam at his place, but he's banned me."

Jack tried for an offended frown, and failed miserably. "Yeah, I can see why. You doubled my score." As he stood, he threw a small, decorative pillow at her head. "I'm going to make some sandwiches and regroup. You hungry yet?"

Tori got herself under control, wiping the tears of laughter from her cheeks. "I don't know. I guess I could eat." Tori followed him into the kitchen and pulled out a beer along with the sliced turkey and cheese. "Want one?"

"Grab me a soda."

"Suit yourself." Tori set his drink on the table and added a couple of bags of chips from the cabinet.

Jack joined her at the table with their plates. "What do you want to try this afternoon? And you better not try to sand bag again."

Popping the tab on her beer, Tori took a long drink then looked at the clock above the window and sighed. "Kill me now before the confinement makes me crazy."

Jack grinned over his shoulder. "No way. My boss would never give me another case."

Tori shoved away from her desk and paced her small bedroom. Three days into their isolation and, besides their crappy chase, they'd been out of the house one time to hit a grocery store, and at Tori's insistence, a liquor store. Where the hell were her storms? They were her only refuge, her only way to get out of here for a while. The maps were so quiet she wondered if she'd get enough material to even produce an entire season of shows.

And why hadn't Mr. Sims responded to her email?

Pulling her dusty yoga mat from her closet, Tori cleared a spot near her bed and began stretching. She'd be sore tomorrow, but she didn't care. At least she could zone out and escape the tedium for a little while.

In the middle of a routine that she was surprised she remembered, her phone buzzed letting her know an email had been received. Sweat dripped from her brow onto the mat as she debated cutting her routine short to check the message. She'd become conditioned to darting to her phone to check every buzz, but she wasn't one of Pavlov's dogs, and she wasn't going to disrupt her workout for another disappointment.

Although the question of the email's sender was never far from her mind, she finished her workout, guzzled some water, then took a shower before she sat down at her desk to open her browser. Then she swore at herself for not opening it sooner.

Mr. Sims responded that he would check his schedule and advise when he would be in town. He also stated that, because of privacy concerns, he didn't offer his phone number until after he'd met face to face with prospective business partners.

What a loser. But at least it was something to talk about.

Tori unplugged her laptop and found Jack in the living room. "Finally got a response."

Jack glanced up, surprise lighting his face. "Let me see."

She dropped onto the sofa and handed her computer over. Jack's brow furrowed as he read the message. Then, as he scrolled down and read her second message, his frown turning into a scowl.

"What's this?" He pointed at the screen. If his scowl hadn't been a warning, his tone surely was.

"What?"

"You sent him a second message. Without my knowledge."

He sounded like her father. Agitated, Tori threw up her hands. "Oh, my God, Mathis. If you weren't here, that would've been a perfectly normal question for me to ask him. Wouldn't it?" She stared at the ceiling, attempting to corral the burst of anger surging through her. "All I was trying to do was move things forward. You may like hanging out and twiddling your thumbs for days on end, but I don't."

Jack stood and shoved his hands in his pockets. "I don't like the waiting game any more than you do, but you know what I like even less? Surprises, Tori. I don't like surprises."

His entire body was strung tight and, in such close proximity, Tori was having a hard time focusing on anything but the fire flashing in his eyes. She wasn't used to being challenged, and if she were honest, it felt good to have a worthy opponent.

She stepped back when what she really wanted to do was move closer, just to see what he would do. But her ego wasn't ready to take the hit.

Jack sighed and handed her the computer. "It was a good idea. Just talk to me. You're not in this alone. We're a team here."

Tori tucked her laptop under her arm, her anger evaporating. She'd been so focused on her own frustration, she hadn't noticed his. "I know. I'll work on it."

He grinned. "Speaking of twiddling our thumbs, you want to pick a movie?"

She sighed. "I don't care. Avengers or Man of Steel."

"Seriously?" He turned sideways to look at her.

"What? Tell me you didn't expect me to say The Notebook or something." She shuddered. "Too sappy. You obviously don't know me as well as you think you do."

"Give me some time. I'm working on it." He winked at her, then got up and loaded the movie. "Well, if I'm picking, I'm more of a Marvel guy."

"Fine by me. Plenty of eye candy either way."

Tori released a small sigh as Jack's fine backside came into view. A wink should *not* make a legion of butterflies take flight in her stomach. And according to Jack's stupid protocol, he shouldn't be winking at her anyway. She should call him on it, but the slow, lazy smile that had accompanied it just might mean he was finally getting comfortable. Hopefully comfortable would lead to naked and horizontal.

Talk about taking care of the boredom.

Her mind replayed some of the more interesting fantasies she'd created until she realized Jack was staring at her quizzically. His eyes darkened to a deep brown and darted to her mouth. He swallowed hard and swiped the remote from the coffee table before squaring his shoulders and settling next to her on the sofa. He could've chosen the recliner, but didn't.

She'd have to call that progress.

After the movie, Tori glanced at Jack over the thin space that separated them. He was stretched out, hands crossed behind his head, his long legs filling the space in her tiny living room. Something about him made her almost wish she was the kind of girl who snuggled on the couch, holding hands, watching chick flicks. She sat up and hit the remote to turn off the DVD player, shaking off the threatening melancholy.

She picked up her beer bottle and painted a smile on her face. "Has it occurred to you that we've done nothing for days but eat, watch movies, and play games?"

"Yeah. And?"

"I don't know. I guess I expected FBI work to be more exciting. Bet you don't use stuff like this in your recruiting materials."

"Why not? Think about it. Eating, watching movies, playing games? Who wouldn't want that to be their job?"

She laughed. "Point taken. Somehow I don't think that's your motivation, though. So why do you do it?"

Jack studied her for a second. "I went to college with the expectation of running the family business when my dad retired. That was my parents' expectation more than mine, but I didn't fight it, either. Didn't really know what I wanted to do. But, after college, I needed to make my own way. The Bureau was recruiting on campus and that's the direction I went."

"Oh, wow. How'd your parents take it?"

"They understood at the time. But to them, it was just a phase. I think they expected me to come back."

Tori opened her mouth to ask why, but the glimpse of pain in his eyes surprised her. He blinked and it was gone. Or maybe she'd only imagined it.

"It sounds like you get along with them."

"Yeah. They're great people."

Tori jumped off the couch. Last thing she needed was for Jack to steer the conversation to her own family. "I'm going to grab another beer and some munchies. You want anything before I take another run at you on Call of Duty?"

"I'll take a beer. Or several. So I won't feel so bad when I don't win a single round and have to hand over my man card. Again."

Tori laughed from the kitchen. His man card was in no danger of revocation. No worries there at all.

Jack's fingers tapped on the table as he waited for Tori to make her move, mesmerized by the way her fingers idly twisted her hair as she studied the board. He added the slow, rhythmic process to the growing list of ways she turned him on.

Yes, he was chronicling them. This was number seventy-two. Many of them had come from seeing her in action during four chases over the past three weeks, or her dry humor, or simply listening to music with her. He'd hoped that acknowledging his attraction would help keep him from acting on his fantasies, but all it had done was give him a freaking reference guide. And these entries were the worst. The little, unintentional things that were uniquely Tori. Like the half smile on her lips when she was engrossed in her painting, or the soft strawberry scent of her shampoo that made him want to bury his hands in her hair and expose her long, graceful neck for his pleasure.

He was losing the constant battle to maintain a professional detachment from her, giving ground every day. When she was in the room with him, he wanted to touch her, to taste her. And when she wasn't in the room, he wanted her to be.

"What?"

And he'd just been caught staring at her. "Nothing. Waiting for you to make a move. You only have three possible options. The decision can't be that hard."

She raised one eyebrow then, with a sly smile, moved her rook. "Check."

Jack's eyes widened. "Damn. That wasn't one of the moves I saw for you."

Tori was as smart as she was sexy, and the way she was looking at him now, along with the edge of black lace peeking out from her tank top, had his brain short circuiting on multiple levels. He checked the board again. If there was a way out, he couldn't see it. Either way he went, she had him.

He stumbled over the thought. The broader implication caused a greasy drop of faded guilt to slide down his spine. He hadn't meant it that way. Back-pedaling, he forced his head back into the game.

"You're going to beat me."

Tori laughed. "Don't sound so surprised. You're a good teacher."

Raw and jumbled, Jack conceded the game and stood at the same time Tori rose. They were chest to chest and, despite the battle in his head, it took every last bit of Jack's willpower not to pull her into his arms and find out exactly how sweet she tasted.

The quickening of her breath and the heat in her gaze told him she wouldn't stop him if he tried. And she was between him and the freedom of the back door. Or the living room. It didn't really matter. He just needed to get away from her. Fast.

His hands clasped her exposed upper arms, forcing her to the left so he could squeeze around her. If his hands lingered on her softness a little longer than necessary, that was a small prize for adhering to his principles.

She moved and he accidentally brushed her breast, sending a jolt of electricity shooting up his arm and eliciting a sharp intake of breath from Tori.

"If you're going to start something, Mathis, I hope like hell you plan on finishing it."

He stared at her, energy sizzling through him as he grasped for any kind of justification. She called to him on every level, making him wish their meeting had happened at a different time and place. And for a different reason. But, as it was, he had no right to pursue Tori. Not now. He wouldn't allow himself to think about after. Because he had no idea what *after* meant.

As he jerked past her, the disappointment in her eyes mirrored his own feelings. With more force than was necessary, he yanked open the back door. "I'm going to get some air. I won't be far."

Jack walked the perimeter of the house at least a half dozen times, his blood cooling with each pass. What was he doing? How could he effectively protect her if he was distracted by his own desires?

Maybe he should remove himself from the case.

His fists clenched as a wave of protectiveness crushed him. No way in hell. No way was he leaving Tori's life in someone else's hands. He would finish this job. But for now, he owed Tori an apology, and a recommitment to act in her best interests. Even if she disagreed on what that meant.

He stepped onto the front porch, anxious to clear the air, as his phone buzzed in his pocket. Sitting on the stoop, he took the call from Virginia.

"Hey, Josh. Got anything new for me?"

"Nothing exciting. You check your email?"

"Not in the last hour. What's up?"

"Director Collins sent out an email pulling Heather from the case. Said he needed her on a different project."

Jack wasn't surprised. Budget cuts had a lot of people being shuffled around. "Unfortunately, there wasn't much for her to do on this case. Everything she got me on the family was exactly what Tori had said I should expect. And the ball's in the perp's court now, anyway."

"You still think the dealership meet-and-greet is a good idea for tomorrow?"

Jack pushed a hand through his hair and blew out a breath. "I don't know. I think so. It's been over a week since we've gotten any communication and still no firm commitment on a time for Tori to meet him. He's either not here, or he is. But I don't believe he'll do anything in such a public venue. Too far away from everything his profile says about him. No way to leave a note, no way to put his signature on it. But it might be a way for him to get a look at her. That's what I'm hoping. See if any red flags go up."

"Let me know if there's anything you need from me. I'm assuming you've talked to the locals."

"Yeah. They've increased surveillance, but there's not much else they can do."

Jack hung up and walked into the quiet living room, tossing his phone on the table next to the small lamp Tori had left on. She hadn't waited up for him. And why should she? In the shadows, he studied his favorite of Tori's paintings. He finally understood what people meant when they said art spoke to them. Because this one spoke to him. It reminded him so much of its creator. Light and shadow. Anger and humor. Depth of color from black and blues to yellow, with bold lines that resonated strength.

Closing his eyes, Jack let his head drop against the back of the sofa. He'd needed that call from Josh to reset his focus. His perspective had gotten twisted during the past few days. It had been all too easy to slip into a routine with Tori that almost made him forget there was a mad man waiting in the wings.

Chapter 9

Tori stood in front of the full-length mirror in her room and ran a brush through her hair, which was getting too long to manage easily. She considered putting it up in a ponytail or even braiding it, but it wouldn't look right with the simple black wrap dress.

Stepping into the red pumps that matched her chunky jewelry, Tori walked past the bathroom where Jack was showering and wandered into the kitchen. She checked the time. It was too early to head over to Whitey's. Maybe she could try her hand at making breakfast. She pulled up a recipe website on her phone, but every one she found looked complicated. She knew her limitations.

Instead, she pulled out bread to toast, and unearthed a few eggs from the fridge while the coffee brewed. She turned and saw Jack in the doorway. His slow perusal made Tori forget to breathe. It also made her want to forget his little talk with her first thing this morning about his job and his priority.

He was going to be the death of them both.

Tori turned back to the stove and stirred the eggs, biting her tongue to keep from opening the door he said he wanted to keep closed. Coming up next to her, he ripped open the bacon like it had personally insulted him and laid the strips in the skillet.

"Your guard better be up today. Anything or anybody that feels out of place to you, you let me know. Got it?"

His voice was loud in the awkward silence. And angry. Tori couldn't help but smile a little knowing that she was at least partially responsible for his frustration. Served him right.

A knock sounded at the front door.

"That would be Dwayne. Always right on time."

"I'll get it. You keep an eye on the bacon."

"Hurry back. I can't get grease on the only decent dress I own."

Dwayne followed Jack into the kitchen a few seconds later. "Smells good." He glanced around the room. "Where's Cam? I thought he'd be here today."

"Morning, Dwayne. He called yesterday to let me know he wouldn't be able to make it. He's got an online test he needs done by noon today. I told him not to worry about it since you and Jack would be here."

"Could've used another pair of eyes," Dwayne grumbled.

"Never hurts," Jack agreed. "But we've got local plain clothes police in the area. I want you at the front door. I'll be with Tori. And just like I told her, anything doesn't set right with you, let me know."

Dwayne popped a piece of bread into the toaster. "You got it."

———

Tori walked into the dealership with Jack and Dwayne flanking her. The table display was set up with the stack of next year's calendars ready to be signed and given away. Before she'd taken three steps, a booming voice filled the showroom as Whitey rushed forward.

"There's my girl. You're better for business than a hail storm."

With his shock of thick white hair, Whitey's name did him justice. He reminded her vaguely of her grandfather, but with a few extra pounds and a bucket of false charm. She didn't resist when he wrapped her in his signature giant hug. Then, with as much grace as she could muster, she extricated herself from his grasp and introduced him to Jack.

A few minutes later, people started to form a line. Jack stayed on her like a second skin. She wanted to push him away, but it was an exquisite kind of torture to have him that close, to catch his scent when he moved a certain way. She found this position odd, and oddly fascinating. She couldn't remember the last time she'd wanted something or someone like she wanted Jack. And for the first time in a long time, she wasn't sure what the outcome of their obvious power struggle would be.

Within minutes, she was forced to push those unsettling thoughts away as she was whisked to the front of the line where she signed calendars and posed with kids and adults, eight to eighty, against a backdrop of a raging twister.

After the first session, Whitey's office manager, a tiny girl with a sweet smile and a huge chest, motioned for them to follow her. "Whitey said to come get you for your break. So, here's our break room if you, you know, want to take a break."

Tori caught Jack's sardonic eyebrow lift and smacked his arm as they followed the girl. "Thank you. We only have one more session, right?"

The girl checked her clipboard and nodded. "That's right."

As soon as the door closed behind her, Tori flopped onto the hard couch and closed her eyes. "Forty-five more minutes. You can do this."

"Personal pep talk?" Jack flipped around a chair and straddled it, resting his arms on the back.

Sighing, her head fell back. "Something like that. Not really much of a people person. It's all I can do to get through these events. Sad thing is, I was actually looking forward to this."

"I know. But you could've fooled me. If I didn't know better, I'd think you were having a good time out there."

"Yeah, well. That's why they pay me the big bucks," she mumbled.

Tori enjoyed a few minutes of blissful silence, appreciating the fact that Jack seemed to understand that's what she needed. Sitting up, she put her hands on her knees. "I'm ready to go one more round. Anything suspicious to report?"

Jack rose and extended his hand, but he was quick to release her once she was up. "You'll be the first to know."

She shook off the little tingle his fingers left behind and refocused her attention on the task ahead. They left the break room and turned right down the long hall that led to the main show room. Around the last turn, Tori stopped short causing Jack to come up hard behind her, his hands tight on her waist as he steadied her.

She crossed her arms and glared. "Wow, look who crawled out of his lab. What are you doing at my publicity event?"

"A guy can car shop, can't he?" Glenn Pritchard's lean frame shoved off the wall, his eyes straying to Jack. "Looks like you found a new goon. Dwayne not doing it for you anymore?"

"You never could figure out what did it for me, could you, Glenn?"

His pale face darkened all the way to his blond roots. "You've got two things going for you, Tori. You've got great tits," he paused, squinting. "Second one slipped my mind." His smirk smacked of superiority. "There's nothing special about what you do, you know. You don't research, you don't promote scientific advancement. All you do is chase and look good in front of a camera. Oh, and speaking of cameras, thanks for passing on Tricia Chalmers. She shot some great footage for me on that first storm. Can't wait for next week to really see what she can do."

Tori seethed. Not that she hadn't heard him use the same tired lines a hundred times before, but Jack overhearing them changed the dynamic. And on top of that, Tricia went with Glenn? How the hell did he maneuver that?

Normally she'd walk away from his petty bullshit, but he pushed all the right buttons today. "Well, it's a good thing for you that I chase, Glenn," she said in her sweetest voice. "Because if I didn't, you wouldn't have a snowball's chance in hell of figuring out where to go, despite all your scientific equipment. I'll see you on the road. In my rearview mirror. If you'll excuse me, I've got work to do."

"Work?" he scoffed at her back. "You're taking pictures with people."

"Fans, Glenn. They're called fans. Good luck trying to find enough to keep your lame ass show on the air."

"Fuck you, Tori."

"In your dreams, sweetheart." Tori grabbed Jack's arm as he made to turn around. "Leave it," she hissed under her breath. "Do *not* make a scene here."

Jack allowed Tori to lead him to the show room, and didn't speak until he was able to unclench the fists he'd somehow managed to keep at his sides. She did a good job putting the prick in his place, but Jack wanted to follow it up with a right hook to his face. He released the tension in his jaw. "What the hell was that?"

She looked flushed and there was fire in her eyes, but she kept walking. "I'd call it asshole on parade."

The small tremor in her voice told him she was more affected than she wanted to let on. He stopped in front of her, forcing her to stop. She tried to side step him, but he took her elbow and walked her away from the waiting crowd. "Details, Tori. Now. That guy just guaranteed himself an invitation to meet one-on-one with the FBI."

Sighing, Tori shook off his hand. "Don't waste your time. He's just a guy I went through the meteorology program with. His name is Glenn Pritchard. We were competitive back then, but he had no complaints about me until I told him I wasn't interested in dating him. Then somehow, I turned into an airhead bimbo bunny. It kills him that I've got a successful show. So this year, he got a rival network to float him for a season. They're selling it as reality TV for smart people." She glanced over at the growing line. "Can we hurry up and get this over with so I can get the hell out of here?"

Jack released her. From the corner of his eye, he watched Glenn's grim expression from the other side of the show room until a salesman approached him and he left. *Car shopping, my ass.* Jack texted Josh to get him everything they could find on Glenn Pritchard.

As the crowd dwindled, Tori surreptitiously checked her watch then smiled at a young boy clutching his dad's hand. "Hi there, buddy."

His face lit with a nervous smile. "Can I have one of your calendars for my room? The Beast is so cool."

"Sure thing." She signed it then passed it over to him.

The father leaned in. "Archer loves to watch your show. His mom thinks it'll give him nightmares, but it hasn't so far."

"It's very exciting, but we do everything we can to be safe." Tori looked at Archer. "Do you guys have a plan at your house if a tornado comes?"

"Yeah, we don't have a basement, but my dad says we should go to the bathroom because there's no windows. Is that right?"

Tori smiled. "Your dad's a smart guy. That's exactly what you should do."

"Archer wanted to get his picture with you. Do you mind?"

"Not at all." Tori motioned the boy over then smiled as his dad snapped a couple of photos. "Thanks for coming to see me today. You stay safe, okay?"

The boy nodded, beaming ear to ear as they left the table. "She was really nice, Dad."

Jack smiled at the boy's loud whisper and wondered how Tori would take that assessment. She didn't want to be sunshine. But man, was she substance. Thick and rich and potent. During their time together, Jack had watched her canvases come alive with color and passion. He'd seen her feeding squirrels in the backyard when she thought he wasn't watching. And he'd seen the fierce protectiveness of the people closest to her.

Jack blew out a breath. He was in trouble. And then she'd gone and delivered a knock-out punch this morning with that dress. After his initial reaction to the little black number and how her fiery hair glowed against it, he'd tried all day to keep from noticing. But every unconscious move and sway accentuated her curves and lit him up all over again.

Finally, the last fan left and Whitey congratulated Tori on a job well done.

Jack picked up Tori's bag and handed it to her. "You ready to go?"

"You have no idea," she said quietly.

Jack's attention was drawn to the doorway where Dwayne was talking and gesturing to a man who looked like he was trying to get past him and into the showroom.

"This day just keeps getting better and better," Tori mumbled under her breath. "I don't have any patience to deal with him today."

Jack monitored the situation for a few more seconds. Chuck Patterson was thinner than he'd been in his mug shot from January and his movements were animated, almost erratic. Cam's comments about the drug use filtered back to Jack. Looked like Patterson's stay in jail didn't do much to dissuade him from using. Or from staying away from Tori.

Dwayne shook his head and crossed his arms. Jack couldn't hear the exchange, but it was apparently enough to convince Patterson to leave.

Tori released a sigh. "Let's get out of here."

After visiting briefly with the plain clothes officers, Jack joined Tori and Dwayne in the car. He glanced at Tori. "You want me to drive? You look beat."

And she did. But she threw the car in gear and made her way out of the lot. Guess that was his answer.

Jack turned so he could talk to Dwayne. "What happened with Patterson?"

Dwayne shrugged. "He's a mess, man. He knew Tori would be at the dealership today and wanted to ask for his job back. Gave me a big old sob story. I told him he had to leave, that it wasn't a good time."

"Was he tweaking?"

"No doubt. I knew he used a little when he worked with us, but he was usually a pretty decent guy, decent camera operator. Never seen him like he was today though – all sweaty and out of control."

Jack didn't mention the issue Tori had with Patterson in January and from the look on her face, that was the right call. She looked pissed. He wasn't sure what was going on in her head, but he decided to tread lightly.

"Idiot's going to end up killing himself if he doesn't get his shit together," Tori said.

Jack had Dwayne stay with Tori in the living room as he swept the house then did a perimeter check, but she was nowhere to be found when he came back inside. Jack crossed his arms and waited until Dwayne disconnected his call.

"That was Cam. Checking to see how today went."

"Where'd Tori go?"

Dwayne motioned down the hall. "Taking a bath. She's does it after public events. Has for as long as I've known her. She won't be out for a while."

Jack accepted the beer Dwayne offered him and sank onto the sofa. He thought about Glenn Pritchard and got fired up all over again.

"I've been spinning my wheels for weeks waiting for any kind of direction. What I'm trying to figure out is why I've never heard of Glenn Pritchard before today. Why didn't his name ever come up?"

Dwayne frowned. "Guess I never thought about somebody like him being a murderer."

"Somebody like what?"

"You know. Smart, educated. I think he'd have a lot to lose."

Jack considered some of the cases he'd worked. "You'd be surprised how many serial murderers are college educated with careers. Or married with families. It would blow your mind. So tell me about Pritchard. The guy's obviously got an ax to grind with Tori."

"He's a first class asshole."

"Got that part," Jack interjected. "What else?"

Tipping his beer back, Dwayne took a long swallow. "I know he hates Tori. And he's gotten a lot of his cronies against her, too. Guys who used to like her and get along with her. Way I see it, he's kind of made her the outcast of their old group. All out of jealousy, I think. But it don't seem to bother her."

Josh's report on Pritchard couldn't get here soon enough. Could he have a connection to the other victims?

"Who else is on his team?"

"Not sure. I did hear that he hired Tricia Chalmers, but I wasn't about to tell Tori."

"Yeah, he mentioned that to her today."

"He did? Holy crap."

"Seemed to light Tori's candle. Who is she?"

"She was going to be our second camera operator 'til you got here."

Jack paused, absorbing yet another price Tori had paid. And another strike against him. "Does Tori know her?"

"Personally? I don't think so. Tori checked out her portfolio though and pushed to hire her." Dwayne leaned forward in his chair, his beer dangling from his fingertips between his legs. "So, you think Glenn's our guy?"

Jack held his groan. Dwayne had watched too many TV crime dramas where everything wraps up nice and neat in an hour, minus commercials. "Don't know yet."

Finally, Tori emerged in a robe and a towel wrapped turban style around her head. She looked pale, almost fragile wrapped in the white terry cloth, and it called to every basic protective instinct Jack possessed.

She headed for the kitchen without looking at either of them. Jack heard ice clink into a glass, then she came into the living room and sat down, her tumbler filled to the rim.

"Feel better?"

She took a sip of the amber liquid and closed her eyes briefly. "I will soon."

"Good. So, I'm checking into Pritchard. Anything else you can give me on him?"

Tori shrugged. "We worked on several projects together, and he did some chasing with me early on. Like I said, he was cool until I wouldn't date him. Then he got hateful. Don't know much about him now. We don't exactly pal around together. My personal motto is to avoid weird guys." She looked over at Dwayne. "Unless they're my weird guys. Then I put up with them."

Dwayne laughed. "I'll take that as a compliment." He rose. "I gotta scoot. I get Cassie tomorrow through Sunday night. We're good 'til then, right?"

Tori nodded. "I think so. But next week could get crazy. Finally. So be ready."

"You know it." Dwayne let himself out.

With a heavy sigh, Tori leaned back in her seat.

Jack waited. He was learning to give her time. She took another sip, her tongue darting out to catch a drop on the lip of the glass. Jack looked away. It was either that or kiss her.

"Today was strange."

His brow furrowed. "How's that?"

"I was thinking about this in the tub." Her weary eyes met his. "Before you came, it could've been like every other day. I could've run into Glenn. I could've fended off Chuck if he'd have come in. But you make everything strange. You make me think that the boogey man's around every corner."

Maybe it was exhaustion allowing her to speak honestly. She'd been poring over her computer for days and today totally drained her. She was such an enigma to him. Becky had always gained energy from being around people, but it was obvious that Tori was the complete opposite.

Jack froze, his bottle almost to his lips. He had no business drawing any comparisons between Becky and Tori. God, he must be tired, too. He shook his head, pissed that he'd gone there, and his words came out more forcefully than he'd planned. "Look, you may not like it, but at least you're aware. The other women, the victims, they never had a chance to be aware. It's a small price to pay if the weirdness saves your life."

Tori's eyes flashed, but she didn't speak as she stood and set her empty glass on the coffee table. Just before her bedroom door closed, her faint words reached his ears.

"If you say so."

Jack finished his beer and plunked the empty bottle next to Tori's glass. He sat on the edge of the sofa, fighting the urge to call her back. She wanted to say more. He'd have bet his life on it. But that would've meant opening up, being real. And that wasn't in her playbook. At least not with him. Not yet.

He sighed, and let his head fall back against the stiff cushion. Playing the waiting game obviously wasn't her forte, and it wasn't his either, but he'd wait as long as he had to for the bastard to show himself.

His eyes closed and, for a second, Tori's lifeless body superimposed over the crime scene photos in his mind. He jumped up and paced the room until his speeding heart rate slowed. With a deep breath, he drew back the curtain from the window and stared out at the inky night. In his head, he repeated the words that had become a daily litany, trying for a sense of conviction.

She's the job. *Only* the job.

The light behind him shifted his focus to his reflection in the glass. He looked long and hard at himself. He was staring at a liar.

Chapter 10

Anticipation sang through Tori's veins as she shifted in her bedroom chair and studied the laptop screen. Everything was setting up beautifully for a monster storm tomorrow in Northwest Kansas and Southwest Nebraska. April had given them a few interesting chases, but she'd been waiting for a set up like this one since the beginning of the season. Not only should it offer some powerful shots for the camera, but she was more than ready to get her focus off of Mr. Sims. And off Jack.

She resented his assumptions about her. And he certainly didn't have the right to tell her what was or wasn't a small price to pay for her life. He didn't get to ascribe value to her. He could believe whatever he wanted to believe, and he was there to do his job and protect her, but he didn't know her. The people who *really* knew her wouldn't have ascribed any value at all.

The comparative data analysis in front of her blurred as unwanted tears filled Tori's eyes. Squeezing them closed, she swatted away the moisture from her cheeks then took a deep, shuddering breath to rein in the unexpected rush of emotion.

Her parents' presence filled the room as surely as if they were standing behind her, crowding her with their pressure and condemnation. How many times had she heard them express their anger, their disappointment in her? Their words assailed her like poisonous arrows, hitting the intended target.

"Why can't you be more like your sister?"

"We've should've stopped at one."

"She doesn't look like the rest of us. What are the odds they switched her at birth?"

Tori's hands shook as they squeezed against her head, trying to drown out the noise. They didn't deserve space in her head. Hadn't she read that in a book somewhere?

Shoving out of her chair, she left her data, and her demons, and marched to the kitchen where Jack sat at the table in front of his laptop. His eyes tracked her, but she ignored him. Pulling out the first frozen dinner she touched, Tori popped it in the microwave.

"I was going to start dinner in – "

"Count me out. I'll be busy tonight."

Heavy silence filled the room as Tori counted down the slow seconds on the oven.

The legs of Jack's chair scraped against the linoleum and then he was next to her. She looked up and caught his worried frown.

"You okay?"

The caring look in his eyes sent weakness spreading through her, tempting her to dump every unwanted emotion she'd had since last night straight into his lap. She looked away as the microwave beeped. What was wrong with her? She was ready to clutch his shirt and cry like a damsel in distress.

She straightened her shoulders and met his gaze. "Sure. Fine. The data's fluid right now so I want to keep my eye on it." She pulled her meal out and grabbed a fork on her way out of the room. "Get some sleep. Tomorrow should be good."

Jack pulled his clothes out of Tori's dryer and dumped them into a small basket. He'd tossed and turned all night, and it had nothing to do with the sofa. He'd gone so long without a woman in his life for more than a date or two, he assumed that would be how his future played out. He certainly hadn't planned on finding someone who challenged him and turned him on in so many ways, especially in the middle of a murder investigation.

He wanted to know so much more about her, and he'd kicked himself all night for not pushing to get her to open up to him yesterday. And in the kitchen, her red-rimmed eyes made him want to wrap her in his arms and take away whatever it was that made her so sad. Would it always be like that? Would she ever be able to open up that side of her, the emotions she kept hidden from the world? And if she wouldn't or couldn't, could he accept that and still make something work between them?

He pulled his last T-shirt out of the dryer and a small thong came with it. He glared at the tiny slip of lace as if it withheld the answers from him, then flung it back in the dryer.

Jack shoved his clean clothes into his bag then checked the time on his phone. The bureaucratic wheels always turned a little slower on the weekend, so when Josh's call came in, Jack was more than ready.

"What do you have for me?"

"Just sent you the files on Pritchard. Looks like a boy scout from here. Literally. Eagle Scout. Let me know if you're going to bring him in. I can't see a reason."

"You didn't see him at the dealership."

"True. In the meantime, I'm still looking for anything that might link any of these girls together through the university, but so far, no club connections, no sorority connections. Nothing except the meteorology program. Curious though, our guy is picking off his victims in graduation order. Did you know that?"

"What do you mean?"

"Each victim graduated the year after the previous victim. All the way up to our current target. More affirmation that we're on track, I'd say."

"There's no question. But that's interesting." Jack studied one of Tori's paintings. "Start looking for anybody who dropped out of the program during the years in question. Remember, we're dealing with an ego-driven killer. He wants us to know he's better than the women he's killed."

"And we're sure we're dealing with a guy, right? I've gotten caught up on the other files and I know the killer's always chosen to represent himself as a male in the emails, but no sexual assault. None. Which doesn't quite fit the standard profile."

Jack had considered that as well, but every time it came back to the hands. Just like the Minneapolis strangler case. "Go back and look at the bruising in the autopsy photos. I'd bet my life that the killer is a right-handed male." He released a harsh laugh. "That narrows it down for us, doesn't it?"

Josh laughed. "Yeah. Case can practically close itself."

Jack ended the call as Tori entered the living room.

"You ready?" she asked.

Whatever it was that had her sideways yesterday had vanished. She was all business. It was there in her bold stride, and no-nonsense movements as she chomped a bagel in one hand and loaded her backpack with the other.

"Just about."

When the crew showed up minutes later, Tori waved them in. "Jack set out bagels and fruit if you're hungry, but hurry up. We're burning daylight."

All but Reece made a quick trip to grab food in the kitchen. Jack watched from the corner of his eye as the young man sauntered over to where Tori tucked her laptop into its bag.

"I hope today kicks some serious ass."

Tori offered a distracted nod. "Yeah. Me, too."

Reece rocked back on his heels and shoved his hands in the front pockets of his jeans. "So. You…uh…I mean would you – "

"Time to go." Tori straightened as the others ambled back into the living room. Thank God. She didn't have the time or desire to deal with Reece at the moment, and she sure wasn't interested in however he planned to finish his sentence. She grabbed her bag and stepped around him, intent on herding everyone out the door.

As they merged onto the freeway, anticipation began to flood her senses. If she was right, they were in for a couple of hot days of chasing. And after spending most of yesterday in a place she didn't want to be, battling herself and corralling voices from the past, she was more than ready.

At least Jack had proven that he wouldn't be a hindrance in the field. Despite the faint praise she'd offered him, she was truly impressed with his skill, especially if he really hadn't filmed in years. He was definitely a natural. And Cam was progressing, too. Between the two of them, they could get some remarkable footage today.

A few hours into the trip down a two-lane Kansas state highway, a familiar pit settled in Tori's stomach as they passed the sign that showed Cimarron ten miles west. She looked out the window and tried to blow out the tension in quiet, deep breaths. She'd been through this area dozens of times over the years, but knowing they were this close to her home town and the graves of her parents and sister never sat well.

"Tori grew up just down the road," Cam explained.

"Cimarron, right?" Jack asked. "How big a town is that?"

Tori hated talking about that town or anything to do with her time there, but she figured Jack was just trying to make conversation. "It was about two thousand when I left. Doubt it's changed much since then."

"And still no tornadoes since they got that state-of-the-art siren system," Cam said. "I think the storms are afraid of it."

"Did they not have a system before?" Jack asked.

Tori shot Cam a look and felt Jack's stare from the seat behind her.

"It was old and didn't work." She looked out the window. "How about we focus on today's storms instead. Probably a better use of our time."

After the mental altercation she'd had with her parents yesterday, she needed to keep a tight lid on the guilt and shame that were synonymous with Cimarron, Kansas. When a conversation sprung up about football and the argument of whether the Patriots or the Cowboys were the better team, Tori relaxed into her seat and leaned her head against the window. Her anxiety slowly ebbed and as they pulled into the hotel, and she was the first one out of the truck, glad that part of the trip was behind them.

"I'll get my bag in a minute." She jogged inside to secure their rooms, but she had to make a pit stop first. As she washed her hands in the strange place, familiar excitement bubbled up inside. She released a deep breath and smiled at her reflection. "It's go time."

She stepped out of the bathroom, but stopped short as Jack blocked her path, his scowl fierce.

"Don't disappear on me like that again."

She met his frown with one of her own. "I went to the restroom, Mathis." She grabbed her bag from his hand and marched to the lobby where Cam and Dwayne stood waiting. "How far is truck two behind us?"

Cam checked his phone. "I got a text from Reece a few minutes ago. They were only about ten minutes out."

Tori took care of the rooms and handed out the key cards as Justin and Reece entered the lobby.

"Data I saw looked strong. Ready for a good chase today?" Justin asked.

Tori shot a quick glance toward Jack. "More than ready."

She held her tongue as the group rode the elevator to the third floor, but before she made it three steps down the hall, Jack nabbed her key and swapped it with Dwayne's.

"Dwayne, you and Cam take the room down the hall to the right, next to Justin and Reece. Tori, you're at this end of the hall to the left, across from my room."

Tori watched, mouth open, as Dwayne acquiesced to Jack's highhandedness without so much as a blink. Did Jack seriously think Sims was going to follow them to Nebraska? No one except her crew even knew where they were headed.

Reece frowned, but didn't say anything as Dwayne put an arm around his shoulder. "Jack just did you a favor. Tori snores."

Rolling her eyes, Tori walked away. She'd obviously acclimated during their time together to Jack's presence, maybe too well. There were more than a few times that she'd forgotten the real reason he was there. But if he thought he was going to control her chase, he was dead wrong.

In a few strides, Jack caught up with her. They made it to the end of their hallway, out of earshot from the others, before she rounded on him. "We need to be really clear on something, Mathis. I don't particularly care which room I sleep in, but once we're out in the field, I am the only person in charge. It has to be that way."

"What name did you reserve the rooms under?"

Tori blew out a breath as she processed the implication of his words. "The show name."

"And how hard would it be for a motivated person to find that information?" Jack paused, then squeezed her shoulders and offered a conciliatory smile. "Remember our first night together when we bonded over Master Chen's?"

Tori rolled her eyes at his choice of words. "Yes."

"I promised I wouldn't try to tell you how to do your job. But, you've got to cut me some slack here. It's not about being in charge. I'm not going to tell you how to chase tornadoes. As crazy as it sounds, chasing may be the safest place of all. But the rest of the time? When we're not in the field? You've got to trust me, or I can't keep you safe."

The concern in his eyes, and the sincerity in his deep voice pulled her. And repelled her. She'd gotten her answer, hadn't she? So why was she still standing there, staring at him like a simpleton?

"I'll be ready to go in ten minutes." Tori slid her key into the door and made her retreat.

Not two minutes later, a knock sounded. She didn't need to check the peephole to know who stood on the other side, but she did it anyway, and the view wasn't disappointing. Despite the hint of a frown, Jack was, without a doubt, the hottest guy she'd ever known.

"Let me in, Tori."

His words stopped her hand before she turned the handle, her frown matching his. *Is that what she was doing?* Letting him into her life like Cam had slipped in? Except, Jack wasn't Cam. Jack wouldn't stop, wouldn't accept boundaries. He'd push until he knew all of her.

And she couldn't accept that.

Anything that might happen between her and Jack would be strictly physical. She paused, allowing herself one more view through the peephole. *Physical, and likely mind-blowing.*

She shook her head to clear it. "No bad guys in here, Jack. And I'm trying to get ready. Storm should start blowing up within the hour."

Another knock.

"Would you go away if I told you I was naked?"

A pause. "If the goal was to get me to leave, you suck at this game."

Tori couldn't keep the smile away that teased her lips. Good Lord, was she in high school?

"Fine." She pulled open the heavy door. "But I'm not really naked."

For a second, the look in Jack's eyes as he walked past her made her wish she was, but he was all business as he made a quick check of the layout of her room. He stood by the window, watching the parking lot.

"People are taking pictures of the Beast. Do you ever wonder what locals think when you come rolling into town in your armor-plated vehicle?"

His laugh sent an unexpected dart of heat straight through her. Maybe it was the impending storm, but everything felt more potent, more alive in the thick afternoon air.

"They're thinking 'oh shit, we're in for some crazy weather'." She plugged in her laptop to charge and even that simple action felt sexual. Jesus, she needed to get laid.

"What do you like better? The anticipation or the storm?"

Did he really lob her that softball? She stopped in the midst of her unpacking and turned to him, unable to resist. "The anticipation is a blast, Mathis. But when you're in the middle of the storm, there's nothing better."

If she'd wanted him to squirm, she was sorely disappointed. He turned from the window, but instead of avoiding her innuendo as she'd expected him to do, he surprised her by playing along.

"I have a feeling the storm would be incredible."

Her eyes darted to his. Nope, he didn't misspeak. By the heat in his gaze, he knew exactly what he was saying. At least she hoped he did. Maybe the coming storm had him thinking crazy, too. She wasn't going to complain, though.

She lifted her hands and sifted fingers through her hair, gathering the long tresses into a pony tail. If the movement just happened to draw his attention to her hard nipples, so be it. "It would be."

The heat in Jack's eyes turned to raw hunger as his fists clenched at his sides. "I need to go."

She savored the regret in his tone. "Says you."

She would've bet money he was seconds away from finally relaxing his ridiculous standard when a soft knock at the door cracked like a sonic boom. Tori wanted to punch whoever was on the other side of it. The magic, heady spell that had spun around them shattered, and in a flash Jack's gaze returned to the window, but not before Tori saw the self-recrimination in his eyes.

Damn it. One step forward and two back. Tori slowly released the breath she hadn't consciously held as she walked over and met Dwayne at the door. "What's up?"

"Hey, you two." Dwayne's raised brow to Tori was enough to send a little heat to her cheeks, but he didn't speak again until he tossed a map onto the bed and ironed it out with his hands. "Justin said it looks like I-80 straight west for about thirty miles then north about fifteen. What do you think?"

"I don't know." Tori bent over the map as she flipped her focus. "I thought we'd probably give it another twenty minutes, see how things shape up. But I'm guessing you might be able to jump off here and head north a little sooner."

She checked radar and aligned it with Dwayne's map. Oh yeah, this was going to be a great ride. She straightened and caught Jack's slow perusal of her backside. He was wavering. Hmmm. If she played her cards right, she might be in for more than one great ride tonight.

They ate a quick meal at the truck stop next to the hotel, but Tori barely tasted it. When she'd told Jack that she could feel the storms, she wasn't kidding. And this one was going to be awesome. They piled into the Beast, then did an equipment double check and headed west.

Cars whizzed by heading east, headlights on, like rats on a sinking ship. The sky was like nothing Jack had ever witnessed before. Near the horizon the sun shone bright but higher, a huge dark blue monster swallowed the light. Even to Jack's untrained eye, the striations in the clouds swelled with power like a living thing.

"North from here," Tori barked. "Stay ahead of the rain. We've got minutes, Dwayne. Go."

Her intense words punctuated the tension in the air. Everything was moving fast and slow at the same time. As they drove, the clouds seethed in a slow dance that belied the power building in them.

Then there was no more sun as darkness surrounded them, charged and thick. "Stop, here. Look over there! Cam, Jack. Now!"

None of it made sense to Jack. He'd been watching the sky, he swore he was, but when he followed where Tori pointed across a field it was just there. And huge. So huge he could barely even tell it was rotating. On the fucking ground.

He grabbed his camera and raced around the front of the Beast, Tori's ragged words reaching him over the howling wind.

"This is Tori Whitlock. There's a mile-wide wedge tornado near 65 Highway and Rock Road traveling east, northeast. Alliance is in the path of this storm. Advise all citizens to take cover immediately."

Wind rushed past him, buffeting him, like the storm was sucking in every bit of energy it could from its surroundings, but he never took his eye off the twister. It was different than any depiction he'd ever seen. Not like any of them ever felt harmless, but this one looked like a killer.

The reality of the situation crashed down on him as Tori's words replayed in his head. People could die from this storm. Would Tori's alert allow them enough time to take cover?

Jack zoned in on his work, trying to ignore the questions he had no way to answer. He followed Tori's lead, positioning as she directed. He wasn't sure how much time passed before driving rain forced them back into the Beast. Jack had just slammed his door closed when the first golf-ball-sized hail stone hit.

"Dwayne, get us the hell out of here," Tori's head whipped around, her eyes focused on the road washing out behind them as hail battered the vehicle. "That bitch is rain-wrapped and changing direction. She's been on the ground for at least twenty-five minutes. Our window's closing to get in front of her again." She checked her laptop. "Head east and south. That's our best bet. Where's truck two?"

"Out ahead of us. I've got Reece on the cell," Cam held up his phone, yelling over the noise.

The wind buffeted them as Dwayne slammed into reverse. Rain came in torrents and adrenaline raced through Jack's blood.

"Punch it, Dwayne! It's practically on top of us."

Jack fought a wave of panic. His job was one of split second, life or death decisions, but he'd never felt like this. So out of control. So unsure of his fate. He tried to take cues from the people around him who'd lived through this situation time after time, but all he could feel was the intensity of the storm.

His shoulder slammed against the side of the truck as Dwayne swung it around. As fast as the Beast could accelerate, they screamed south, away from the storm.

Suddenly, like someone had flipped a switch, they were out of the rain, and the sky calmed and lightened. Jack chanced a look behind him and saw the swirling storm from a distance. Had he really just been in the middle of that?

"Yes! That's what I'm talking about!" Tori slapped the dash. Jack caught the grin that broke out on Dwayne's face and decided they were all insane.

"Fucking A," Cam echoed. "What do you think? EF-4?"

"EF-3 at least," she nodded. She swiveled between the storm to their north and the radar on her computer. "Damn, I thought we might have another shot, but it's weakening."

There was a tinge of disappointment in her voice, but Jack barely heard it. He was trying to make sure he hadn't pissed himself. Was this normal? Holy hell, the range of emotions he'd just experienced blew him away.

As they hit the main highway, Cam shot him a sidelong grin. "So, what'd you think?"

Could he even articulate what he'd experienced? Jack settled into his cramped seat and shook his head. "I think I need a beer."

Tori opened the cooler and dug in, passing beers to the crew. She loved the afterglow of the chase. It was almost better than post-sex. Almost.

She flopped into the crappy hotel chair and flung a leg over the side before raising her can in a toast. "To incredible storms." She took a long swallow.

Reece sat on the floor at Tori's feet and raised his can. "And incredible storm chasers."

Tori tapped her can to his. "We made a good team today." As soon as the words were out, she wished she could suck them back in. "I mean all of us. Together. That was a hell of a storm."

"You watch any film yet? Did Jack hold his own?" Dwayne asked.

"Not yet. I texted him to bring it. But I'm guessing he probably shot well."

She took a long pull, enjoying the ice cold brew sliding down her throat. Jack had surprised her by staying right there in the thick of it, even when she figured he'd duck into the Beast and hide.

As if on cue, knuckles rapped at the door and Dwayne stood to open it.

"Did Tori–" Jack's angry voice reached her ears seconds before he burned her with his glare. "You were supposed to wait for me to come with you."

Tori grabbed another beer from the cooler and tossed it to him, letting his overbearing attitude slide by. Nothing was going to upset her postgame buzz. She crumpled her can and rattled it into the plastic trash can. "Score," she cheered, before grabbing another for herself. Jack was still frowning at her. "You can relax. Reece came down and got me, and I was ready to get the party started. You must've still been in the shower when I knocked on your door."

With a sigh she knew cost him dearly, he plunked into the chair next to her and popped the top on his beer. "Next time, you wait for me. I thought we had this discussion already."

Jack's tone was hard and his frustration rolled over her in waves. Out of the corner of her eye, she saw Reece's shoulders tighten. Tori matched

Jack's sigh with one of her own, trying to dial down the burgeoning testosterone threatening to bubble over. "Look, I'm sorry. I'll try. Okay? I'm not very good at taking orders."

"That's the truth," Cam said, as he and Dwayne nodded from their beds.

Reece mumbled under his breath about no one having to take orders from Jack, but Tori pretended she didn't hear him.

"Nobody asked you, Cam," Tori said. She slugged him in the shoulder as she stood and grabbed her laptop. Hooking it into the TV on the wall, she looked up, grinning at them as Jack handed over his thumb drive. "Okay, fellas. Let's see what we got."

She queued up Jack's file first and heard his sharp inhale and, quick as that, he was back in the moment. She could see it on his face and knew the feeling well. The power screaming from the video filled the small room.

"Look right there." Tori pointed to the screen. "See that? I didn't think you'd caught the debris field. And the way you pulled back to wide? Perfect capture. That shot's going on a teaser for the season."

"That was unbelievable. Never thought of myself as much of an adrenaline junkie, but son of a bitch. This is addictive." He continued to stare at her. "And you were amazing. I'm in awe of how you knew exactly where to go."

His high kick of energy hit her right in the gut. A little further south, actually. And it wasn't just that. The look in his eyes, like admiration, respect, and lust made her want to kick everyone out and jump him right there.

She was supposed to respond, wasn't she? Whether it was the beer or Jack, her brain was operating in slow motion. Fortunately, Dwayne piped up.

"It's her gift. The rest of us just go along for the ride."

After they watched Cam's film, Jack dropped into the shabby chair next to hers, as if he'd suddenly realized he'd been standing all through the footage. Tori stayed out of the conversation, preferring to relive the better chases in her head, but she smiled as the guys rehashed every play like it was the Super Bowl.

Her eyes strayed to Jack as he laughed at something Cam said. He looked so comfortable slung out in his chair, it surprised her how well he'd insinuated himself into their little group. Maybe that was Jack's gift. Where ever he went, he fit. Except for Reece, who was in a testosterone-induced pissing contest, the rest of them could've been high school buddies.

Checking the time on her phone, Tori was surprised to realize that more than an hour had passed. She stood and stretched before tossing her fourth or fifth can in the trash. "Well, I'm out. We'll head east in the morning. The storms are supposed to fire again tomorrow late afternoon near the Nebraska-Iowa border. We can't miss them."

Through sheer willpower, she resisted an accidental rub on Jack as she squeezed past him and Dwayne. But, damn he had her engine hitting on all cylinders tonight. She could try to blame it on the chase rush, but she was an arm girl and his biceps were fierce and on full display against his black T-shirt.

She'd resisted the urge more than once to lean over and squeeze them. Or lick them. And, did he really need to be so tan? Guess she probably had his sauce-making Italian grandparents to thank for that. She'd replayed her initial meeting with Jack at least a hundred times over the past few weeks and, if he were here for any reason other than to play babysitter, she would've had him in her bed already. The look in his eyes, the instant chemistry that sparked between them, still thrummed through her veins. And he'd felt it, too.

"Forgetting something?" His deep baritone jarred her as she reached for the door handle.

She turned, keeping her hand on the cool metal. "You're going to insist on walking me to my room, aren't you?" She tried to sound annoyed, but the tremors in her belly made it difficult.

"I could walk you back," Reece offered.

"Stay here and enjoy the celebration," Jack said.

He was speaking to Reece, but his eyes never left hers as he rose from his chair. Moving around her, Jack pulled open the door and, with a light hand at her back that set off tingles of pleasure, he propelled her out of the room and down the hallway then took her key card and slid it into the lock.

"You're welcome to come in. I might have something for a night cap."

"I *am* coming in, Tori," he said, slightly exasperated. "But not for a drink." He followed her through the door, then checked her small bathroom before walking to the window and testing the lock.

She wanted to misunderstand his words, wanted to walk right up to him and put an end to her frustration, but instead she busied herself folding the clothes she'd strewn around after her shower. God, did he taste as good as he smelled?

She was so lost in her thoughts that she didn't hear him walk up behind her.

"I think we're good —"

Without giving herself a second to think, or him time to step away, Tori turned and pressed her lips to Jack's. The muscles in his arms tightened against her palms as they gripped him, his lips hard and unyielding. Then, as if he couldn't or wouldn't fight it, his arms circled her, crushing her to him. Restraint gone, Jack dove in, releasing every second of the past weeks' frustration.

And all she could do was hang on. Holy hell, he could kiss. His hands splayed across her back felt oddly protective, but there was fire burning through his fingers, igniting her to the core. Then they moved lower, cupping her backside, pulling her up hard against him. Breathing became optional as every curve and soft place collided with his strength.

He broke from her lips and began trailing fiery kisses down her neck to the curve of her shoulder. Her arms slid around his neck as every touch of his lips sent new sparks through her. She was jelly, powerless to control the passion swirling around them.

His lips returned to hers, his low sexy growl competing with his plundering tongue for space in her mouth. It was the kind of kiss that decimated any girl's silly fantasy of a perfect kiss. Hard and soft, wicked and wonderful, Jack rocked her off her foundation until she was flying and hoping she'd never land.

A moan that Tori barely recognized as her own filled the room as Jack's teeth nipped her earlobe then the skin of her neck. Next, he tendered soft kisses to replace the tiny sting, and she almost dropped to a puddle on the floor.

"Yes," she groaned. "Please, Jack."

Jack tensed then pulled back as Tori's words penetrated his foggy brain. As Tori's eyelids fluttered open, he met the heat in her gaze. He was in big trouble. The insane hunger exploding through him was seconds away from taking over any hope for rational thought. Tori was a beautiful, single woman who wanted him. A woman he needed like he hadn't needed in a long time.

And a woman you're supposed to be protecting, not seducing.

As much as he wanted to, he couldn't silence the truth. With more willpower than he knew he possessed, Jack overrode his own need and gripped Tori's arms, separating their bodies.

Cool air filled the space between them as their harsh breathing filled the quiet room. "That shouldn't have happened. I'm sorry."

She stared at him, the passion that had turned her blue eyes to a stormy gray replaced by a cool challenge. "I'm not. I should get a vote, too. And I think you should stay."

Logic. Protocol. Objectivity. He dropped his hands and closed his eyes against her argument, letting the words pound his brain like a war drum. "Good night, Tori," he couldn't keep the regret from his voice. "I'm sorry."

The five steps between her door and his were the hardest he could remember taking. Because every single one of them took him farther away from what his body craved, what his mind told him he shouldn't take.

How many times had he told himself this case was one hundred percent hands off? In his entire career he'd never crossed that line. Never even been tempted. So what made this different? Was it Garrett in his head about getting into a relationship? Maybe. Because as much as he hated to admit it, he'd avoided his friend's calls for weeks. More likely, it was enduring Reece practically panting at Tori's feet for the last hour.

Yet here he was, frustrated as hell because the kiss he'd envisioned with Tori was nothing compared to what just happened. He wavered between another shower, this one much colder, or pulling out his laptop and digging into Glenn Pritchard's file. God, anything to get his body to accept his mind's mandate. He grabbed his computer, then his phone buzzed in his pocket.

Tori's number lit up the screen, instantly putting him on high alert for a threat.

"Is everything okay?"

"Not really. I think your no sex rule is stupid."

Jack's shoulders relaxed slightly and the corner of his mouth twitched up. "Tori," he groaned a warning.

"Seriously. What harm could come from it? I'm sitting here on my bed, and if you don't come back over here, I'm going to have to take care of myself."

Oh, shit. Can I listen? He bit his tongue hard to keep the words from coming out. "Did you hear that? It was the sound of me beating my head against the wall. You don't play fair."

"Well, at least I'm playing." She paused. "You know, I've never stooped to asking for sex, but you're cramping my style. It's not like I'm free to hook up with someone at a bar and bring them home."

Her casual words sent a quick stab of something too close to jealousy coursing through him. He had no right to go there, but that knowledge didn't make it go away. Shoving his hand through his hair, he heaved a sigh. *Please don't ask me right now because I don't think I'd say no.* "It's not forever. When this is all over you'll be free to do whatever or whoever you want."

"What if whoever is you? Would there still be a reason you'd say no?"

Would there? He'd grappled with that question. It wasn't like he hadn't had sex or dated women since Becky died, but he'd never been interested in more than a date or two, or a hook up or two. But he couldn't fit Tori into that mold. She was different.

"That's your answer then?" Tori's sharp words brought him back to reality.

Memories of Becky flooded him, paralyzing him. But he refused to lie. "I don't know," he answered.

Tori's frustrated exhale carried over the line, and her words were clipped. "Got the message. Loud and clear."

Jack stared at the phone for a long minute after Tori disconnected the call then leaned back, knocking his head against the wall. Jesus. Not only was he not taking her to bed, he just moved them from being good with each other to a major disconnect. *Shit.*

He glanced down at the laptop in his grip and pulled up the file. At a glance, Glenn looked as vanilla as Josh had indicated, but Jack couldn't get his mind off the woman across the hall. Tori was at the center of everything that was disrupting his well-ordered life. He needed to find his killer and either get the hell out of there for good, or undo the damage he'd just done and figure out a way to extend his stay for a good long while.

Chapter 11

Jack knocked once, lightly, on Tori's door and waited. He checked his phone then rapped louder. Looking out the hallway window at the bright morning sunlight, he thought about how the small town might've been ravaged if the tornado hadn't turned sharply yesterday. If he hadn't been in the middle of it, he could almost believe he'd imagined it all.

But he hadn't imagined that kiss. The feel of Tori's body crushed to his had made sleep hard to come by. And where was she, anyway? Anxiety hit him first, followed quickly by anger. Would she have gone to the lobby without him? He raised his fist, ready to pound on the door until everyone on the floor was awake.

Just then Tori opened her door, slung her bag over her shoulder, and walked past him without a look. He took a deep breath, and shoved a lid on his own frustration. The last thing he needed was for someone else to pick up on it and start asking questions.

As they entered the lobby, Jack spied their group at the hotel's complimentary breakfast bar. Tori headed straight to the coffee machine as Jack walked up to Cam. "You look like crap this morning. You and Dwayne burn the midnight oil?"

Cam's bleary eyes crinkled. "Midnight? I wish we'd stopped at midnight. That fat bastard can drink. Too bad for him he has to drive. I'll be crashed in the backseat."

Jack laughed. "Don't think you're going to use me as a pillow."

Dwayne behind the wheel probably wasn't a great idea, but what the hell. Jack was only along for the ride. And maybe, if he was busy making sure Dwayne stayed awake, he wouldn't be so damn focused on the guilt that had stayed with him since last night.

Shoveling in his waffle, Jack watched Tori sprinkle granola over a yogurt cup. Her ball cap hid part of her face, but her eyes were shadowed. And she'd acknowledged the group with only a brief nod.

After grabbing a bagel to add to his smorgasbord, Cam sat down in the chair next to Jack and tilted his head Tori's direction. "Looks like she had a rough night."

Jack's chewing slowed. "Yep."

"She dreams, you know. Sometimes. After the storms."

The wisest course of action was to say nothing, so Jack simply nodded and took another big bite of his waffle. Cam watched him for another second before pouring his carton of milk over his cereal and digging in.

Tori ate standing up then grabbed a bottle of orange juice and messed with her phone until everyone else finished. She was itching to get on the road and put last night behind her. She was still pissed at Jack, but she was even more pissed at herself. She never willingly gave people power over her, but she'd practically begged Jack to have sex with her last night.

And still, he'd refused.

She glanced up from her phone and realized every member of her crew was watching her, waiting. It was past time to get out of there. Reaching for her bag, she tossed a look at them. "Grab your gear. It's time to go."

Tori surveyed the sky over eastern Iowa as they rolled in to a run-down gas station. The sinking pit in her stomach was no match for the ball of anger and frustration that still had her shoulders in knots. Screw Jack for kissing her the way he did and invading her dreams. She needed this damn chase today, needed the energy release. Because no matter how much she wanted to erase last night from her memory, nothing she'd done for herself had even come close to taking the edge off.

But the system was dying. Or more correctly, it never reignited like it should've. Dwayne hopped out to fill the tank and Cam headed into the whitewashed building. They'd all given her a wide berth during the drive over. Thank God. The last thing she wanted was some bullshit useless conversation.

She pulled up the maps on her laptop again, hoping for a data refresh that would give her hope, but nothing had changed. If a super cell was going to happen at all, it wouldn't fire until late that night. Too damn late to be of any use to her, and too dangerous.

Stepping out of the truck, she leaned against the hood and stared at the mocking cumulus clouds to the west, willing them to create the necessary fuel for a chase. Damn it. Not only would the chase have been a release, it would've prolonged the inevitable moment when she found herself alone with Jack. But she wouldn't be stupid enough to throw herself at him again. He wanted her, damn it. But if his pride and protocol were that much more important, he could sleep with them.

Ultimately, she had no choice. And that pissed her off more than anything else.

She straightened her shoulders as Cam and Jack approached. "Break time's over. We've got to go."

Dwayne replaced the fuel nozzle. "We going farther east?"

Anger surged again. "No. If you need relief, I'll drive. But we're going home."

Dwayne held up a hand. "I'm good. Just checking."

It was well after midnight when they pulled into Tori's driveway. Jack suspected the guys' quick departure had as much to do with Tori's surliness as it did the lateness of the hour, but only Jack knew that he was at least partially responsible for her obvious frustration. Exactly why he'd tried to avoid opening that door in the first place.

He walked in ahead of Tori to check the house and as he went from room to room, he battled the insane urge to pull her into his arms and forget everything behind them and everything between them until there was nothing but her.

"You want the shower first?"

She didn't bother to look at him, but he couldn't miss the dark shadows under her eyes. She dropped her bag at the foot of her computer table. "Go ahead."

After showering, Jack was so beat that Tori's god awful couch actually looked comfortable. A man wasn't designed to spend that many hours in a cramped vehicle. But before he made it two steps into the small living room, his eyes were drawn to Tori as she scanned chase footage on her monitor. Despite his bleary state, he was instantly turned on. By the content on the screen, and the woman studying it. As road weary as she had to be, her intensity about her project compelled him. If that wasn't already on his mental list, it needed to be.

The realization of how much of her was woven into every scene and every angle of the finished product fascinated him. *She* fascinated him. In a dangerous way. A way that he'd assumed had died with Becky. And as much as part of him wanted to run from it, the bigger part of him wanted to explore it. Despite knowing that potential tragedy could follow him here.

Just go to sleep. Walk directly to the sofa. Do not go anywhere near her.

He stepped behind her, close enough that he caught her faint strawberry scent. He absolutely would not touch her, but he needed to be near her. Maybe he could just keep it professional. "You know, if you transition from one to two about thirty seconds later, you're going to get a much better look."

Tori's hand froze on the mouse. As much as she wished she could deny it, she'd been aware of Jack's presence since the moment the bathroom door opened. Aware of every movement, even with her back to him. And when he walked up behind her, she silently cursed her body's reaction.

But when the first thing out of his mouth was about her editing? *Her editing?* She saw red. Shoving away from her desk, she went toe-to-toe with him.

"You know what? I'll finish this tomorrow, when you're not around. Oh, wait. You're *always* around." Her chest heaved. "Don't you have some file you can go read? Or maybe you should take one of your walks outside. That should help."

"Christ, Tori. It was just a suggestion. Forget I mentioned it."

Oh, she'd forget it all right, but he wasn't getting out of this that easily. "What the hell makes you think you can just walk in and turn my life sideways, kiss me like we kissed last night, then act like nothing in the world has changed?"

He'd started to turn away, then came back, nostrils flared a mere inch from her face, forcing her against the computer table. She didn't fear him, but if the vein ticking in his neck was any indication, she probably should have.

"Everything in the world has changed." His deep voice was quiet, restrained. "It changed for you the day that email showed up in your inbox. You didn't ask for that. I get it. But that doesn't change the facts."

She opened her mouth to interrupt but he was on a roll.

"This is exactly why I've done everything short of castration to try to keep my hands off of you. You think I'm immune to whatever this is? You think I don't lie out here at night torturing myself with the knowledge that you're thirty feet away from me, warm in your bed? Well, think again. Some nights, that's all I think about.

"But having sex with you would complicate everything. Hell, that kiss turned my brain to mush. You intrigue me, fascinate me, draw me in ways I haven't felt in a long, long time. I want time to know you. The real you. I won't risk your life by getting sloppy. You can get angry with me all you want, but I'd rather have you alive and pissed off than dead on my watch."

Tori wanted to stay angry. She wanted to burn him with her words. But the fire in her chest was doused by his raw emotion. And, as warning bells jangled in her head, she realized she'd made a huge tactical error. Jack wasn't looking to hook up. He was talking about a relationship.

Tori ducked away to the right to put some space between them. When had that happened? Had she sent the wrong signals? She tried to think back, but her brain was too fried. God, how could he take something so simple and straight forward and complicate it?

The irony of their situation wasn't lost on her. Jack was going to win their little war, because he was either really smart or really damn lucky. He would win, but they would both lose. Relationships were nothing more than chains that turned two people who might've cared for each other at some point into, at best, polite strangers.

And that was the one thing she absolutely wasn't interested in. She'd rather never start a committed relationship than be trapped in one that sucked the life out of her. So, if Jack thought sex with her was a door to something more, it really was better left unopened.

Tori straightened her shoulders. For the first time since Jack had walked into Mack's garage, she reluctantly let go of her fantasy.

Turning to him, she met his gaze. "I see your point, Mathis. And I agree with you. I'm sorry I put you in such an awkward position." Jack's stunned expression would've been comical if she didn't feel like she'd lost out on something that could've been damn good. "See you in the morning. Tomorrow we make a fresh start."

Jack sipped his coffee at the kitchen table and tried to digest the report on Glenn, but his mind kept going back to Tori's one-eighty last night. He should give up trying to figure out what goes on in her brilliant head, but he couldn't let it go. And while he was relieved, he couldn't deny the disappointment that lurked below the surface.

Maybe the keen disappointment was his answer to the question of what would happen after the case was over. A smile worked its way onto his lips as he thought about what it would be like to date Tori. She'd always keep him on his toes, and he found that thought quite intriguing.

Jack dove back into the report, more anxious than ever to get this case behind him. But even after a second review, there was nothing. No criminal background, Eagle Scout, and high school Valedictorian. *Damn it to hell.*

He pulled up his spreadsheet comparing Tori's emails to the schedule of the other victims. It had been too long since Mr. Sims had been in touch. The question was, what did his lack of communication mean? He'd already broken patterns of geographic location and the victims' profession. Was this simply another pattern change?

Jack went to the window and watched three squirrels chase each other from Tori's yard to her neighbor's. He rolled his shoulders and tried to clear his head. Were they playing into the killer's hand by sitting still?

His phone vibrated in his pocket and Garrett's number blinked from the screen. Letting the call go to voicemail, Jack grappled with how much he could share with Garrett about the case. And about Tori. But Garrett was a good friend, and Jack could use a good friend right now to get his head on straight. He hit the button to retrieve the message.

"Call me back. Rachel's seriously starting to worry about you. I told her you were a big boy, but you know how she is. Oh, and Lily wants to make sure you know we're coming to Kansas City for your mom's thing. Rachel talked me in to going so she can spend some time with her family. Before the baby comes." The message paused. "Yeah. If you'd called me back before, you'd have already known. Ass hat. Call me."

Jack smiled as he speed-dialed Garrett's number.

On the first ring, Garrett picked up. "About damn time. Guess I should've left that message sooner. Where you been hiding?"

Pushing the guilt aside, Jack laughed. "In Oklahoma chasing tornadoes and psychopaths. Congrats, Big Daddy. Great news."

Tangible excitement sang through the phone line. "Thanks. Took us by surprise and Rachel's making me wait until after the baby comes to make an honest woman out of her. Said she doesn't want a shotgun wedding. I'll do whatever she wants as long as we get to say 'I do'. Which is the other reason I was trying to track you down. I'm going to need a best man. You up for that?"

Jack's smile was bittersweet as the squirrels continued their game. He wondered if Garrett realized those were the exact words he'd used when their roles had been reversed. And just like Garrett, Jack didn't hesitate. "Name the date. I'll be there."

"Good deal. I'm guessing late October or early November, so keep the weekends open and I'll let you know. Rachel and her sister are supposed to start planning during our trip to KC. You're going to be there, right?"

"We're going to try. Told mom I'd do my best, but I don't get to make the rules. The only advantage I have right now is I know who he's targeted, and I'm with her until we catch the son of a bitch."

"From the sound of your voice, he probably ought to give up now. So who's the unlucky girl who has to put up with you and a crazy psychopath?"

Jack cringed. "She's feeling pretty unlucky right now, that's for sure. The sooner I get out of here, the happier she'll be. You'd trip if you met her, though. She's amazing. She chases tornadoes for a living. Does a regional show here called Vortex. You should check it out."

"Give me a sec. I'll pull it up." A pause, then a low whistle. "Whoa. She really look like this in person?"

Jack pushed aside a ripple of possessiveness. "She's gorgeous, but it's not just that. She's so damn smart and quick. And she's become a hell of a chess player."

"Okay. If I didn't know better, I'd swear I was getting punked. The Jack Mathis I know would've given me a hundred reasons why this girl, or any girl, wasn't a good fit for him. What gives?"

Rolling his eyes, Jack shrugged. It wasn't like he didn't expect Garrett's ribbing. He was only telling the truth. "I don't know what's going to happen. Certainly nothing before the case is solved, but after... I don't know."

"Rachel's never going to believe me."

"She's not going to know, because you're not going to say anything to her. If we make it to KC, I don't want Tori to feel like she's under a microscope."

Garrett chuckled. "You remember your mom's going to be there, right?"

"Then it's a good thing there's nothing going on between us. Not yet, anyway." Jack thought about Tori's statement last night and frowned. "Maybe not at all. I don't know. I need to get going. Tell Rachel and Lily I love them and will hopefully see them next week."

"Sounds good, brother. Take it easy. And watch your back."

Jack smiled. Talking to Garrett reset his brain. And, if things worked out, he'd see him next week. That was a good thing. He'd used his best friend as a sounding board more times than he could count, but in recent months, he'd shut him out. And the reason was so obvious, it embarrassed him. Garrett's life had evolved into something incredible while Jack had been stuck in neutral.

Stepping outside into the sunshine, an unseasonably cool breeze brushed across his skin and he realized he was starting to think about the future. A future with Tori. Maybe he was shifting gears, too.

But everything came back to finding the killer. With that in mind, Jack dialed Josh's number. "You got anything else for me on Glenn Pritchard? He's too clean."

His inside guy responded. "Agreed. I'm not done digging. Any new emails to send me?"

"No. And, his silence is odd. Are we getting close to figuring out where they're coming from?"

Josh sighed. "Unfortunately, no. Whoever this guy is, he knows his way around. Definitely not your run of the mill onion router user. There are so many relays, and the switch backs are sending us down one rabbit hole after another. But keep them coming and maybe the computer forensics guys will get lucky."

Jack kicked a pebble into the grass. "Will do."

"Oh. Hey, Jack?"

"Yeah?"

"Just a heads up. Director Collins came by the other day, asking some pretty pointed questions about the case's progress."

Jack stiffened. *Shit.* "Okay. I'll touch base with him."

He disconnected the call and ran a hand through his hair. He didn't have anything against Collins, but he'd been out of the field so long that his expectations had become skewed. And with the pressure of the new budget watchdog, Jack should've known that conversation was coming.

He checked his watch then returned to the table and fired off an email to the director with an update on the case. He spun the timeline as well as he could, be it was hard to paint it in a good light when he was frustrated as hell with it.

Jack's thoughts ran forward to the coming days, as worry pricked him. Surely they'd hear from Sims soon.

With a low growl of frustration, he opened his browser. If nothing changed, he'd be seeing his mom in a week, and she'd expect him to have information on Hope's place. He clicked on the organization's website as Tori walked into the kitchen and made a beeline for the coffee pot.

After her first sip, she turned to him. "Thanks for making a pot."

It took Jack a second to realize what was different about her. She was wearing a full-length bath robe. He wanted to appreciate that she was respecting his wishes, but he hated the damn thing on sight. He grunted a reply, pissed at himself for his current bipolar tendencies, and returned to his computer screen.

Tori came up behind him and peered at the screen. "What are you working on? Anything new on the case?"

Her voice was light, but Jack heard the underlying thread of impatience. "No such luck. I'm checking out a place my sister Hope wants to lease. My mom's convinced it's a mistake and wants me to prove her right."

"She in college?"

"No, she's a couple years older than me. Hope has Down syndrome and has always lived with my parents. She wants a place of her own."

"What have you found out so far?"

Jack rolled his shoulders and offered a sheepish grin. "That I'm a horrible procrastinator. Haven't looked up a thing about them. I guess I feel like if Hope wants to do it, I want her to do it. If it ends up not being a good idea, then she'll learn from it."

Tori nodded. "Makes sense. Email me what you've got. Maybe I'll take a look, if that's okay with you." She opened the fridge and pulled out eggs and bread. "You want French toast?"

"You'd do that?"

"I've watched you make it. It's not that tough."

"No, I mean look at Hope's thing?"

"Sure. I've got time. Why not?"

"You're a lifesaver." He tapped a few keys. "Just sent you the link to the company's website. That's about as far as I've gotten." He shut down his computer and took the eggs and milk from her hands. "If you're willing to do my dirty work, the least I can do is make breakfast."

"Well, make it good. I'm hoping it'll be our only meal until dinner. There's a system developing about eighty miles west of here that I think might produce later today."

Hours later, Cam and Dwayne laid sprawled out on Tori's sofa as Jack grabbed beers out of the fridge for everyone. "Another decent chase."

Tori nodded. "Can't wait to edit. I think we got some great shots today." She looked up from her seat and took the can Jack offered. "Thanks. You seemed more comfortable out there today."

Jack grinned and nodded. "I fake it well, apparently." He passed drinks to the guys, then dropped into the chair closest to the sofa and popped the top on his can. "How long will the season stay active?"

"We've got another six weeks or so of favorable conditions. After that, we'll have to get lucky to get a good opportunity."

"Tired of chasing already?" Cam laughed.

"Yes. But not tornadoes." Jack tried to shake the sense of foreboding that settled between his shoulder blades. He was running out of time to net results. The end of the season meant the end of the hunt for Tori, and probably for him. He closed his eyes against the exhaustion that threatened. *Give me something here. Some direction. I'm shooting in the dark at nothing but air.*

Chapter 12

The house creaked and popped as it settled for the night. Jack was down for the count, and Cam and Dwayne were long gone. Tori envied them all. She'd punched her pillows at least twenty times trying to get comfortable, but her mind continued to race.

The storms had been intense today and, if she didn't take the edge off, nightmares would plague her. It wasn't that she didn't appreciate the storms. They kept her going. But she needed time in the quiet aftermath to separate today's chase from the howling, vicious winds of her past.

Giving up her fantasy of a dreamless sleep, she threw back the hot, sticky blankets and climbed out of bed. She found a small empty canvas on the floor in her closet and plunked it onto her easel then pulled the half-empty bottle of bourbon from her bedside drawer. Surveying the room, she found a single glass.

Shrugging, she poured turpentine in the glass, and tipped the bottle for a healthy swig of the bourbon. After squeezing a variety of oils onto her palette, she let the brush take over as vibrant color flowed onto the canvas, freeing her mind to process the storms.

As she painted, thoughts about Jack occasionally intruded. She tried to mute them with repeated sips from the bottle, because having him here was unhealthy. And confusing. What kind of guy wasn't open to a few nights between the sheets with no strings attached? It didn't have to be anything more. Couldn't be anything more.

She splashed more color onto the canvas. This needed to end soon. All of it. Jack needed to leave. And the killer needed to finish what he started.

Stepping back from the canvas, she shook her head as the room began to spin. That wasn't what she meant. The killer needed to be stopped. Jack would stop him, though. He'd made her invincible.

A goofy grin spread across her face. He wanted to date her, didn't he? Isn't that what he implied?

They could go to movies and the park. They could ride bike trails, and she could introduce him to her other favorite restaurants. Or maybe they could travel. She'd never been to the beach. He could be her very own Prince Charming.

Twirling and spinning, she pretended she was in a fancy gown, all dressed up for the ball. Tori tripped on the leg of the easel, but caught herself on the footboard and avoided a face plant. Didn't spill a drop, either. She laughed at that.

After three tries, she screwed the top back on the bottle and balanced it on the table, then flopped on the bed as logic seeped in to her fantasies. Jack couldn't be her Prince Charming. He didn't even own a horse.

And he didn't want to date her. He didn't know her. If he did, he'd run. Tori closed her eyes and hoped the room would stop spinning so she could get some rest. God, she was tired.

Hopefully, the storms wouldn't chase her.

Jack woke to a dark room. Disoriented, he looked around and found his phone. Two-thirty. Yep, he'd fallen asleep. Cam's text confirmed it.

Good night, sleeping beauty. Catch up with you later.

Well, hell. He was never going to live that down.

A faint hint of turpentine greeted him as he stood and stretched his back. On his way to the bathroom, quiet sobs coming from Tori's room put him on high alert. He grabbed his pistol and crept down the hall. At the door, he listened again as the cries turned to moans.

He twisted the door handle and slid into her room. His eyes quickly adjusted to the darkness as Tori thrashed, trapped by her twisted blankets.

The relief he should've felt knowing she was safe was short lived as he spied a nearly empty bottle of bourbon standing sentry at her bedside.

Tucking his gun behind his back, a pang of something akin to sympathy nudged him. Man, did he know that feeling. He stepped closer, smoothing a lock of hair away from her face. *What demons are you trying to exorcise?*

His chances of getting that answer wouldn't be any better when she woke. He still knew little about what she'd experienced as a kid – the tornado that killed her family, or the aftermath. He knew exactly as much about her as she allowed him to know, and every small revelation was calculated to close off any further discussion. In the light of day, she'd retreat behind armor as thick as the layer covering the Beast.

Touching Tori's shoulder softly, he leaned down and whispered to her. "Tori, wake up. You're having a bad dream."

She rolled over with a muttered groan, exposing her fine rear view. Jack closed his eyes with a groan of his own. Avoiding temptation, he moved to the other side of the bed. She seemed to have calmed down, which should've been his cue to leave. But something about the way her eyebrows were knit together even in sleep arrested him.

From the dim streetlight filtering through her lacy curtains, the canvas on the easel caught his attention. The room's deep shadows highlighted its darkness and hid its depth. There were walls and broken glass. Did the bright red symbolize blood? Or anger? He wished he'd been able to watch her paint it, to know her thoughts as she created the piece. She was a complex woman. There was nothing perfect about her, but she was incredible in her imperfection.

The bedsprings creaked as Tori winced and opened an eye. "Mathis?" She leaned up on an elbow, and pushed her hair off her forehead. Frowning, she looked around the room. "What are you doing in here?"

"You were having a bad dream."

Jack once again tried to ignore the view as Tori struggled to untangle her legs from the sheets. Failing miserably, she flopped back on the pillow with a groan and flung her arm over her eyes.

"Oh, my God. I'm such an idiot."

Jack didn't respond, and he sure wasn't going to cast a stone. Instead, he left the room and returned with a bottle of water and three Tylenol. "Here take these."

Tori cracked an eye again then sat up, frowning at the pills. "Three?"

"Two never did it for me."

She dug the pills out of his palm and tossed them back with the water. Jack untucked the bottom sheet allowing Tori to disentangle herself. With deliberate caution, she swung her legs over the side of the bed.

"Need any help?"

A slow shake of her head as she stumbled out of the room. "No. Just need to use the restroom. I'll be right back."

Jack gave her a few minutes, and was starting to wonder if she'd passed out in the bathroom when she returned and laid down on the bed without a word or a look his way.

As her breathing evened out, Jack knew he needed to leave. Because what he really wanted to do was crawl into bed next to her and hold her. He'd struggled with alcohol after Becky's death. How many nights had he called Garrett, drunk off his ass, his heart broken and bleeding?

And even though he still hadn't figured out how to deal with the anniversary of her death, he had a support system. His family and Garrett had kept him from tumbling headlong into a dark abyss that he wasn't sure he would've ever recovered from.

But who did Tori have to bring her back?

Jack straightened the covers and pulled them to her shoulders. Was it his place to say anything? Hadn't he just told her they needed to keep their relationship professional? And hadn't she just accepted that?

He'd be smart to leave things alone. There was little doubt in his mind that any attempt to broach the subject would backfire. And he wasn't about to alienate her. Not now.

Maybe he could talk to Cam.

Jack closed her door and leaned against the hallway wall.

What was he doing?

Tori had a problem with alcohol. He'd clued in almost immediately to the signs. There was a fine line that separated a drinker from a high functioning alcoholic, and she'd crossed it. That should've made her even more off limits. But it didn't. Every instinct in his body told him she was worth fighting for, that he could help her through it. But would she let him?

Several moments passed before Jack's ears processed a scratching noise against the back door. He flipped the safety off his pistol, the hair on the back of his neck standing at attention. From his vantage point, he could barely make out a dark figure against the darker night. Crawling to the living room, he kept his senses tuned to the sound as he located his phone and dialed.

"911. What's your emergency?"

"Home invasion in progress," Jack whispered. He gave the address. "There's someone breaking in through the back door."

"Understood. We have someone on the way. ETA five minutes. What's your name, sir?"

"Special Agent Jack Mathis, FBI."

"Stay on the line until they arrive."

"Will do."

The lock he'd replaced on the screen door popped and the door knob rattled. Jack slowed his breathing and crouched near the entrance to the kitchen, gun trained on the door. Surely Sims wasn't this stupid. If he'd been around already, he'd know Tori had someone living with her.

But he'd become unpredictable, so maybe Jack was going to get one hell of a lucky break. He thought about Tori, blissfully unaware of what was going on. As tough as this case had been, he'd be glad to see it end here. Tonight.

"Agent Mathis, are you still there?"

"Yes," he whispered.

"Patrol will be there in less than a minute."

Moments later, wood cracked and the lock broke. Jack set the phone down on the floor as the man entered the kitchen. A few more seconds. Hold for a few more seconds.

Jack slipped around the corner into the kitchen. As the man began rummaging through the kitchen drawer, Jack flipped on the light switch.

"Freeze."

Jack heard the officers' approach, but never took his eye off his target. "Jack Mathis, FBI," he yelled to the officers.

In a flash, the man's hood fell away from his face as he grabbed a knife from the block on the counter and lunged at Jack. Jack sidestepped the attack and brought the butt of his gun down at the base of Chuck Patterson's head, knocking him to the floor.

The officers surrounded Jack, guns ready, as he rolled Patterson onto his stomach. Jack remained where he was, with a knee in Patterson's back, until one of the officers cuffed the unconscious man.

"Stand and produce your badge."

Jack holstered his gun and followed the officer's order. "This residence belongs to Victoria Whitlock. This man is Charles Patterson. He is a former co-worker of Ms. Whitlock, and she has a restraining order against him."

Patterson groaned from the floor and tried to roll over. One of the officers hooked him under the arm, pulling him to his feet.

"You have the right to remain silent," the officer began.

Patterson shook his head and moaned. "You don't understand. She took everything from me. I wasn't going to hurt anybody. I just need money."

"Anything you say can and will be used against you in a court of law."

As the officer continued, his partner addressed Jack. "How is it that you were here tonight? And is Ms. Whitlock present?"

Jack ignored the territorial tone. He'd encountered it from local law enforcement more times than he could count. "I've been in communication with your Chief about the case I'm working on involving Ms. Whitlock." He ushered them toward the front door and pulled a card from his briefcase then handed it to the officer. "Ms. Whitlock is currently sleeping. But she and I will both be pressing charges. Call me tomorrow and we'll be happy to come down to the station."

───────────────

Between the pot of coffee he drank, and trying to get his anger under control, sleep evaded Jack the rest of the night. He calmed down enough to scratch out a list of supplies he'd need to fix the broken door jamb then got fired up all over again thinking about what might have happened if he hadn't been there.

The sun had been up for a few hours, and he'd started to zone out when the front door opened and Cam let himself in, his anxious eyes darting around the room. "Hey. Got your message and tried to call you back, but I kept getting voicemail. I got everything on your list." He paused. "You going to tell me why you need a two-by-four and a screen door lock?"

Jack rose from the recliner and stretched his tight muscles. "Follow me." He led Cam into the kitchen. "Last night, Chuck Patterson thought he'd help himself to whatever Tori might have of value lying around the house."

Cam's face went from perplexed to furious. "Where's Tori?"

"She's in her room, still asleep. She's fine."

Cam inspected the busted wood and broken lock. "Son of a bitch. How'd it go down?"

After explaining the chain of events, Jack asked Cam to have a seat. "I could've told you all of that on the phone. Could've had the supplies delivered. But I wanted to talk to you in person. About Tori."

For all of Cam's trust in him, Jack sensed his defenses rising. "What about her? I thought you said she was okay."

Beating around the bush wasn't going to help anybody. "She is. She's fine. But here's the deal. Tori has no clue what happened last night because she passed out. Wasted." He didn't know another way to state the obvious. "I care about her, Cam. And I know you do, too. She has a problem with alcohol. A problem I'm not sure she can control."

A muscle twitched in Cam's jaw. Again, Jack waited. He wasn't sure if Cam was going to walk out or throw a punch.

Cam stood and poured himself a cup of coffee. After adding milk and sugar, he returned to the table. "Has Tori told you how we met?"

"No."

Cam nodded. "You know my story. Or at least the big picture. After my mom died, I was passed around from foster family to foster family until I aged out of the system. I spent a few years drifting and, by that point in my life, I was a mess. So was Tori. We met in a laundromat in Atchison at two in the morning. I was there, screwing around with shit, and I saw her walking. I was kind of keeping an eye on her because she was out there alone, plus I had nowhere else to be. She walked in and told me she'd just had a deep discussion with Amelia Earhart. I busted out laughing but didn't have the heart to tell her she'd been talking to a statue.

"Anyway, we were both wasted, but somehow struck up a conversation. At the time, I didn't know who she was, or what had brought her there, but she was the first person I'd felt a kinship with in a long time. So we're talking and I tell her my name is Cameron. She thought I said camera so she told me she was looking for a camera guy. We both laughed at that."

Jack frowned. "Were you really a camera guy?"

Cam smiled at the memory. "Well, that would be a no. But I picked it up pretty quick. Started taking college classes once I moved here. I liked it a lot, and Tori told me from the beginning that I had a good eye."

Setting his cup on the table, Jack shook his head. "Wait a minute. You're telling me that she hired you to be her camera operator because of your name?"

"It sounds a little crazy when you say it out loud, but yes. That's exactly what happened. I left Atchison with her crew the next day and I've never gone back." Cam eyes misted as they met Jack's. "Tori saved my life and gave me a reason to live. And I've spent every day since then trying to figure out a way to return the favor."

Cam smiled sadly. "So to answer your question, yes, I know she has a problem with alcohol. But she's going to have to figure out her own reason to get past it. Nothing you, or I, or anybody else can do will change it."

Tori awakened to a wicked pounding headache and a stomach on the edge. She groaned and rolled over, but the pounding didn't stop. If anything, it got louder. She opened bleary eyes and realized that the noise wasn't in her head.

Following the sound, she covered her ears as she stumbled into the kitchen and found Jack in a pair of jeans and a gray T-shirt that had seen better days. He was standing in the open space where her back door used to be.

"Mathis?" The hammering continued. "Mathis," she yelled, triggering a wave of nausea. "What's going on? What on earth are you doing?"

Her screaming must've penetrated his ear plugs, because he took them out and turned to face her.

As he opened his mouth to respond, Tori's stomach heaved. "Be right back," she mumbled as she ran for the bathroom. After a few minutes, she brushed her teeth and brushed away the remainder of her excess. Damn, she hadn't tied one on like that in a while.

She rounded the corner to the kitchen and saw a fresh cup of coffee waiting for her on the table. She grasped it like manna from heaven and took several sips.

"How you feeling?"

The sympathy in his eyes made her surly. "Like shit. What happened to my door?"

"You might want to grab a seat." Jack's chuckle was at odds with his serious tone.

A pit formed in Tori's stomach, but she followed his suggestion. She had a feeling she wasn't going to like whatever he was getting ready to say.

"Chuck Patterson paid you a visit last night."

"Seriously?" She motioned to the mess. "Did he do that?"

"Yes. I'd just left your room – "

Tori frowned. "Wait. You came into my room while I was sleeping?" She stared at him, trying to remember anything from last night. Her stomach rolled at the void in her head. God she hated blackout nights.

"I did. You were crying out, and I assumed there was a threat, but you were only dreaming. Then after you calmed down, I was in the hallway when I heard some noises from outside the back door. Long story short, he broke your doors. I called the cops and we apprehended him."

Tori heard the words, but had a hard time processing them. Dark anger mixed with a sense of relief. "I don't get it. I thought there was no way he could be the guy you were looking for?"

Jack sighed. "He's not the guy I'm looking for. Patterson was here for money, or something he could sell."

His words stole her relief, but her anger remained. Taking a deep breath and rolling her shoulders, she managed to contain it in a tight knot deep in her gut. "So what you're saying is that I'm the lucky girl who has two crazy people out to get her."

Jack reached across the table and closed his warm hand over her cold ones. "*Had* two. Technically, we're down to one."

He was trying to make her laugh, or at least smile, but she didn't have it in her. Not now.

"I'll let you know when I hear from the police. We'll need to go down there to press charges."

Tori nodded then stood and cinched her robe tight as she walked out of the kitchen. She'd planned to edit yesterday's film, but that could wait. Her nerves could use a little soothing, and her head still felt like the anvil under a relentless sledgehammer. A long bath, some Tylenol, and maybe a little hair of the dog sounded like a lot better use of her time.

Chapter 13

Jack practically had to jog to keep up with Tori's sharp steps as they left the police station.

"Hey. Going to a fire?"

She got to the car then turned on him, her eyes a dark, stormy blue. "Why didn't you tell me Patterson came at you with a knife?"

Jack opened her door, but she didn't budge. "It wasn't important. He was strung out and clumsy. No big deal."

She didn't look mollified, and her words were little more than a hiss. "You have some kind of hero complex. You know that? You make a living risking your life for other people. It's stupid if you ask me."

Jack stared for a long moment, fascinated by the cool fire in her eyes. After a moment, a slow smile tugged at his lips. "You were worried about me."

Tori huffed as she put on her sunglasses and sank into her seat. "Don't flatter yourself, hot shot. I'm pissed because you didn't tell me the whole story. Period."

He came around to the driver's seat. It shouldn't matter that she was concerned for his safety, but he couldn't deny that it felt good.

Her frown was still in evidence when he chanced a glance her way. He hid a smile. "How about Master Chen's as a truce?"

He thought she might not answer, but finally, she cocked her head his direction as he pulled out of the lot. "I can live with that. Just promise you won't do something that stupid again."

"Only you think it was stupid. I thought it was judicious."

He wasn't sure, but she might've rolled her eyes behind her shades.

The evening and the dinner reminded Jack of the first night he'd stayed with Tori. Except her eyes were missing their speculative gleam. There was certainly no sexual banter, or even innuendo for that matter.

And damn if he didn't miss it.

He helped pick up the empty containers and dumped them in the trash, chewing on the idea of how to convince Tori to go to Kansas City next weekend.

"When's our next chance to chase?"

She glanced at him as she filled the sink with water. "It's hard to say. Something may pop east of here tomorrow. Beyond that I'm not sure. Why?"

Tori wasn't a fan of new people, or new situations that didn't include a massive weather event, so Jack needed to proceed with caution. He crossed his arms and leaned against the fridge.

"If it ends up working out in the schedule, what do you think about a different kind of road trip?" The immediate skepticism he'd expected skittered over her face. "My family is going to be in Kansas City next weekend. If there's nothing going on, I'd like to bug out and catch dinner with them Friday night."

Tori dipped a glass into the sudsy water. "Go for it, Mathis. But I'm not going to intrude on something like that."

"Either we both go or we don't."

Her chin came up. "Why? Can't someone else babysit while you're gone?"

"No." *No way in hell.*

Shaking her head, Tori resumed scrubbing. "I can't imagine why you wouldn't want a day or two away from this monotony."

"Why wouldn't you? Just a nice, quick break."

After a minute, a heavy sigh escaped her lips. "The weather pattern is destabilized right now. I have no way of knowing what's going to happen between now and Friday."

Jack willingly took the small concession. "My family is easy. We have a week, and we can decide as late as Friday morning and drive up."

Her shoulders visibly relaxed, and Jack knew she was thinking she had an out.

"Okay. We'll play it by ear and see if any more systems become active between now and then. I'd hate to commit and then not be able to go."

"Sounds fair."

Jack picked up his computer from the table and left the kitchen. Dropping into the recliner, he opened the screen, but his mind wasn't on the display. The circumstances were odd, to say the least, but Jack couldn't help thinking if she agreed to go, Tori would be the first woman he'd introduced to his family since Becky died.

Ambivalence filled every space in his heart and mind. Maybe this wasn't a good idea. His family would be only too eager to make assumptions about who Tori was to him when *he* didn't even know the answer to that question. All he knew for sure is that she made him feel, really feel, in ways that he'd forgotten. He didn't want to send a bunch of mixed signals to anyone, but then again, mixed signals had pretty much defined his experience with Tori from the beginning.

He opened his email to find a message from Director Collins. His eyes scanned the content, an uneasy pit forming in his stomach.

By Saturday morning, Tori had worked herself into a panic. She needed a storm system to come along as far away from Kansas City as possible. She didn't want to read anything into meeting Jack's family, especially since Jack was only wanting to drag her along out of obligation to the case. He'd made it more than obvious since the night they kissed that he was all business. So why did she feel like she wanted to be sick?

She pulled her gaze from the kitchen window back to the computer model she thought might put up a storm in Arkansas today, but the system had weakened considerably.

Squeezing her eyes closed, she tried to keep the frustration at bay, but it was all too much. The weather. The wait. The worry. She got up and shoved her chair hard enough to move the kitchen table. Reaching around a stack of frozen dinners, Tori pulled out one of the bourbon bottles and slammed it on the counter.

"What the –" Jack stormed into the room like he was ready to kill someone, but stopped short as he looked from the bottle to her face. His tone softened. "Hey. Everything okay in here?"

Tori turned away and reached for a shot glass. "It's fine."

Even with her back to him, she knew he hadn't left the room. Of course, he hadn't. He was her self-appointed, one-man savior. Couldn't leave a damsel in distress.

His soothing voice quieted even more. "No chase today?"

She fought back tears of futility as resentment bubbled up until it almost choked her. Releasing a heavy sigh, she poured a liberal amount into her glass and tossed it back. "Doesn't look that way."

A tear slipped down her cheek as her fist connected to the counter top. "This nowhere land can't go on forever." Jack came up beside her and she whirled on him. "What did I do wrong? It's been weeks since he's communicated with me. You told me he'd never gone more than that between messages. What if he changed his mind?"

Jack started to reach for her, but she took a step back as the kitchen started to shrink around her.

Shoving his hands in his pockets, Jack released a deep breath. "All I have to go on is my gut. That I'm at the right place, and this is the right time. I can't quantify that to you, but I feel it."

"You *feel* it? How's that conversation going to go with your boss?" She challenged. "The calls haven't started yet, or maybe they have. The knife attack proved you don't tell me everything." She was unfairly provoking him, but Jack was a convenient target, the only one she had. "You know as well as I do the clock is ticking. If there isn't an imminent threat, it's only a matter of time before they pull resources."

She opened the back door, the summer humidity smacking her in the face. Closing her eyes, she took a deep breath of the hot, heavy air, trying to get herself under control.

Jack followed, his low voice taking on an edge. "They're not pulling resources. They're adding them."

A dollop of anxiety plopped squarely in her chest as she whirled to face him. Her voice was weaker than she'd hoped. "What does that mean?"

Jack's sigh filled the tiny backyard, but he didn't speak as his eyes continually surveyed the area. Tori stared at him, waiting.

"I got an email from Virginia. My director is changing up the plan. He's bringing in an agent named Sheila Graham. I checked her out. She's similar to you in build and features, but an observant person, especially a serial killer with a target, is going to know she's not you."

A sick knot formed in Tori's stomach as she absorbed the implication. "Why would she –"

"It's the job, Tori. It's what we do."

She collapsed into a metal patio chair, head in her hands. His dispassionate words bounced around in her head as visions bombarded her of the danger this woman would be in. "This is insane. Call her off, Mathis. Chasing is out of the question for someone who's untrained." Her eyes filled, imploring him. "I'll move. Far away. Please. She could get killed without even provoking him. I can't carry that. Don't make me carry that."

His jaw tightened. "She's not going to chase. They're bringing her in to try and draw him out, see if they can get him to make a move on her."

Jack's tone told her he didn't like the idea any more than she did.

"How?" Tori cried. "He's got us on his schedule. Not the other way around. How do they not see that?"

Unable to remain still, she stalked back into the kitchen, hands shaking as she poured bourbon into her glass. Slamming it, her eyes slid closed as she focused on the heat expanding in her chest.

Cool fingers wrapped around hers, gently taking the glass as Jack stood before her, his face a mask of concern.

"I don't know. But trust me, there's no answer at the bottom of the bottle, either."

Tori swallowed the sharp retort that sprang to her lips. Maybe not, but it might keep her from giving a shit. Which, right now, was the next best thing.

Jack continued in the same, low murmur. "Other people are going to be in harm's way until we find this guy. The only thing that will change is their names. Yes, I'm uncomfortable with the decision, but my director's taking a hard line. I don't always get to make the rules. And as much as it drives you crazy, neither do you."

His words and tone did nothing to calm her. Tori's breath hitched as they stared at each other for long minutes. What could she say to that? He was absolutely fucking correct.

Finally, she shoved both hands in her hair, and lowered her gaze. "God, I hate this," she whispered.

She also hated her weakness. The insistent pull that, once again, had her wishing she could hide inside the circle of Jack's strong arms.

"I know, and I'm sorry." He paused. "I need you to pack. We're leaving late tonight."

Tonight? She squashed the flare of anger at Jack for not telling her sooner. Did it even matter? With a nod, she left him in the kitchen and dragged a dusty suitcase out of her bedroom closet, hoisting it onto the bed.

I need you to pack anything you want to salvage. We leave in the morning for Dallas.

The unwelcome, forgotten memory of her aunt's emotionless dictate punched her, a stark reminder that her life had never been anything but an endless loop of uncontrollable circumstances. Tori threw clothes into her suitcase and finished off the last few swallows of bourbon from her bedside table before shoving the luggage to the side and crawling into bed.

Silent tears flowed. She'd need a few more drinks to make them go away.

———

The low rumble of male voices woke Tori from her unplanned nap. As she rolled away from the noise, the angle of the late-evening sun was long across the hardwood floor. Time was almost up. On edge, she rose and stretched, then shuffled to the bathroom where she splashed cold water on her face. But it didn't do any more than the nap had to relieve the dark circles under her eyes.

She made her way to the freezer and poured bourbon over ice before joining Jack and Cam in the living room. It might not fix the looming situation, but it couldn't hurt. Anything to offset the anxiety blooming in her chest.

"Hey. How you feeling?" Cam asked.

Jack's frowning glance slid away from Tori's glass, raising her ire. Twice in one day was twice too many times for him to be acting like her parent.

So she lifted it in the air in a mock salute before taking a drink and responding to Cam. "Peachy. Did Jack tell you the exciting news? We're leaving. Running off in the night. Hiding like cowards."

Jack stood abruptly, his features stony. "I'm going to shower. We need to leave by ten."

Cam sighed as Jack left the room. "He told me the plan so I didn't show up unannounced and get blind-sided."

Plopping down on the sofa next to him, she let her head fall against the cushion. "Jack knows this is a mistake, but he's doing it anyway. I don't understand that."

Crossing his arms, Cam's scrutiny made her wish she'd never opened her mouth. "Because he has to, Tori." He stood and paced the small room. "I know you're frustrated, but you're not the only one stuck in the middle of this situation. Jack is too, you know. He's spent months here, given up his life back home, to try to catch this guy. Cut him some slack." He stopped in front of her. "And you should apologize for that crap you just pulled. You sounded like a first-class bitch."

Cam's condemning words struck her like a fist. She wanted to hurl the empty glass across the room, wanted to strike him, make him take it back. But her anger struggled to prevail under the weighty truth of his words. She'd never stopped to consider what Jack had sacrificed. It was his job, sure, but his family hadn't seen him for months.

She really was a first-class bitch.

Cam pulled her to her feet and wrapped her in a hug. "I'm sorry. I know you're in the middle of a shit storm. That was out of line."

"No. You're right," she whispered to the button on his shirt as a layer of guilt took its rightful place with all the others. "Now, go home."

Cam tilted her face up and placed a kiss on her forehead. "Trust him, Tori. Jack's one of the good guys."

Chapter 14

Tori counted the streetlights as they whizzed by. It was easier than trying to figure out what to say to Jack. He'd given her a couple of brief instructions, but his white-knuckle grip and the set of his jaw told her he wasn't interested in filler conversation.

She wasn't either.

Jack checked his rearview mirror repeatedly as they meandered through the city, until he finally pulled into the underground parking garage at the Hilton and drove down to the third level. Seemed odd that they'd stay somewhere so public.

"You do realize you passed about thirty open spaces, right?"

He didn't respond, even after they parked. Her hand reached for the handle, but Jack stayed her. "Not yet."

A few moments later, a dark car pulled up in the spot next to Jack. He got out of the car as the passenger side window rolled down.

"You got the address?" Jack asked, leaning in.

"Right here, sir."

Jack received the piece of paper and swapped keys with the agent. "Thank you." He opened the door to their backseat and grabbed their suitcases. "Let's go."

She latched the seatbelt in the generic black sedan, then before Jack turned the ignition, she put a hand on his arm. He looked at her sharply.

"Wait. Before we go wherever we're going, I need to apologize." She paused. "What I said earlier, when Cam was at the house, was rude. I've been ugly and out of sorts about this whole mess. It's not your fault, and you're paying a price, too."

His eyes were shadowed in the dimly lit garage. "It's no big deal."

"Yes, it is. And you need to learn how to hold a grudge."

He raised an eyebrow. "Is that so?"

"Absolutely. You're too nice for your own good."

"And you're the most perplexing woman I've ever met."

"But never boring, right?"

Silence filled the car, but she was so attuned to him, she could feel his anger slipping away. She grinned as a smile quirked the corner of his lips. Her hand squeezed his forearm.

"Never boring," Jack repeated, covering her hand with his. "I wasn't so much angry with you as I was with the circumstances. There's nothing to forgive. Seriously. I'm supposed to deal with this for a living. You didn't ask for any of this."

Tori reflected on his words as he cranked the ignition, her bullshit meter quiet. Was forgiveness really that easy for him?

After another twenty minutes of driving, Jack exited the highway at Edmond and found the cross street he needed. Cruising slowly down the quiet, well-lit suburban street, he peered at the house numbers stenciled into the curbs until he found the right one.

From the driveway, he hopped out and punched in the key code to the garage door. After pulling the car in and setting the exterior alarms, Jack dumped their bags at the base of the staircase then set out for the kitchen.

He was still shaking his head over his conversation with Tori. He'd been around her long enough to know what that apology had cost her. And she deemed that cost worth paying. With a smile, he replayed the conversation in his head. Nope, never boring.

"I have a few things to put away in here," he said. "Then we can crash. I'm sure you're exhausted. I know I am."

Tori folded her arms and leaned against the door jamb, her watchful gaze heightening his awareness of her.

"You brought the coffee."

The quiet lilt of her voice, not guarded, pulled him. He rubbed his eyes. She was just making small talk. His filters were down and several unsuitable replies jumped to his lips.

"Come on. Let's go find your room." At the top of the staircase, he opened the door on the left, exposing a master suite. "This works."

Tori opened the door to the ensuite bathroom. "Oh, my God. A Jacuzzi tub. Do you think they'd mind if I used it? My bathtub looks like a thimble compared to this."

Jack stifled an inward groan as his mind filled with an image of Tori, surrounded by nothing but bubbles and water, her gorgeous hair piled on top of her head.

"No one will mind. I'll let you get settled. It's been a long day."

Jack set his case inside the room adjacent to hers. He should've gone downstairs, but he couldn't get himself to do it. Walls might separate them, but he could still hear the occasional comment or happy groan.

"Jack?"

He'd almost drifted off to sleep, and it took him a moment to realize that Tori was standing in his doorway. He scrambled to his feet. "You okay?"

"I'm fine. Just a little wired. Is there any liquor here? I could use a drink before bed."

The hallway light behind her hid her features, but he didn't want to see the need on her face. "Come in for a few minutes, then I'll go see what I can find downstairs."

She walked into the room, her bare feet silent on the thick carpet. He patted the bed. "Lay back."

At her quizzical glance, he smiled. "Just going to rub your feet."

The furrow didn't leave her forehead as her eyes followed him into the adjoining bathroom where he grabbed a bottle of lotion from the vanity.

"You're really going to rub my feet."

The skepticism in her voice saddened him. He'd bet fifty bucks no one had ever so much as offered to pamper her.

He sat down on the edge of the bed and set her right foot on his thigh. "Why not? Pretend you're at the spa." With his thumbs, he began to knead the arch, eliciting a low groan from Tori.

"I'll give you a year to stop doing that," she mumbled.

A low chuckle was his only reply. He took his time massaging one foot and calf then the other, until the tension left and her muscles went slack. She looked so beautiful, so peaceful.

Carefully, he repositioned her on the bed so he could pull the comforter over her. He laid next to her, above the covers, promising himself it would only be for a few minutes.

She was in his bed. Her even breathing lulled him into the fantasy he'd tried so hard to squash. How many nights did he lay on her couch, rock hard and nowhere near sleep, thinking about the things he wanted to do to her? He'd done everything he could to evade the pull she had on him, but it was always there, in the background.

And in these unguarded moments, when she didn't feel that innate need to protect herself from the world, he was more tempted than ever to stop resisting whatever was happening between them. There was no doubt she recognized his attempt at diversion, but she let him succeed. She let herself relax and sleep instead of fighting him on the alcohol.

A smile lifted the corner of his lips as he rolled off the bed and went to the other bedroom. He could help her if she'd let him. And maybe it was time to let her help him, too.

Tori leaned up on her elbow and pulled her hair away from her face to survey the cream-colored room in the morning light. The beige and dark blue accents almost gave it a hotel feel, but the bed was comfortable and she felt more rested than she could remember.

And, oddly, not hungover at all.

She scooted out from under the covers, surprised that she'd fallen asleep in Jack's room. Sleepovers weren't her thing, but the last thing she remembered was his strong hands working magic on places she hadn't even realized were tense. She stopped herself from thinking about all the other places his hands could work magic. No use tormenting herself.

In her room, she pulled on a pair of jean shorts and an old Nike T-shirt before wandering to the kitchen to find Jack at the table in front of his computer, phone pressed to his ear.

"She's in place now." A pause. "Yeah, I'll give it a week. If nothing changes by then, I'll go around him as far as I have to. We're running out of storm season and time." He looked up, quickly hiding the surprise that flickered in his eyes. "Hey, Garrett. I'll touch base with you in a few days. Not sure whether I'll see you on Friday."

Tori didn't say anything as she looked away and stared out the bay window. Didn't know what to say. She'd been upstairs thinking about sleep and sex, and he was here, talking about murderers and foolhardy plans.

The disparity of real life versus the caricature they were experiencing jolted her. To anyone bothering to look, they would appear to be like any other upwardly-mobile young couple in their perfect house, with their perfectly manicured back yard. She swallowed hard to dislodge the unexpected pang of yearning that landed somewhere in her chest, but it had taken root, her mind running with the folly.

"Good morning. How'd you sleep?"

Tori looked at Jack, and the quiet timbre of his voice and the sincerity in his gaze only deepened the fantasy. What if they were those people? For now, she didn't want to remember what had brought them here. She didn't want to be on guard. As trite and ridiculous as it sounded in her own head, she wanted to believe that Jack was her guy and that she was his girl.

She cracked a smile. "I slept well. In your bed. Where did you sleep?"

"I suffered in the master suite."

"Poor guy." Tori took eggs from the stocked refrigerator and moved to the stove. "Hey, Mathis?"

"Yeah?"

"Can we not talk about the case today?"

He studied her. "Sure."

"Or chasing? I need to be a different person in a different world today. That probably doesn't make any sense, but it's what I need."

Jack continued to watch her as if he was weighing something in his head. "It makes perfect sense to me." He came up next to her and nudged her. "Any chance you'll be a person who likes cooking?"

She laughed out loud, relieved. Maybe he understood, maybe he didn't, but she'd give him points for going with the flow. Walking around the kitchen, she peeked into a few of the cabinets, impressed by the full array of cookware and bakeware. A vertical drawer housing cookie sheets gave her an idea.

"I never really learned how, but I'd be willing to try my hand at baking. Last time I baked cookies was with my grandma. I was probably seven or eight."

Jack took the sheet from her. "What's your favorite cookie?"

Memories of her grandma's cluttered kitchen made her smile. When they finished, there was always flour everywhere and a huge serving plate of cookies.

"Peanut butter." The smile in Tori's voice surprised her.

"Okay." He grabbed his phone from the table. "Let me find a recipe."

Three hours and a few burnt cookies later, Tori lifted the last of the batch from the baking sheet onto the rack to cool. Her stomach hurt from laughing at Jack's exasperation over her incessant barrage of questions, but it had been a long time, and she wanted to make sure she did it right.

"I think we made more cookies than we'll ever eat." She turned off the oven and set her mitts on the counter. As she pivoted, she almost jumped back. Jack was close. Closer than she'd expected.

"Hold still. You have a little flour here," he brushed her nose, "and here." His fingers lingered on her cheek, almost caressing, as the spark of humor in his eyes was eclipsed by something much more serious. "I know you wanted to be a different person today. But you aren't, Tori. This is still who you are. When you let everything else fall away, this is you. This hysterical, relaxed, unguarded person is you."

His soft words met her ears. Of course, they weren't true, but everything else was a fantasy today, so why not them, too? She didn't even realize she'd closed her eyes, but when she opened them again, Jack was still there, and there was no hesitation in his eyes.

"Let me know the real you."

Her legs quivered like she'd run ten miles, and heat pooled low and deep in her belly. "What about your protocol?"

Was she an idiot? Why did she just say that?

His finger traced her lips, his words low, urgent. "When you came into my room last night, I ached with wanting. What's happening here defies everything I've ever known. I can't run from it anymore." His finger traced her lips, parting them. "I don't want to."

Tori didn't move. She barely breathed, afraid she'd snap whatever fragile logic had brought Jack to his decision. She wanted him with a ferocity she'd never felt before. And she couldn't predict the future. She may never get the opportunity to feel it again.

Justification. Rationalization. She didn't care what it was called. They'd arrived there together, and everything else faded away. The world was simply her. And him.

"My answer is yes," she whispered.

Jack stared into her eyes, but the image of her spread out before him dominated every part of his brain. His breathing matched hers and every fantasy he'd had of her, of this moment, rioted through him like lightning, electrifying his senses. His first compulsion was to hoist her onto the countertop, but it would end much too soon. And he didn't want that. More than anything, he needed to savor her.

Jack's fingers moved to trace her temple then the gorgeous curve of her jaw before traveling the length of her neck to the high point of her collar bone. She shivered, her pupils dilating.

His hand traveled to cup the back of her neck, drawing her into a whisper of a kiss, soft and tender. He restrained his desire, slowly exploring one corner of her mouth then making his way to the other side. From every point of contact, Tori's passion was almost vibrating in its intensity, but she didn't rush him.

His tongue flicked out, lining her lips, drawing a soft moan from the back of her throat. And that was all it took to break the hold he'd kept on his desire. Jack crushed her to him, and their tongues dueled, driving him mad.

Her hands roved over his back, sending a trail of energy everywhere she touched. He was raging for her, his body demanding release. He broke their kiss, his breathing ragged. "Upstairs. Bedroom."

"Yes." Tori nipped at his lips, suckling. "Now."

Jack didn't waste another second. He couldn't. Shifting, he cradled her to himself. Tori's husky laugh as he bounded up the staircase had him racing to the master suite. As he lowered her to the floor next to the bed, the clothing between them that kept her skin from his touch became his nemesis.

But Tori's mouth, red and swollen from his kisses, drew him like a drug. His lips found hers again, and his forceful advance drove her backwards until her knees hit the edge of the mattress.

Between kisses, he applied a touch of pressure on her shoulders. "Lay back for me."

Tori obeyed and, with efficient precision, Jack started at her feet, torturing them both. But today, he didn't stay there long. His hands and his lips teased her sensitive inner thighs until the denim of her shorts stopped his exploration.

"You're killing me," she whispered.

Jack rose, leaning over her. "I'm killing us both." He captured her lips again, gently raising her arms above her head. He then gave his full attention to the small expanse of skin exposed below the rise of her shirt. His mouth placed tiny kisses while one finger teased beneath the top of her shorts.

He loosened the button, and Tori sucked in a breath. As he slid the denim slowly from her hips, he almost lost it. The red, lacy covering he left behind was damp with her desire. He'd been determined to wait, to prolong this moment, but he couldn't stop his fingers from dipping underneath the fabric. Her scorching heat radiated to his cock, and as his thumb found her most sensitive spot, his fingers plunged inside of her.

Her low moan of pleasure incited him. His pulled the lace away and his mouth replaced his thumb while his fingers continued their assault. Tori's hips matched his rhythm, undulating, her legs spreading to give him unfettered access. And he took full advantage.

Tori's cries rent the air as she came apart around him. Relenting, Jack again occupied his hands and his mouth with the soft skin of her thighs, tasting and touching, giving her time to come back to him.

"I could die happy now." Her languid voice floated above his head.

"Oh, baby. We're just getting started." Jack smiled and placed another kiss against her heated skin, but he was desperate to be inside her.

Tori seemed to understand exactly what he needed. Jack could only watch as she sat up, pulling her arms out of her shirt then releasing the front clip of her bra, allowing her full firm breasts the freedom they deserved.

He reached for her as she stood, but she side-stepped his hands. "Uh-uh. Two can play that game."

Jack fisted his hands at his sides as Tori pulled his shirt from his pants and painstakingly unbuttoned it. With each incremental gain, her fingers played over the skin of his chest, heightening his pleasure. Next his belt buckle released, and her hands were on him, stroking him, caressing him.

He gripped her hands, stilling the motion. "Holy hell, Tori. Give me a second." He was rasping like he'd run a marathon. "I need to be inside you. Please, baby."

Her Cheshire grin let him know she wasn't finished with her exquisite torture. And he forgot why he cared. Dropping to her knees, she removed his socks and shoes, then pulled his khakis from his ankles. Her mouth, poised a breath away from the head of his cock, was the most beautiful thing he'd ever seen.

Then he was inside her. Her tongue laved the sensitive underside as she consumed him. He was seconds away from exploding when she relaxed the magical rhythm. She licked and played along the tip allowing his clenched muscles a moment of reprieve. How was he still standing upright?

She began her onslaught again, but he gripped her head to slow her down. No way he'd survive a second round.

"Tori," he groaned in warning.

Rising to her feet, Tori kept her hand firmly wrapped around him. The fire in her eyes as she teased and stroked him sent his need to the next level. His arm came around her, crushing her soft breasts to him, as his mouth descended to hers.

In a flurry of kisses and touches, they landed on the bed. Jack positioned himself over her, begging at her entrance. He held steady until Tori's passion-filled eyes met his.

"I've wanted you from the first moment I saw you," he breathed. With shaking fingers, he brushed back a fiery tendril of hair from her forehead. "You called to me on every single level."

Her legs wrapped around him, urging him forward with her hips. "I'm here."

She snaked her arm around his neck, her mouth rushing to his, kissing him into oblivion. And there was no more time for words or thoughts. He drove into her with a ruthlessness her body relished. With every stroke, he rode higher. And she matched him, stroke for stroke, crying out seconds before he found his own release.

He collapsed next to her and wanted to shout, but the best he could manage was a weak smile as Tori laughed.

"I should be so mad at you, Mathis," she panted.

He rose up on one arm to look at her, his fingers drawing circles around nipples that puckered again at his touch. God, she was so incredibly responsive.

"Why?" he murmured as his mouth dipped to follow his fingers.

Her back arched against him. "Could've. Been...doing this...for months."

Jack groaned then suckled her again. "Then I better make up for lost time."

Oh, and he did. Tori stretched against the soft cotton sheets as rarely muscles twinged in protest. She'd hate to tell Jack it had been worth the wait, but it had been. As he dozed, her fingers idly circled the smattering of dark hair on his chest.

"Mmmm…you know what that will get you, right?"

His hand closed over hers, stilling her movement. Tori was captured by his hooded gaze, his eyes darkening by the heat she'd stirred in him. Heat, and something else. Something that scared her. Slipping her hand from beneath his, she sat up, pulling the sheet with her.

"I'm hoping food. Except for cookies. No cookies." She laughed at his crestfallen expression. "It's your fault. You wore me out, and now I'm starving."

Jack's stomach rumbled in agreement. With a grin, he threw off the covers. "Fine. You win."

"I'll come help."

With one knee on the bed, Jack leaned in and brushed her lips with a kiss that promised more. "Stay right here." He pulled the sheet down, exposing her breasts, and sampled her pebbled nipples with soft swirls of his tongue. "Just. Like. This."

As he teased her, Tori relished the soft, rocking pulses that rippled through her. God, would it always be like this? So effortless and so thorough? Her eyes followed him as he pulled on his slacks, fascinated by the play of muscle in his back and arms. So much power there, but she'd felt nothing but secure and treasured in his arms. He was an incredible lover, patient but demanding at the same time. She'd lost count of the number of times she'd come for him.

He turned and caught her staring. "If you want food, you better stop looking at me like that."

"I'm debating."

Shaking his head, he chuckled. "I'll be right back."

Tori let her head fall to the headboard as she studied the pattern in the paper on the opposite wall. Her smile faded along with her delusion. What was she doing? There was no "always" for them. There was only right now. This fantasy.

She took a deep breath and sank into the mattress. *Calm down, Tori. This doesn't change anything. There's no harm, no foul here. Just a couple of consenting adults killing time.*

Chapter 15

Jack rolled onto his back with a resigned sigh, his hand feeling the warmth of the sheets where Tori had been moments ago. The pattern hadn't varied for the past two nights. As soon as she thought he was asleep, she left him.

Their first night together, he'd gone back to sleep, too sated to think. He'd assumed she was using the restroom or getting a drink of water. It wasn't until last night when he'd woken again to find her gone, that he'd checked on her and found her in the kitchen, nursing a drink.

He hadn't interrupted, although he wanted to chuck the bottle through the window and watch it shatter along with his irrational hope that she didn't need it like he knew she did. She hadn't stopped. Instead, she was waiting until the middle of the night to get her fix.

Which meant she still didn't trust him. Worse, she felt like she had to hide from him.

Sitting up on the side of the bed, Jack ran a hand through his hair. How could he prove that he only wanted to help her? That he was on her side? He walked to the window and stared out at the quiet cul-de-sac.

The neighborhood looked similar to the suburbia he and Becky had talked about living in. Great friends as neighbors, nice schools for the kids. That all seemed like a lifetime ago, those pastel dreams and whims paper thin now.

What would shared dreams and visions look like with Tori? Vibrant, bold images, like her paintings, leapt to mind. But how could he get her to trust him?

Do you trust her?

The unbidden question popped into his mind. Of course he did. He'd shared the most intimate details of the case, but the truth nagged at him. He'd talked about the case, yet he hadn't talked about his past. Only pried into hers.

Could talking about Becky open a two-way door?

He didn't go downstairs this time. Didn't want to see how far gone she was tonight. But tomorrow, he'd take the next step.

Jack clicked the remote to shut off the television, then settled back into the sofa next to Tori.

Tori's voice was quiet. "Is it good or bad that there isn't anything on the news? Have you gotten any updates on Agent Graham?"

For the most part, she'd stuck to her plan of not talking about the case, but at least a couple of times a day, this question came up anyway.

"Same as yesterday. They've been in communication via email but nothing else has happened."

Tori nodded and sat forward, her head rubbing against the arm he'd extended along the back of the couch.

"I was just wondering because Minnesota's starting to set up for this weekend and I need a few more good chases to give Alan a strong finish to the season."

He let her rationalization go by. She wanted to believe that she was asking because of the chase, but he'd watched her anxiety about Graham grow by the day, seen the fear in her eyes, and heard it in her voice.

"I wish I could tell you yes, but I don't know. I'll check in on Friday and see what's going on." He paused. "Speaking of Friday, if it's still quiet, I've gotten approval for us to go to Kansas City."

"Oh." He could almost hear the gears turning in her head. "Is it a formal thing? Because I wouldn't have anything to wear to that."

"It's not. It would just be dinner with my parents and sister, and my best friend and his family. Not sure if my brother's family is coming in."

"Hmmm...You guys do that very often? Get together for dinner?"

139

He accepted the turn in conversation. At least she hadn't balked completely. "Not as often as my mom would like. I told you before that they used to think I'd run the company at some point. That came along with expecting all of us to stay close to home as adults. But I bolted."

"After college. I remember. You never mentioned why you changed your plans."

Jack took a slow, deep breath. It had been a long time since he'd said the words out loud. "I'd gotten married to my college sweetheart."

Tori sat up. There was no accusation in her blue eyes, just curiosity. But she didn't speak. She simply waited for him to continue.

"A few months later, she started complaining of headaches. She was a runner, so we thought it might be a pinched nerve or something in her back. We started going to the chiropractor, but the treatment was only marginally helpful, and then not at all."

Jack looked away from Tori, focusing on the watercolor above the fireplace, as he swallowed past the tightness in his throat. "By the time we went to the campus doctors, they ran tests and determined that the cancer had spread from her brain into her lymphatic system and her lungs. Their prognosis was six months She made it four."

He looked down at his hands and realized that Tori's fingers were laced with his. Tears shimmered on her lashes. "I'm so sorry."

Jack took another deep, shaky breath. "My parents wanted me to take off the semester and come home, but I couldn't go home after that. Becky's parents asked if she could be buried in their family's plot a couple of towns over from where I grew up, and I agreed. After the funeral, I spent a while trying to figure out how to survive. Spent a lot of nights that semester black out drunk."

The darkest memories of that time – watching Becky die and remembering how close he'd come to drinking himself to death – battered him.

"Then what happened?" Tori's quiet words pulled him back from traveling too far down that road.

He found a smile. "The FBI happened. It helped me center myself. Forced me to sober up, gave me a physical outlet for my grief, and a sense of purpose. The day I graduated from Quantico, I looked up to the sky and told Becky that I'd do everything I could to make her proud of me."

Tori leaned in to him and rested her head on his shoulder, her words not much more than a whisper. "How could she not be?"

The house was finally quiet. Jack was sleeping next to her, but Tori's mind was racing. Learning that Jack had been married shouldn't have been a surprise. But knowing that he'd lost his love had unsettled her. Not that she believed in love, but it was obvious from Jack's tone that he did. Which made her wonder why the hell she was still lying there.

Climbing out of bed, she tiptoed down the stairs and, once again, raided the liquor cabinet in the den. After her first long swallow, she plopped down on the couch and waited for the soothing calm to settle over her. There was no reason to get sideways about Jack. He'd go home when this was all over, and she could get on with her life. And it would be okay.

Tipping the bottle back again, she closed her eyes, until she finally felt nothing.

"Care for a glass?"

Tori jumped at the censure in Jack's voice. She bolted forward, setting the bottle on the table with an unsteady thud as he walked into the room. His spiked hair looked like he'd run his hands through it and his boxers rode low on his hips.

He was angry. It was there in his stance, and his eyes drilled into her. Had she been too loud? "Sorry. Didn't mean to wake you."

"I was awake when you left the room." Tight lines bracketed his mouth. "I know you've come downstairs every night to quiet whatever your demons are. But this isn't the answer. This isn't real."

Did he want her to agree? If he did, he didn't know her very well at all. If he was trying to convince himself, it was better to dispel that notion here and now. "Doesn't get much more real than this."

"Bull shit." Jack's nostrils flared as he picked up the bottle and shook it at her. "This doesn't define who you are."

Jumping to her feet, fury rose up in her, quick as lightning. She reached for the bottle, but Jack stepped back.

"What the fuck is wrong with you, Mathis?" Chest tight, she crossed her arms, refusing to play his stupid keep away game. "You have a hero complex *and* a daddy complex?"

For long seconds, the only sound in the room was her breathing as they faced off.

"I'm not your father. Far from it. But I care about you, damn it." His voice quieted but his eyes were full of challenge. "And you're not in control of this area of your life."

Tori fumed as her anxiety rose. She resisted the urge to lunge for the bottle. "Sorry to tell you, but we can't all be as perfect as you."

"Fuck that. The reason I recognize what's going on with you is because I know how it feels to have shit happen in your life. I told you that. I know how it feels to lose yourself in the bottle. It was the hardest thing I've ever lived through. And it almost broke me."

Her head buzzed as she fought off his empathy. His story was tragic, but it wasn't the same. "But it didn't. You're strong, and you made it through. That's your story, Mathis. Not mine." She reached across the table, doing her best to be civil. "I'd like my bottle back, please."

He looked like he was about to refuse. "One condition. You know my story. I want to know yours."

"What are you talking about? You already know my story."

"I know what's in your file. Tell me the rest."

Tori turned toward the liquor cabinet. "No, thanks. I'll find something else. I'm not looking for therapy hour."

He stepped in front of her, blocking her path.

She looked him up and down. "Really?"

His voice low and calm, he held out the bottle to her. "I'm not going to hurt you, Tori. I promise. Tell me what happened."

Anger simmered behind the bright sheen in her eyes. She jerked the bottle from his hand and took a long drink. "Fine. You want a damn story? I'll give it to you." Her voice dripped with disdain.

"My sister Vanessa was the good one. The one who should've lived." Tori turned her back on Jack and walked to the wall of books, the titles on the spines blurring. "My parents and I never got along. Every single thing I did was a disappointment to Dr. and Mrs. Righteous. But not Vanessa. She was beautiful. And so accommodating, but not on purpose." She waved her hand in his general direction. "Now that I think of it, you would've been a perfect match for her."

Tori paused as memories of that awful night bombarded her. "She'd been crowned prom queen the week before. But she wasn't just beautiful. She was good, you know? Like nice-to-old-people-and-puppies good. Everyone loved her. She didn't deserve to die."

Her voice did hitch then, and Jack was next to her in a heartbeat, gathering her into his arms. He let her cry, all while dropping small kisses in her hair and rubbing tender circles on her lower back.

"I know. Shhh. I know."

Arms at her side, Tori hiccupped against his chest, the guilt crushing. "But you don't. You had no choice. I did. That's the irony." She bit the inside of her cheek and tried to stop the flow of tears. "I was in the basement when that storm came through because I was passed out. Drunk. I'd had a huge fight with my parents because I'd embarrassed them at their stupid country club spring dance. I was so keyed up, I knew I wouldn't sleep, so I went downstairs and raided my dad's liquor cabinet."

She pulled back and looked up at Jack. "I never heard the storm come through. Vanessa died wrapped up in my blanket, which means she came to my room to find me. And I wasn't there."

Jack's hands cupped her cheeks, swiping at the tears with his thumbs, his own eyes damp. "Holy hell, babe." He released a deep breath then his voice took on a sense of urgency. "Listen to me, Tori. You wouldn't have saved her by being in your room. You would have been one more tragic life lost."

She flung his hands from her face and took another long swallow. "You think you're the first person to tell me that? But you don't *know* that. And I'll never know if I could've done something to save her. She would've changed the world, done something that mattered."

"And you aren't? What about the work you do to improve early storm detection? Or the thousands of dollars you give storm victims from your trust?" Her eyes narrowed. "You think I don't know about that? You think that doesn't matter? Tell that to the people you've helped."

Anger swelled in her chest all over again. He said he understood, but he didn't. He couldn't. "You mastered your grief. And your dependence. Good for you. But that doesn't qualify you to make value judgments against me because I haven't."

He reached for her, but she moved behind the desk, putting the physical barrier between them. She plunked the bottle down hard on the wood surface and gripped the edge to still her shaking hands. "You got your story, but I didn't ask for your analysis. And I don't need a keeper."

Jack watched her for a minute longer, his eyes darker than she'd ever seen them. "I wasn't judging you, Tori. You don't judge people you care about. You try to help them."

His low, deliberate words punched her in the chest. Her breath came in quick rasps as he walked away. Jack was at the door when she finally got the words past her throat.

"Don't care about me, Jack. You said you wouldn't hurt me, but I can't make the same promise to you."

Chapter 16

Tori woke to the soft sunlight bathing the study through the two long windows that flanked the large desk. With a groan, she sat up on the sofa, working the kink from her neck. She spied the empty bottle on the table. *Had she finished it last night?*

The sick roll in her belly said the answer was probably yes, or maybe it was a result of her confrontation with Jack. She felt raw and exposed in ways she hadn't felt in years. She rubbed her hands over her face. Damn it, she would *not* feel bad for pushing him away. She'd just saved him. How could he not see that?

But she didn't want to be at odds with him, either. Memories of the relative peace, and the great sex, of the last few days flitted through her mind. Such a rare escape from their reality. Why did he have to change the dynamic?

Tori stepped into the entry hall and listened for movement, but only the quiet tick of the hall clock greeted her. Hopefully, Jack was still sleeping. She needed some time to figure out the best way to smooth things over.

After brewing coffee, Tori settled into a chair in the breakfast nook. She opened her laptop, but it didn't hold her attention. Staring out the bay window at the potted flowers on the deck, she took a deep breath and tried to think logically about how things had gotten so screwed up last night.

He tried to get too close.

That stubborn thought had plagued her almost incessantly from the moment she woke up. She swallowed hard against the panic that tightened her chest. Having sex with him had probably been a huge mistake, although she was loath to admit it. He'd obviously read too much into it. She wasn't capable of the kind of relationship he'd experienced.

The fantasy was over, she conceded. The best course of action was to pretend that the past few days – the wonderful parts, and the awful parts – had never happened at all.

Jack shoved a hand through his hair, his eyes burning as he stared at the case notes on his screen. The next update should be coming through this morning, and after last night, he wished like hell he was out there in the mix instead of fucking things up here with Tori. What little sleep he'd gotten was haunted by the look on Tori's face just before he'd left her downstairs.

He had to walk away. Because if he hadn't, she would've run.

So, not only did he botch an opportunity to have a legitimate conversation about her drinking, he coerced her into telling him her past. Fucking brilliant. And his past hadn't connected with her at all.

Closing his eyes, he tilted his head back and arched against the desk chair to stretch his kinked muscles. The bed had been much more comfortable when Tori had shared it with him. With a groan, he stood. That line of thinking wasn't going to help him focus, either.

Jack's phone buzzed. "Mathis."

"Hey, Jack. Lewis. Graham got hit last night."

Replaying the words in his head, Jack knew he hadn't misheard. *Holy Hell.* He fucking knew putting her in as a decoy was a bad idea. "How is she?"

Lewis' sigh rang through the phone. "Not good. Last I heard, she was still in surgery. Sims isn't a ringer, or she'd be dead."

"What happened?"

"She had an email thing going with him. They'd made arrangements to have dinner at her place where we could contain things. So she went out to the grocery store, under protection, and got hit twice. Long range rifle."

Jack slammed his fist on the desk. *Damn it.* "Did we get him?"

"No. We're chasing ballistics now. Trying to get something from the shooting site. But Collins is going to be calling you to revise strategy."

Yeah, no shit.

After hanging up, Jack paced the room, willing himself to think. Telling Tori might do more harm than good. But was it right to keep it from her?

He was still grappling with the decision when the call came from Collins.

"Have you heard?"

Jack sat down on the edge of the bed. "Yeah. Talked to Lewis. Any update on Graham?"

"They moved her to ICU, still in critical condition. Got hit twice. Back and shoulder."

Guilt plagued Jack. He should've resisted more, maintained control of the plan. The entire case might be screwed because there was no telling what Sims would do.

Closing his eyes, Jack centered his breathing and tried to keep the frustration out of his tone. "So what now? He obviously knows we were trying to pinch him."

"He does. I don't know how, though. When we took over email communication, he was reactive from the get-go. I thought we just hit on good timing. He was responsive to Graham, even went so far as to suggest dinner. We thought we had him. Then he blindsided us."

Jack shook his head. Why was Collins surprised? "He wasn't fooled."

"Not at all," Collins growled. "What's worse is that not only did he know we were dumb FBI mother fuckers, to quote him, he knows you. By name. Said to tell you hello. Also wanted to let you know that sloppy seconds aren't his style. Cocky bastard."

And getting bolder. Jack's mind raced. "We have to assume he still wants Tori. There's no reason to suspect otherwise. Who can you give me to help cover? Tori said we should have a chase this weekend, and we're going to have to expose her, but I'm going to need another set of eyes and ears that can move with us."

"Lewis is good. I'll let him know that you'll be in touch to coordinate."

Jack rubbed a hand over his face. He's was going to have to tell Tori they were going to chase, and there was no way she'd let it go at that. She'd want to know everything. And, if she was going to be prepared, she had to know.

He walked into the kitchen, his eyes drawn to her as she studied her computer at the table. Sunlight turned her deep auburn hair to glistening fire, catching the brilliant red strands. Her jaw was locked, her posture stiff.

"Good morning." Jack busied himself pouring a cup of coffee. He needed a task to help get the words right. "How are the chase conditions?"

He glanced at her over his shoulder, but she didn't look up from her screen. Her voice was tight with forced cheerfulness. "Looking good."

"Good." He couldn't wait any longer. She had to be brought up to speed. "Tori," he began.

She still didn't look at him. "Let's not, okay? I've thought about this a lot already. Yesterday is over. Let's leave it there. We're going to be stuck with each other for a while longer, and it doesn't make sense to feel all weird about everything."

Jack hadn't forgotten about last night, but in light of the conversations he'd had today, he'd forgotten that would be foremost on her mind. And every damn word out of her mouth was contrary to what he wanted her to say. What he wanted to say to her. And he wished more than anything that was all they had to work through.

"We can talk about that later."

Tori looked at him sharply. "What? That makes the most sense –"

"We need to talk about the case. The dynamics have shifted."

It wasn't the words so much as what Jack wasn't saying that made her rise from her chair, dread seeping into her bones. She stared at him. "Tell me," she whispered.

"We're going to chase."

He was being evasive. He knew what she wanted to know. Which meant it was bad. "Why?"

Jack started forward, but her hand came out. "Stop. Tell me what happened."

The stress that twisted Jack's face said all she needed to witness. The words were barely heard over the roaring in her ears. "He got to her. Agent Graham. She's in ICU."

The quaking started in Tori's hands and quickly consumed her entire body. Her vision tunneled as Jack moved toward her. She couldn't stand still. Couldn't let him touch her.

She lunged for the back door, ripping it open, her legs propelling her across the back yard. Sprinting, chest heaving, she barely registered the soft grass under her bare feet.

"Tori."

Jack screamed her name, but she didn't dare look back. The gate loomed large in front of her, twenty feet away, then ten. She didn't know where she'd go, just that she couldn't be here anymore.

The prison of Jack's arms circled her, as he knocked her to the ground, his shoulder and back taking the brunt of the fall. Rage so thick and dark it almost choked her rose in Tori's throat. She kicked and thrashed, but Jack forced her onto her back, one leg trapping hers, while his hands shackled her wrists.

She saw nothing and heard nothing as she bucked and fought, until finally, her energy spent, she lay still underneath him, her breathing ragged. "How could they? They knew this would happen," she cried. "*We* knew this would happen."

His hand released one wrist then brushed the tear-soaked hair from her face. "Shhh," he murmured. "She'll be okay."

Tori squeezed her eyes closed. *Please, please don't let another person die because of me.*

Jack pulled her to her feet and held her hand, ushering her into the house like an errant child. Once inside, she stepped away from him and walked directly to the liquor cabinet, stopping only long enough to grab a glass from the kitchen.

Jack fell into step behind her, and her shoulders tightened, preparing for the confrontation ahead. She didn't want to fight him. Didn't even think she had the energy to do it. But as she brought her drink to the sofa, he met her there, no condemnation, no judgment. He simply held out his arms to her.

Damn it. She closed her eyes for a moment, warring with the decision. She shouldn't encourage whatever this connection was between them. It couldn't end well. But, she found herself slipping into his embrace, against every self-preservation instinct she possessed.

Jack pulled her down to sit with him on the sofa, his soothing fingers combing through her hair. Long, quiet minutes passed, until the edge of panic that had sent her running abated. She sipped her drink then let her head rest against Jack's muscled arm.

"That was really stupid of me. I don't know what happened. It wasn't even a conscious decision."

He continued to stroke her hair, and the liquor mellowed her. She drifted for a few minutes before Jack's quiet reply met her ears.

"I know. But I need you to stay with me. No matter what happens."

She let him believe she'd fallen asleep. He should know her well enough to know she didn't make promises. Especially ones she knew she couldn't keep.

Jack woke to the sound of his phone ringing from the bedroom. He checked his watch to get his bearings and realized it was past noon. He looked down at Tori's sleeping form, and scooted out from beneath her as gently as he could. He hadn't planned on falling asleep with her on the sofa, but he'd bet neither of them had slept too well last night.

He grabbed a bottle of water from the fridge then climbed the stairs to retrieve his phone. He'd missed calls from Collins and Lewis over an hour ago, surprised that he'd crashed so long. He decided to call Lewis first.

"Any new information from our perp?"

"Haven't gotten any new updates from Collins, except that I'm on point with you starting now until this thing is over. So, what's the plan?"

Jack was going to need Tori sober and focused for this. "I don't know. Tori should have better data on the travel plan by tomorrow. I'll let you know as soon as I hear. What's the word on Graham?"

"She's at OU Medical Center, which is the best of the best in the area. But they haven't upgraded her status."

Jack paced the room. "Damn. Okay. I'll touch base with you in the morning."

He finished the call, then after a brief conversation with Collins, Jack connected with ballistics and the CSI team, but by dinnertime, he had precious little new information.

He jogged downstairs and helped Tori pull together a Caprese salad and some angel hair pasta with olive oil for dinner. Tori uncorked a bottle of chardonnay, pouring a single glass as she reviewed the chase data and picked at her meal. Brow furrowed in concentration, she didn't look at him or speak to him.

"You've barely eaten."

Tori looked up, her eyes bloodshot and tired. "Not very hungry tonight. And I'm done with this data for now. I can't even read it anymore."

Jack got up from the table and squeezed her shoulders. "It's been a long day. Why don't we get some rest and see how things look tomorrow?"

"Can't argue with that plan."

Tori went upstairs, took a shower, then changed into pajamas. She figured, after the past twenty-four hours, Jack would be asleep in his room, but when she got out of the shower, he was sitting on the edge of her bed in blue boxers and a white T-shirt. "What are you doing in here? I thought you were going to bed."

"Wanted to make sure you're settled."

Tori removed the towel turban from her head and shook out her damp hair. "I'm not going to run again, Mathis. I told you that was a gut-reaction. I didn't think."

He didn't budge. Just sat there watching her. That should've made her anxious, but she found his presence oddly comforting. She started to rebuke that notion, but didn't have the strength to deny it. Not now.

After drying her hair as best she could, she folded down the sheets and climbed into bed and rolled onto her side away from him. "Good night, Jack."

She closed her eyes and waited for the soft click of the closing door. But Jack instead pulled down the sheets on the other side of the bed and scooted in beside her. She scrambled to sit up, looking at him with a frown. "What are you doing?"

"Caring about you. Deal with it."

She'd had enough wine to take the edge off, and her eyelids were heavy. "Fine. But I toss and turn a lot, so you'll probably need to leave after I fall asleep."

She laid back down on her side, and Jack pulled her into his chest, his arm setting around her stomach. "Thanks for the warning."

Chapter 17

Tori woke in the exact same position she'd gone to sleep in, and Jack's arm still embraced her. She wiggled from underneath it, careful not to wake him.

She tiptoed down the stairs to the kitchen, her head jumbled. Except for Vanessa, she'd never spent the entire night in bed with another human being before now. She squashed the tiny flicker of hope that dared to come to life. That had never been part of her plan.

Neither was being the target of a serial killer. She was anxious for Jack to wake, so he could get an update on Agent Graham. Tori's insides bunched up in a knot, just thinking about the word they might receive today.

She should've been prepared for the possibility that Graham would get hurt. She'd practically predicted it. But it hadn't been real then. Not until yesterday. But she refused to cower. Sims won if she cowered, and she wasn't going to let that happen.

She logged in as administrator on the Vortex website and announced the likely location of the chase in Minnesota. God, she hoped that it came together because she was ready for this bastard to go down once and for all.

Jack walked downstairs right after she'd posted on the website. She walked up to him. It felt good to feel strong again. Good to have a plan.

"Get some rest?"

"I did," he replied. "How about you?"

"Feeling better than I have in a long time. This is going to be a good chase." He started to turn away. "And, Jack?"

He looked at her over his shoulder. "Yeah?"

The sacrifices he'd made for the case, for her, loomed large. She owed him the opportunity to see his family. "We're going to Kansas City first."

Jack threw clothes in his bag and shoved his dress shoes in the side before gathering his computer. He listened as Tori recapped recent events to Cam on the phone and updated him on the schedule.

Ambivalence filled him. On the plus side, they now knew that they didn't have the tactical advantage of surprise that they thought they had. But by every indication, time was up. Jack was hours, or maybe a few days at most, from the killer's attempt to take Tori's life. And he wasn't any closer to having a viable suspect than when he arrived three months ago. No subtle gut checks. No lucky guesses. And, so far, no forensic evidence from yesterday's crime scene, where the bastard had proven to have skill with tactical weapons.

How the hell was he supposed to protect Tori when he had no idea what was coming?

Burning resolve coursed through him. *No matter what happened after, he would not lose her to this mad man.*

Jack knocked on Tori's bedroom door, anxious to get them out of there. "Ready? We need to be in Kansas City by five."

Tori watched Jack from the corner of her eye. As they headed north on I-35, he called his mother and told her they were coming. Up until the last few days, she'd thought *she* was the master at hiding emotion. She should've taken notes. From the sound of his voice, his mother probably thought he was at a picnic in the park.

But stress emanated from his stiff posture and white-knuckle grip on the steering wheel. Not to mention the way his eyes darted to the rear view mirror every few minutes. She was feeling it, too, but as the miles passed and they closed in on Kansas City, a different kind of stress enveloped her.

In less than two hours, she'd be meeting everyone who mattered in Jack's entire world. She released a slow, deep breath. What she wouldn't give for a shot or two of Wild Turkey right now. A huge part of her wished she hadn't committed so they could bypass Kansas City and meet Cam and Dwayne in Minnesota tonight instead of tomorrow. But that wasn't fair to Jack, and there was nothing she could do to make the storms fire early. And they might not fire at all.

"I looked up the Hope for Down Syndrome event online. Looks like it'll be very successful."

After a short pause, Jack answered. "Always is."

"It's tomorrow night though, right?" She owned absolutely nothing that would work for a black tie event.

"Yes. Tonight's just the dinner with the family."

Tori nodded. She knew what that meant. There would be nowhere for her to hide.

Jack pulled into the first available space in the parking garage beneath their hotel. After he cut the engine, he tugged her cold hand from her lap and offered a genuine smile. It was the first she'd seen since he told her about Agent Graham.

"You'll be fine. They're pretty cool people. I think you'll like them." He released her, then grabbed their bags from the backseat and jogged around to her side of the car.

But would they like her? The question plagued her as they checked in and made their way to their fifth floor room. She couldn't decide if she was more anxious about the answer, or about the fact that, on some level, it mattered to her.

She rummaged through her bag and pulled out her simple black dress and heels. Fortunately, the fabric traveled well. She stayed in the shower as long as she thought she could get away with, then took an insane amount of time to blow dry her thick hair until it fell in soft loose curls down her back. She wasn't much for make-up but applied mascara, a hint of blush to her cheeks, and lip gloss. That would have to be good enough.

As she emerged from the bathroom, she heard Jack on the phone. His back was to her as he stood by the window, giving her time to study him. He'd changed into khaki slacks and a navy blazer that fit his shoulders so well, it had to be custom-made.

Those shoulders were tight though, and she stifled the urge to walk up behind him and knead them until their worries were lost behind a haze of passion. There, they could get lost. But his words snuffed out her budding fantasy.

"Okay, we'll meet you at seven." He turned, eying her sharply. "What? Yeah. We're close." He hung up the phone, and while his stare made her uncomfortable, the look in his eyes enflamed her. "You look beautiful."

"Thank you." She walked past him to her bed and plucked her purse from the white duvet coverlet.

He took her elbow and guided her out of the hotel, his voice hard. "We've got about a block walk to the restaurant. Stay close to me and stay vigilant."

"Okay."

Jack's arm weighed heavy against the small of her back as they walked past the row of brightly lit upscale shops and restaurants. His tension only added to hers, overshadowing the laughter from other patrons and the lively strains of street musicians.

With no time left, Jack led her under the black and white stripped awnings of Brio. A young hostess with an engaging smile welcomed them. Tori's eyes were drawn to the beautiful people and the beautiful presentations beyond. As she glanced at her simple dress, a couple laughed behind her sending heat rushing to her cheeks. Had they noticed her lack of style? Or in the brisk breeze, had her hair blown into tangles during their walk over?

For a moment, as Jack spoke to the hostess who led them toward a staircase toward the rear of the restaurant, panic gripped her and her stomach roiled. Could she tell Jack that she wasn't feeling well and needed to go back to the hotel?

Damn it. No. This was not that time, and you're no longer that awkward person. She straightened her shoulders. For tonight she would play a role. She'd be a confident, self-assured woman, adept at small talk and social niceties. And with a glass of wine or two with dinner, she might even enjoy it.

They climbed the stairs and entered a large private room dominated by a horseshoe shaped table, raucous noise, and happy smiling faces. A cute little girl with strawberry blond curls shrieked. Jumping out of her chair, she launched herself into Jack's arms. "Uncle Jack!" She smacked a big kiss on his cheek. "I've missed you. You were supposed to come over and play video games with us."

All eyes turned to them as Jack squeezed her in a hug. "Hello, Lily! I know I was, but the snow got in my way. I'll get there soon. I promise."

Chairs scraped, and Tori and Jack were instantly surrounded by the entire group. After a round of hugs and hearty back pounding, everyone quieted, waiting with expectant faces for introductions to be made.

"This is my friend, Tori Whitlock. Tori, these are my parents, Barbara and Stuart Mathis."

Tori had expected some version of her own parents. And while the cut of their clothing, and certainly Barbara's simple but quality diamonds spoke of their social station, there was warmth and welcome in their gazes.

"Very nice to meet you both." Tori shook Stuart's hand, then allowed Barbara to fold her into a brief hug.

"You too, Tori," Barbara offered. "We're so glad you're able to stop on your way north."

"I'm Lily," the little girl piped up from her perch on Jack's arm. "That's my mom and dad."

Tori leaned, following Lily's pointing finger, then shook hands with the attractive couple as Jack introduced them.

"Garrett and I have been friends since we were kids. And this is Rachel, who's absolutely too good for him."

Garrett smiled. "No argument there."

Barbara gestured to the table. "Let's give them some space and find our seats, shall we? Jack, you and Tori come sit by Dad and me, then you can finish introductions."

"Uncle Jack, can I sit by you, too?" Lily pleaded. She hopped down and pulled her chair from between her parents, scooting it next to Jack.

Tori smiled and found her seat next to Barbara. Before she could even remove the tented napkin on her plate, a suited server leaned in and placed the napkin on her lap.

"May I get you something to drink?"

"House Merlot?"

The server nodded then turned to Jack. "For you, sir?"

"Iced tea with lemon, please."

Tori glanced under her lashes, sighing under her breath in relief at the other glasses of wine on the table. Jack touched her hand, drawing her attention.

He motioned to the other side of the table. "Next to my dad is my sister Hope, then my brother Ben. Next is Ben's wife, Holly." He looked around the room then under the table skirts. "Where are Tucker and Tanner?"

Holly smiled. "They're with my parents in Boston." She leaned in a bit toward Ben. "My parents were begging for some time with them this summer, so Ben and I have been doing a little national sightseeing. We're touring Route 66, and we were close, so we came up this morning and are staying for the wildly successful gala tomorrow night." She tipped her glass toward Barbara.

Barbara held up crossed fingers. "The last one we hosted here was very well attended, so we're optimistic. Aren't we, Hope?"

Hope's gaze dipped to her plate briefly before she mustered a smile for the table. "It will be fun."

After they placed their orders, Tori was hoping to fade into the background and allow the family to catch up. But the first question was lobbed to her before the waiter even left the room.

Rachel leaned in. "So Garrett tells me you're a meteorologist and storm chaser. I grew up in this area, and used to love it when the big storms came. Did I hear Barbara say you're on your way to a chase now?"

Tori smiled. "There should be some good conditions in southwest Minnesota starting tomorrow afternoon into Sunday. We're going to try to hit the road early and make it up there ahead of them. Our crew left tonight to head up."

Throughout dinner, conversation flowed as Tori answered their questions and talked about some of her more interesting chases. She felt included, yet detached, like an actor in a movie.

"Give the lady a chance to eat her dinner," Jack chided. "She's barely had time to take a breath."

Tori forked a bite of her salmon, waging a battle against her inner turmoil. She sensed Jack's worried gaze on her more than once, but did her best to ignore him. She didn't want him to read her so easily, so after her second glass of wine, she doubled down and threw herself back into the conversation.

After the dishes were cleared and dessert ordered, Barbara crossed her hands on the table and leaned back. "I can't remember the last time we all had dinner together. This was nice." She turned to face Jack. "So, what did you find out about the Beneficial Life people?"

Tori bit her lip at Jack's sheepish look and hid her smile. She found their mother-son dynamic fascinating, and oddly charming.

"I, uh," he paused. "I really think – "

Tori pulled her phone out of her purse and opened the notes she'd emailed to herself. "Jack knew I had some extra time on my hands, so he asked me if I'd look into this opportunity. I hope you guys don't mind."

She could feel Jack's stare through her wine buzz, but ignored it. "I found eight other similar properties owned by the same firm. All of them have A+ ratings with the Better Business Bureau, and seven of the eight are at maximum occupancy. The eighth has a single vacancy because two of their residents just recently married, but they have a waiting list, so I'm certain they won't have that vacancy for long.

"The company is based in Wisconsin, has been in business for almost thirty years, and is privately held. I went back to its inception and can't find a single law suit filed against them, which I personally thought was beyond extraordinary. Even more amazing, they've never had so much as a formal complaint filed against any of their supported living facilities."

"Would you care for coffee, ma'am?"

Tori looked up from her notes and nodded to the server. "Sure. As strong and black as you've got it. Thank you."

She was about to go back to her notes, but as she glanced around the table, every single person was staring at her, mouth agape. Hope had a huge grin. Tori quickly looked to Jack, but he wasn't any better.

"I like doing research. Was that too much information?" she whispered.

He leaned in, his warm breath teasing her ear. "Thank you."

Everyone started talking, but it was Stuart's voice that drew the table's attention. "Thank you, Tori. We got much the same information, although not to such fantastic detail. I think we've all been putting off making this decision, and waiting for some kind of validation that we're making a good one. And it looks like we just got it. Hope, we'll speak to the contract coordinator when we get home."

Hope threw her arms around her dad, tears streaming down her face. Barbara placed a hand over Tori's. "Thank you for taking the time to find all of that out."

"It was my pleasure." And it was true. Tori had enjoyed ferreting out the facts and was pleased by the result. She sipped her coffee and surreptitiously studied the people around the table, fascinated. Did they really enjoy being around each other? Their constant conversations and smiles seemed genuine enough.

"What's it like being behind a camera again, Jack? Enjoying yourself?" Stuart winked at Tori. "Is he doing an okay job for you? I always thought he was quite exceptional."

Tori sensed the almost imperceptible tightening of Jack's shoulders. "He's really very good. He and Cam, my other videographer, are putting together a heck of a season."

Jack jumped in. "And Tori's way too modest. Her show lives and dies because of her eye."

Stuart offered a mock-dramatic sigh and spoke to Tori. "Knew he would be. I keep thinking that someday I'll get to retire, but Ben can only do so much. One of these days, Jack's going to surprise me and tell me he's coming back. To run the company, of course, not a camera."

Ben concurred. "My degree is in accounting. I'm a passable Chief Financial Officer, but I'd be a lousy Chief Executive. No people problems for me, thank you very much. Numbers work just fine. If I make a mistake, I can always go back, find it and fix it. Not true with people."

Holly patted his arm. "Now look who's being modest. You know your entire department adores you."

Jack stood. "Excuse me. I'll only be a minute." He leaned in to Tori. "Don't leave the room without me."

Garrett stood and followed Jack out of the room. "Hey, Jack. I'll join you."

Tori almost jumped up too, as Jack walked out. She had no doubt his exit was intended to allow his father's line of questioning to die, but he'd left her surrounded by virtual strangers. Her coffee wasn't nearly strong enough for her liking, but she sipped it anyway, hoping to blend in behind the cup as she listened to the boisterous conversations.

Barbara set her napkin on the table and leaned toward Tori. "So what keeps you busy when it isn't tornado season?"

"Oh. Uh. Independent research, mostly."

"That's wonderful. Do you ever vacation? If you can get away, you'll have to come visit. We'd love to have you as a guest. In fact, autumn is particularly lovely near us."

Rachel plopped into the seat Jack had vacated. "It is beautiful country in the fall, so much gorgeous foliage. Garrett's mother still lives in that area."

Tori twisted her napkin in her hands, hiding her surprise at the invitation. "That sounds nice."

"Slick escape. But you know your dad's never going to quit asking."

Jack turned as Garrett joined him on the balcony overlooking the bustling street below. The wind had picked up enough to keep other patrons inside, so they had the area to themselves.

Jack rested his elbows on the wrought-iron balustrade and offered a lop-sided grin. "Sad part is, I've been having a blast behind the camera, but I can't tell him that or he'd only get worse."

Several moments of companionable silence passed before Garrett spoke again. "Tori's a heck of a girl. Saved your ass at least twice in there."

"Nice segue. Nonchalant with a hint of indifference."

Garrett shrugged. "I tried." He paused. "But she is. And she did."

With a sigh, Jack straightened, gripping the railing. No way was Garrett going to let it pass. "I know. And I know."

"She's also a vibrant, beautiful woman who you haven't kept your eyes off of all evening."

Gritting his teeth, Jack stared out at the twinkling lights on the Spanish style building across the street. "I know."

Garrett let out a low whistle. "Son of a bitch."

Jack rolled his shoulders. "I don't know what's going to happen. I don't even know where her head's at most of the time. But, it's damn hard to think about a future when I'm consumed with whether or not I'll be able to protect her from a killer. If I lose my focus, it could cost her life."

Garrett nodded. "So what you're saying is that if you were in love with her, you'd be *less* vigilant?"

Jack scoffed. "Of course not. And I didn't say I was in love with her."

Garrett was quiet for a long minute, then he spoke quietly. "You look at her the way I look at Rachel."

The tension Jack had tried to release invaded again in full force. He wanted to deny, but the words wouldn't come. "Tori isn't anything like Rachel. And she sure isn't anything like –" He stopped, his eyes widening at the comparison he almost made out loud.

Garrett met him eye to eye. Jack's vision misted, but he couldn't look away from the raw compassion on Garrett's face.

"It's okay, brother. She doesn't have to be."

Garrett pounded his shoulder then went back inside as Jack let Garrett's words settle over him. Could he really get a second chance at love? They'd have things to work through, but would Tori give them a chance once this nightmare was over? He stayed outside a few more minutes wrestling with the questions, but the answers were as elusive as the wind that whipped around him.

He walked back into the room and found Tori surrounded by his mom, Rachel, and Lily. Although Tori was smiling and chatting, the lines around her eyes told him she'd just about maxed out her people energy reserve.

"Ah, Jack. I was just telling Tori about our lovely autumns in the northeast." His mom patted Tori's hand. "You have an open invitation any time you want to visit."

Tori offered a smile. "Thank you."

Jack walked over to Tori and put his hand on her shoulder. He should've known that leaving Tori with his mom was a bad idea. "You about ready to head back? We have a long drive ahead of us tomorrow."

The tightness beneath his fingers belied her carefree tone. "Sure. If you're ready."

After fifteen minutes of good-byes and well wishes, along with another open invitation from his mother, they made it out of the restaurant. Jack could almost hear Tori's shields crashing to the ground. She'd played her part well, and she'd done it for him.

"Thank you for that," he said softly.

"What?"

"For everything. The research for Hope, deflecting my dad's mission. Having dinner with a roomful of strangers." He nudged her with his shoulder as they trekked back to their hotel, his eyes watchful of the surroundings. "Don't know how to repay you."

She frowned up at him. "You deserve to get your life back, and besides, you're trying to save my life. I'd say that's payment enough."

Tori's statement hit him squarely in the chest, as his conversation with Garrett tumbled through his head. Jack didn't want a quid pro quo relationship with Tori. He didn't want her to feel like she owed him.

Then what do you want?

Jack walked next to Tori with a hand on her back, her unconscious sensuality drawing him closer to the point of no return. But could he save her? And could he survive the loss if he didn't?

She picked up the pace. "It's a little chilly. We need to get back."

As soon as he opened the door to their room, Tori found her bed and flopped onto her back, closing her eyes. "You take the bathroom. I'll change out here."

By the time he finished, Tori was in basketball shorts and a T-shirt and looked as sexy as he'd ever seen her. She pulled a small bottle of Wild Turkey from her bag and poured shots into two hotel glasses. She left his on the table.

He wanted to walk away from it, but he didn't. No more than he could walk away from her when this was all over.

"Here's to catching a crazy person and life getting back to normal."

He stared at the tumbler a moment before clinking it against hers. Tonight wasn't the night to rock the boat. After he slammed the shot, he refilled their glasses. "My turn." Raising his glass to her, he smiled. "Here's to the future, and finding a new normal."

Chapter 18

Iowa's endless maze of cornfields was behind them, and the ominous wall of clouds to the west mirrored Tori's mood. The dark swirling mass grew, absorbing the energy from the sun that had joined their journey an hour earlier.

She'd rolled away from Jack's prying, caring eyes last night, trying to shut her mind down against the multiple attacks on her defenses. It had been a long time since she'd thought about being part of someone's family – never seen a family function like Jack's did. There was no artifice or veiled backhanded compliments. The whole group genuinely enjoyed their time together, and they'd completely sucker punched her with their kindness. Who offered their home to a complete stranger?

She recognized the jealousy for what it was, but she never expected to feel it so keenly. Despite doing her best to shut it down, she'd tossed and turned, and witnessed every hour of the night on the bright red bedside clock display. A drop of sadness landed somewhere near her heart, repulsing her with its intensity. Jesus, what was wrong with her? No strings was what she wanted, wasn't it?

"You're awful quiet this morning."

Jack's voice startled her out of her thoughts, and Tori scrambled for a suitable reply. He'd been all business since they left the hotel, barely looking at her. She could've said the same of him.

"If you're anxious about how all of this will go down, no one would fault you for that. But we're going to make it through this. And when it's all said and done, the world is going to be minus one lunatic."

Ten more miles until they'd meet up with the rest of the crew, along with Agent Lewis, in Worthington. Tori looked out the passenger window as her foolish thoughts mingled with Jack's words in her head.

The world might be minus one crazy person, but would it be Sims? Or her?

Tori pretended to pick at the eggs and bacon on her plate. She'd been ravenous when they arrived at the truck stop, since neither she nor Jack had felt like eating when they left Kansas City, but her appetite had all but vanished as her eyes strayed to the conversation between Jack and Agent Lewis.

They stood by the men's restroom door, far enough to be out of earshot, but Tori read Jack's body language like an open book. Something wasn't right. When his eyes flashed to hers, she caught her breath from the sadness she saw there, and shook her head.

She didn't want to know. Not now. Not with a chase upon them. After a swallow of strong coffee, she muscled through her plate then pulled out her laptop. She couldn't control anything else, but she could control her focus. And for now, she was not going to let anything get between her and the brewing storm.

Within a few minutes, she offered a low whistle, causing everyone to swivel their attention her direction.

Reece spoke up. "It must be looking good. Your eyes are lit up like a little girl at Christmas."

"It's better than good. You guys about finished? This storm's turning into a beauty. Looks like it's going to fire soon and if we're lucky, it'll continue to redevelop throughout the day."

Dwayne threw down his napkin. "Well, what are we waiting for? Let's go get this mother."

Jack stepped next to her and dropped a tip on their table, but Tori didn't look at him. She couldn't. Not at close range. After paying the cashier, they left their cars behind, piled into the trucks, and headed west.

A few minutes down the highway, Tori had Dwayne pull onto the shoulder so she could do a full visual check. Horns honked and her head whipped around in time to see Glenn Pritchard's crew fly by them on the highway. For a split second, she second guessed her decision, but she shoved aside the doubt and jumped back in the truck. Glenn wouldn't dictate her actions.

"Take the next exit, about a mile ahead, and turn right."

And then, everything – Glenn, Jack's family, the killer – fell away as she focused on the swirling, seething sky in front of them. She hopped out of the truck, and energy blasted through her as she took in her surroundings. She'd anticipated the dry line perfectly.

Within minutes, the moisture and the instability in the atmosphere aligned and played right into their hands. Tori's adrenaline spiked as a monster wedge tornado formed and skirted the little town of Lucerne, giving them some of what she knew would be their best footage of the year. By the time it dissipated, Tori was hoarse from screaming instructions, but she couldn't wait to see how Jack and Cam had fared. And she was sure Reece had plenty of opportunity to film them in action.

"We need to head east toward Owatonna," she said as they loaded into the truck. "How long 'til we can get there?"

Dwayne checked his watch. "Probably close to one. Will that work?"

Tori looked at her screen. "We'll have to stop back in Worthington for the car, but we should be fine. I think the storms will re-fire later in the afternoon. Probably around three or four. But I don't want to take a chance on missing it."

The guys' excited conversation echoed around her in the truck, but Tori reveled in the power and freedom she'd experienced today. From the minute they left the truck stop, her mind had been almost singularly focused on the storm, and it had been incredible. God, she'd missed it. Missed her life.

Maybe it was the endorphins from the chase, but Tori couldn't keep the grin off her face. She knew the day wasn't over – not by a long shot.

They rolled into Owatonna closer to two o'clock and grabbed motel rooms at the first Super 8 they came across. They had just long enough to dump their bags when Dwayne pounded on the door. "Hey, Tori. We got time to go eat?"

Opening the door, she checked the time on her phone and patted Dwayne's ample belly. "If you insist. We've probably got an hour or two at most."

Bubba's Brisket Palace was across the parking lot from the motel. It smelled delicious, but Tori wasn't hungry. She could've used a beer, but that would've broken her cardinal rule: No drinking before a chase.

Tori was flanked by Jack and Agent Lewis at a round table in the corner and, within minutes, their dinners arrived in red plastic baskets. She chatted with Justin about the data shifts and was about to pop a French fry into her mouth when the door opened.

"Oh, shit," she muttered.

All heads turned as Glenn and his crew lumbered in, their boisterous laughter crowding the already tight quarters.

"I think I may be sick. The jerk even follows us for food."

Cam nudged her knee with his own. "Put away your claws, Tori. Just because he tries to bait you doesn't mean you have to take the hook."

Tori stuffed the fry in her mouth and turned her chair to avoid having to see Glenn's group. She was still pissed about Tricia Chalmers. "Yeah? We'll you're too nice. He probably didn't even want Tricia. But since I was going to hire her, he just had to grab her up."

Cam rolled his eyes. "What does it matter now? You have Jack."

Jack watched Glenn and his five crew members settle into a corner booth at the other end of the restaurant. Tricia's hair was different than the photos in her report, but there was no mistaking her dark, almond shaped eyes.

Lewis leaned in. "You want me to take him? That guy's been dodging for weeks."

"I've got it." Pushing his chair to the table, he looked at Tori. "I'll be right back."

Glenn eyed Jack as he approached and, as the other members of the group followed Glenn's frowning gaze, the looks on their faces varied from curious to concerned. Jack motioned to the guy on the end to scoot around and to Jack's surprise, he obeyed.

Lacing his hands on the table in front of him, Jack zeroed in on Glenn. "You're a busy guy."

Glenn shrugged a shoulder. "I speak at symposiums across the country. I've got a show to put together, and data to interpret. I don't have time to waste."

"So responding to a request from the FBI is a waste of time?"

The tennis match might've continued, but Tricia leaned in to Glenn, alarm on her face. "What's he talking about?"

"Nothing to worry about." He draped an arm around Tricia's shoulder.

Jack was done playing games. Pulling his badge from his back pocket, he slid it to the middle of the table. "Cut the bullshit." He looked hard at Glenn. "After that stunt you pulled at the car dealership, you're lucky I didn't haul your ass in."

The color drained from Tricia's face. "What stunt?"

Glenn's gaze hardened. "Irrelevant. Tori and I've had our differences, but I've never wanted her dead."

A hush fell over the table as Jack studied him, looking for any hint of deceit. He was a smart guy, but even the smartest were often bad liars.

"Why were you at Whitey's that day?"

Tricia frowned at Glenn and shoved his arm away. "I don't understand. What's going on? Why *were* you there? And why didn't I know about it?"

Jack cocked an eyebrow. The dynamic between Glenn and Tricia didn't appear to be employer/employee based.

Shifting in his seat, Glenn clenched his teeth. "As I said, irrelevant. I was just checking out the competition."

Apparently, his answer didn't appease Tricia. Her voice turned brittle. "What else is there to check out, other than her ass? God, I'm so sick of your stupid, competitive infatuation." She rolled her eyes. "I'm glad I didn't end up working for her, because three's a crowd and I'm not into that."

Glenn's pale face reddened and if his glare could've killed, Tricia would've been dead in her seat.

Jack suddenly understood why Tricia had been nervous. He stared at her, anger blooming in his chest. "You were going to sabotage her season, weren't you? If you'd been in her truck, you'd –"

With wide eyes, she looked at Jack like she'd just remembered he was at the table. "It wasn't even my idea."

"Shut up, Tricia," Glenn ground out.

Jack glared at Glenn. "You want to give me one reason why I shouldn't bring you in for further questioning?"

The silence around the table erupted into questions and defenses of Glenn, their words fairly tripping over each other. Glenn slammed his hand down on the table, shocking the rest of his group into silence.

"Because I'm not an idiot. Since the first phone call came right after the car dealership, I surmised that it likely had something to do with Tori.

FBI plus meteorologist. It's not all that difficult to do a google search and find what I was looking for."

The waitress interrupted with baskets of stacked beef, turkey and sausage, but no one dared touch their food. After she left, Glenn continued. "The FBI has four dead female meteorologists. Tori's next on the list."

Tricia gasped. "Why didn't you tell me?" She was looking at Glenn as if she'd never seen him before.

His brows furrowed. "Why would I? It didn't have anything to do with you." He looked straight at Jack. "Or me. I can provide you with alibis for each of the murders if you need it. My alibi for the killing in January is sitting next to me."

"A girl died while we were in Bermuda?" Tricia looked like she was going to be ill.

Jack might've had pity on her, but he chanced a glance at Tori, who was watching the proceedings with an eagle eye, and Jack was furious all over again about Tricia's part in the deceit she and Glenn had planned.

Jack exhaled long and slow. Everything about Tricia and Glenn disgusted him, but he couldn't pass up the opportunity to dig for more information.

He refocused on Glenn. "I already know your whereabouts. And if there'd been one single anomaly, you wouldn't be sitting here right now."

Once again, he looked into every face around the table, hoping to appeal to their humanity. "I'm not asking you to defy your allegiance to Glenn. I'm asking you to put your petty, bullshit pride on the shelf for a minute. We're talking about life and death here."

The group shifted uncomfortably in their seats, until finally one of the other meteorologists spoke up. "What do you want to know?"

Jack relaxed a little in his seat. "What I want are names. Anyone who was in the program that dropped out of sight or lost a job. Anyone who might have a motive."

The conversation floodgates opened as the group tossed around a few names of former classmates. Glenn sat back against the tattered red vinyl with a dramatic sigh. "Fine. I'll play along." He crossed his arms. "You're sure it's someone in the industry?"

Jack frowned at him, surprised at his participation. Then again, he probably couldn't stand not being the center of attention for long. "We don't know. Right now, OU is the only link we have to all four victims."

"I'm sure I would've heard if something major had happened to someone in the school. It's an elite program and we were all tight when we went through."

Jack pocketed his badge, biting his tongue. *Tight, my ass. You trash talked Tori until she was an outcast.* Standing, Jack had had all of Glenn's ego he could stomach. "If anyone comes to mind, get in touch with the local office. You have the number."

He returned to the table, but his cold brisket sandwich and soggy fries held little appeal. Before he reached for a fry, Tori's took his hand, and inspected it. "Well, you still have all of your appendages," she joked. "Probably should wash them though."

Dwayne laughed, but Reece frowned at Jack from across the table. "Fraternizing with the enemy?"

Tori looked at Reece sharply as Cam frowned. "Chill out, man. We're on the same team."

Jack shoved back from the table and motioned for Tori to join him. "Give us a minute."

Reece continued to grumble at the table as Tori stepped in front of Jack, and he directed her around the tightly-packed tables.

Around the corner and down the hallway toward the restroom, Tori turned to Jack. "I don't know what Reece's problem is…"

Jack shook his head. "I don't give two shits about Reece."

Tori's eyes widened. "Oh."

Her tone was light, but anxious eyes darted to his. She was waiting for him to tell her the news he'd received this morning, but now wasn't the time. And maybe he didn't have to talk about Glenn or Tricia, either. Before he could speak, she continued.

"Well, don't let Glenn get to you," she muttered. "He's a piece of work."

Her soft, and wholly inadequate, assessment made him smile. The corners of her eyes crinkled in response like they'd just shared some kind of inside joke. The part of Tori that she tried so hard to keep hidden, the part that cared about others, was evident in her eyes and her tone. Jack thought about the scam Glenn and Tricia had almost played on Tori, and his skin crawled.

He didn't think around the burst of protectiveness that consumed him. Cupping her cheeks in his hands, his mouth descended, capturing

Tori's in a long, searing kiss. When he finally pulled back, Tori blinked up at him, and the small wrinkle between her eyebrows begged to be kissed.

"What was that for?"

Because people are assholes. And you're so strong and independent despite all of the shit you've been through.

His hand slid from her neck down the length of her arm until his fingers twined with hers. He couldn't say any of that to her. She'd shut him down in a heartbeat. Instead, he shrugged. "Just needed something good."

Tori crowded into his line of vision. "What aren't you telling me?"

Could she really read him so well? He cringed. "Probably nothing worth mentioning."

"Uh, no. You don't pull me away from the table, kiss me like you mean it, then go all quiet on me."

He swore under his breath, but he owed her the explanation.

Crossing her arms, Tori took a step back. "Mathis. Does he know something about the case?"

Jack shook his head. "No. But, Tricia Chalmers is in some kind of relationship with Glenn."

"Oh, really?" Tori watched him with interest. "For how long?"

Damn, she didn't miss a thing. "A while. Before she submitted her resume to you." He paused. "Sounds like the plan was for her to share intel and possibly sabotage your season."

Tori lips curled up in a thin smile, but now that he knew how to spot it, she couldn't quite hide the hurt in her eyes as she patted his arm. "You need to finish your lunch. We'll need to be ready to roll by four."

As Tori predicted, the storm reset and bore down on the outskirts of Owatonna. As they raced through the town to meet the storm, Cam leaned out the window with a bullhorn, yelling out instructions to take cover.

Just outside of the city limits, Tori ground them to a stop as the massive wall cloud filled Jack's entire line of sight. The wind bowed two tall oak trees in front of a nearby farmhouse. Tori hopped out of the vehicle about a hundred yards north of the house and surveyed the sky.

Massive streaks of lightning illuminated the sky to Jack's left, and the monstrous thunder that followed shook the ground. Thank God Lewis was with him. His one and only job was to be on the lookout of Sims. Jack looked over at Tori, waiting for her to make the call to start filming, but she was fifty feet away, headed for the house.

Taking off after her, Jack yelled to get her attention, but the words were whipped away on the rising wind as soon as they left his mouth.

Justin yelled from behind him. "It's on the ground, coming straight at us."

Jack did a one-eighty as the fear in Justin's voice registered. And there it was. A massive twister, no more than three hundred yards to the north, bearing down on them.

"Where'd Tori go?" Cam yelled. "We gotta get out now!" He waved furiously at Justin, signaling him to cut and run with the Explorer.

Jack screamed at Lewis. "Did you see anything?"

"No. She just took off."

Jack could barely hear Lewis's words as the energy consumed everything around them. He motioned at the house, but there was no time to explain. Truck two pealed out. Jack pointed to the Beast. "Lewis, get to Cam. Now!" he shouted.

He watched Lewis long enough to make sure he'd heard him then raced after Tori. Her jog had turned into a sprint. *What was she doing?* He could barely see her in the torrential rain pummeling him. His heartbeat pounded in his ears as mud sucked at his shoes, slowing his progress.

He'd swear she slipped in the front of the house, but he couldn't be sure. He had no choice though. The intensity of the wind and the horrendous, violent sound behind him drove him to dive through the open door.

But there was no reprieve. The north side of the house creaked and bowed, tossing glass and furnishings like projectile missiles as the storm slammed through the structure. Jack was thrown against a wall and landed on his stomach in the dining room.

And that's when he saw her lying prone, half-way down the hallway. Her eyes were closed, and there was blood on her forehead and a fractured piece of wood paneling sticking out of her left arm.

"Tori!" he bellowed.

Panic gripped his chest when she didn't respond. He shoved displaced furniture out of the way, keeping as low to the ground as he could. Glass shattered behind him as the picture window imploded, projecting a million shards into the living room. Jack dove next to Tori then scooped her up against his chest and ran down the hall in search of the bathroom.

She moaned as he laid her semi-conscious form in the tub and crawled on top of her. He'd sell his soul for a mattress to cover them, but there was no time. He grabbed a few towels from the closet next to the tub and burrowed underneath them. They wouldn't help much, but maybe they'd keep glass from getting through.

Intense pressure pulled at Jack, ripping the towels away, trying to suck him out of the tub and out the bathroom door like a giant vacuum. The screaming wind whistled, and Jack knew the house couldn't hold up much longer.

Squeezing his eyes closed, he clung to Tori and to the brass shower handle above his head. As slow, torturous seconds ticked by, he prayed. Prayed that Tori would live. Prayed for the storm to end.

He had no idea how much time has passed before the powerful winds subsided. Seconds? Minutes? In the aftermath, a gentle rain fell, and the sun peeked out from the clouds, the calm almost surreal. Jack cupped Tori's face in his hands and touched his lips to hers, rubbing his thumbs over her cheeks to chase away the rain drops.

Her lips spread into a weak grin. "Kissing me twice in one day?" Her eyes slid closed. "I'm just resting for a minute."

Jack barked out a laugh and kissed her again gently before removing his weight from her. In that moment, he conceded the battle. He wanted her in his life, not just for a few days or weeks. Despite the issues they surely had to face, despite everything he'd done to avoid falling for her, he couldn't deny it anymore. Didn't want to deny it anymore.

He was in love with Tori Whitlock.

The guilt and dishonor to Becky's memory he'd been so certain would condemn him didn't materialize. In fact, all he felt was freedom. And a sense of absolute rightness he'd only experienced one other time in his life.

Gently, he helped Tori to a sitting position then assessed the injury to her arm where blood still oozed. Next, he checked the goose egg near her temple. "Uh-uh. Come on, baby. No sleeping. We need to get you to the hospital. You may have a concussion."

With one arm around Tori, he pulled his phone from his pocket as Cam's voice reached his ears.

"Jack! Tori!"

"We're over here. Bathroom," Jack yelled. "Call 911. Tori's hurt."

The other men's progress was marked by the sounds of shifting rubble and Dwayne's conversation with the 911 operator. Cam finally lumbered into the bathroom, followed by Lewis who still looked a little shaken.

Cam took one look at Tori and was on his knees next to the tub examining the wood protruding from her arm. "How bad is it?"

Tori shrugged, then groaned through the pain her action caused. "Could've been worse," she said through clenched teeth.

"Ambulance is on the way," Dwayne declared, filing into the already small space.

Tori shifted against Jack's chest, trying to sit up straighter, hissing when she accidentally bumped her injury.

"You guys okay?" she asked Cam.

"We're fine. Anchored the Beast and hunkered down there."

"Hey," Jack said. Tori leaned back and made eye contact. "Why the hell did you run off? You could've gotten yourself killed."

As if a spell had been broken, Tori tried to scramble out of Jack's arms.

He pinned her squirming body against him, careful not to hit her arm. "Whoa. Hang on, Tori."

"No," her eyes filled with fear. "There was a little boy. Check the bedrooms."

Jack watched her for another second for signs of confusion, but Tori's eyes were clear. Still, he wasn't about to leave her side. "Lewis?"

"On it."

"He came around the side of the house. I followed him to get him to safety, but I was too late. I couldn't find him."

Her worried words ran together. Jack pulled her close again, soothing her hair with his free hand. "Shhh. It's going to be okay."

A few minutes later, Lewis hollered. "I found him! He's okay!"

Tori's rigid frame relaxed against Jack as Lewis made it back to the bathroom, beaming from ear to ear. The boy he held, maybe nine or ten, was pale and shaky but didn't appear to be wounded.

"He was huddled in a closet. Damnedest thing. Wall was blown out on that side of the house, but the closet was perfect. Clothes were still on their hangers." He squeezed the boy. "Hang in there, buddy. Hear those sirens? That's help coming."

Within minutes, police, fire and rescue crews were on scene. Jack listened with one ear as the police calmed the boy, but his eyes never left

Tori as they lifted her through the side of the house to get her out as quickly and safely as they could.

Jack hopped into the back of the ambulance alongside her, his hand on her leg. Once the crew had stabilized her, Jack leaned down against her ear. "And you thought *I* was the one with a hero complex."

Chapter 19

Tori sipped from the water jug the hospital had sent home with her as a parting gift after awarding her twelve stitches in the arm. Well, not home exactly. Cam had upgraded them from the Super 8 to a two-bedroom suite at the Hyatt near the hospital. By the time she was released and had spoken with the parents of the little boy they rescued, she was glad for the short drive and the hefty pain medication she'd received.

Jack, Cam, and Dwayne were perched around the room like mother hens anxiously watching their chick.

"Justin and Reece made it out okay, too. Right? I didn't see them at the hospital."

Cam nodded. "Once we knew you'd be okay, I told them they could stay over or head back. Reece wanted to stay, but Justin was anxious to get home to his wife, so they left around five."

"What about Lewis?"

"Stationed outside the door."

The local television news playing low in the corner caught Tori's attention as scenes of the destruction on the north side of town flashed on the screen.

"Can you turn that up?"

Dwayne snagged the remote and increased the volume as the on-scene reporter began speaking.

"About one-third of the city was affected, but the northern edge took the brunt of the storm. As you can see from the video, dozens of homes were decimated, and many others sustained damage. Officials estimate that as many as three hundred families have been displaced. The Red Cross and Samaritan's Purse are on hand and ready to assist. We'll have the links on our website to donate to disaster relief."

Knowing she wouldn't be able to rest until she'd done what she could, Tori's eyes darted around the room.

Jack came to her side, holding her laptop. "Looking for this?"

From the corner of her eye, Tori saw Cam and Dwayne exchange glances.

She frowned at them. "Can a woman have no secrets?"

Dwayne came to her bedside and kissed her on the top of her head. "I think what you do is sweet. Proud of you, girl."

Shrugging, Cam followed suit. "Some things that are said over a shared bottle of bourbon just kind of stick." He closed the door behind him, leaving Tori alone with Jack.

He yawned and stretched out on the bed next to her. "Yeah, tell the families you're getting ready to help that what you do doesn't matter."

For once, she didn't push the words away, letting them settle over her, warm her. She'd always treated her donations as a kind of a survivor's penance, but Jack made her think differently, feel differently. With a sigh, she rested her head against the wooden headboard. The slippery slope she was on with Jack was getting steeper and slicker by the day. And, to make matters worse, she couldn't see the bottom.

By the time she finished the transaction on her computer, he was sound asleep next to her. She traced the worry lines around his eyes, then brushed back the hair that had fallen onto his forehead. "I don't know why Sims didn't show up today, but you need to find him, Jack," she whispered, hating the sadness in her voice. "You need to go back to your real life."

The next morning dawned bright and clear as it often did after a storm, like a power washer had come through and scoured the sky clean. Tori slid from Jack's embrace and tiptoed to the bathroom.

Aside from the knot on her head that had ripened to shades of purple and green, and the bandage on her arm, she was good as new. She took her time in the shower, carefully avoiding wetting her bandage, and by the time she was dressed and ready, the guys were up and room service had arrived. After three separate assurances that she was fine, one for each of them, she lifted the silver plate cover and dove into her pancakes and bacon.

Cam's phone vibrated next to his water glass. He glanced down on the screen and hit the speaker button.

"Morning, Alan. You're on speaker."

"Good. Good. How's Tori?"

Tori rolled her eyes. "She's fine. We're getting ready to head out."

"Okay." He paused. "Is Jack in the room with you?"

Alan's stark tone had an edge of nervousness to it.

"Of course."

Jack's frown mirrored everyone at the table. "What's going on?"

"The front page headline in this morning's paper reads: *Meteorologist Targeted by Serial Killer*. Did you leak the story to the paper?"

Jack set his fork on his plate with deliberate precision. "Hold on, Alan." He looked at Dwayne. "Get Lewis." After the other agent was roused from sleep and standing next to Jack, he continued. "Hell no, I didn't. Send me the link to the article. Who do they source?"

"I'm emailing it now. Source was anonymous. But the article is thorough. The other girls, the tie-in to OU. It's all there."

Tori tried to read Jack as he read the article. His shoulders tightened with every paragraph. "I could've written this article myself."

"Who would do this?" Cam asked. "And, why?"

"I have a pretty good idea," Tori mused.

Jack watched her. "You think Glenn did it."

She crossed her arms. "Well, yes. Probably. Or he talked someone in his group into it. Think about it. You confront them yesterday, and boom. The story's in the paper this morning. Seems a little too coincidental if you ask me."

"Alan, we'll let you know our travel plans as soon as we figure them out." Jack jerked his head toward Lewis, then pulled his phone from his pocket and stalked out of the room. "Come with me. We'll need to make a couple of phone calls."

Lewis drove in the car behind them during the long drive home. Jack barely acknowledged Tori, except to ask about her injury. Tori pledged not to pepper him with questions because she recognized that his furrowed brow was a byproduct of the gears turning in his head.

But by the time they reached the outskirts of Oklahoma City, she was stretched thin. "Talk to me, Mathis."

He shook his head. "Glenn's an asshole. I get that. But more than that, he's a narcissist. Why would he shine a light on you? What's in it for him?"

"I don't know. Maybe he thinks it's bad press. That it'll turn people off. I gave up trying to figure him out a long time ago." She paused. "I mean talk to me. About your conversation with Lewis yesterday morning. At the truck stop."

Jack glanced over at her, the truth in his eyes before he even opened his mouth. "Agent Graham died yesterday morning. She coded in the hospital, and they weren't able to save her."

At least he hadn't sugar-coated the truth. Or lied. Tori nodded slightly then closed her eyes, barely registering Jack's fingers as they laced with hers. In the darkest corner of her mind, she already knew. Had known since Jack received the news.

Numbness invaded her body like sludge, thick and dark. A woman she would never meet died trying to protect her from a madman. A woman who probably had a life, a family, a future.

She turned her face toward the passenger window as a tear slid down her cheek, wishing she could scream to the world that the tradeoff hadn't been worth it. But she didn't have it in her to scream, barely had the energy to continue breathing.

Tori swallowed another pain pill and drifted in and out. She no longer knew what was worse, the nightmares in her sleep, or the one she was living.

"Tori, we're here."

She jumped at Jack's quiet words, surprised that they were already back in Oklahoma.

Jack ushered her into the house and upstairs to the bedroom. Pulling the blankets back, he shuffled her into the bed. "Try to rest. Agent Lewis will be downstairs. I'll be back in a few hours."

Tori winced at the pain in her arm as she tried to sit up. "Where are you going?"

"I'm meeting with Director Collins at the office. We're making a public statement in response to the article." He kissed her on the forehead. "Take a nap and I'll probably be back before you wake."

Jack stood behind the podium and stared out at the sea of faces as a hush fell over the room. Almost a hundred reporters from all over the country had descended on the Hyatt Ballroom in Oklahoma City, like a plague of locusts. He hated them all. Hated this part of the work. They couldn't add anything to his investigation, only waste his time.

"Good evening. The details in this morning's newspaper article are factually accurate. We are working diligently to track all leads and will advise when a break in the case presents itself. We will take a few questions at this time."

A female reporter spoke over the others. "In the article, the source seems convinced that this case is connected to the three other women. Are you certain of that? And if so, how?"

"We aren't at liberty to discuss the specifics of the case, but yes, we are certain this case is connected to the others." He pointed at a man on the third row. "Go ahead."

"We understand Ms. Whitlock has been the target for several months. How is she holding up under the pressure?"

The tangible sorrow that had accompanied them on the trip back from Minnesota hit Jack hard. Tori was the strongest woman he knew, fearless for herself, yet broken, because of the senseless deaths in her life. His skin itched to get out of there. He didn't want to be standing here like a puppet on a string, doing a song and dance for these people. He wanted to be with her, holding her, protecting her.

It was all he could do to keep the irritation from his tone. "She's doing as well as can be expected. She's a very strong-willed woman and she's looking forward to the day we capture the suspect, as are we."

"Speaking of the suspect, do you have one? Any leads?"

"Again, I'm not at liberty to discuss the specifics of the case. We have time for just a few more questions."

After fifteen minutes of sharing what little information he was willing to part with, Jack was ushered by Collins off the stage and toward the exit door. As most of the reporters packed up their equipment, a man walked over to Jack.

"Agent Mathis, do you have a second?"

Jack and Collins turned toward the reporter making his way to the front of the room.

The man extended his hand first to Jack then to Collins. "Good evening. Ken Johnson. I'm with Internet Intelligence." He paused. "We're an internet news agency. I've been following this case for quite a while now."

"What can I do for you, Mr. Johnson? You obviously heard my statement. I have nothing further to add at this time."

A vigorous nod. "I did. And I'm sorry to even ask this, but my boss said I had to."

Jack stared at him, waiting for him to continue.

"Yes. Well. Since I'm here on this assignment until something happens, would it be possible to do a storm chase with you guys and –"

"No."

"My boss said it would be a great feature article. Good publicity for her show. We could –"

Jack had zero patience. "Tell your boss he's an idiot. And you can quote me on that." He strode toward the door, uncaring whether Collins followed or not. He'd had his fill of this circus.

By the time he returned to the house, he was more on edge than he'd been in weeks, and that was saying something. After checking in with Lewis and relieving him from his post, Jack found Tori in the bedroom, staring out into the night, her stance rigid.

She didn't turn from the window. "How did it go?"

He came up behind her and wrapped his arms around her middle. She let her head rest on his shoulder and that simple act fortified him like no words could have. They stood like that for long minutes before he finally spoke.

"About like I expected it to. Bunch of vultures looking for food."

She nodded, the top of her hair rubbing his chin. "Jack?"

"Hmmm?"

"Did Agent Graham have kids?"

His eyes closed. The dejection in her voice made his knees weak.

"She didn't. Her parents are still living, but no husband, no kids."

"They must be devastated."

"I know. But Graham was doing what made her happy, just like most of us." He squeezed her a little tighter. "She didn't die because of you, Tori. She wanted this assignment. Collins said she practically begged him for it. She didn't want this scumbag on the streets, preying on innocent women."

He hoped Tori was hearing him. But not just hearing him. He hoped she knew he was speaking the truth. This wasn't her burden to bear.

"I want you off the case," she whispered.

Jack tensed. She hadn't heard a word he said. He understood her logic, her unspoken fear for him, but the thought of leaving this case, leaving her, turned his blood cold. "No."

Tori stepped out of his arms and poured a splash from the bottle of bourbon on the bedside table. She tossed it back before meeting his gaze, her eyes distant. "I'm not strong enough to watch you die, too."

The irony of her words struck him like a fist as he watched her pour another drink. He rolled his neck, trying to dispel the low pounding at the base of his skull. She cared about him, but would she ever care enough?

The energy required to try to answer that question didn't exist tonight. With a short shake of his head, he strode toward the door. "You won't have to."

———

Everything was the same, but different. Tori talked to him, watched a movie with him, and even cooked with him, but she was detached, indifferent, mostly inebriated. Lewis was there, and Tori engaged with him, too, a caricature of her normal self.

Which was why he was glad for the chase opportunity in Texas. Unlike the past several mornings, Tori had awakened bright and ready to face the day. As Jack trotted down the steps, she paced in the doorway, already in hard core meteorologist mode.

"The trucks are headed down already."

Lewis emerged from the kitchen, bagel and coffee in hand. "We're all set. I'll be right behind you."

Jack nodded then picked up their bags and slung them over his shoulder. He ushered Tori to the car. "Think we'll get to chase?"

She slid into the passenger seat, keeping her attention focused on the computer models. "I'm keeping my eye on the dry line. We're going to need to see a lot more instability this evening to get some real potential for tomorrow."

The comfortable silence that descended felt good. He missed spending time with *this* Tori. As they continued south on I-35, thick white clouds began to develop to the west. Funny how he noticed. He probably wouldn't have given it a second thought a few months ago.

"Jack?"

"Yeah?" His head swiveled.

"I'd like to set up a scholarship in Agent Graham's name in her hometown. Do you think her parents would be okay with that?"

He reached for her hand. "I'm sure they would."

She nodded then looked out the window, but didn't say anything more.

After a few minutes of letting her slide, Jack's squeezed her fingers then released them. "How's the data looking now? Will Dallas be in the storm path?"

She started, then refreshed her screen and toggled from one map to another. "It's hard to say yet. We'll watch it over the next few hours."

He gave her points for trying, but he knew her mind was still on Agent Graham.

"Dallas is where your aunt and uncle live, right?"

Jack was watching the road, but from the corner of his eye, Tori's shoulders stiffened.

"They live in Westlake."

"You going to try to see them while we're here?"

"No." Tori didn't hesitate, and the look she tossed him discouraged any more questions.

His grip tightened on the steering wheel as silent minutes passed. He wanted to know why, but more than that he wanted her to choose to tell him.

"Safe harbors aren't always safe."

Her words were quiet, but Jack heard the unmistakable sadness in them. His hand drifted to hers again, clutching her cold fingers. And she didn't pull away. He didn't need to know more right now, and he knew she needed to focus on the chase. "Whatever happened, I'm glad you got out of there."

They rolled past the city limit sign for Sanger, Texas, but Jack wished like hell they could just keep driving to the Gulf of Mexico. And they could stay there and talk, and love, and play, until their worlds were right and their hearts were healed.

Had anyone ever loved Tori unconditionally? Certainly not her parents, and apparently not her aunt and uncle. Her sister, maybe. But Tori was convinced she was responsible for Vanessa's death. Resentment rippled through him at the circumstances and the people who had scarred her so deeply.

If he could convince her to give him a chance, he'd show her exactly how it felt to be loved. But there was no convincing with Tori. She'd have to come to that place on her own. All he could do was give her time, and do what he could to show her he was worth taking a chance on.

Chapter 20

As the Holiday Inn in Sanger came in to view, Tori shoved aside their conversations. She glanced at the map one more time, hoping to see some maturity in the cells out west, but they were moving slowly and not showing a lot of promise yet. At least from this location, they weren't fully committed to the Dallas area. If the storm veered north, they could ride straight back up I-35 and catch it.

There was already a crowd at the bar across the street from their hotel, and Tori's attention was captured by a short cowboy with a tall hat escorting his girlfriend around the haphazardly parked cars. He stole a kiss and pulled her into his side before opening the door where laughter and music spilled out to greet them.

A few months ago, she would've rolled her eyes at them. Today, a pang of jealousy riffed through her, which was completely idiotic and one hundred percent Jack's fault.

Turning into their hotel, Tori forgot all about the twosome, groaning when she spied Glenn's intercept entourage lining one side of the small parking lot. Apparently, he'd had the same thoughts about the storm's direction. For a split second, she considered finding a hotel in Denton, but she'd never let him change her chase plan before, and she wasn't about to start now.

In such a small hotel, Tori knew avoiding their group would be next to impossible, but she hadn't expected them to be right smack in front of her when she walked in, either. With Jack and Lewis flanking her, Tori watched Glenn hold court in the atrium seating area, while more than a few curious guests listened to his impromptu weather lesson.

"Fuck," Jack muttered under his breath.

Her thoughts exactly, but she was surprised Jack voiced it. "What?"

"There's a reporter here from the news conference. He covered the cases in Los Angeles and Duluth. He'd wanted to shadow our next chase but I told him no." Jack frowned. "Looks like he found another way to get his story. Guy's resourceful. I'll give him that."

Tori stopped, placing her hand on his forearm. "You don't like him?"

Shaking his head, Jack turned back to the counter and dropped his card. "I just don't want any press. We don't need national attention here, and reporters are like cockroaches. If you see one, there's probably twenty more you don't see."

Tori glanced at the clock, surprised that it was only seven-thirty. She rubbed her face with her hands and let her head fall back against the headboard. She was pumped that the conditions were starting to come together like she'd hoped, but the thrill was tempered. Truth be told, she missed the way things were with Jack before Agent Graham. She missed the banter. And the sex. Man, did she miss the sex.

As if he sensed her ambivalence, Jack rolled over and raised up on one elbow and glanced at her laptop screen. "How's it looking?"

Complicated.

That was the only word that fit. All she knew at the moment is that she wanted them to be back on even footing. Could they find a middle ground that would make them both happy?

Snapping the lid closed, she slid it onto the bedside table then scooted down the bed so they were face to face. With her arm tucked under her head, their eyes connected. For long moments, she simply stared at him. And he stared at her.

"Tori –"

The conflict in Jack's eyes was real and raw, matching the angst churning in her chest. She rested three fingers against his lips, silencing him. She didn't want to know what he was going to say.

"We don't have to go backwards," she murmured, as her hand slipped to the sheet between them.

"No, we don't." His hand joined hers. His thumb slid over her knuckles, the movement both soothing and provocative. "But we can start from here. Build something amazing."

The resonance of his voice touched Tori somewhere deep. She took a small shuddering breath, pushing back the fear that fought to control her thoughts. They didn't have to define what came next, did they? Maybe the past few days had tempered Jack's feelings and they could find a way to be benefit buddies after all. A small smile played at her lips. She might've just coined a new phrase.

"We can? Like right here, right now?" she teased.

Jack's eyes lit with a devilish gleam as his fingers trailed a path up her arm, leaving gooseflesh in their wake.

"Yeah. Like right now."

Jack leaned over, planting his hands on either side of Tori's head. His lips lowered to hers, playfully at first then with a force and passion that made her dizzy. She returned his kiss with everything she could give, leaving them both breathless.

Their moans mixed, forcing a giggle from Tori. "Shhh. Lewis is right outside."

"Don't care. I want to taste you everywhere." Jack shifted lower on the bed and pushed the hem of her night shirt up tight against the swell of her breasts.

Eyes closed, it took immense willpower to lie still as he started with her left knee and kissed his way to the cloth barrier. He made his way across the flat of her stomach and was teasing her hip bone with his tongue and lips when her stomach grumbled so loudly she heard it through the haze.

Jack's head fell onto her stomach as he burst out in laughter. "Talk about killing a vibe."

"You're the one who stopped." Tori reached above her head and tossed a pillow at him, making him laugh even harder as he sat up on the side of the bed to catch his breath.

"What?" she cried. "I can't help it. I'm a big eater. And I was barely able to stomach anything at dinner with Glenn at the other end of the restaurant."

"Come on. We need to get you something to eat. I have plans for you and, besides, you'll need your energy for the storms."

Tori arched her foot against his thigh. "Nothing's open now unless we go into Denton, and I'm not getting dressed to make the drive."

Jack took her foot into one hand and ran his index finger slowly along the underside then up her calf, teasing her sensitive skin.

"Mmmm...I can eat later."

"You're a temptress," he growled, a mix of heat and humor. "There was a vending machine downstairs off the lobby with cold sandwiches and chips. If you promise to stay right here, just like this, I'll go grab you something."

Tori's stomach rumbled a response, prompting another laugh from Jack.

"Guess that's my answer then."

As Jack stood, Tori stretched out on the bed. "If you insist, but I have a strong aversion to botulism, so choose wisely."

"Very funny. I promise I won't bring back anything I wouldn't eat myself. Holler at Lewis if you need anything."

"Holler?" she laughed. "You've been in Oklahoma too long. Besides, I don't think I can ask him for what I need right now."

"Anything but that. That's all for me to give."

His soft words, combined with the heat of his stare, sent a flush of heat to her skin. "Then hurry."

Tori listened to Jack's short exchange with Lewis, then laid back down and closed her eyes. Her skin still tingled where Jack had touched her, as her mind played out different scenarios for the rest of their evening.

A thud against the door startled her out of her thoughts and, moments later, the key card slid into the lock and the door re-opened.

"Let me guess. They were all out of chicken salad." The smile died on Tori's lips, and her heart almost beat out of her chest. "How did you get in here?"

She scrambled off the bed, her brain working overtime to rationalize. "Lewis?" she screamed.

"Shut up," the man hissed. "He's taking a nap right now."

Blood rushed from her face as the reporter Jack had mentioned earlier moved into the room. He pulled a pistol from the waistband of his jeans and trained it on her.

"You stupid, brainless bitch," he sneered.

Everything clicked in Tori's head, and she was in deep trouble. But more importantly, Jack was going to come down the hall any minute. Her stomach rolled as the stranger made his way around her until he was between her and the bedside table where her phone sat, utterly useless.

"Make one sound, and I'll plant a bullet in your head. Got it?"

Tori licked dry lips and nodded. "Yes." She whimpered as he grabbed her injured arm and shoved the gun muzzle under her rib. She had an inch or two in height on him, but he was wiry and the death grip he had on her wound made her see stars.

Pulling her to the room's entrance, he nodded toward the door. "Open it. Nice and easy."

Tori almost tripped over Lewis as she looked left toward the elevators and said a silent prayer of thanks that Jack wasn't there.

"What did you do to him?"

Johnson jerked her to the right. "Down the stairs."

Tori stumbled, trying to slow their pace, but he squeezed her arm tighter. "Keep moving. If your boyfriend comes running, you can watch him die first."

Pain and panic gripped her. Where was he taking her? Lightning flashed to the west as he opened the hotel's side door. The storm's intensity was building. Down the short flight of cement stairs, he led her toward Glenn's intercept vehicle.

For a split second, she rebelled on sheer will alone. Glenn's vehicle? She was going to die in Glenn's vehicle? This couldn't be happening. Where was Glenn? Was he involved? Shocked, Tori stumbled again before she was jerked back to her feet.

As if he'd read her mind, the man spoke low in her ear. "I'm a little disappointed that we won't be able to use your Beast. It would've been more authentic, but Glenn was so accommodating. All it took to get his keys was a little GHB in their drinks. Nice folks, but damn, they talk a lot."

She heard the superior sneer in his voice over the rising wind, but could she slow him down by playing in to it?

Think, Tori. Think.

But her brain wouldn't function, except to register the residual heat that still warmed the asphalt under her bare feet as she walked to her execution.

He shoved her against the side of the truck as he dug in his pocket for the key. How was this even possible? She'd always believed that she'd own her destiny. That she would go out in an epic battle with Mother Nature, just like Vanessa had. But she'd be damned if she'd go willingly with this bastard. If he was going to take her out, at least it would be quick, with a bullet, on her terms. Not his.

She whirled on him, staring into his beady, dark eyes. "I'm not getting in that truck."

Before she could prepare, his fist holding the gun connected with the side of her face, knocking her to the ground. He swung open the door, his strong hands pulling at her as she tried to scramble away. "Oh, no you don't. Get back here, bitch."

Jack whistled as he punched the elevator button to force the door closed. Hope for a future had taken root all over again in the last few minutes. He wouldn't be a fool this time, though. He'd take his time, nurture trust, build on what they already had together.

And what they had was incredible.

The bell dinged and he stepped out of the elevator. He'd gone two steps before his mind accepted what his eyes were seeing. *No. No. No.* The dark lump on the floor by his room was Lewis. Dropping the food, he unholstered his gun and crept toward the door. Jack felt the other man's neck for a pulse, relieved to find it strong and steady.

Jack listened through the door, but couldn't hear anything inside. He didn't have time to wait though. With one motion, he slid in the key and shoved open the door.

Silence greeted him. Unnatural silence.

"Tori?" Fear edged his voice, thick and raw.

Her phone and computer sat on the table where they'd been when he left. He made a quick, fruitless search of the bathroom as every one of his worst nightmares blew into his brain with the force of a tornado.

Minutes. He'd only been gone minutes. Which meant they couldn't have gotten far. Jack raced out of the room and down the hotel stairs, panic gripping him. *He would not be too late to save her.*

Heart pounding, he pushed open the exit door and jumped the short flight of stairs to the ground. Then he heard the screams.

"Help! Help! Please!"

Tori shrieked at the top of her lungs as she flipped over, kicking at Johnson's vice-like grip on her ankle.

"Tori!" Jack's bellow of rage filled the air.

In the patterned lighting of the parking lot poles, Jack raced toward them, his face contorted in a mask of pure anguish. Scrambling, the man took advantage of her distraction and grabbed her hair, dragging her to her feet in front of him. The gun pressed hard against her temple, forcing Jack to a grinding halt about thirty feet away.

"So help me God, I'll kill her right here!" Spittle from his mouth sprayed Tori's cheek. He shifted the gun, pointing it at Jack, and Tori froze.

Jack held out his hands. "Put down the gun. No one has to die."

"You put down your gun. Now!"

Lightning jagged across the sky, and Tori saw even more clearly the harsh lines of Jack's face, the fear in his eyes. He would never forgive himself if she died. He was a good man. He didn't deserve to have another woman's death on his conscience.

With every bit of strength, she possessed, Tori reared her head back. The crunch of cartilage and bone accompanied the man's shriek of fury as her skull met his nose. Blood sprayed everywhere.

"Tori, move!" Jack shouted.

She was off balance with the force of the hit and, with momentum propelling her backwards, she landed hard on her hip and arm. Pain shot through her wrist as she struggled to push herself up.

This is how she would die. He would simply turn and shoot her.

To her horror though, he didn't turn. He stood still, staring straight at Jack, and centered his gun. Blood dripped on the pavement in front of him, in time with some universal clock, ticking in slow motion.

Tori's mind screamed at her body to move, to break his aim, but before she could even blink, shots fired like twin cannons and the reporter stumbled backwards, tripping over her legs, and landing with a lifeless thud next to her.

Her head whipped to where Jack stood, but he wasn't standing there.

Her blood ran cold as she pushed the man's skinny legs off of hers. People trickled out of the hotel lobby as gasps and shouts filled the humid air.

"Call 911!" she screamed, racing across the lot to Jack.

Tori skidded to a stop on the blacktop, kneeling next to his prone body. With two shaking fingers she checked for a pulse, sobbing with relief when she found the steady beat. Tearing away at his blood-soaked shirt, she discovered the bullet wound just above his belt line. A few fat raindrops hit the muscled surface of his chest.

The torn, angry flesh made her stomach heave, but Tori stripped down to her bra, using her night shirt to apply pressure to his wound.

He groaned, but his eyes didn't open.

"Jack," she cried, as the onlookers gathered around. "Jack, please. Please, stay with me."

Cam and Dwayne busted through the group with Reece and Justin right behind them. "Everybody, get back."

They swooped in around her, forcing back the onlookers. Dwayne ripped off his shirt and draped it around Tori's shoulders. "Is he okay?"

"Get an ambulance," Tori cried. "He's been shot!"

Cam held his hand over her blood-soaked one, increasing the pressure. "They're coming. They've been called."

Tori nodded, her eyes never leaving Jack's face. Like a hawk, she watched for any sign that he was waking, or that he wouldn't.

A multitude of sirens strained in the distance then raced into the parking lot. Policemen first, then a pumper truck, and finally two ambulances. Jack's blood had soaked through her shirt, thickly coating her hands as paramedics swarmed around her.

"Back away. We need in here."

Dwayne's strong arms came around her, lifting her away. Tori stood in rapt attention, watching them assess Jack, barely daring to breathe as they moved him in quick time to the waiting ambulance.

Then Cam was next to her, forcing her arms through Dwayne's shirt, his voice firm. "He's going to be fine."

She winced from the contact.

"Holy hell, you're bleeding. Did you get hit?"

Tori shook her head.

A policeman tapped her shoulder. "Ma'am? I'm Sheriff Doug McNeely. Let's get someone to take a look at you." He whistled and motioned to a paramedic from the other ambulance.

Reece handed her a pair of sweat pants, but her eyes never left Jack's ambulance until the EMTs sealed up the doors and drove off. "Where are they taking him?" she whispered, as the rain began in earnest.

"Denton Regional," the Sheriff said over the rising wind. "Let's get you inside. I hear there's a pretty nasty storm coming."

She allowed Cam and the Sheriff to lead her to the lobby, but not before pointing to the white-sheeted body in the lot. She looked at the officer. "You better make sure he's dead. Because if he isn't, I'll kill him myself."

Cam helped her into her sweats and the paramedic rewrapped her upper arm. The sheriff took her statement and, by the time they finished questioning her, the paramedic was urging her into the ambulance.

"Ma'am, your left wrist is broken and your stitched wound has reopened."

She shook her head and looked at the paramedic, his words barely registering. "Can't Cam drive me?"

"Are you refusing transport?" the EMT asked.

"She is. But she'll be there right away," Cam said.

Dwayne, Reece, and Justin surrounded her, their gazes filled with equal measure of tragic sadness and awe at what had happened.

"You go get yourself fixed up," Dwayne said as he gently wrapped her in a bear hug.

Justin pecked her on the cheek. "Call us when you find out about Jack. We'll be praying for him."

Reece stared at her. "I can't believe that just went down. I feel like I was on an episode of Cops. Oh, and I brought your flip flops, too."

Tori looked at him, unable to digest his words. Nothing he said made sense.

Cam took the shoes from Reece and dropped them to the ground, guiding Tori to slide her feet into them. Then he took her elbow and steered her toward the car, with a backwards look at Justin. "You guys get the equipment home. We'll call as soon as we can with an update."

Tori stared out the window into the rainy night as numbness settled over her. Cam had listened to her recount the events to the sheriff, and she was thankful he didn't press her for more. She was incapable of more.

Rain pelted the ground, hard and fast. It ran like the blood. There was so much blood. She couldn't stop it. Despite the pressure they applied, she could feel Jack's life draining through her fingers. Vanessa had died trying to get to her, to save her. Now, Jack would, too.

The constant drum of those words in her head made her stomach churn. He was so full of life, had so much love to give, and he might've wasted it all. He was such a fool!

Fury speared her, the urge to lash out at him almost overwhelming. How dare he? She never asked him to do that. Never asked him to care about her. And there was no way that his fucking FBI protocol said that he should've barged out of the hotel like a crazy man, drawing Johnson's fire.

Hadn't Jack always said he would lose objectivity? But she'd pushed and pushed, and finally gotten her way. And he'd pay for her folly with his life.

Cam pulled the car under the portico at the emergency entrance. Opening her door, he ushered her inside where a nurse met them.

"They said you were coming in."

"What about the man they brought?" Tori looked at her hands again, stained with Jack's blood, and her heart rebelled against asking the question. But her mind had to know if Jack had survived.

Chapter 21

Tori stared at the nurse, willing her to say that it had all been a misunderstanding. That Jack hadn't taken a bullet. That his blood hadn't spilled all over the ground.

The compassion in the nurse's eyes was almost Tori's undoing. "I don't know, sweetie. They rushed him into surgery and he's still in there."

Cam followed them back to the examining room where the nurse rechecked Tori's vitals and told her to sit tight. For long minutes, Tori read and re-read the hand-washing instructions over the little sink, as if they held all the world's secrets. It was easier to do that than think.

"Tori." Cam's deep voice held a hint of challenge.

She read faster. Why couldn't he go away? Why couldn't everyone go away and leave her alone?

"Talk to me."

"You saw him. What do you want me to say?" She whispered, closing her eyes. "He should've called for back-up. But he didn't. He —"

"Did his job. He was brought here to protect you and find the killer. And he did. That's not on you."

He sounded like Jack talking about Agent Graham. And he was lying, just like Jack had been. The words in front of her began to swim and she closed her eyes. "I don't want to talk about it right now," she whispered.

Moments later, the doctor entered their curtained space. He assessed her arm, clucking his tongue. "Definitely need to get that taken care of." He nodded to his nurse who was pulling out suturing supplies. Another technician rolled an x-ray machine into the room. While she took pictures of Tori's wrist the doctor shined a light in Tori's eyes. "Heard you had a pretty hard hit to your head, too. I'd like to run a scan to make sure there's no concussion."

Tori shrugged. "Okay."

She knew she didn't have a concussion, but it gave her a valid reason to stay here, stay close, until they could find out about Jack.

Cam touched Tori's arm. "I'm going to run back to the hotel and grab your stuff in case they need to keep you, okay?"

More out of relief than necessity for her items, she nodded to Cam. "Good idea."

She had no idea how long she sat in the emergency room between the stitching and the scans. She asked about Jack several more times, but there was still no word.

Cam returned with her purse and phone, Dwayne in tow. Dwayne offered a gentle bear hug. "How you doing, girl?"

Tori couldn't form the words, so she simply nodded, the glisten in her eyes matching his.

"Glad this damn mess is over."

He rubbed her back absently until the nurse came back. When Tori was finally stitched, casted, and deemed concussion free, the woman directed them to the waiting room on the fourth floor.

"Your friend has just been moved to recovery. The doctor will be out soon to visit with you."

As Tori watched the nurse leave the waiting area, the constriction in her chest loosened slightly. In recovery implied successful surgery, didn't it?

The waiting room was empty except for them. Tori paced, and Dwayne and Cam sat in relative silence, save for the almost imperceptible classical melody playing through the ceiling speakers. A few minutes later, two suited men entered the room.

"Victoria Whitlock?"

Her nerves jangled and for a split-second she wondered if she was going to be arrested. "Yes."

Cam stood at her side. "Can we help you?"

"I'm FBI Director Collins. This is Agent Dan Owens. We've been working with Agents Mathis and Lewis on this investigation. We'd like to ask you a few questions."

Her back stiffened. Would Jack's director be looking to get Jack in trouble for how he'd handled the situation? Was that what they were angling for? Her mind was exhausted, and the pain pill they'd given her for her wrist and arm dulled her senses.

"I don't know how much I remember. It all happened so fast."

"That's what Agent Lewis said, as well. The only thing he remembers is a sting in the back of his neck before he went down." The director gestured to the sofa. "We're not here to grill you. Please, sit down and relax. You've been through a very traumatic situation. We won't take much of your time."

Tori sat ramrod straight on the edge of the cushion as they lofted questions at her, but before long, she realized they were simply routine questions, meant to fill in the blank spots in their reports. Both men looked immensely relieved to have this case behind them.

They filled in some gaps for her, too. Apparently, the reporter had stolen a master key from housekeeping to get into her room. The agents also mentioned that Glenn and Tricia were both recovering from being drugged. As much as she didn't like or respect them, Tori felt a tiny twinge of guilt that she hadn't even thought about them. In light of all that had happened, the rest of everything else, including their petty grandstanding, was of such little significance.

"Do we even know who this guy was or why he killed all those women?" Dwayne asked.

Director Collins deferred to his agent.

Owens shuffled through some notes. "His name was Leonard Norris. We have a team of people analyzing his residence in Tulsa. From what we've been able to determine thus far, he'd attributed his rejection from the OU's program to their diversity practices. Apparently, he blamed a woman for taking *his* spot in the program. So for each graduating class, his notes show that he deemed himself the *selection committee* and chose one woman, randomly, as payback for their misdeeds."

Tori stood. She didn't want to hear about that bastard. He didn't deserve to be a thought on her mind. She paced, swearing the clock on the far wall hadn't moved since she'd arrived. At least the agents had stopped asking her questions, but they were still there, talking quietly near the window.

They might be done with her, but no way would they leave before hearing an update on Jack's condition. Of course they'd want to know. Everyone who worked with Jack would care about him. He was that kind of guy.

Tori was just about to go in search of someone, anyone, who could give them an update, when a man in green scrubs opened the doors and walked over to her. "Are you Jack Mathis' family?"

Tori stood between Cam and Dwayne as the agents walked over, trying to ignore the stab in her heart from the doctor's words. "No. But they're on their way from the east coast. "How is he?" she whispered.

"Mr. Mathis' wound required extensive internal repair, and he lost a significant amount of blood. Fortunately, the bullet avoided bone, but it nicked his kidney. We're waiting to see if a second surgery will be necessary."

The worry lines on the agents' faces softened slightly. Tori's knees buckled, as Cam's arm came around her waist.

The doctor frowned. "Are you ill?"

Tori shook her head sharply. "I'm fine. Where is he?"

"ICU. It'll be another few minutes before he's ready for visitors."

The elevator dinged faintly from down the hall, and Barbara and Stuart Mathis flew into the waiting room.

Barbara's eyes landed on Tori, and she and Stuart took turns scooping her into a hug. "Oh, my God. Look at you. Your arm. Your wrist. Are you okay?"

Tori nodded, stunned. "I'm fine. The doctor's just out of Jack's surgery."

Barbara turned fear-filled eyes to the physician. "How is my son?"

The doctor patiently relayed the information again, then left the room. As the agents visited with Jack's parents, Tori found herself struggling to look at them. *Why weren't they screaming at her? Didn't they understand what happened? Why it happened?*

Too soon, the agents excused themselves, and Tori took a deep breath. "Stuart, Barbara, this is Cam Tate, my other videographer, and Dwayne Davidson, my driver." She was surprised her voice sounded so normal.

What should've been a few minutes turned into forty-five as they continued to wait. Cam and Stuart struck up a conversation about Mathis Productions, while Tori fidgeted and bounced her leg. Barbara paced the length of the room, back and forth.

Finally, a nurse came from the same hall the doctor had earlier. "We can allow one or two members of the immediate family back now."

All of the rooms' occupants jumped and Barbara's anxious eyes met Tori's. "We won't be long, I'm sure."

"We'll be right out here." Again, Tori marveled at how level and calm she sounded. Anxiety welled up inside her. Was it enough to know that Jack was out of surgery? Did she really need to see him lying still as death and unconscious?

She eyed the short hallway that led to the elevator bank. She couldn't do it. Couldn't see him. She stood to leave, as Barbara and Stuart returned to the waiting room. Tori's heart broke for them. They'd aged ten years in the last ten minutes. Barbara was speaking and Tori shook her head, trying to catch up to her words.

"Stuart's going to grab us some coffee. It's going to be a long night, I'm afraid. Let me walk you back, so you know where you're going."

Neither Cam nor Dwayne touched her, but Tori sensed their silent pressure, forcing her forward. She followed Barbara dumbly as the wide double doors swooshed open. And with every passing step, the pressure in her chest tightened until she thought she might pass out. Shallow breaths, in time with the slap of her flip-flops on the vinyl tile, marked her progress.

Barbara opened the door to room 413, but Tori's feet were rooted to the floor. She motioned to Cam. "You and Dwayne go on in. I'll wait out here."

Cam looked like he wanted to challenge her, but his gaze pivoted to Barbara who was watching, her brow furrowed. "We won't be long."

Tori breathed a tentative sigh of relief as she leaned against the hallway wall, listening to the low rumble of their voices. She let her mind drift along the soothing tones, unwilling to process their words. Too soon, Cam was in front of her, nudging her. Her eyes popped open as he leaned in.

"Your turn. It's not going to get any easier."

All eyes were on her. Dwayne's. Cam's. Barbara's. Tori swallowed the bile that rose in her throat as Barbara took her hand and ushered her into the room, past the small sitting area near the door. Both recliners were stacked with pillows and blankets, Jack's parents' beds for the night.

Beyond that, the curtain was partially drawn and all that was visible was the foot of a bed.

"Come on. He'll want to know you're here, that you're all right."

Tori wanted to vomit, her insides curdling, as Barbara led her to Jack's bedside. Her vision tunneled, and all she could see was his broken, bloody body, lying on the asphalt.

You can do this. You have to do this.

Squeezing her eyes closed, Tori waited for the words to take root. When she opened her eyes again, Jack was still there, wan and weak, buried under a layer of blankets and surrounded by a series of tubes and beeping machines.

Barbara touched Jack's face lovingly, her fingers trembling slightly as she brushed the hair off his forehead like she'd probably done when he was a toddler. Tori recoiled as guilt smothered her.

She'd almost cost this woman her son.

Barbara motioned her to come closer, and Tori reluctantly obeyed. The older woman's face was a paradox. Tears and a smile.

Tori cleared her throat, her own eyes filling. "I'm so sorry, Barbara," she whispered.

Barbara took her hand and squeezed. The motherly love pouring out of her almost broke Tori right there.

"I'm just glad he's going to be okay. And I'm glad you're okay." She turned toward her son again, adjusting the edge of the blanket. "And I'm *really* glad this case is over, once and for all."

"I'm alive because of him," Tori whispered.

"Yes." Barbara's voice took on a tinge of awe. She continued to squeeze Tori's fingers as they stared at the steady rise and fall of Jack's intubated breathing. "I think I'm finally starting to understand why he does what he does." She dabbed at her eyes with the tissue in her other hand. "I'll leave you two alone for a few minutes. I'm sure he'll love to hear your voice and know that you're safe."

Tori didn't want the intimacy that his mom's words implied, yet she did. Scooting the chair next to the bed, her pale fingers skimmed his arm as memories assailed her. Memories of smiles, of good times they'd had despite everything, and she realized just how far Jack had destroyed her defenses. She'd never let anyone in to the level she'd let him in, not even Cam.

Her shoulders shook as quiet sobs filled the room. She laid her head next to his hand, her fingers curling around his cool ones as the fear and the guilt worked its way through her heart and flowed down her cheeks.

"Thank you for saving me, but you should've run, Jack. You should've called the cops. Anything but this."

She lifted her head and studied his face, memorizing the tiny lines around his eyes, remembering how they crinkled when he laughed. She stood and carefully traced his forehead and down the length of his jaw.

Replaying their last conversation in her head, she stumbled on the conviction in his eyes when he said they could build something amazing.

"If I knew how, I would love you." She whispered, the words foreign on her tongue. "You made me want to believe impossible things. But, I'm a mess, Jack. You deserve so much more."

With a shuddering sigh, Tori wiped her tears and forced her unwilling fingers to release his hand. She didn't look back as she walked out of the room.

Cam and Dwayne stood as she entered the waiting room, along with Stuart and Barbara. She painted a smile on her face and hoped like crazy that her face wasn't puffy and red.

Barbara circled her in a hug. "You have to be exhausted."

And she was. Bone-deep, empty-to-her-soul exhausted. "Sleep sounds like a great idea."

"Dwayne snagged us a room at the motel on the corner, so we'll be back tomorrow."

"We'll see you tomorrow, then." Barbara pecked Tori on the check. "Get some rest."

"You too."

Stuart drew her into a hug. "You take care of yourself, you hear?"

Tori's laugh sounded brittle to her ears. "Yes, sir."

He turned to Cam. "You think a bit more about our discussion. I'll look forward to talking to you more."

Cam smiled and shook Stuart's outstretched hand. "I will."

With bright eyes, Barbara thrust a piece of paper in Tori's hands. "Before I forget, here are my numbers. Home and cell. If you need anything, don't hesitate to call. When he gets discharged, I imagine Jack will be recuperating at our home for a good while."

Tori ignored the undisguised hint, but took the paper. "Thank you. Again, I'm so sorry. You two raised an incredible man with a huge heart."

After a few more hugs, Tori watched with dry eyes as Jack's parents headed back toward their son's room. Her heart felt like a stone in her chest as she stepped out of the elevators and walked behind Cam and Dwayne toward the exit, almost bumping into Cam when he stopped suddenly.

"Well, shit," he mumbled.

Tori struggled to see around them. "What?"

"There's a gaggle of reporters right outside the entrance," Dwayne muttered. "Let's go around to the emergency room. See if we can slip out that way."

Jack's contempt for the media played in Tori's head. More than anything, she needed to close this chapter. "No. They'll just keep at it. If I give them something now, I think they'll move on."

Cam looked skeptical, but followed her lead. As they approached the entrance and heads swiveled their way, Tori took a deep breath. She stepped through the revolving door and, immediately, one of the female reporters tossed a comment to her camera operator before sticking a microphone in Tori's face.

"Ms. Whitlock. A harrowing day for you. What can you tell us about your experience?"

Tori swallowed past the sudden lump in her throat. She could tell them that there was an incredible man who didn't deserve to be in a fight for his life. She could say that crazy comes in all kinds of packages. She could tell the reporter to fuck off. But, she wouldn't. Saying anything provocative would only prolong these vultures' interest.

With as much disdain as she could muster, she stared into the camera. "It happened. And it's over." She paused. "I'd like to thank the FBI for their hard work. Other than that, I have nothing more to add. Thank you."

More questions were vaulted toward her, but Cam took her elbow and guided her past the reporters toward their car, with Dwayne on her heels. "Short and sweet."

"Yep."

They drove around the corner to an economy motel. Low hanging clouds shrouded the effect of the tall halogen lights, and Tori resisted the urge to look for anything or anyone that seemed out of place. It would probably be a while before her mind accepted that the drama was really over.

"Been a hell of a day," Cam muttered.

Tori knew that tone. Cam was fishing, taking her temperature, but she wasn't biting. She followed him and Dwayne down the dingy motel hallway, hoping he'd take her silence as the warning she intended.

Cam slowed, waiting for her. "How long do you want to stay? At least until Jack wakes up?"

The shock and the helplessness of the day's events overwhelmed her yet again. She looked at Cam, but barely saw him. "I don't know. I don't know!" She paused, her eyes filling. "Can I just have thirty minutes to figure out what comes next?"

Cam's arm came around her shoulder as he pulled her into his side. "Yeah. Of course. I'm an ass. We'll figure it out tomorrow, okay?"

Tori nodded and swiped at the stupid tears streaming down her cheeks. Despite her utter exhaustion, she dug through her bag for clean clothes then cranked the shower. With her one good arm, she scrubbed every inch of available skin and hair to remove the evidence of the horror she'd experienced. Except she couldn't rinse away the memories. They were there every time she closed her eyes.

After brushing her teeth and swallowing another pain pill, Tori stretched out on one of the beds.

Dwayne rose from the upholstered chair. "I got next dibs on the bathroom."

Cam shrugged from the bed. "Go for it."

Dwayne pulled out a pair of shorts from his bag. "You going to follow up with Stuart?"

Cam paused. "Don't know yet."

Tori cracked open an eye. "About what?"

Shrugging, Cam got up and walked to the window. "It was nothing more than polite conversation. He said Jack was impressed with my work and that Stuart could use someone like me in his business."

Tori stiffened. Whatever she'd expected to hear, that wasn't it. Mathis Productions would be a hell of an opportunity for him, but she couldn't help feeling a tiny bit devastated as her world continued to unravel.

She forced words over her dry lips. "Wow. That's cool."

"I'm sure he was just being nice."

The mellowing effect of the pain medication soothed her, but she couldn't let Cam lie like that. "Bullshit," she mumbled as she rolled on her good side. "You've come way too far, and you're way too good, to film storms for the rest of your life."

Chapter 22

Tori woke to the rumbles of thunder. She sat up, her eyes adjusting slowly to the strange room. Cam and Dwayne were matching freight trains from the bed on her left, their feet and ankles dangling over the bottom.

Yesterday's chain of events crashed over her with the power of a tsunami. Scrambling to stand, Tori winced as her casted wrist connected with the corner of the bedside table. "Shit. Shit. Shit," she whispered as she cradled the arm close to her chest. Her pain medicine had worn off, so she went to the bathroom and gulped down another pill. She looked at the bottle. Maybe two would be better than one. Might help her sleep better, too.

Muscles twinging in protest, she hobbled to the hotel window and pulled the thin curtain aside. The storm continued in earnest, as sheets of rain pounded the side of the building. There were no warnings lighting up her phone and, although she should, she had no desire to check the weather pattern on her laptop.

Wandering back to her bed, she lifted the scratchy sheets and crawled beneath them. Staring at the dark ceiling, she replayed every horrific detail of her experience in the Sanger hotel parking lot.

The gun steel pressing against her side and her temple.

The sound of the gunshots.

Norris' body hitting the ground.

And the blood. Jack's blood streaming from his abdomen.

Once again, she struggled to sit up as panic squeezed her chest. She reached for her cell phone and google searched the hospital's number. Then she remembered the paper Barbara had given her. Should she call? She didn't want to disturb her, but maybe she could leave a message.

With her back against the headboard, Tori took deep calming breaths as she dialed the number. To her surprise, Barbara answered on the first ring.

"Barbara Mathis."

A pit formed in Tori's stomach from Barbara's tight tone. "Um, hey Barbara. This is Tori. I couldn't sleep and –"

"Oh, Tori. I'm sorry. I didn't know who was calling. I thought about finding your number and calling you, but things have been hectic."

"Hectic?"

Barbara's voice rose, and Tori could tell she was trying to keep it together.

"They took Jack back into surgery about an hour ago," she cried. "Bells and alarms started going off, then there were nurses everywhere and they took Jack away. One of them told us that Jack was bleeding internally. He's in surgery right now." Her voice broke. "They're not telling us anything, and it's been over an hour."

"Oh, my God." Tori whispered. "I'm so sorry. I'm so sorry."

The room spun, and Tori's fragile hold on rationality shattered. Jack was going to die. This was exactly how it happened to Agent Graham. Pain stabbed through her chest, so deep and dark it filled her vision.

"I'll call you as soon as we hear from the doctor. Please, pray."

Tori didn't remember saying goodbye. She didn't remember grabbing her purse and the car keys from the cheap hotel desk, and she didn't remember stopping at the liquor store on the way out of town. But as she drove north on the highway through the town of Sanger, she remembered everything else in sickening detail.

There was no destination, no plan. She just had to leave, to escape the abyss licking at her heels. Because if she fell in, she knew she'd never make it back.

Somewhere along the way, she had no idea if it had been minutes or hours, a tiny gas station just off of the highway reminded her that she needed to pee and she needed gas. She hadn't touched the bottle yet, but it sat heavy and solid next to her hip.

As she stood outside her car, pumping gas, the darkness of the two-lane road leading to nowhere beckoned. She finished up at the station, but instead of getting back on the highway and heading toward Oklahoma, she took the rambling country road.

With no one around for miles, she opened the lid of the bottle and tossed back a big swallow, letting the liquid burn its way down her throat as she drove into the inky darkness. Sometime later, she pulled the car over, narrowly missing a fence post. After cutting the engine and the lights, she got out of the car and stumbled into a field. The stars in the night sky pressed in on her, so heavy she could almost feel their weight.

Swinging her arms in a wide arc, her eyes strained to see, but there was nothing. Her breathing changed, coming in sharp, panicked gasps as the pressure that had been building inside of her exploded. Her high piercing screams of utter desolation shattered the night, destroying the illusion of nature's peace.

Tears streamed down Tori's face. The screams might have lasted a minute or an hour, but the night absorbed the sound like she'd never made it. She didn't know how to make a deal with the devil to save Jack's life, and she didn't believe there was much chance of God listening to her either, so she sat in the middle of the growing rows of wheat and took another swig of the bourbon as despair swallowed her, like the night had swallowed her screams.

"It's jus' you and me," she whispered to the bottle. "Jus' like it's always been."

Tori wished she was dead. Or maybe she *was* dead. She lay still for another minute then when she tried to move, sharp pain shot through her arm. She cracked her eyes open and stared at the cast on her wrist. The ferocious pounding in her head kept time with the painful pulsing beneath it.

As gently as she could, she raised her torso from the hard ground, but that only lasted a moment before she curled into a fetal position as snippets of last night took shape. She was lying between rows of winter wheat. Alone. More alone than she'd ever been.

Her stomach heaved, spilling what was left of the contents on the dry ground. Bright red blood mixed with yellow bile, sending her heart racing. She spied the empty liquor bottle near her feet and cried harder.

If this was all there was, she didn't want it anymore.

Her phone chirped a low battery warning next to her hip. Through teary eyes, she reached for it and saw a missed call from Barbara. Her stomach turned, and she would've heaved again if there'd been anything left to give.

For several moments, she laid on her side staring at the phone, fingers shaking. Could she listen to the message and hear the words she'd dreaded for months?

Fresh, hot tears slid sideways from the corners of her eyes as she squeezed them closed. She swore she'd never allow someone as close to her heart as Vanessa had been, yet Jack had firmly disregarded her convictions. He'd simply been there, unwilling to allow her to push him away.

Finally, her eyes were dry, and she was numb everywhere from the inside out. Before she could change her mind, she hit the button to retrieve Barbara's message and put the phone to her ear.

"Good morning. I hope you got a little sleep." Her voice hitched. "Jack's stable, Tori. The doctors believe he turned a corner last night. His prognosis is improving. I knew you'd want to know. Stuart or I will call you later with an update. Thank you for praying for him."

Tori stared at the screen as it went dark, the words barely registering. Jack was alive. Tori didn't move, her breathing shallow, as if the slightest movement might alter the words, make them untrue.

Jack was alive and healing.

And she was in the middle of a wheat field, dying.

Rolling onto her back, Tori stared up at the sky. Twinkling stars were giving way to the light gray of a new day, but depression swamped the metaphor.

When Tori woke again, the sun had broken the plane of the horizon, warm on her cheeks. Heads of grain rustled all around her in the early morning breeze. She played Barbara's message again and released a shaky breath, relieved that she hadn't imagined it.

Jack was alive.

She let the truth settle over her, even warmer than the sun. A curious bird called to her from a solitary tree across the road, a simple reminder that her world hadn't ended.

A whisper of resolve floated through her mind. Did she have the power to change her destiny? Was it possible? She scooped up her phone and stood slowly, acclimating to the strange notions taking root. Jack was in

CONVERGENCE

the hospital fighting for his life. Maybe it was time that she fought for hers, too.

She glanced down at her phone, ignoring the low battery warning, and dialed Cam's number. After three rings, his groggy voice came on the line.

"Tori?" The bed creaked and Tori envisioned him searching the room for her.

"Yeah. It's me. Listen. My battery's going to die, but I just got a message from Barbara. Jack had a second surgery overnight. He's out now, and they think he's going to be okay, but will you check on him again before you leave? And can you get a ride home with Dwayne?"

"Where are you?"

"I took the car." She paused. "I had to go."

"Are you at home?"

"Not yet." She pulled the phone from her head as it buzzed another warning, then spoke again. "But I will be. Please let Barbara know I got her message."

"Are you okay? You don't sound like it."

She bit her lip. The concern in his voice almost undid her. "I hope so. I've got to go, but I'll call you later when I get things figured out."

Her phone died before she heard his reply. She shoved it in her pocket and listened once again to the bird's peaceful song as images of Jack filled her mind. He believed she was worth fighting for. *They* were worth fighting for. On shaking legs, Tori crossed the field to the car she'd left barely on the road. She wasn't convinced she could fix her broken places, but she had to try.

By the time she pulled into her driveway, every part of her body ached. She unlocked the front door, drawing a sharp breath as memories of Jack assailed her. Her gaze landed on the sofa and without a thought, she stretched out on it, burrowing into the pillow that carried his scent. She could almost pretend that he was there with her still.

Except it was different, so quiet. Too quiet.

She thought she might sleep, but her head still pounded and her mind was too keyed up. So she decided to implement phase one of her plan, starting with the freezer. The cold bottle in her hand felt so familiar, and the insidious voice of reason in her head told her that one drink wouldn't hurt.

She twisted off the cap and sniffed the bottle, closing her eyes against her body's learned response. Jack would be so upset if she took a drink

207

right now. He'd tell her that it wasn't the answer, that it was the problem. His features crossed her mind, disappointment lurking deep in his brown eyes.

But it had never stopped her before. And it didn't stop her now. She put the bottle to her lips and allowed the liquid to slide down her throat. Just a small sip. Didn't mean a thing. And if she was going to get help, this would be her last taste. Before she had even another second to contemplate her decision, she dumped the remaining contents of the bottle down the sink.

She followed the same routine for the other bottles she'd stashed around the house. One last drink, then dumped the rest. After she finished, she sat down with her computer at the kitchen table and with renewed concentration, and a slight buzz, she studied the websites of several in-house treatment facilities.

The website photo galleries of her favorite so far, Cherokee Ridge, made the rooms and surrounding grounds look like an upscale resort, and the treatment plan included everything from meals to exercise, along with individual and group therapy.

But her determination waned in the face of what she'd have to do there. Sharing her past with a room full of strangers? And she'd have to have a roommate? She hadn't had a roommate since her freshman year at OU.

A knock sounded at her door, causing her heartbeat to race. She shook her head as she marched to the living room. "There's nothing to be afraid of anymore," she mumbled.

Cam stood on the porch, his face a mask of worry. "You didn't answer your phone this afternoon."

Tori opened the screen door. "I'm sorry. I've been a little out of it. Come in." He followed her to the kitchen where he joined her at the table. "Did you see Jack today?"

"Yes. He's still sleeping, but his color was better. Barbara said they would probably keep him sedated for another day or two to give him a head start on healing. I told Barbara that Alan had called you back to Oklahoma. She seemed to accept my explanation."

"Thank you."

"Now, explain it to me."

She paused only a moment before sliding the laptop around to show him the Cherokee Ridge website, and his eyes darted from the screen to her face. "This was kind of the plan I was thinking about."

"Was?"

Tori sighed. "Am. I just…"

Cam leaned in. "What?"

"I don't know. I was driving home with conviction in spades thinking I could do this for Jack," she whispered, staring in disgust at the now empty glass on the table. Because she'd justified one more glass. "He was so strong, and I thought I could be strong, too, you know? This morning I wanted it so badly. But now…"

"Jack can't be your motivation." His intense eyes bore into her. "I've been there, Tori. You know I have. You found me and believed in me. You made me want to believe I could be better, that I could matter. But ultimately, I'm still the one who had to own it. It's the same with you. Jack can make you want to be better, but it still all comes down to you wanting it for yourself."

Her vision swam as fear swarmed her. The abyss last night was nothing compared to what she faced now. Alcohol had been her constant companion for years. Comforter. Encourager. Devourer. Controller.

What if she couldn't beat it?

Cam took her cold hand into his warm one, pulling her back. "Let's give them a call, okay?"

Tori stared at him, the fear growing, choking her. But somehow she managed to nod. In a fog, she listened to Cam's side of the conversation with the facility. Surreal. Was this really happening?

Cam disconnected the call. "They're ready for you now."

"What?" Tori jumped from her chair. Now? She'd expected next week, or maybe tomorrow, but now? The urge to run from the room filled her, but Cam's calm, steady gaze halted her.

"Do you think I can really do this?"

"You're one of the toughest people I know. I believe you can if you choose to," he said quietly. "I'll help you pack if you're ready."

Was she?

Memories of last night crowded her mind. She could've wrecked the car. She could've stayed on the road and hurt or killed someone else. And she was surely killing herself.

Despite the cumbersome cast, she linked her fingers to keep them from shaking as she pursed her lips and nodded. "Okay."

A list of worries bombarded her as Cam drove west toward Cherokee Ridge. She chewed her thumbnail as she stared out the window.

"What about the rest of the season?"

"No sane person is going to expect you to finish the season. I'll talk to Alan. Justin can run lead. He's almost as good as you, and you know he'll want to help."

Tori was silent. So many times during the season, Justin had given her his opinions and insights. And Cam was right. Justin was good.

More miles passed until Tori broke the silence again.

"Mathis Productions could be a huge opportunity for you. You need to interview with Stuart."

Cam smiled. "We'll see. Maybe after the season."

Thirty minutes later, they turned off onto an asphalt driveway. If she hadn't looked to her right, she might've missed the small, unobtrusive sign identifying their destination. The panic that she'd worked to contain bubbled to the surface again.

"Online, it said they'd take my phone. Will you be able to communicate with me? Let me know how Jack is recovering? I just need to know that he's healed."

"We'll make sure of it." He pulled into a visitor parking space and cut the engine. He turned to her. "You okay?"

She pondered the simple question before answering. "I don't know if I'll ever be okay, Cam," she whispered, hoping he could see the honesty in her eyes. He'd been there for her, had her back, was the closest thing to a brother she'd ever known. "But I want to thank you –"

He held a hand up, silencing her. "Hey. None of that. Let's stay focused on the goal of getting you healthy."

She shook her head. "Jack's not the only one who saved my life. You did too, by turning in the emails."

"Even though you were ready to kick my ass that day."

She sniffled around the answering smile that broke across her lips. "True."

Cam's eyes turned from humorous to solemn. "There's nothing wrong with letting people love you. And letting yourself love them back. I'm going to consider myself in the club, but I'm not the only one who wants in."

Tori shifted in her seat, staring ahead at the finely sculpted bush in front of the car. "Jack deserves a good woman who can love him the way he can love her."

Cam's calloused hand rubbed her neck. "Jack's a big boy. And I've seen the way he looks at you. You think I can tell him not to love you?"

"You have to convince him he doesn't." Her voice rose. "He doesn't know who I am without alcohol. *I* don't know who I am without alcohol." *Maybe nothing but dust.* "You have to tell him not to wait for me, Cam. Promise me." He opened his mouth to voice the objection on his face, but she cut him off. "And please don't tell him what I'm doing. I can't handle the pressure of him holding onto hope when I don't know if there is any."

Cam sat quietly for so long, Tori thought he might refuse. Finally, he sighed. "Okay. I'll do my best."

Tori pulled her phone from her purse and typed the text she planned to send to Jack. The last communication she might ever have with him. Her thumb fumbled over the pad until she finally had the message she wanted. She re-read the words on the screen.

Thank you for everything. I still think you're crazy to do what you do, but I'm glad you did. Take care and get well soon. You deserve nothing but the best.

Simple. Grateful. Final.

She stifled the stab of regret that pierced her heart. Jack was far better off with his freedom than hoping for a future with a woman who only knew how to cause him pain.

Tori took a deep breath and hit the send button.

Chapter 23

A steady, rhythmic *beep-beep* infiltrated Jack's groggy head. As he shifted further into consciousness, his heavy eyelids opened for less than a second before bright sunlight forced them closed. He swallowed past the soreness in his throat as he tried to think.

"Jack? Honey?"

His mom's voice. *Why was his mom here?*

With concerted effort, Jack squinted toward the sound of her voice. "Mom?" he croaked.

"Oh, thank God. You're back."

As her cool palm brushed his cheek, he tried to make sense of the tears that filled her eyes.

"They said they'd dialed back the sedative and you'd wake up on your own, but we were so worried. It's been three days."

Three days? Three days since what?

More of his surroundings began to materialize. The needle taped to the back of his hand, the soft pillow under his head.

"Glad to have you back, son." His dad stood next to his mom, a broad smile diminishing the dark circles under his eyes. "About time you joined us. Are you hurting anywhere? Need anything?"

Jack tried to move, but his languid muscles wouldn't obey. "Water?"

After his mom raised the straw to his lips and he swallowed the cool liquid, his head fell back, the effort sapping his energy. He frowned as snippets of memory floated in the periphery of his mind. A storm. His gun. Falling…falling.

He'd been shot.

He scanned the pile of white blankets covering him. "What's the damage?" he whispered.

"You took a bullet to the left side of your abdomen. It was touch and go for a little bit." His dad's calm words were at odds with the sheen in his eyes.

As the room came into focus, Jack looked at the assortment of balloons and flowers that adorned the long shelf in front of the window. But, something wasn't right. Drifting, he closed his eyes and relaxed against the pillows, freeing his mind to allow the fractured memories to coalesce.

His eyes snapped open as reality crystallized and crashed over him.

"Where's Tori?" He struggled to look around his parents, anxious to see if she stood behind them.

Their eyes met, and the non-verbal exchange wasn't lost on him. Ice filled Jack's veins as fear sucked away his breath. He was almost certain his shot had been true, but what if he'd only wounded Johnson…what if the son of a bitch had gotten to Tori after all?

"Is she okay? Mom? Dad? Tell me." He gasped as he tried to sit up, ignoring the pain in his side as panic raced through him. God, he was so weak.

"Settle down." His father's hand on his shoulder stilled his futile effort. "She's fine, Jack."

A nod from his mother reinforced the information. "She had to get her arm re-stitched and she broke her wrist, but other than that, she's fine."

"Is she still in the hospital?"

Another glance between them. "No, honey. You've been out for several days. The doctors felt it best to keep you sedated to give your injury a good start at healing. She left the morning after your surgeries. Cam told us she was needed back in Oklahoma."

The incredible relief that washed over him was fleeting as he processed his mother's words. Tori had left. Hadn't even waited until he woke up.

He had to talk to her, had to see her. "I need to –"

"Rest," his mother finished, with a hard stare. "You need to heal. Everything else comes after that."

Jack tried to attribute the pain stabbing his chest to the injury that lay beneath the layers of white blankets. "Did you talk to her?" he whispered.

"Briefly, yes."

Jack closed his heavy eyelids, the lethargy in his body overcoming his need to move. "What did she say?"

His mom's words floated over him. "...saved her life...you're a wonderful person..."

He drifted half-asleep, his meandering thoughts circling around Tori. He'd call her. Straighten everything out. In a few minutes.

Tori stood outside the door to Dr. Leanne Carpenter's office and pulled tight the black cardigan that had become her constant companion. Two things she'd learned after five days of detox: She went from burning up to freezing in no time at all. And she never, ever, wanted to experience anything like that hell again.

She'd been moved to the main residence and met her roommate, Lyn. The stylish woman told Tori she'd come to Cherokee Ridge because she'd filled her empty nest with wine bottles and had spent so many years being a mom, she'd forgotten who she was. Tori liked Lyn's straight-shooter attitude and realized maybe the roommate thing might work out after all.

But it was time to begin her first individual therapy session. She took a deep breath in through her nose and blew it out pursed lips. The nurses and aides in the detox unit insisted that her time with them would be the hardest she'd have to get through, but at this moment Tori wasn't convinced.

She tapped on the open door before her courage deserted her. "Dr. Carpenter?"

A tall, African-American woman walked out from behind her desk, palm extended. "Good morning, Tori. Come in. Please, call me Leanne."

The room was an array of bold colors and Tori was instantly drawn to the abstract on the wall. "Is that a Delauney?"

Leanne smiled and nodded. "A print, but yes. I love his work. Do you paint?"

"A little. Not as much as I used to."

"Would you like to paint here?" Tori swiveled her head back to the doctor. "You look surprised. A lot of our guests find wonderful creative outlets here. Not only painting, but ceramics, loom work, you name it."

Tori glanced at the painting once more and nodded. "I think I would."

"Excellent. I'll show you the spot where I've been told has the best light is in the whole facility. But once we get you some supplies, you're free to paint anywhere you like."

A tiny streak of ambivalence shot through Tori as she remembered how many times painting was accompanied by straight shots of bourbon. Leanne directed her to a seating area with two overstuffed chairs and a low table between them.

Tori raised her hand. "On second thought, maybe I should hold off on the painting."

Leanne nodded. "Okay. What changed your mind?"

"I don't know. I should probably make a clean break from the past. And painting is part of my past."

Leanne relaxed back into her chair. "I see. Everything feels a bit different here, doesn't it? A bit foreign?"

"Yes."

"That's not uncommon. My best advice is to give yourself time to just be. And if you decide tomorrow or two weeks from now that you want to paint, then you paint. Sound good?"

"Yes." She was starting to feel like a parrot.

Silence filled the room before Leanne spoke again. "How are you feeling today? Physically?"

Tori followed Leanne's lead and settled into the chair's cushion. Her first thought was to default to the standard answer. But she wasn't here for idle chatter, and Leanne didn't look like the kind of woman who was willing to listen to it.

"Yesterday was the first day I haven't felt like throwing up, pulling my hair out, or punching someone in the face. So, I guess I'd say better."

Leanne's smile was warm and genuine. "I'd say so." She paused. "I spoke with the detox group and they only had positive things to say about your time with them."

Tori waited in the silence, unsure where to take the conversation. But Leanne continued in the same, soothing tone.

"I spent the morning reviewing your intake file, and there was something that stuck out to me. I'd like to discuss your relationship with your parents. Is that okay?"

Tori straightened in her seat while consciously relaxing her shoulders. Might as well start from the beginning. "Sure."

"People might think that admissions process is too lengthy, but it's extremely helpful in allowing us to get a broader picture rather than a current snapshot."

Tori recalled the hours of questions and couldn't disagree. "Yeah, that was a long night."

"You mentioned that your father always had a stocked liquor cabinet in the basement, that you frequently hid down there to drink."

"Yes." The parrot was back.

"Do you ever remember seeing your dad drink?"

Tori paused, allowing memories to filter through her mind. Dad at the club with a highball. Dad at the barbeque with a beer. Dad in the basement, staring into nothing, a glass in his hand. She raised wide eyes to Leanne.

"Always."

"I gathered as much." Leanne said. "Was he ever violent toward you?"

Tori swallowed but didn't answer. Could she really tell a virtual stranger the truth? The truth that she'd never said aloud?

"I know this is heavy for our first time together, but you're safe here, and I promise that acknowledging the pain in your past and accepting that it can't hurt you anymore, is critical to your success."

The familiar urge to run whispered through her. They told her when she checked in that the doors would never be locked, that she could leave whenever she wanted to. She took one deep breath. Then another.

She would not let him stop her now.

"Yes." Tori paused, tasting the bitterness. "But he was a doctor so he made sure the bruises were never visible." She took the tissue Leanne offered and wiped the tears from her cheeks. She didn't want to cry. She didn't want to feel anything about him.

"What about your sister and mother?"

Tori shook her head. "They were appeasers. They walked on eggshells around him all the time. I always thought my mother was too worried about what the town gossips would say to ever confront him. She was constantly on me to behave, but maybe she was afraid. He was a big man."

Leanne switched topics, but throughout the hour circled back around to Tori's family and home life. And every time, Tori checked her desire to hold back and answered the questions as honestly as she could.

When their time together was almost up, Leanne offered another tissue and allowed the silence to lengthen. "I'm going to leave you with a few thoughts to ponder. One, alcoholism is a disease. As surely as heart disease is. And even though your father was a physician, they're often the last people to acknowledge their own illnesses.

"And two, your father can't hurt you anymore. But he'll still have power over you as long as you hold on to the anger and the hatred. I'm going to encourage you, through your recovery, to do your best to let that go."

"Okay." Tori nodded, but her insides curdled. It would be a cold day in hell before she forgave her father.

"One more thing." Leanne produced a leather bound journal. "Not to sound trite, but today is a very important day. The first day of your recovery phase. I'd like you to use this to begin journaling. Writing out your thoughts and feelings is a very valuable tool toward recovery."

Tori didn't have any more desire to write in a journal than she did to forgive her dad, but she took the book from Leanne. "Is this required?"

Leanne stood and ushered her to the door. "Nothing is required. If you feel like writing in it, write in it. If you don't, you don't have to."

Tori marched down the hall, shaking off her sweater as she went. It had to be eighty degrees in this part of the building. As she entered her suite, Lyn looked up from the magazine on her lap and waved. "Hey. How'd it go?"

Dabbing at the sweat on her forehead, Tori stifled her frustration. It shouldn't be directed at Lyn anyway. "It was fine. And awful."

Lyn sipped from her iced tea. "Sounds about right."

"And she wants me to figure out how to journal." Tori dropped the book on the glass top table before plopping in the chair adjacent to Lyn.

"I had a hard time with that at first. It felt like empty words on a page. So after about a week of trying, I scrapped it and decided to simply write a letter to my husband, instead of calling it a journal. It worked so much better for me."

Tori's energy was gone. Another byproduct of detox. With a yawn she couldn't hide, she stood and grabbed the journal. "I'll think about it. Right now, I need to crash."

Of course, naps were different now, too. Just like everything else. Tori rolled over, thinking she'd slept for a couple of hours, but it had been less than thirty minutes. Still, her mind was alert and jumping as she stretched out on the soft down comforter.

Her hand skimmed the covers and bumped into the journal. Maybe she could write to Jack. Not that he'd ever see it, but somehow it made the most sense to write to him. Grabbing a pencil, she settled into one of the chairs that looked out over a beautiful blooming flower garden and rolling hill beyond, and tucked her legs underneath her. After opening the cover of the journal, she started at the empty lined page.

Dear Jack,

Her hand stilled. Leanne said to write thoughts and feelings, but the ones bubbling to the surface all stemmed from her earlier session, not the beautiful scenery, or the hope she was supposed to feel. But, she couldn't write those. Could she?

Desolation washed over her. If she couldn't be honest, there was no point to any of this. And he'd never see it, so why not write what she wanted? After a moment's hesitation, the pencil slid back to the second line on the paper, the scratch of the graphite as raw as her exposed nerves.

Here's what I SHOULD say to you: I have you to thank for the journey I've begun. Not only did you save my life, literally, you challenged me like no one I've ever known.

But here's the real feel of the moment. Pain sucks. Getting scabs ripped off sucks. Facing the past sucks. I detoxed for five days and every single hour, I wanted to die.

Then for kicks, I got to talk about my abusive, asshole father who apparently still controls me because I won't magically forgive him for YEARS of hurting me. Oh, and he was an alcoholic, too. Surprise, surprise.

So bottom line, I'm here. I hope you're healing, because I need to know that one of us is going to end up okay through all of this.

Chapter 24

Searing pain burned his side, jolting Jack from sleep. The hospital room was pitched in darkness except for a small sliver of light from the bathroom that illuminated his sleeping parents.

He must've made a noise because his mother was next to him in a flash. "What is it, honey?"

"My side," he said through clenched teeth.

She fumbled near his pillow, then pushed a small black button on the device in her hand. "Morphine. Do you remember the nurse showing you this? She told you to keep ahead of the pain by pushing it when you need it, but you must've been sleeping hard."

Jack's short nod was his only movement as he waited for relief. By infinitely small degrees, the pain lessened from mind numbing to nearly bearable. When he could take a full breath, he looked at his mom. "What day is it?"

His mom flicked her wrist, checking her watch. "Technically, it's Friday morning."

"You've been…in those chairs for almost a week." His couldn't seem to make it through a sentence without having to rest. "Won't keep me much longer."

Barbara grunted. "This is what parents do. We've always wanted to be there for you, even when you didn't want us to be. And, I might remind you that, until you got that wonderful little infusion, you were in severe pain. The doctors warned us that recovery would be slow on wounds like yours. You're going to have to be patient."

———————————

Jack was anything but patient as the days wore on, but he made it a point to hit the button fewer times every day. The physical therapists stretched and tortured him regularly, and they'd gotten him up and walking, which his doctor promised was one of the major hurdles to jump through before being released.

He picked at the turkey and mashed potatoes on the plate in front of him. He'd been poked and prodded in ways he'd never imagined. He'd spoken with the case agents and with his team in Virginia, who'd worked with the local guys to wrap up the final details. He'd even spoken with Cam, who'd called into his dad's phone a few times for updates on his recovery. But every time Jack tried to bring up Tori, Cam offered single sentence replies about her readjusting to her life, then conveniently had to end the call.

His only communication from Tori was a text he'd received almost a week ago. He pulled his phone out of his pocket and reread it for probably the twentieth time.

Thank you for everything. I still think you're crazy to do what you do, but I'm glad you did. Take care and get well soon.

Messages didn't get much more generic than that. So, either she really didn't give a shit about him or she wanted him to think she didn't. Neither one of those notions sat well.

After lunch, Jack stared out the window counting cars as they entered and left the parking lot below. He'd sent two responses to Tori's text and left her a couple of voice messages, but she hadn't replied to any of them.

How was she coping with everything that had happened? Was she processing it at all? Or was she lost in the bottom of a bottle?

The television he left playing drew his attention as a commercial aired for the upcoming season of Vortex. It was the third one he'd seen because, as he'd hoped, the weather channel promoted them. But the two previous ones had just been cut scenes, not live action. Jack sat down on the edge of his bed as he recognized his footage. And there was Tori, barking out instructions in the face of the storm.

She was so compelling. He couldn't look away – just like the first time he'd ever seen her videos in his office in Virginia. After the commercial ended, he grabbed his laptop and pulled up the Vortex website again, revisiting several of her old chases.

His perspective on the videos was vastly different from when he'd watched months ago. He'd been enthralled before, but now he noticed more than the storms. He considered how he'd framed the shots, and how perfectly she'd edited the scenes.

Jack settled back onto his pillows. With nothing but time on his hands, he finished the videos on her site then searched YouTube for more of her chases. The first video wasn't a chase, though. It was from a Dallas news station reporting on the case.

He clicked on the file and listened as the news anchor read the teleprompter, her cheery and modulated tone so at odds with the words she was speaking. As he was about to close the screen, the story cut away to Tori, flanked by Cam and Dwayne as they exited the hospital. His stomach clenched. Between the bandaged arm, partially hidden in a sling, and the dark circles under her eyes, she looked so lost, so empty.

"Ms. Whitlock. A harrowing day for you. What can you tell us about your experience?"

Tori's cold, emotionless eyes stared straight into the camera, straight at him. Her words were even colder than her eyes. "It happened. And it's over. I'd like to thank the FBI for their hard work. I have nothing more to add. Thank you."

Jack took a deep breath then replayed it again. And again. She was obviously still in shock. And more than ever, he sensed that she was handling this the same way she'd dealt with the death of her family. Bury it, and drink to forget it. Maybe Cam was shielding him from that truth.

He watched the video one more time. Was she talking to him? About him? His jaw clenched as he wiped a hand across his face. He recognized the look. It was the same look she'd leveled at him when he'd gotten too close.

Difference was, she couldn't avoid him now. She may end up hating him for it, but as soon as he physically could, he'd force her to confront the situation head-on. That would be his only shot. Because the further she distanced herself from him, the more convinced she would become that there had been nothing between them at all.

And if that wasn't motivation to get the hell out of the hospital, he didn't know what was.

On Saturday afternoon, almost two weeks after he'd been admitted to Denton Regional Medical Center, Jack breathed a sigh of relief as his father wheeled him down the ramp and into the first class section of the waiting Boeing 737 that would take him to his parents' home in New York.

Garrett, Rachel, and Lily, along with Hope and Ben's whole family, waited at the gate. Jack swallowed hard past the lump in his throat at the identical looks of relief that flooded their faces as his dad pushed his wheelchair down the gangway and into the terminal.

Lily and his nephews were the first to reach him. As he braced for impact, Garrett and Ben corralled them.

"No climbing on Uncle Jack today," Ben scolded. He reached down and hugged Jack. "Jesus, don't ever scare us like that again."

Garrett kissed Jack's mom on the cheek, then took over the job of getting Jack through the terminal. "You're riding with me and the girls. Ben's got your parents and Hope. None of them want to listen to me rip you a new one for taking years off of our lives."

His words were laced with humor, but Jack heard the worry underneath. "It's all good. Probably deserve it."

By the time they made it Jack's parents' house to enjoy the feast that Holly, Hope, and Rachel had prepared, the effect of the medicine has worn off, and Jack was exhausted.

"You guys went to too much trouble."

"Nonsense," his mom said. She touched his cheek, her eyes misting. "It's so good to have you home."

He gutted out the party for close to an hour before the pain in his side became too intense. He stood, ignoring the momentary dizziness, and found his mom in the kitchen. "Hey. Hate to be a killjoy, but I need to lie down for a little bit. Where do you want me?"

Her brow furrowed. "You've lost your color. The doctor said as few stairs as possible for the next few weeks, so the office is your makeshift bedroom. Of course, once stairs aren't as big an issue, your old bedroom is available upstairs."

Jack longed for the privacy of his old room, but more than that, he needed a pain pill and some sleep.

He followed his mom into the office and found not only a large bed in the corner with a mountain of pillows, but a wardrobe with his clothes in it. "How'd you manage that?" he asked.

"Garrett and Rachel offered to drive up and stop in Virginia to pick up some of your things."

Jack smiled. "Thanks, Mom. Don't know what I'd do without you."

"Good to hear you talk some sense. I know if you had a choice, you'd be at home alone."

Jack sat down on the bed, testing the mattress, as his mom's soft words rang in his ears. He'd spent years running from them, and from his past. He'd shut them out for too long. Tori had helped him understand how fortunate he was to have their love and support.

Stretching out on the bed as best he could without causing his side to cramp and pull, he accepted the pain pill and water Hope brought for him.

She hugged his neck. "I'm so glad you're home."

Despite his desire to see Tori again, Jack couldn't think of a better place to be. "Me too, Sis." A yawn escaped and his eyes began to droop. "Tomorrow I want you to tell me more about your plans, okay?"

Her eyes lit up. "Okay. Get some rest."

Jack woke to the dusky summer sunset casting long shadows on the dark paneled walls. It took a minute to get his bearings, but the stinging pain in his side said he'd stayed in one position too long. Cautiously, he sat up on the side of the bed and waited for the slight dizziness to subside.

His stomach rumbled, reminding him that his most recent meal had been breakfast at the hospital. Had he really been discharged just this morning? Looking to his left, his lips twitched as he spied an apple and a package of nuts next to a bottle of water. The note next to it, written in his mom's flourishing script, said to join them on the patio if he felt up to it.

Jack stood slowly then took a long drink of water as he surveyed the room where he'd played countless games of chess with his dad and brother. Even the faint scent of cigars and furniture polish was familiar.

The pain in his side notwithstanding, he could almost believe the last few months had been a dream. Except for one giant exception.

Chapter 25

Dear Jack,

I talked to Cam today and he told me you went home to New York. Not going to lie – I cried when he told me. And you know me. I'm not a crier.

As you can probably tell from my letters, I feel a little stronger every day. And I might be starting to figure things out, but I'm a long way from success.

I've been working hard at looking at my addiction honestly, and it's crazy how insidious it is. I still find myself mentally searching for a bottle every once in a while. They promise that will go away over time.

They also say that one of my goals is to work on acknowledging my regrets and mistakes, then releasing them. I'm trying. But I'm afraid that pushing you away might be my biggest one yet. Not sure how to let that one go. Writing to you every day probably isn't helping, but Leanne thinks it's good for me. All I know is that I feel close to you through these letters. And I want to feel close to you. For better or worse.

Tori closed the journal and set it on her bedside table, her thoughts on Jack. What would the next weeks and month look like for him? A small smile played at her lips as she sifted through memories of their time together. Probably lots and lots of Xbox. Her smile broke into a grin. He might actually get good enough to challenge her.

Jack had stretched himself today. He'd walked two miles along the path behind the house, twice the distance he'd gone yesterday. The image of Tori's hauntingly empty eyes during that interview, the image he slept with at night, drove every step. The faster he got cleared by the doctors, the sooner he could get to her.

But where was she?

His frustration with Tori's unwillingness to communicate was compounded by his dad's inability to get information out of Cam. Of course, his interest had more to do with interviewing Cam for a position with the company than data gathering for his son, but Cam's vague responses were now sounding alarms in Jack's head.

Was there something wrong that no one wanted to tell him? His mind had played out dozens of different scenarios, none of them good.

And it wasn't as if he hadn't tried to communicate with Cam directly. He'd called multiple times since he'd arrived at his parents' house, only to get Cam's voicemail. The only time Cam had returned the call, it was the dead of night, and his message said that Tori was doing well, back in Oklahoma and working hard.

But he was done with the half-answers and avoidance. After grabbing a bottle of water from the fridge, Jack returned to the office and sat down at his dad's desk. He punched in Tori's number first.

Like he expected, the call went to voicemail. He let the entire message play, just to hear her voice, then ended the call without leaving a message. The invisible band around his chest tightened a fraction more.

Next, Jack dialed Cam's number. Also, voicemail. But Jack didn't care. He'd blow up Cam's phone for as long as it took until he finally answered.

It only took eleven calls before Cam's artificially cheerful voice came on the line.

"Hey, Jack! How you feeling? Your dad said you got released last week. Man, that's awesome."

Jack had missed talking to Cam, but he wasn't interested in pleasantries. "Thanks. Glad to be out of the hospital. I know you're busy with the season, but the message you left a couple of days ago said Tori was back working in Oklahoma. I had my guys there check, and she hasn't been part of the crew since Sanger. And she won't return my calls or texts."

That old familiar circling of the wagons sang through the phone line without Cam saying a word. Cam knew exactly where Tori was. Jack would bet on it.

"Oh. Yeah, um…she's on hiatus. Justin's leading the show and Dwayne, Reese and I are making do. It's going pretty well. We caught a monster storm in Southern Colorado. You might've seen it on the news –"

"Cam." The sigh in Jack's ear confirmed that Cam didn't miss the low warning in his tone. "Do you know where Tori is?"

Silence filled the line, and Jack wished he could read Cam's face.

"This freaking sucks," Cam finally groaned. "I've done everything I could to avoid talking to you about her because I knew when I did, I'd have to honor her wishes."

Jack's fingers stilled on the desk. "What wishes?"

"She said to make sure you knew that she wants you to move on with your life. To not wait on her."

The sucker punch to his gut was swift and vicious. Jack took two slow, deep breaths, trying for a normal tone. "Were those her words?"

"Pretty much, yeah."

The misery in Cam's voice only added to the resentment building in Jack's chest. Move on, she said. Just like that. Despite everything, he never believed she'd simply walk away, without so much as a final conversation. Or maybe she considered the one bullshit text good enough. Then again, running was her default.

Cam was still talking, and Jack pulled himself out of his morose thoughts to catch up.

"Listen. I'm supposed to interview with your dad as soon as we have enough chase footage to finish the season. But if this is going to complicate that, I can –"

Jack gritted his teeth. He wanted to make the false threat to back Cam into a corner, but screw it. If he had to coerce and threaten just to find out where she was, what was the point?

He reined in the tumult coursing through him. "Of course not. Nothing has changed since I suggested Dad talk to you. Mathis Productions would be lucky to get you."

Cam was silent for a moment. "God, I'm sorry, Jack. I wish like hell it didn't have to be this way."

What could he say to that? "Not yours to own, man. Call me when you're in town and maybe we can grab dinner."

Jack left the phone on the desk and walked to the tall windows facing the backyard. His hands squeezed fingerprints into the wooden frame as he stared out at nothing. Why had he thought it would end up any other way?

He'd avoided making this mistake for seven years. Seven years of insulation, seven years of isolation. Why had he opened his heart at all? And why hadn't she opened hers even a little?

Stalking to the liquor cabinet, Jack poured a finger of scotch. He downed it with a grimace, then slammed the glass onto the wooden bar, the taste bitter in his mouth. He stared at the glass for a long moment, hating it for the power it had wielded over him for the years he'd turned to it instead of his family. Hating it more for the power it had over Tori, her first and best love.

He resisted the almost overwhelming urge to chuck the glass across the room, and it was a good thing because Hope chose that moment to knock on the door and step into room.

"Good morning." She glanced around the room with a frown. "Is everything okay?"

Hope was more intuitive than almost anyone he knew, so Jack painted on a smile he hoped was good enough. "Sure. How's my favorite sister?"

"I'm your only sister." She laughed as she entered the room, carting an armful of papers. "Do you want to see my new house?"

The light shining in her eyes was the distraction Jack needed, as he shoved his thoughts about Tori into a box he could unpack later. "You bet. Show me what you've got."

He gave Hope his full attention, directing her to the desk where she precisely laid out artist renderings, floor plans, and fact sheets about the company and the building. Her knowledge and understanding of some of the more obscure concepts blew him away.

After her presentation, he beamed at her with pride. "You've really done your homework, haven't you?"

She nodded. "But your friend helped, too. She helped a lot."

Jack hadn't expected Hope to remember Tori's contributions, and remembering them himself dug at him. He wasn't interested in being charitable toward her at the moment. And he wasn't about to have a conversation about her with his sister.

"So, when's the big move in party?"

"I'll have to ask Mom. She knows more about that stuff." Hope paused, watching him over her pile of papers. "Are you hurting? Your face looks like you're sad."

Jack erased his frown with a smile. "I'm fine. Took a long walk this morning. Probably overdid it a little bit."

Jack pored over the two computer monitors, intent on finding anomalies in the data. There was always a paperwork backlog, so it hadn't taken much effort to talk his director into funneling some his way, even though he wasn't technically supposed to be working.

He never wanted to be a desk jockey, but it was vastly better than the alternative. The less time he had to focus on what a fool he'd been, the better. And since he still had a few months before he could be tested and cleared for active duty, he'd better learn to love it.

"Burning the midnight oil, son?"

Jack looked up in surprise, blinking at his dad in an attempt to refocus his eyes. "What time is it?"

"Little after two. You know they don't pay you overtime, right?" He chuckled and selected a cigar from the teakwood box on the desk.

Jack leaned back in the chair and stretched his kinked back. "Better open the window. Or has mom relaxed her rules on smoking in the house?"

By way of reply, Jack's dad opened two of the three windows, allowing in the cool nighttime breeze. "As long as the door is closed and the windows are open, I stay out of the dog house."

Jack thought about the tenure of his parents' marriage and the highs and lows he knew of, certain there were plenty more he didn't know about. He liked the comfort level, the inside jokes that only they understood. He even liked that they could still gross out their grown kids by talking about sex.

He hated that he envied them.

His dad settled into one of the chairs across from Jack and propped his feet on the desk, and Jack glanced around the office that he'd made his temporary home.

"Looks like I've taken over in here. I need to give you your office back."

"I'm not in any hurry."

"Well, at least trade me seats."

"I'm good right here. And I'm enjoying the company, so don't worry about it." He paused. "You giving much thought to what happens after recovery?"

Jack sighed. He wasn't up for the fight. Not now. And he wasn't even sure of the answer anymore. He'd replayed the Sanger hotel scenario in his head a hundred times and knew that if any one of a multitude of variables had changed, he'd be dead and so would Tori.

He'd lost a lot of sleep thinking about how close he'd come to blowing it completely. He should've never left Tori alone in the hotel room. He'd vowed to protect her, and had almost gotten her killed.

Restless, he stood and stretched his back and side. "I talked to my director last week. Hiatus is a minimum three months, but I don't know. It's still a ways out. I'm not ready to consider options yet."

His dad was quiet for a few minutes. "I don't think you should."

Jack stopped mid-twist, certain he'd misunderstood. "Should what?"

"Consider your options. I think you're doing exactly what you're supposed to be doing."

Jack raised an eyebrow, waiting for the catch. This conversation always turned into an argument. Was he so tired he hadn't heard him correctly?

"Don't get me wrong. I'm proud of our company, and I think we do outstanding work. But you saved lives, and you neutralized a madman. I can't, in good conscience, ask you to give that up to appease a stubborn old man."

At another time, Jack might have rejoiced that his dad had given up the fight, but tonight he chewed on his dad's words, then sighed heavily. "I don't know, Dad. I fucked this one up pretty good. I got in a lucky shot. Otherwise, this thing could've ended a whole lot differently." The doubts he'd harbored for weeks were finally spoken. It felt good to get them out. "I've wondered more times than I can count if I'm really doing what I'm supposed to be doing."

His dad took two puffs on his cigar, the smoke wafting around him. "I think it's natural to look at things in hindsight and let all the what ifs cloud your thinking. But I'll tell you one thing. If I needed someone at my back, I'd sure as hell want it to be you." He stubbed out his cigar and rose. "Get some sleep, son. You need rest to heal."

Jack waited until he heard his dad go upstairs then headed to the kitchen to make coffee. Sleep didn't equal rest. Rest would be a dreamless black place, uninterrupted by visions of what could have been with Tori. Maybe his dad was right. Maybe he needed to let go of all of the what-if scenarios.

As the coffee began to brew, the strong, familiar aroma filled the room. Seemed like a hundred years had passed since he'd first tried it in Tori's tiny kitchen. Would it be a hundred more before he'd stop associating the two? If so, he needed to dump the whole damn box down the sink.

Chapter 26

"Headed out this morning?"

Jack's mom's question stalled him with one hand on the knob of the back door. "To the gym. I'll be back in a couple of hours."

Since coming home, the gym had become a haven of sorts. He couldn't work out like he wanted to, but it was a great place to shut off his head and focus on muscle and breathing until there wasn't room to think about anything else. And it felt good. Getting stronger felt good.

"Perfect. You'll be back in plenty of time to get cleaned up."

Jack turned. "For what?"

"We're going to watch the fireworks over the lake tonight. You'll go with us, won't you?"

There was a thin line between hurting his mom's feelings and telling the truth. "Let me think about it. What time are you heading over?"

"We're all meeting here at seven for dinner, then riding over together."

"Who's we?"

A smile spread across her face. "Well, I was hoping to keep it a surprise, but Garrett, Rachel and Lily will be here late this afternoon. They're flying up for the holiday weekend. Rachel called me last week and asked me if you were up for company, so we put this little plan into action."

Jack had a sinking suspicion that his parents had called in the reserves. "Interesting timing."

His mom picked up a tea towel and wiped the spotless counter. "Isn't it? Your dad and I were just talking about how tired you looked and how you needed a break from all the work you've been doing."

He gave her a pointed stare, but she continued to speak.

"They're planning to join us here for dinner. Your dad's going to put some steaks and veggies on the grill. Then around eight-thirty or nine, we'll head over to the park."

Jack studied her for a second longer, but decided against calling her actions meddling. Wouldn't have done any good anyway. Closing the door with a soft click, he took a deep breath. He needed to start making plans to get out of there.

Jack showered and dressed in cargo shorts, a red T-shirt and flip-flops, and by the time he'd gotten through the process, which was still slower than it should've been, he'd gotten rid of the worst of his mood. It wouldn't kill him to spend a little time with friends. In fact, he hadn't even talked to Garrett since he'd left to break ground on his company's construction project in China.

So, he put on a smile and walked toward the commotion in the entry hall. "I think I hear a Lily-bug out here. Someone call the exterminator."

"Uncle Jack!"

Her shriek of excitement was a balm on his soul in a place he didn't know it hurt. She came running toward him, and he knelt to receive her hug, strategically shifting her away from his side. Jack found his first real smile in weeks as he wrapped her up.

He stood, with Lily still on his good hip and slid an arm around Rachel, dropping a kiss on her cheek. "Hello, gorgeous."

"Glad to see you up and around."

After getting bags unloaded, Jack's mom shooed everyone out to the patio. Garrett clapped Jack on the shoulder and leaned in. "Looking a little ragged, man. You're on medical leave, but Rachel said you've been putting in sixteen-hour days. What gives?"

Jack shrugged. "Just passing time 'til I can get off the desk."

The night was a rush of fun, food, and fireworks. Ben's boys ate everything they could get their hands on, and Hope and Rachel talked apartment decorating. Jack's stomach ached. Could've been from laughter, or all the food he'd consumed. Either way, he couldn't remember the last time he'd had such a normal, carefree evening, before or after Oklahoma.

He hated to admit it, but his mom had been right. He'd needed this.

Sipping on a glass of sangria, his mom leaned against his dad's shoulder. "What a fun night. We'll have to do this again during fall festival." She turned to Rachel. "Think you can travel that soon after the baby comes?"

Rachel started to speak, but after a startled look, Garrett jumped in. "That may be too soon. The baby will only be about two months old by then, right?"

Rachel joined Jack's mom in a laugh. "Garrett's a little nervous. Can you tell?" She patted his arm. "We can play it by ear, honey."

Barbara grinned. "Sounds perfect. And, Jack, if Tori's chase season is over, you should see if she'd like to come, too. She seemed excited about it when we discussed it."

Jack's good humor came to a screeching halt. His mom had mentioned Tori a few times after he'd been released from the hospital, but he'd done his best to close the topic quickly. Now, all eyes were on him.

But it was Garrett's he felt most keenly.

Jack set his glass on the table with a loud thud. "I'm sure she was just trying to be polite, Mom. But you need to let it go. Like I've told you, Tori was part of a case I worked. Nothing more. Nothing less. Certainly not someone you should be planning on bringing to future family gatherings."

Rachel's chair scraped across the flagstones as she stood. "I better go check on Lily. Make sure she's all settled for the night. I'll probably hit the hay myself." She leaned down and kissed Jack's mom on the cheek. "Thanks for everything. Tonight was fun."

Jack's parents stood next. His dad feigned a yawn. "We're right behind you. Been a long day."

Unintentionally, Jack had cleared the entire patio in thirty seconds, leaving him alone with Garrett. Jack wished Garrett would excuse himself, too, but he knew he wouldn't get off that easy.

Long minutes passed before Garrett spoke. "Cicadas are out in full force tonight."

The insects' songs, like the humidity, were so intertwined with Jack's memories of this place, he didn't even realize how loud they were. He stopped to listen. "That they are."

Garrett balanced his metal chair on the back two legs and crossed his fingers behind his head. "Great fireworks, but I'm glad Rachel took off Lily's 'ears' before the big ones started. They were loud enough, I almost wished I could remove mine, too."

Jack nodded. "She's come a long way in a year. Her speech is amazing."

Lily and Rachel had had a huge impact on Garrett's life. He'd been on a collision course with vengeance before they came and shook up his whole world. Looking at him now, Jack almost couldn't remember the calculating, driven man Garrett used to be.

He also couldn't remember him being this slow to get to the topic at hand.

"Anything else?" Petty shot, but Jack was already on edge.

Garrett let the front legs of his chair fall to the ground. "You okay?"

The sincerity in Garrett's tone kept Jack from rolling his eyes, but God, he was sick of being asked that question. There were a lot of reasons Jack needed to get on with his life. But not having to answer that question nonstop had to rank right up there.

Jack had spent time, too much time probably, analyzing everything that had happened with Tori. And with Becky. Maybe putting it out there would take it from his mind and move him toward closing the door to his past once and for all.

Still, Jack hesitated. It would be impossible to explain the end without exposing Tori's most private demons. And her past. But he trusted Garrett with his life. And he could use some perspective.

"She's gone."

Garrett frowned in the light of the citronella candle. "Gone?"

Jack shared the story, and the moon was high in the sky when he was finished.

Garrett's quiet voice filled the void. "She hasn't had it easy, has she?"

"Not by a long shot." The grip on his glass should've shattered it. He hated that telling her story could still make him feel something for her.

"But you haven't either. And neither have I. Or Rachel. Or anyone who's worth a shit."

"I know."

Garrett tossed back the last of his drink. "Well, wherever she is, I hope she's figuring it out."

"Me, too. But I'll never know for sure. And I'm trying like hell to be okay with that." He paused, searching for the words to voice what he'd contemplated during the past weeks. "You know that Becky was my world, and I was hers. We were inseparable. Had our whole lives planned out down to where our retirement beach house would be." He paused. "When she died, I was angry."

Jack met Garrett's solemn gaze. "You, more than anybody, saw that firsthand. I was angry at God. Angry at her for leaving me. Angry at myself because I couldn't do anything to fix it. But this was different. I fell hard for Tori, but she didn't trust me enough to give us a chance. It shouldn't have the gravity it does, but it's been hard to get her out of my head."

"Like watching a train wreck?"

Shaking his head, Jack stood. "It's wasn't like that."

Jack had seen glimpses of who he believed was the real Tori. Not who she let the world see, and not who she would even admit to, but a person with incredible passion and compassion for others. Someone whose fear and worry was always for others, never herself. That was the woman he'd fallen in love with. He figured that the rest was just stuff to sort through, but she obviously hadn't seen it that way.

"There was a lot going on. You've got to give her that."

Garrett's comment dragged Jack back to the conversation. He frowned. "You're defending her now?"

"Not at all. But you weren't crazy. There was something there between you two. Rachel and I both saw it. Your mom obviously did, too. Tori did something in a few months that no other woman did in seven years."

Jack stood and paced the patio as anger bubbled beneath the calm surface. "What are you saying? That I should sit around and stare at my phone, hoping for a call that will never come?"

"God, no. Like she said – you have to move on. But your life isn't over. I just don't want you to shrink back into that place where no one can touch you. You've got to live. That's all."

How many times had Jack replayed those words in his head?

Move on. Move on.

It was a fact. Non-negotiable. Regret knifed through him, but not the white hot pain it had been. The blade had worn, leaving only a dull ache.

———

Tori wiped off the wet metal bench and sat down in the center of the arboretum, gripping her cell phone loosely. This was her favorite place to be after the rain. She loved the smell. Loved to watch the flowers as they opened up to the hoarded drops from the broadleaf trees overhead.

It felt like new beginnings. And she was starting to believe in new beginnings.

She glanced at her phone again. In the two months since she'd used it last, she'd held everything from paint brushes, gardening tools, and cooking utensils, to golf clubs, knitting needles, and even a therapy dog.

She'd talked in depth about repressed memories, worked hard to understand her triggers and how to avoid them, and she and Leanne had started mapping her aftercare plan.

Because of her progress, she was in her final phase of recovery at the center, so the restrictions they'd agreed upon at the outset had been lifted. But still, the phone felt strange in her hand.

Her first thought was to call Jack, probably because he'd become such an integral part of her recovery. She hadn't spoken to him in more than two months, but she talked to him daily. She was on letter fifty-eight in her journal. Some detailed her progress; some revealed parts of her that she'd never shared before coming to Cherokee Ridge. Most asked about him and how he was doing, physically and emotionally. But none of them asked the question that mattered more to her with each passing day.

Would he open his heart to her again?

As she continued to stare at her phone, it began to buzz in her hand. She jumped, dropping it on the ground by the bench. She scrambled and answered Cam's call before it could go to voicemail.

"Cam?"

He paused. "Tori? You have your phone?"

She grinned. "Got it today. I was thinking about how odd it felt. How are you? Did the season end okay? Did you get enough footage?"

Cam laughed. "Good. Yes. And yes. We finished pretty strong. I think Alan's happy with Justin as the lead."

"That's a huge weight off my shoulders, because I'm done chasing." She hadn't meant to blurt that out, but it felt good to say it. Made it even more real.

"Wait. You're serious?"

"Yep. I've learned so many things about myself here, Cam. I could spend hours telling you. Like chasing isn't healthy for me. It's one of the main things that kept me tied to my past." She took a deep breath and released it. "I'm working on leaving my past completely behind me."

"You sound good. And happy."

"I'm feeling good. You probably won't believe this, but I've started cooking. And baking," she laughed. "I actually have sort of a knack for it. The staff recruits me to make cinnamon rolls at least once a week and Bella, the head chef, thinks I should try my hand at culinary school."

"Sweet. Literally. Sounds like we're both heading in new directions."

Tori absorbed the implication of his words. "You got the job," she whispered, excitement singing through her veins. "Cam. Did you?"

"They just called with the offer." He let out a whoop. "I got the job."

Tori could almost see his fist pumping in the air. "That is awesome! I never doubted it. When do you start?"

"I'll tell you on one condition."

She paused. "Okay?"

"That you promise to let me know when you're coming home, because I want to be there waiting."

Tori's eyes filled. She'd sure gotten lucky at that laundromat in Atchison. "Deal. So do you have a place there yet?"

"I interviewed last week, and Mr. Mathis said I should look around the area." He laughed. "Not very subtle, but I took his advice and found an apartment I liked within a few miles of the office."

Cam was wound up like a kid at Christmas, and Tori smiled, trying to keep up with him.

"I'm going to call the leasing company next. They want me to start next week if I can. Next week. I don't have a ton of stuff to move. I told them yes. I can't believe this, Tori." His voice filled with awe. "I'm going to work for Mathis Productions."

"I can't think of anyone who deserves to follow his dream more than you, Cam."

As she continued to listen to him detail the facilities and what his job would entail, she noticed that he skipped over his evening activities. She bit her tongue to keep from asking if he'd seen Jack while he was there. Of course he had, or would. It was Jack's family's company.

And since Cam worked for them now, it was highly likely that, at some point, she would run into Jack again. The thought filled her with equal parts trepidation and joy.

Chapter 27

Jack strode up the sidewalk toward the manicured shrubs and potted flowers surrounding Garrett's front door. The brick two-story was a far cry from his old penthouse suite, but Jack had a feeling it was much more of a home.

He barely raised his fist to knock before the door flew open and Garrett stepped aside to let him in.

"I'm glad you're here." Garrett's hair waved in every direction and his clothes looked like he'd slept in them.

Jack did everything he could to keep a straight face. "How's it going?"

"Shhhh," Garrett whispered. "We just got Sam to sleep. Finally. Rachel is a superstar and has way more patience than I do. I don't think I've slept four hours straight since we got him home last week. It's like he's got a sensor that goes off every time we lay down."

Jack did laugh at that. And it felt good. Most of the flight down from New York had been a mental tug of war. He was absurdly happy for his best friend and his family. But he wouldn't deny that he was also jealous as hell.

"The place looks great. Glad I'm finally getting to see it."

"It's been a dream project for Rachel. And, I'm sure when Lily wakes up from her nap, she'll want to show you her playset out back." Garrett led the way through the spacious open floor plan, then on to the kitchen where he pulled a couple of sodas out of the fridge and handed one to Jack. "This may be the only quiet time the whole weekend."

Jack popped the top on his can and raised it in a toast. "To Sam, the newest member of the Staker clan. May he bring you a lifetime of joy."

Garrett joined in, his tired eyes crinkling at the corners. "And night times of sleep." He slammed his drink then laughed at the look on Jack's face. "What? I need the caffeine, man."

"Yeah. Sorry I'll miss the all-nighter. I'm headed to Virginia on the red eye. The only time my director can meet me this week is early tomorrow morning."

"At least try to sound sincere," Garrett groused. "What's up with the director?"

"I initiated. I'm going to ask to transfer to the Albany office."

Garrett's chair scraped across the hard wood floor as he rose and tossed his can into the recycle bin. "Really? You used to say you'd never move back."

Jack joined him. He shoved his hands in his pockets and shrugged. "My mom drives me crazy sometimes, and there's no way I could live next door, but it's been good to be around the family again. Didn't realize how much I'd missed them."

"That's a damn good deal for me," Garrett laughed. "Let me know where you land, and I'll be over whenever we come to town to visit Helen. Lily and Rachel love visits to Grandma's house, but I can only handle so many tea parties and shopping trips."

Jack laughed at the vision Garrett planted as a plaintive infant wail reached his ears. Scooping up his can, he dumped it and followed Garrett to the staircase. "Tell you what. You bring the little guy, and I'll see what I can do about the man cave."

Jack juggled the bag of burritos and rapped on the door to the apartment. It was his second house call in two weeks, but no less important.

"Just a sec," came the muffled reply from inside.

Jack hadn't called ahead, on the off chance that Cam would ignore the calls – like he'd ignored Cam's a few weeks prior.

A thud and a muffled curse followed before Cam appeared at the door. His eyes registered surprise for a few seconds before he smiled. "Jack."

He shouldn't have doubted. Cam couldn't hold a grudge if his life depended on it. "Congratulations, Cam. Dad told me you got the job. He also told me your address, so blame him for me tracking you down."

"Come in. The place is trashed, though. I've been going through orientation this week, and my evenings have been a crash course in furniture assembly." He stepped to the right. "There's a path this way."

Following Cam's big body through the IKEA maze was good for a chuckle. Fortunately, they both made it to the kitchen without breaking furniture or bone. Jack was relieved to see the kitchen table and chairs already put together.

He dropped the bag on the table. "Best burritos around. This will be one to put on speed dial." He unloaded the foil-wrapped monsters, guacamole and chips, while Cam reached into the fridge and grabbed a couple bottles of water.

"I'd offer you a beer, but all I've got is water."

"Water's great. I quit drinking a while back."

Cam turned so fast, he hit his head on the freezer handle. "You did? Why?"

Jack raised an eyebrow. "Felt like the right thing to do."

Cam tossed him a bottle and closed the door. "Cool."

Jack watched him for another second then dove into his burrito. Silence descended as food was devoured until they both came up for air.

Cam spoke first. "So, what brought you by?"

Swallowing the last of his burrito, Jack washed it down with a swig of water. "Mostly to welcome you to town, since we're going to practically be neighbors."

"How's that?"

Jack explained the transfer to the Albany field office. "I'm going to start looking for a place in the next few weeks. But that's not the whole reason I stopped."

"No?"

"The other reason was to apologize. You called me a few times when you were here to interview, and I didn't take the calls. That was a dick move."

241

Cam shook his head. "Don't sweat it. One dick move deserves another. I think we're square."

Jack laughed. "Fair enough." He pushed the bag of chips away, groaning. "So what'd you think? Good, huh?"

"Amazing. I'll have to remember this place when Tori comes to visit." Cam's voice trailed off, his face ashen. "I'm a fucking idiot –"

Jack ignored the jolt, more surprise than sadness. It had been awhile since her name had come up in casual conversation, and what she did was none of his business. Still, he shook his head to dislodge the mild curiosity about Cam's comment. "She's not in my life anymore, but that doesn't mean she's not part of yours."

Regret lurked in Cam's eyes, but Jack ignored it and walked into the living room. "What do you say I stick around and help you get some of this stuff together? At the rate you're going, it'll be Christmas before you're done."

Cam followed him after banking his burrito foil into the trash can. "That soon? Awful optimistic, aren't you?"

Jack surveyed the chaos. "Or plain stupid. Besides, I'll need you to return the favor in a few weeks."

Tori pulled on the shirt and denim skirt she laid out the night before. Everything else was safely stowed away in her suitcase, ready for the trip home.

And she was ready, too.

Lyn came back to Cherokee Ridge earlier in the week, as she'd promised, and "mothered" her through a salon and spa day. Tori's dark auburn hair, parted slightly to one side, now fell in layered waves just below her shoulders. She couldn't resist a slight shake of her head which set the shimmering mass in motion.

Staring at her reflection in the mirror, her hair was one of many changes. Her skin had gone from sallow to healthy, and she'd gained weight and muscle, smoothing out her sharp angles.

Had it really only been three months?

Looking around the bedroom, now devoid of her personal touches, she pondered the season she was completing today. She sniffed away tears as profound thankfulness flooded her. Where would she be now if not for Cherokee Ridge?

She pulled back, acknowledging the futility of that line of thinking. What mattered now was the future, and although she wasn't ready to make final plans, the staff had convinced her that she had a gift in the kitchen. She was looking forward to exploring new paths, and she had friends to help her. She had Leanne and Lyn. And Cam.

She also had her journal to remind her just how far she'd come. She leafed to the last entry.

Dear Jack;

Sometimes pills are bitter to swallow, but the effect is so worth it. One of the most important things I can do to heal is to ask for forgiveness from those I've hurt. And I hurt you. So many times. When all you ever tried to do was love and protect me.

I don't deserve your forgiveness. Just like my dad didn't deserve mine. But I gave it up last night. All the hate. All the anger. Everything that tethered me to the darkness of the past. And it felt incredible. I can't even describe how I feel right now.

And I'm coming to you soon. Because I'm hoping for your forgiveness, too. But not just your forgiveness. I'm going to ask you to love me, and let me love you.

It's been three months since that horrible night in Texas. Three months since I believed my world had ended. But I'm stronger, and more alive than I've ever been, and, even though I know you won't take the credit, I want to thank you for believing in me.

You really were my Prince Charming, and I love you.

Tori

P.S. I'm bringing the Xbox.

With a smile, she turned from the window and grabbed her bag. It was time to go.

She'd called Cam like she promised a couple of days ago to make sure he knew she'd be home this weekend, and expected him to arrive either late tonight or tomorrow morning. But when the center's car service pulled into her driveway, he was already there. Waiting.

Tori couldn't contain her smile as she jerked the door handle and bounded out of the car. In seconds she was engulfed in Cam's giant bear hug as they rocked and swayed and cried right there on the front stoop.

"I expected you tomorrow," she cried.

"No way was I missing this." He pulled back, holding her at arms' length. "Wow. Look at you, Tori. You're stunning."

"I'm healthy. For the first time in my adult life, I understand what healthy feels like. It's amazing."

"I'll grab your stuff. Go on in."

She shouldn't have been surprised that the house was cool and clean. Cam had probably worked on it all morning. "What time did you get in? And how did you get off work?"

"Flew in late last night. I was hoping to beat you here."

"Well, dinner's my treat then. I haven't had Master Chen in months. What do you say?"

"Sounds great."

She paused, then set her phone on the kitchen counter. "Wait." She grabbed his hands in hers and forced him to hold still. "For the past two years, you've had my back in every way imaginable. You wouldn't accept anything less or more than my true friendship, and you said things that needed to be said even though I didn't want to hear them. I'm sorry for the heartache I put you through, especially this year. I know I worried the shit out of you. And I want you to know that I'm so thankful for you and for our friendship."

He enveloped her in another hug, his chest hitching. "You done now? I'm a dude. I'm not supposed to blubber like a baby."

Tori laughed and nodded against his chest. "I'm done."

The food arrived and Tori was even more shocked to see that Cam had stocked her fridge with water, tea, and soda. "You thought of everything."

The evening flew by in a rush of conversation and laughter. Tori couldn't have imagined a better homecoming.

"When are you coming to New York to check out my place?" Cam stifled a yawn. "Still sounds weird to say that I live in New York."

"It does, but you're happier than I've ever seen you."

Another yawn. "I am."

"We can figure out travel plans later. You're exhausted right now."

Cam rubbed his hands over his face. "No way. I've got to leave tomorrow to be back for a shoot in the city on Sunday morning, and I'm not leaving until we ink plans. Next weekend is my only free weekend until October. Would that work for you?"

Tori considered what she still needed to finish in Oklahoma. A week would give her plenty of time to catch up with Alan and the show crew and touch base with Leanne. And a week to figure out exactly what to say to Jack. "Sure. That sounds good."

Tori turned off the GPS on her phone as she found a parking space in the parking lot of the trendy complex. She fished the piece of paper out of her purse with Cam's apartment number, but before she found it, she heard her name shouted from the second floor balcony.

Cam raced down the stairs, taking her bag and rolling it ahead of her as he led her to his place. "Let's throw your stuff in here." He motioned to the bedroom on the left. "It's a futon mattress, but I slept on it a couple of nights before I got my bed put together, and it's not bad."

"It's perfect." Tori smiled as she toured the apartment. "Nice place, Cam. Mathis Productions must be treating you well."

"Better than I'd even hoped. Speaking of employers, how did Alan take the news?"

Tori pulled a bottle of tea out of the fridge and took a sip. "He had a bit of a freak out, but I took Justin and Dwayne with me to help convince him all would be well. By the time I left, he was convinced that *his* idea for Justin to lead the crew next year was perfect."

Cam grinned. "Same old Alan."

"Yep."

"So what's next for you?"

Tori followed him to the sofa and settled next to him. How should she answer that? She'd looked at a couple of different schools, but had hesitated to make plans until she talked to Jack. "Don't know. My only anchor right now is staying connected to my therapist. I've discovered a lot of new interests, but she agrees that I have time to explore them before I commit to anything."

"Jack's still here. He's staying."

Leave it to Cam to read her mind anyway. Tori paused. "I know."

"How?"

"I have friends." At his perplexed look, her lips twitched. "I got with Director Collins last week and finalized a scholarship in Agent Graham's honor. He mentioned that Jack had asked to be reassigned here."

Cam sobered. "You miss him?"

More than I ever thought I could miss anyone.

She didn't want to create false hope, for herself or Cam, so she hedged his question. "I want to see him while I'm here. There are things I need to say to him."

Chapter 28

Tori rubbed sweaty palms against her pant legs as she approached the white columns of the early colonial. The red brick front and neat black shutters of Jack's parents' home spoke of a cultured refinement that reminded her so much of them.

The well-rehearsed words that she thought she'd committed to memory flew out of her head. How would they react to her showing up unannounced on their doorstep? If she'd called ahead, would they have refused to see her?

Her stomach cramped. *Was Jack even here?*

She rang the bell, and before she could think twice and dive for the sculpted bushes on either side of the black painted door, Barbara Mathis was there, mouth agape and eyes wide.

Or maybe Tori only imagined her response. When she blinked again, Barbara's face was a mask of serenity, but her squared shoulders and sharp eyes silently urged Tori to run.

"Hello, Tori."

Tori hadn't expected a warm welcome, but at least Barbara hadn't slammed the door in her face. So far so good. She clutched the strap on her shoulder bag. "Is Jack here?"

"I'm sorry. He isn't."

After all the mental preparation Tori had done, Barbara's clipped words almost brought her to her knees. She closed her eyes to keep the tears away, and when she opened them again Barbara was looking at her, studying her. Then the older woman released a sigh.

"Jack is with Hope today. They're moving some things to her new place. You're welcome to come in and wait for him. He should be back within the hour."

Tori was even more torn. Was this a sign that she should leave him be? Despair wormed its way into her heart. He'd obviously moved on, just as she'd first thought was best. Was she being selfish by trying to reopen a door between them?

"Maybe this was a bad idea."

Barbara's eyes narrowed. "So you came all the way from Oklahoma to walk away?"

"Well, I –"

"You obviously have something to say to Jack. I'd suggest you stick around and say it."

Tori's head was jumbled. Should she stay or shouldn't she? Barbara opened the door wide and motioned her into the cool foyer. The classic natural woodwork in the home should've been impressive, but Tori was having a hard time believing she was walking through Jack's childhood home. Probably wouldn't have quite believed it, except for the pictures of him and his siblings that were proudly displayed on tables and walls.

Barbara led her to the kitchen and pointed to a wooden stool at the bar that separated the cooking space from the large dining area, and Tori dutifully sat as doubts plagued her. Could Jack forgive her for what she'd done? Was she opening his old wounds in an effort to soothe hers?

Barbara rummaged through a cabinet, her back to Tori. "I have a wonderful selection of teas, if you're interested. Wind's got a bite to it this afternoon."

"Oh, thank you. I'm fine. More of a coffee girl, myself."

"Well, I'll apologize in advance then." Barbara said. She fished around for another moment then turned to Tori. "All I can offer you is some God-awful blend that Jack seems to have fallen in love with. It's all he drinks."

Tori's heart hammered in her chest as she stared at the familiar packaging, and she couldn't help the ray of hope that sprung to life deep in her chest. "Oh, that's perfect. Thank you."

"Are you certain? It really is strong."

"No. I love it, too. It's the kind I drink at home."

Barbara's hand stilled. In a beat of silence, her sad eyes met Tori's. "You broke his heart, you know."

Tori couldn't speak around the giant, swelling lump in her throat. Tears threatened to choke her. "I'm sorry," she whispered. How could she explain to this gracious woman about what addiction had done to her? "I'm not here to disrupt anything. I just need to apologize to him for the hurt I caused."

A rush of chilly afternoon air followed Jack in the back door. "Mom," he hollered. "You home?"

"In the kitchen."

"Good." He tossed his jacket on a hook in the mud room and headed down the hall. "Hope said she's missing a box of clothes. Did you –"

Tori.

Jack's chest constricted, and slow seconds ticked by as he tried to reconcile that the woman who'd haunted his dreams was sitting at the counter in his mother's kitchen, drinking coffee. Except this woman was different. Her hair was shorter and styled, her face fuller. But the eyes. Those beautiful, expressive, passionate eyes that looked at him now hadn't changed at all.

Breathe, idiot, breathe.

He'd tried for months to rid his mind of her image. He'd worked like crazy. He'd reevaluated his life. He'd convinced himself that he was better off without her.

She stared at him. Her eyes roaming his face. "Hello, Jack."

Yet, the smoky timber of her voice almost took him to his knees. What was she doing here? Was this some cruel test to see how many times she could walk away before he broke for good?

Jack slowed his breathing, berating himself for his initial reaction. She didn't warrant a reaction at all. He turned to his mother and saw the anxiety that Tori had brought to her, to their home. "Can you give us a few minutes?"

"Of course."

Tori hadn't moved, but Jack watched out of the corner of his eye as she followed his mother's departure. Looking for something to keep his hands busy, Jack poured a cup of coffee. He couldn't have forced it down his throat with a pry bar and jack hammer.

He stood across the counter from her, arms crossed. "What are you doing here?"

"I – I came to see how you were doing."

"Completely healed." He did a quick three-sixty, arms extended. "Check that one off your guilt list. I'm just fine."

She absorbed the shot, twin spots of color appearing on her cheeks. "I'm so glad." She stood, as if sitting was too difficult. "I also came to talk, if you have time."

Talk? After three months of radio silence, she wanted to talk?

Jack could almost feel his shoulder blades touching as he tried to hang on to his temper. He made sure his tone betrayed none of the turmoil beneath the surface. "Got your text and your message via Cam. They were pretty clear."

He walked around the bar, picked up the jacket on the stool next to her, and held it open. The subtle scent of strawberries that wafted through the air was almost more than he could handle. She needed to leave. Now.

Tori watched him for a moment then turned and slipped her arms into the sleeves. "That was all I could say then. But there's more to say now." She turned to face him, her eyes clear and bold despite the way her fingers shook when he handed over her purse. "I spent the last three months getting healthy, learning to control my addictions. Part of my recovery involves asking for forgiveness from the people I've hurt. And I know I hurt you. More times than I can count." She placed a hand on his forearm, searing him through his sweatshirt. "I'm not trying to cause more pain. I just wanted you to know how truly sorry I am. For everything."

As much as he told himself she was part of the past, the words she was saying weren't the ones Jack wanted to hear. He wanted to hear that she loved him, and missed him, and wanted to be with him. What he'd do with that information, he didn't know, but the fact that she was standing here, and had traveled halfway across the country to absolve herself of some personal guilt trip, stoked his anger.

"So I'm a step in your recovery. You're here to clear your conscience. Got it."

She'd followed him to the foyer and stared at him, mouth slightly open. "Yes." She paused, shook her head slightly. "No. I mean, I thought it would be important…" Her voice trailed off.

Jack let out a heavy sigh as he opened the front door. Part of him wanted to be angry, to lash out at her. But he couldn't. She'd done what she needed to do, what he'd hoped and prayed she'd do. Just without him. "Consider yourself forgiven, Tori. I'm glad you got your life straightened out."

He gripped the knob with as much force as he could as she studied him.

With a slight nod, she whispered, "Okay."

He watched her walk down the stairs, his jaw clenched against the words he wouldn't utter. Then he closed the wooden door with a soft click.

Hope's missing boxes could wait. Jack swapped clothes and headed to the gym. With every pounding step on the treadmill, he replayed the scene with Tori. He hated being blindsided, but he'd have been shocked by her either way. He couldn't get past her amazing transformation.

God, did she look beautiful. Healthy. Whole.

And she still had the power to twist him up inside. He ran faster as questions bombarded him. How had she come to her decision? What had her treatment been? What did her recovery feel like? What would she do now?

His side hitched, fair warning that he'd pushed hard enough. After showering, he checked his phone and saw that he'd missed a call from his realtor who'd scheduled his closing for next Thursday morning. He'd deny to anyone who asked that he'd hoped to see Tori's number on his missed call list.

He plugged the appointment into his phone. Today was no different than yesterday. His life was moving forward. And Tori was still in his past.

Tori's hand shook as she inserted the key into Cam's front door. Thank God he was at work so she had time to regroup. She splashed some water from the kitchen sink on her face then flopped onto the sofa.

What had she expected? Jack was more gracious than she would've ever been if the situation had been reversed. But she'd hoped to see some flicker of emotion. Some indication that he still cared. But he couldn't wait to be rid of her.

God, he looked good. His hair was longer, that hint of curl well below his collar. And with the shadow of beard growth on his face, he looked wilder, less restrained, even sexier than she'd remembered.

Ugh. Stop it. Torturing yourself won't help.

Her phone buzzed in her hand, and Lyn's number popped up on the screen. Tori was tempted to let the call go to voicemail, but she'd promised to call Lyn after she met with Jack, and Lyn would worry until she answered.

"How did it go? I want details."

With a groan, Tori sat up and rested her elbows on her knees. "Great news. He said he forgives me, and he's glad I got my life straightened out."

Lyn paused, surely catching the irony in her voice. "That's a good thing, right?"

Tori closed her eyes. "Except for the fact that he was saying it as he was practically pushing me out the door."

"What did he say about the journal?"

Tori bit her lip and Lyn pounced on her silence.

"Did you tell him how you feel about him? Show him the letters?"

Agitated, Tori rose. "Of course not. Like I said, he made his feelings really obvious."

"So in other words, you didn't want to risk your pride when you felt like the odds were stacked against you."

Lyn's words stung, but Tori couldn't deny their truth. She'd hoped, more than anything, that Jack would give her one small opening, one chance to let her say what was in her heart. "I guess so."

"If I was your mother, this is what I'd say." Lyn's voice softened. "Find a way to see him again, Tori. Trust him with the journal."

Tori cringed. "He won't see me again."

"You tried once. Now, try again. You opened your heart to him through that book of letters. Write him one more. If he's the man you told me about, he'll see you."

Jack closed up the lid on the box of clothes, this time his own. It was past time to get away from his parents' place, especially with his mom's worried frowns following him around since Tori's surprise visit. He'd thought about calling Cam to see if he'd help over the weekend, but if Tori was still here, she'd be with him.

Tossing the shirt aside, Jack jammed his hands into his pockets. Cam hadn't made a secret out of the fact that he believed Tori had made a mistake shutting Jack out of her life. And his comment about Jack giving up drinking made a lot more sense now.

Shaking his head, Jack resumed packing. And still, he hadn't made it a day without thinking about her. Cam was a romantic fool. Jack was just a fool.

He growled at the knock on his door. "What?"

His mom peeked into the room. "Don't be so surly. You've got mail." Jack frowned at the envelope in his mom's hand. "It's from Tori."

Ignoring the expectant look on his mom's face, he tossed the letter on the bedside table.

"Aren't you going to read it?"

Jack lifted an eyebrow, but his mom just stared at him and crossed her arms. "Maybe later."

His mom retreated, but her frown told him what she thought of his decision. He shook his head and picked up the shirt again, shoving it into the box. What good would come from opening the letter? If he continued to pick the scab, it would never heal.

He finished packing up the rest of the clothes, then scanned the room for anything else he'd missed. His eyes landed again on the cream colored envelope. His name was written boldly, in capital letters, larger than the address below it.

It felt like a challenge.

He was stronger than whatever was on the inside of that envelope. But by God, if he had to read that she was sorry they'd ever met, he wouldn't be responsible for his actions. Stalking to the letter, he ripped it open and began to read.

Dear Jack;

I'm leaving on Saturday to head back to Oklahoma. Thought I'd start there so you'd read the rest of this letter.

I'm sorry for surprising you, but I was afraid you wouldn't see me. Unfortunately, I screwed up pretty much everything I wanted to say. So no more surprises. I'd like to see you once more before I go.

There are things I still need to say to you. Things you need to hear.

I'll be at Lydia's Coffee Shop, around the corner from Cam's place Friday morning at eleven. If you're willing to come, thank you. I hope to see you then.

Tori

Jack stared at the short letter for another minute, then crumpled it and tossed it back on the table. *Why, Tori? What's left to say?*

Cam. Of course. She'd want to take care of him, make sure things weren't awkward moving forward. For Cam's sake. Jack bagged the regret for what might have been that tightened his chest, cursing himself that it existed.

He'd go and see her. That really hadn't been a question in his mind. Fool that he was, he wouldn't pass up the opportunity to see her one more time. He'd hear what she needed to say and, maybe then, he could let her go for good.

Tori checked her watch as she closed the door to Cam's apartment. The next fifteen minutes would be the longest of her life. Jack hadn't called or reached out to her at all to let her know whether he'd come or not. He might not have even opened the letter.

But she would be there, waiting for him.

As one of the critical components of her recovery, she and Lyn had already planned her next steps if Jack didn't show. She mentally went through the list with every step she took, preparing for disappointment.

She opened the coffee shop's heavy glass door and scanned the room, her heart tripping as she spotted Jack at a small table toward the back of the room.

He was early.

His attention was on the phone in his hand, so she simply watched him for a moment, trying to gather her wits and remember exactly what she wanted to say. She had one opportunity to get out everything that was in her heart.

On noodle legs, she walked toward the table. Ten feet from him, he glanced up and the unguarded look left his eyes as he spotted her. He stood as she approached and held out a chair for her.

"Coffee?"

Tori nodded as she slid into her seat. "Yes. Thank you."

She watched him walk to the counter and order, thankful for the chance to get her rioting heart under control. As he returned, she folded her hands in front of her to keep them from shaking.

"Thanks for coming."

Jack nodded, then took a sip of his brew, waiting for her to continue.

Tori cleared her throat and met his cool gaze head on. She straightened her shoulders. He may not want to hear what she had to say, but she wouldn't, couldn't, let the words go unsaid.

"I came to New York hoping to apologize and earn your forgiveness." He opened his mouth, but Tori held up a hand, cutting him off. "But I was still, on some level, protecting myself." She studied the wood grain in the table as if it could help her articulate the words that she'd so carefully planned. "My whole life, I put people in boxes. Easily manageable, modular units that I could move and manipulate as needed. Until you. You didn't fit in any of the boxes. And I didn't know how to handle that."

He didn't respond, so she lifted her eyes from the table, sadness filling her. He simply watched. And waited.

"I left you that night in the hospital and didn't know if I had it in me to ever see you again."

Aside from the flicker of pain that crossed his features, he didn't move.

"You risked your life to save mine, and I couldn't process that. Two thoughts played on constant repeat in my head. I deserved to die. And I didn't deserve you." She took a deep shuttering breath and ran shaking hands over her cheeks.

"I realize now that until you came into my life, I was waiting to die. But you changed everything. And that scared the shit out of me. You made me dream of things and feel things I'd never thought possible. Then, when I talked to your mom and things looked bad, I ended up in a wheat field in south Oklahoma and drank until I was sick. Then I drank some more."

Jack swallowed another sip of coffee, then stared down at his cup. She wished he'd look at her, give her some idea of what he was thinking.

"Sometime early the next morning, your mom left me a message that you'd turned a corner. That you were going to be okay." A tremor shook her body and her throat tightened. But, she had to get through this. "And I laid there, in the middle of that field, and had to decide if *I* was going to live or die. The path I was on was surely going to lead to death. You knew it. I think I've known it for a long time, but it was what I thought I deserved."

She paused, trying to slow her words and her heartbeat. "I'd tried so hard to let you go, to tell myself that I was better without you. Certain that you were better without me."

Jack's knuckles were white as he gripped his coffee mug. He was silent so long she wondered if he would say anything at all. When he finally spoke, his voice was low and tight. "Why couldn't you trust me enough to tell me that then? I would've moved mountains to help you get better."

Tori's stomach ached from the pain in his eyes. Pain she'd caused. She barely nodded. "I know. But I didn't know who I would be on this side of treatment. Or if I'd even make it to this side. I couldn't let you put your life on indefinite hold. It wouldn't have been fair to you. Or me. I couldn't fix myself *because* I knew you were waiting for me. I had to fix myself for me."

She pulled the journal from her bag and set it on the table in front of him. "But you were always with me."

Jack stared at the leather journal between them, then met her gaze. Her eyes were impossibly blue and brimming with tears.

She nudged the book closer to him. "It's all there. Every single conversation I had with you during my recovery."

Jack hesitated, indecision warring in his chest. If he opened it, he was willingly giving her the power to break him. Again.

In the end, there was only one choice.

With a hand that was less than steady, he slipped on reading glasses and opened to the first page, and Tori's journey sprang to life. Page after page, she opened her heart and her deepest thoughts, all addressed to him. He glanced up as she swiped away tears.

She croaked out a nervous laugh. "I don't know when I switched from believing you'd never read it to hoping and praying that you would."

Jack returned to the journal, captivated and desperate to reach the end. When he got to the last page, it took everything he had to hold it together.

Dear Jack;

Sometimes pills are bitter to swallow, but the effect is so worth it. One of the most important things I can do to heal is to ask for forgiveness from those I've hurt. And I hurt you. So many times. When all you ever tried to do was love and protect me.

I don't deserve your forgiveness. Just like my dad didn't deserve mine. But I gave it up last night. All the hate. All the anger. Everything that tethered me to the darkness of the past. And it felt incredible. I can't even describe how I feel right now.

And I'm coming to you soon. Because I'm hoping for your forgiveness, too. But not just your forgiveness. I'm going to ask you to love me, and let me love you.

It's been three months since that horrible night in Texas. Three months since I believed my world had ended. But I'm stronger, and more alive than I've ever been. And, even though I know you won't take the credit, I want to thank you for believing in me.

You really were my Prince Charming, and I love you.

Tori

P.S. I'm bringing the Xbox.

Jack closed the journal and folded his glasses back into his pocket. He could barely hang on to a single thought with so many things he'd read fighting for prominence. He wanted to read it with her page by page, talk to her more. He wanted this day, and this time with her, to go on forever.

Once again, he met her teary gaze, joy and hope that he thought was long-dead brimming from every pore. "I only have one question."

She stared at him as if she was half-afraid to hear what he would say. "What's that?" she whispered.

He looked around the room. "Where's the Xbox? I still need a shot to win back my man card."

Her eyes crinkled and a hoarse laugh escaped, but he wasn't waiting for her answer. He stepped around the table, and she shoved out of her chair and launched herself into his arms, broken sobs racking her body.

"I'm so sorry," she cried. "So sorry I didn't trust you."

"Shhh, babe. You're here now. We're here now. And I'm never letting go." He squeezed her tight and rested his check in her soft hair. "You couldn't figure out how to love me. And I never figured out how to stop loving you."

She continued to cling to him, but pulled back enough to look at his face, her cries turning softer. "I was so full of distrust and anger and resentment, there wasn't room for anything else. I had to figure out how to lose the hate before I could let myself love."

Jack's mouth lowered to hers, his lips a breath away. "I love your letters. I've never read anything more honest and real. Think you could keep them coming?"

"I think I'd like to try," she whispered.

Chapter 29

Jack kept Tori's hand in his as they walked out of the coffee shop into the bright sunshine. "Guess I'm going to need to sample these cinnamon rolls everyone raved about in your journal."

Tori slipped on sunglasses with her free hand and smiled. "Hilarious, isn't it? I knew you'd laugh when you found out. I absolutely love baking. And cooking. All the spice variations. Who knew?"

They wandered to the local park, and hours flew by as they talked through the good, and the bad, and the future. At dinner, the waiter brought the wine card, but Tori politely declined and asked for iced tea.

When their drinks arrived, Jack raised his in a toast. "To the woman brave enough to fight for the chance we deserve."

"And to the man who's willing to believe in second chances." Tori set down her glass. "I think if you hadn't shown up today, I probably would've hunted you down. I couldn't have left without–"

Jack slid his fingers through hers, his eyes crinkling. "No way in hell I wasn't showing up."

***

The cool air chilled Tori as they stood at the threshold of Cam's apartment door. "Cam texted earlier that he's working late tonight if you want to come in."

Jack wanted to come in almost more than he wanted to breathe, but he shook his head and dipped his head for a quick kiss. "Not a good idea for what I have in mind."

Her eyes darted to his, as heat kindled between them. "What did you have in mind?"

He loved the breathlessness in her voice. "My idea involves waiting right here while you walk through that door, write Cam a note that you'll see him tomorrow, and bring your overnight bag back out to me."

She smiled. That sexy, gorgeous smile. "Oh. I like your idea."

Instead of taking her to a hotel, as she thought he would, Tori looked over at him with curiosity as he pulled into a secluded driveway on the outskirts of town. "Where are we?"

He didn't answer as he walked around the car. He opened her door and led her toward the wide front door. To her surprise, he lifted a key out of his pocket and fitted it into the lock. "This is your place?"

Jack smiled. "As of yesterday. Spent the night here last night for the first time."

Tori walked into the foyer, as butterflies danced in her stomach. She'd barely allowed herself to hope, that Jack would be back in her life. Now she was in his home.

"What made you decide to stay?"

"This is where I belong. Guess I'm a family man, after all."

After a brief tour of the ground floor, he took her hand and led her up the stairs. "Movers won't be here for a few more days, so there aren't any amenities yet. A borrowed bed, a few towels, some toilet paper."

She laughed. "You pulled out all of the stops."

The heat in his eyes made the laughter dry up from her throat. "Believe me, if I'd known how today would end–"

"End?" She reached for him. "It's definitely not over."

Neither had time for words as they allowed their bodies to express everything that needed to be said. Afterward, Tori laid on her side, her fingers trailing a path down his chest to the puckered scar tissue above his left hip. He sucked in a breath.

"Does it still hurt?" she whispered.

He guided her chin until she was looking into his eyes. The love she saw there humbled her. "It did for a long time, but not anymore."

Epilogue

November, one year later...

Jack walked into the kitchen, picked a green bean out of the casserole dish and popped it in his mouth. "Mmm. Delicious."

Tori mock-frowned as he pilfered another one. "There won't be any left if you keep that up." She buzzed from the stovetop to the island. "Come here, though. Tell me what you think about the crusted sweet potatoes."

Jack sauntered over and dipped his head for a quick kiss before picking up a spoon and scooping a small bite. He closed his eyes and moaned.

"Heaven on a spoon."

She cocked a brow. "You sure?"

Jack pulled her into his arms. "I'm sure. Stop being nervous."

"Easy for you to say," she mumbled, squirming out of his embrace to check the turkey. "My Brussel sprouts are overdone, and the custard hasn't set yet. This may be my first and last attempt at Thanksgiving dinner for your family."

"Hold on a minute." Jack grabbed her from behind as soon as she closed the oven door. Tori fidgeted, but Jack turned her in his arms and lowered his head until she stopped and met his gaze. "Deep breath. Who graduated top of their class at the New England Culinary Institute?"

She smiled up at him, appreciating his attempt to calm her down. "Okay. But, that's cooking for strangers. This is your family."

"Our family."

Tori paused at the gravity in Jack's voice, and the air flew out of the room.

"A year ago, you asked me for patience. To give you time to know yourself better, to give us time to be a couple without any background noise." Jack reached into his pocket and pulled out a simple, eggshell blue box. He opened it to reveal a gorgeous haloed diamond ring. "We belong together, Tori. Marry me."

Tori's gaze darted from his hand to his face, and tears pricked her eyes. During the past year, Jack had loved her through the highs and lows of her continued recovery. He'd encouraged, pushed, and simply held her when that was what she needed. She pulled a shaky breath into her lungs. If she was one of those girly girls, she'd pinch herself.

Cam walked into the kitchen at that moment, and grabbed a carrot out of the veggie tray. He grinned at them then proceeded to the refrigerator. "Hurry up and say yes, Tori. We're starving."

A laugh escaped Tori's lips. "Get out of here, Cam."

"Hey, Jack? You going to let her talk to me that way?"

"Get out, Cam," Jack echoed, his eyes never leaving Tori's face.

Cam walked away, muttering, as Jack pulled her closer still, his eyes serious. "Be my wife, Tori."

Tori cupped Jack's face in her hands, eyes shining with love for him. "I love you, Jack." She extended her hand, allowing him to slip the ring onto her finger. "And my answer is yes. A million times, yes."

The End

Acknowledgements

Surround yourself with people who are better than you, and you'll never stop growing and working on getting better. That's what I've done.

My tried and true critique partners – Darlene Deluca and Janice Richards – you two are my lifeline. Thank you, as always, for your time, commitment, and honesty.

Emily Hemmer, you were a breath of fresh air and helped me see from a different perspective. Because of you, Tori and Jack's journey is a better, richer, story.

My writer friends at MARA and MRW – I'm so thankful to be surrounded by such talented people who are so willing to share their experience and expertise.

Becky, Susan, Jill and Genita, my amazing beta readers. I value each of you for your insight, honesty, and encouragement.

My family. Especially my husband, Jim, who takes over so many responsibilities when I'm up against a deadline. I could never express how blessed I am to have your unwavering belief in me and my passion for writing.

My readers. Thank you for caring enough to ask about the next release. And the next. You can't know how much your kind words encourage me to keep telling stories.

About the Author

Michelle Grey is an avid lover of books, and had always thought that someday she would take up her pen and write romantic suspense. In 2009, Michelle was diagnosed with a rare form of ovarian cancer, and she realized that "somedays" aren't guaranteed. This life-changing event motivated Michelle to pursue her dream of becoming an author.

In January of 2013, Michelle released her debut novel, Dangerous Ally.

In September of 2013, the next book in her Long Shot Series, Unspoken Bonds, was published.

Now a cancer survivor, Michelle decided to use her platform to promote awareness of ovarian cancer and its symptoms. In January 2014 she published, Are You Listening: A Personal Journal of an Ovarian Cancer Survivor.

Because it is so important to spread the word, one hundred percent of the proceeds from this $.99 e-book go directly to the Vicki Welsh Ovarian Cancer Fund to support their mission of fighting ovarian cancer through awareness, education, research and support.

Michelle lives in the Midwest with her husband of twenty-eight years and has four amazing and unique children, a wonderful son-in-law, and two beautiful granddaughters. Michelle believes that any day that involves family, writing, or reading is a great day, indeed.

Other Books by Michelle Grey
Dangerous Ally, Long Shot Series, Book 1
Unspoken Bonds, Long Shot Series, Book 2
Are You Listening? A Personal Journal of an Ovarian Cancer Survivor

Join Michelle Grey's Fan Club at: www.authormichellegrey.com
Or Follow Michelle on Facebook or Twitter

Made in the USA
Lexington, KY
08 January 2018